LADY OF THE SHADES

DARREN SHAN

First published in Great Britain in 2012 by Orion Books,
an imprint of The Orion Publishing Group Ltd
Orion House, 5 Upper Saint Martin's Lane
London WC2H 9EA

An Hachette UK Company

3 5 7 9 10 8 6 4

A CIP catalogue record for this book
is available from the British Library.

ISBN (Hardback) 978 1 4091 4360 4
ISBN (Export Trade Paperback) 978 1 4091 4361 1
ISBN (Ebook) 978 1 4091 4362 8

Typeset by Deltatype Ltd, Birkenhead, Merseyside

Printed and bound by CPI Group (UK) Ltd, Croydon CR0 4YY

The Orion Publishing Group's policy is to use papers that
are natural, renewable and recyclable products and made
from wood grown in sustainable forests. The logging and
manufacturing processes are expected to conform to the
environmental regulations of the country of origin.

www.orionbooks.co.uk

For:
Bas – *my* Lady of the Shades.

Edited by:
Jon Wood and Jemima Forrester.

My light in the shades:
the Christopher Little Agency.

PROLOGUE

Jose Nilson dos Linos was brushing dandruff from his hair when he was executed. A committed civil rights campaigner, he had spent the day scouring the records of a local orphanage, seeking proof that it was a front for one of Santiago's largest criminal organizations. He had been dogging the orphanage directors for several months, but had only recently made headway when a repentant doctor sought redemption by turning informer.

Jose had not yet been able to rack up significant evidence against the Chilean crime lords, but he was closing in on them. He was convinced that the truth would soon surface, affording him his triumph in court.

He was thinking of dramatic closing speeches as he climbed the stairs to his humble apartment on the third floor of a crumbling mansion. Letting himself in, he made for a circular window which faced on to the streets of Santiago, and stood there, gaze trained on the people below, idly observing. Then, smiling at the thought of sleep, he turned to his writing bureau to record the day's events in his diary.

The diary was a thick, leather-encased ledger. He laid it on the desk, found where he had left off the evening before and started to write. He got through three lengthy, meticulously detailed paragraphs before pausing. Laying his pen aside, he closed his eyes and stroked the bridge of his nose with the thumb and middle finger of his left hand. Opening his eyes, he pushed the diary away, leant over the bare desk and gently ran his fingers through his hair. Flakes of dandruff fell in front of him like snow. Jose watched, amused, imagining himself somewhere cold and relaxing.

While dandruff drifted through the air, Jose's assassin moved in for the kill, unseen and unheard. His chosen name was Sebastian Dash, and there was nothing personal in what he did. He did not know why he had been hired to eliminate Jose Nilson dos Linos and would not have cared if he had. Sebastian Dash was paid to kill, not to question.

Dash placed the muzzle of his pistol to the back of Jose's skull. It touched so lightly that Jose thought it was a moth settling and carried on stroking his hair. Dash hesitated, surprised by his victim's non-reaction, then squeezed the trigger gently.

Jose Nilson dos Linos's head exploded in a cone of bone, brain and blood. The bullet made a tiny hole upon entry, but emerged in a furious crimson torrent, eradicating Jose's face above his upper lip. The bullet embedded itself in the wall ahead of the men, the cranial matter forming a pearly corona around it.

Dash carefully adjusted Jose's head and laid it to rest on its side, so that it was facing the door through which Jose's wife of eleven years would enter when she returned. The grisly touch had been requested by Dash's employer. Across Santiago, an overly talkative doctor had already been found in a similar state by his beloved. It had been a profitable night for Sebastian Dash.

The assassin strode to the door, made sure the angle was correct, then retraced his steps. He did not bother to remove the bullet from the wall — the gun was untraceable. Instead he bent to adjust Jose's shoes. With a frown, he discovered that the dead man was wearing slip-ons. He quickly examined the apartment and found a pair of laced black shoes in a closet. Jose always wore these shoes to court and would have been wearing them when he prosecuted the directors of the orphanage. Dash was not aware of this. Any pair of shoes would have sufficed, as long as they had laces.

Dash slid off Jose's slip-ons and worked the corpse's feet into the shoes. Once they were on, he tied the lace of the right shoe but left the lace on the left undone. This was his trademark. It was not always possible – there were times when he had to hit and run – but he enjoyed signing his name to a killing whenever the occasion permitted. Even in Dash's sinister, secretive business, it paid to advertise.

When everything was to his satisfaction, Dash took the diary – his employer wanted it destroyed – and crept to the door. Opening it a crack, he swept the corridor with a cool, critical eye. Spying nobody, he stepped out, closed the door and took the stairs. Shoulders hunched, lower face concealed by the lapels of his jacket, eyes obscured by thick glasses – plain glass, as he had 20-20 vision – and hair swept to the left. Not an elaborate disguise, but Dash had found that the more mundane one appeared, the less notice people paid.

Sebastian Dash strolled through the streets of Santiago. He dropped the pistol down an open drain. It was not the best way to dispose of incriminating evidence, but he wasn't intimately familiar with Chile's capital and it was better to be swift than certain. Next he disposed of the diary and his gloves in an incinerator, then headed for home.

Back at his hotel, Dash ran a bath, undressed and immersed his clothes in the water. That was the trouble with blood — it got everywhere. In the morning, when the clothes were dry, he would stuff them in a bag and return to the incinerator.

Dash stood by the window, naked, observing the Chilean

sky, comparing the moon's corona to the one he had created in dos Linos's apartment. He was interrupted by a knock on his door.

'Mr O'Hara?' a woman called. The manageress, Mrs Covarrubias. A local woman, but she'd spent time in the United States when she was younger and spoke fluent English. If Dash had known that before he checked into the small hotel, he would have looked elsewhere for lodgings.

Moving closer to the door, Dash cleared his throat and adopted the thick Irish accent that he'd adopted when registering as Donal O'Hara. 'Is it yourself, Mrs C?' he sang, maintaining the pretence that he was incapable of pronouncing her surname.

'It is,' she laughed. 'Are you decent?'

'I'm afraid not. May I be helping you in any way, or would you rather come back when I'm dressed?'

'A letter came for you,' Mrs Covarrubias said. 'Express delivery. All the way from Swee . . . Swi . . . Swizzerland?'

'Switzerland,' Dash corrected her. That would be Antonia. To hire Dash, one had to go through Antonia. She was the only person apart from his employer who knew that he was in Chile.

'Mrs C,' Dash said, 'would you be a darling and slide the envelope under the door, assuming it fits?'

'It's quite thin, so let me try.' He heard the crinkling of the woman's dress as she bent and pushed the envelope through the crack at the base of the door.

'Many thanks, good lady,' Dash said in his Irish brogue. 'Well, I must be off to dry my hands. I was just out of the bath when you knocked.'

'I thought I heard the water running,' Mrs Covarrubias said. 'I'll see you in the morning, Mr O'Hara.'

'Indeed you will,' Dash chuckled, then listened with an

irritated frown as she walked away, not bending to retrieve the envelope until he was sure she was gone.

A plain white envelope nestled inside the larger one. A first-class British stamp and a London postmark. Antonia had opened the letter, read it, then resealed it. Dash slit it open again with a fingernail. He took out a sheet of paper and unfolded it to discover a handwritten message. Dash always insisted on handwritten requests — an extra insurance policy.

The note was from Mikis Menderes, better known as the Turk. Menderes had been born in Turkey but had lived in London for most of his life. He'd hired Dash twice before. On the second job, Dash made the kill – a crooked police officer who wouldn't be missed – but also took out the target's mistress, who was in the wrong place at the wrong time. The Turk was furious — a genuine inquiry had been instigated and he'd had to spend a lot more on bribes than he'd bargained for in order to keep his name out of it. He blamed Dash and demanded a refund. Dash refused, since the target had been eliminated, and the pair had engaged in an ugly war of words until Dash relented and offered a twenty-five per cent discount. The Turk argued him up to a third and they hadn't been in contact since.

Dash read the letter while standing by the door, and again a few moments later, sitting down. It was curtly written, in the style of the Turk's previous letters.

My woman has been seen on the arm of another man. Not happy. Want to talk with you about it. Lodgings set aside for you. If you're agreeable, move in and wait. I will be in touch.

It was signed Mikis Theopolous Menderes, and there was a north London address printed beneath.

Everything seemed straightforward. The Turk's wife or mistress – Dash wasn't up to date with Menderes's personal life – was having an affair, and he wanted Dash to kill either his woman, her lover or both.

Dash was reluctant to accept the assignment. Hits could get messy when a loved one was involved. Employers could have a change of heart and act irrationally. He liked it when his paymaster was as cold and calculating as himself. He usually turned down revenge-seeking husbands.

But if Dash rejected the hit, the Turk might think that the assassin held a grudge. Dash did a reasonable amount of business in London and didn't like the idea of the Turk bad-mouthing him. He had worked long and hard to establish himself as a discreet, detached killer. If clients thought that he let personal feelings get in the way of his decisions, business might suffer. He didn't like the Turk or what he was being asked to do, but if he accepted the assignment, the bad blood between them would be erased and he need never again worry about turning down the tight-fisted gangster.

Dash slept on the matter, then went online early in the morning and changed his flight. He had been booked to fly back to Switzerland – he hadn't touched base in two months – but home could wait. Business was business.

Next, he rang Antonia and told her he was popping over to London for an arts festival.

'Will you hook up with your Turkish friend?' Antonia asked.

'I imagine so,' Dash replied.

'When can I expect you back? I'm missing you.'

Dash grinned. Antonia was as emotionally distant as himself. It always amused him to hear her acting human. 'I'm hoping it won't be more than a week or two.'

'And if anyone asks after you while you're away?'

'Take a message. Tell them to be patient.'

They said their goodbyes and hung up. Dash stood over the phone a moment, thinking of Antonia and the Alps, then sighed and shook his head. He was working too hard. What use was money if you didn't have the time to enjoy it? A few more years and he'd think about retiring somewhere warm. He wouldn't make the mistake of outstaying his welcome. There was good money in killing, but if you weren't careful, it could be the death of you.

PART ONE

ONE

I wake abruptly from a troubled sleep to find the dead pressing in tightly around me. Half a dozen phantoms, teeth bared, snarling mutely, scratching at my face with their insubstantial fingernails. I stifle a scream and bury my face in a pillow, waiting for the last vestiges of the nightmare to pass.

My heart is pounding and I don't move until it's back to normal. When I'm in control, I push myself up and stare blankly at the six ghosts. They've withdrawn now that I'm awake and are simply glaring at me sullenly, the way they do most of the time. They only try to get under my skin when they think I'm ripe for the freaking, choosing their moments with studious care, for maximum impact.

Usually they strike on nights like this, when they see me whimpering and fidgeting in my sleep, when they know from experience that I'll more than likely bolt awake, disorientated and temporarily vulnerable. They can't physically assault me, or they would have ripped me apart years ago. They have to settle for mind games, and they're good at those. They should be. They've had lots of practice.

I get up and shower. The ghosts follow me into the bathroom, passing through the walls as if the blocks were made of mist. I ignore them as I turn the water on cold and shiver in its bite. I'm adept at ignoring them. It's only when they occasionally catch me by surprise that they set my nerves jangling. Not like in the early days, when I was sure they were going to drive me mad. We've fought a battle of the wills, the dead and I, and I've won out. So far anyway. Though I suspect they've got the rest of my life to chip away at me. And, if they're not just figments of my imagination, then maybe far beyond.

I'm in a foul mood. I wasn't able to get back to sleep, so the day dragged. I kept as busy as I could, walking the streets of London, researching, writing up notes. But I couldn't make time pass any faster or rid myself of the headache I often get after an interrupted night's sleep. I tried to avoid people, knowing what I'm like in this frame of mind, apt to snap at the slightest irritation.

As night fell, I thought about postponing my meeting with Joe. We were due to case a house in Kilburn, in north London. Joe wouldn't have cared if I'd pushed it back. But that would have afforded the ghosts a minor victory, and they all add up. When you're fighting for your sanity, you can't cede even an inch of turf. Every slight setback empowers your foes, and there's no telling how little it might take to tip the scales.

It's shortly after eleven p.m. on July 2nd. Joe and I have been camped out in the abandoned house for the past couple of hours, waiting for its alleged spectral inhabitant to make an appearance. Joe sensed my dark mood and has kept small talk to a minimum.

I've cheered up over the course of our watch. It's times like this, when I'm immersing myself in the murky world of the dead, that I feel most at ease with my own situation. I'm a man in search of answers, and I find a certain measure of relief and peace of mind when I'm focused on my ghostly research.

Joe's gone upstairs to the toilet. It doesn't work – no water in the cistern – but he's too polite to piss against a wall. I have no such qualms. Even if I had, I'd rather risk my dignity than my life on those rickety stairs. I hope Joe doesn't expect me to haul him out of the rubble if he crashes through the planks. I don't risk my life for anyone.

The stairs creak. I slide into the corridor to watch Joe make his descent. He's less optimistic coming down than he was going up. Keeps to the edges and tests each step several times before easing his weight on to it. The sight brightens my mood another few notches. 'You should hop over the banister,' I smirk.

'And plunge through the floor?' he snorts. 'No thanks. I'll take my chances on the stairs.' Joe's from northern England and has a thick accent. I had difficulty understanding him when we first met, but it's been four days now and my ear has adjusted. I even find myself unconsciously mimicking him sometimes.

Joe makes it back safely and lets out a grateful breath, as if he'd returned from a bombing raid on Berlin. 'I could murder a cup of tea,' he mutters.

'Then you'd need to piss again.'

He nods glumly. 'We should hire a Portaloo.'

'Or you could just piss against the wall.'

'I'm a Geordie,' Joe sniffs. 'We're more civilized than that.'

We return to the drawing room. I used to think such rooms were so named because people drew in them. Joe put me right. It's short for 'withdrawing'. Goes back to the time when men and women used to withdraw from the dining room to spend the night talking, reading and praying for the invention of television.

'Any action?' Joe asks, sensing the change in the air, feeling free to chat now that I'm not scowling like Rasputin.

I try my best Geordie. 'Norra bit've it.'

Joe winces. 'Do that again and I'm off.'

'You don't think I could pass for a native?'

'In Australia, perhaps.'

We settle down in a pair of busted chairs to wait for the ghost. The chairs had been dumped in the yard out back. We dragged them in during our first night on watch, when we grew tired of standing.

We've spent the last three nights waiting for the ghost to show. (My first night in London was devoted to a traditional pub crawl, which wasn't as rowdy as it sounds, since Joe only drinks non-alcoholic beer and I rarely allow myself more than four pints.) The restless spirit is meant to put in regular appearances – once or twice a week, according to the lady who owns the place – but so far it's been elusive.

I'm a writer. All of my books have been about ghosts. It's not because I can't think of anything else to write about, or because I have scores of fans hungering for my next supernatural tome. Each book has approached the nature of poltergeists in a different way. Each has been an attempt to explain how ghosts can exist. Or, more accurately, how *my* ghosts exist.

I'm not stupid. I know they're probably the workings of a deluded mind. I accept that I'm most likely hovering over the abyss of an insane pit, and that the spirits are nothing more than the projections of a deeply troubled psyche. But I don't *want* to be crazy. I refuse to accept that I'm a loon. I want to fight this thing and find my way back to normality.

Most people would seek psychiatric help, but that's not an option in my case. So I've gone a different route. I'm trying to prove that ghosts are real. If I can do that, I can hopefully come to terms with my own retinue, maybe even find a way to banish them.

The ghosts terrified me when they first began to appear. My world turned on its head. I had screaming fits. I sought escape through alcohol and drugs, but the ghosts followed me everywhere. I almost blew my brains out, just to get away from them. I'm sure I would have, except that one night, in the middle of my mental anguish, I had the (probably crazy) idea that I might not be imagining the shades, that they might be real. That slim possibility gave me the strength to pull body and soul together, and my life since then has been a quest to prove to myself that we live in a world of wonders.

When I first started looking for proof, I read lots of ghost stories, hoping to find something that might set me on the path of true understanding. I found myself having ideas for stories of my own, based on what I had read and my experiences in the field. Having a lot of dead time to fill (pun intended), I began tinkering with the ideas, fleshing them out. The writing helped me blank out the ghosts. It served as an anchor to reality, gave me the sense that I was doing something meaningful, let me believe I wasn't the raving lunatic that I fear I am.

Short stories led to longer stories, then a rough draft of a novel. Out of curiosity, I submitted samples of my work to a few agents, to see what they'd make of my ghostly ramblings. To my surprise, a couple reacted positively and I signed with one of them. Thus Edward Sieveking the author was born, though I wasn't known as that back then.

Joe is one of my more avid fans. He's read all three of my books several times and remembers more about them than I do. In the pub that first night, he was talking about characters and events that I only dimly recalled. It's been six years since my first book saw print. I throw myself completely into a novel while I'm working on it, but when it fails to produce any answers to the riddles that plague me, I publish it, put it behind me and move on.

Joe thought that writers carried each and every book around with them for life. He doesn't understand how I can spend two or three years working on a story, then forget about the finer details overnight. He's a bit disappointed. I'll have to look

15

through my old notes when I get home and email him a few background scraps and discarded plot lines, restore his faith in me.

'It's freezing,' Joe says, breathing warm air down the neck of his jumper.

'I noticed.' It shouldn't be. It's a balmy night outside.

'Maybe the ghost's coming. The temperature drops before an appearance, doesn't it?'

'Sometimes,' I nod. 'I was in a room once where it plunged twenty degrees in the space of a minute.'

'Did a ghost appear?' He's smiling. He's never seen a ghost. Doesn't really believe that we're going to find anything here.

'I don't know. I had to leave. It got too cold.'

Joe rubs his hands together. He's wearing a chunky grey jumper and a duffel coat, but is shivering worse than me, even though I'm only clad in a light shirt. I wouldn't have thought that someone with Joe's physique would feel the chill. He's as muscular as a wrestler. He looks odd, actually, because he's not a big man, with small hands and a neat, oval face.

He notices me studying him and grins shakily. 'Old wounds,' he explains. 'They play up in the cold. You should see me in winter — if I leave the house in less than three jumpers and two pairs of jeans, I have to be thawed out by an open fire.'

I smile sympathetically. Joe told me about his injuries a couple of days ago, when I asked why he was walking around in the middle of a heatwave fully dressed from neck to ankle. His mother grew up in Northern Ireland and they used to go back on regular visits. One day they were out shopping. There was an explosion. Joe was caught in the blast. He nearly died. Doctors patched up the worst of the damage, but his body is a mass of scars and broken skin. He never exposes his flesh in public, ashamed of how he looks. That's why he grew a thick beard — his lower face is scarred too.

'We can leave if you like,' I offer.

Joe shakes his head. 'And miss my big moment? Not bloody likely.' Joe is intent on making this book work. He's thrilled at the thought of contributing to one of my novels. He's determined to assist me in every way possible. He'd probably pump money into the venture if I let him.

'We could bring in an electric fire,' I suggest.

'No good. The ghost shies away from electrics.'

That's what the owner of the house told us. It's why we're sitting by candlelight. Ghosts are shy creatures, loath to reveal themselves. I know from previous studies that they often choose the most inopportune moments to appear, when you're fiddling with your camera or pointing it in another direction. Sceptics mock such failures, but they don't realize how canny the spirits can be.

Canny. I've picked that up from Joe. The new book is set in London. I need to get to grips with the way the locals speak. I'll have to make sure I mix with some genuine Cockneys though — if Joe's my only reference, I won't know if I'm using southern or northern terminology.

'You still haven't told me what the story's about,' Joe comments.

'I'm not sure yet,' I tell him. 'I know some of what I want, but there are still large gaps to be filled in.'

'But you're going with the SHC angle, right?'

'I kind of have to, to keep you happy, don't I?' I chuckle.

'It doesn't matter a damn to me,' Joe says. 'Honestly.'

Joe was the one who got me interested in spontaneous human combustion. He'd read a lot about it and mentioned SHC a few times in emails, told me how scientists were unable to explain how it happened, discussed a few of the differing theories with me. Intrigued, I started to do some research of my own — I've tried to cover every supernatural angle over the years, seeking answers in the most unlikely and unrelated of places. That research eventually led me here.

'It's going to be a horror book, isn't it?' Joe presses.

'Maybe,' I grunt.

'Come on,' Joe groans. 'You can tell me. It won't go any further.'

'You'll be the first to know. But you have to be patient. Sometimes plots come together quickly. More times they don't.'

'It's really not all there yet?' Joe asks.

'No.'

'So . . .' He blushes. 'If I came up with an idea, and it was really good, and you used it, could I get a credit?'

'Sure.'

'Imagine,' he sighs. 'An Edward Sieveking and Joe Rickard book. Your name at the top, mine below, slightly smaller print.'

'Maybe *your* name should be at the top,' I deadpan.

Joe withers me with a look. 'No need to be cynical. I know the book's yours. I was only thinking how nice it would be to –'

'What was that?' I silence him with a sharp gesture.

There's a low rumbling noise. My hopes rise. Joe dashes them.

'Just a cat.' He laughs. 'A tom on the make.'

He's right, and I'm annoyed with myself. I should have made the connection before him. I'm the one with experience.

We settle back into silence. I think about when I first made contact with Joe, nearly a year ago. I was promoting my most recent book, *Soul Vultures*. It was the first time I'd released a novel under my own name. Before then I'd called myself E.S. King. (My original agent thought that Stephen King fans might buy my work on the strength of the pseudonym, but in fact it worked against me and hampered sales.) With *Soul Vultures* and a new agent, Edward Sieveking finally saw the light of day. My first two books, *Nights of Fear* and *Summer's Shades*, were re-released and did better business second time round. I wasn't exactly haunting the best-seller charts, but after a stumbling start, I had a definite feeling that I was on my way.

I took part in an internet chat-room session that turned out to be a damp squib. Several people lodged questions about the new book, but Joe was the only one who seemed familiar with my past work. I sent him a signed copy of *Soul Vultures* and the reprints of the other pair, and we became Facebook buddies. A few months ago, I told him about the start I'd made on my next novel, mentioning the fact that I was exploring the field of SHC, and he talked me into setting it in London.

'This city's spookier than a graveyard,' he vowed. 'Plus I know people in the field who could be helpful.'

It didn't take him long to persuade me. I'd been to London a few times, but years ago, before I established myself as a writer. I'd never explored it with a creative eye. My other novels were set in rural towns – two in America, one in Canada – but a city was vital to the framework this time, and London seemed as good a place as any. Besides, I was looking forward to meeting Joe. I'm a loner and don't have many friends. I thought it would be good for me to team up with an assistant. My agent keeps telling me that I come across too stiffly in interviews. I was hoping that time spent with Joe might loosen me up and help me talk more freely about my work.

Joe leans forward and taps my knee, interrupting my reverie. His dark brown eyes are wide. He points towards the opposite wall. As I turn, a wind gusts through the room and the candles blow out. Fortunately there are numerous holes and cracks in the boards covering the front windows, and enough light seeps in from the street lamps to see by.

Mist is rising from the bare brick wall. No, not rising . . . *emanating*. It doesn't drift like normal mist would. It's bubbling out, as if blown from an invisible pair of lips. Dirty grey mist, coming from within the wall.

'Shit,' Joe gasps, getting to his feet. 'It's real.' He's trembling. This is his first time. Nothing can prepare you for that initial encounter, that moment of confirmation that there really *is* more to the world than what most people ever see.

The bubble has reached its limits. About three feet in diameter, two thirds visible, one third obscured inside the wall. The mist eddies within the translucent boundaries, thick and thin tendrils overlapping, blending into one another. I lay my camera on my lap. According to the landlady, a flash frightens the apparition away and nothing develops, but I've got to try.

'Can you hear popping sounds?' Joe asks, leaning towards the bubble, face aglow, eyes wide with wonder.

'Yes.'

'What are they?'

I shrug. 'Ghosts forming. The mist reacting with the atmosphere. Exploding air bubbles inside the wall. Take your pick.'

I rise from my chair, walk around the ball of mist and study it from the sides. I can see through it, but only barely. Cold air radiates from it.

'Ed,' croaks Joe, and raises a trembling finger. '*Faces.*'

I return to my chair and stand by it. Within the mist, faces – or eerie simulacra – are forming. They aren't clearly defined, but they seem to be human. Glimpses of eyes and ears, open mouths, teeth. I think of the figures hovering behind me but I don't look back to compare their faces with those in the bubble. I don't need to. Those six faces are as familiar to me by now as my own.

I don't show it, but I'm excited. Apparitions are rarely this vivid. This is one of the most astonishing encounters I've yet to experience.

I turn towards Joe. 'Describe what you're seeing.'

He gulps, tugs nervously at his beard, then whispers reverently, almost afraid to speak. 'A woman's face, maybe twenty years old. Long hair. The face is changing now. Losing its shape. Gone.' A few seconds of silence. 'Now another's forming.'

'A boy's,' I interrupt. 'Plump. Short hair, badly cut fringe, what looks like a bruise under his left eye?'

'That's it,' Joe agrees.

'Great. We're seeing the same thing.' It's important to establish that fact. People don't always interpret apparitions the same way.

The faces so far have been small, embedded within the heart of the mist. Now one forms closer to the surface of the bubble, larger than the rest. An old man. We've been told that the other faces vary, but this one always returns.

'This is unreal,' Joe moans as the man's gaze sweeps the room. Joe is shaking badly. He glances at the door and I expect him to run. But then he bunches his fingers into fists and forces himself to stand firm.

'Do you see his pupils?' I ask. Joe stares, then nods. 'I couldn't see any on the others. Their features were blurred. This one's less ethereal.'

'They're real,' Joe mutters. 'Ghosts are real.'

'So they'd have us believe,' I say sourly, then press closer to the bubble. 'Tell me your name,' I whisper. 'Prove you are what you appear to be.'

The ghost doesn't respond. None of them ever has.

We spend a couple of minutes watching the old man's face as his eyes roam. When there are no further developments, I decide to try a snap. 'Seen all you want?' I ask Joe as I produce my camera.

He nods reluctantly. 'Yeah.'

I take a quick shot. The face dissipates instantly and the

bubble loses its shape. Most of the mist is sucked back into the wall. A strong sulphurous stench fills the room. I cover my mouth with the mask I always bring along. Joe also has one – I gave it to him on our first night here – but he seems to have misplaced it. While he fumbles in his pockets and coughs, I take him by the elbow and guide him out into the corridor. Once the coughing subsides, he wipes tears from his eyes and grins weakly. 'Must have left the mask at home.' He stares through the open door at the last of the mist vanishing into thin air. 'You see shit like this all the time?'

'No two apparitions are the same, but yes.'

'Fuck.' He shivers. 'They're really real.'

I arch an eyebrow at him. 'You reckon?'

'After what we've just seen? Of course.' He squints at me. 'Are you saying you don't believe?'

'I want to,' I say softly. 'More than you could imagine. But . . .' I check the camera. Nothing in the picture except the wall and some mist. I show it to Joe.

'So?' He frowns. 'You said ghosts are almost impossible to photograph.'

'Yes. That's why I'm sceptical.' I put the camera away, disappointed as I often am after a sighting, even one as spectacular as this.

Joe is staring at me uncertainly. 'If that's not enough proof for you, what is?'

I pull a face. 'I want one of them to *tell* me it's real. If that was truly the shade of a dead person, I want it to talk with me, answer my questions, confirm that it is what it seems.'

'That's never happened?' Joe asks.

I shake my head. 'I've spoken with the dead many times through mediums and Ouija boards, but how can you trust a source like that? I know most of the tricks that fakes use to fool gullible customers. Even on the few occasions when I've been surprised, when I've not been able to explain what has happened, I haven't found concrete, one hundred per cent *proof*.'

'What about what we saw tonight?' Joe challenges me.

I smile bitterly. 'It was incredible. But what does it prove? People used to think that the Northern Lights were dead spirits shimmering across the sky. Who's to say there isn't a scientific explanation for what we've just seen?'

Joe scratches at his beard. 'But in your books, you claim that ghosts are real.'

'And I want them to be. But I haven't found proof yet.'

'What would prove it to you, Ed?' Joe asks.

'A genuine encounter,' I reply. 'A ghost who'll address me directly, tell me its name, answer questions. One with a verifiable history, who can prove it's every bit as real as you are.'

'That's a big ask,' Joe notes.

'Not if they're real,' I laugh, then smirk at Joe. 'What do you reckon? Has that put you off ghost-hunting? Do you want to leave it here and not push on?'

'Are you shitting me?' Joe gasps. 'That was amazing! It scared me but I loved it. Back out now? Not on your nelly.'

'Not on my what?'

He waves the question away. 'I'll explain later. Where next? I'm hungry for more.'

'That's enough for tonight,' I tell him. 'Let's go home. It's late.'

Joe checks his watch and whistles. 'We've missed closing time. Fancy coming back to my place for a few drinks?'

'Thanks, but no. I want to write this up while it's fresh in my mind.'

'No problem. Are we returning tomorrow?'

'No. This house has revealed all of its secrets. It's time to move on. There's a guy I'm trying to arrange a meeting with. Pierre Vallance. He's a medium but he doesn't believe in ghosts.'

'How can a medium not believe in ghosts?' Joe frowns.

'That's what I want to find out,' I say drily, then lead Joe back to the security of the safe, boring, normal world. Behind us, my six shades glide along after me, as silent, observant and condemning as always.

TWO

It's been a long time since I last visited London. The city has changed in many ways, become more American with its new high-rises and franchised chains of stores and cafés. It's still a different world to mine, with its old grey buildings and its polite but oddly stiff people, but it's not as out of sync with the States as it used to be. There was a time when I felt completely alien here. Now it's almost like visiting any city Stateside. Globalization has a lot to answer for.

Having said that, you can't find a chippy like Super Fish on Waterloo Road anywhere in the States. Or a van parked down a side street that serves jellied eels, like Tubby Isaacs in Aldgate. And I've never seen anything like the Hunterian Museum, where you can find the bones of an Irish giant, pickled penises, old surgical instruments that look more like tools of torture, and a whole lot more. They're all places that Joe has introduced me to, steering me clear of the usual tourist hotspots, giving me an insider's taste of the city.

The other thing I've really noticed this time is that London's landscape is smudged with the fingerprints of the dead. I trudge the streets, lined with houses that date back hundreds of years, built on plague sites and Roman burial grounds, their foundations teeming with history, and it's as if I'm taking a stroll through the largest mausoleum in the world, where phantoms jostle for space with the living. The hairs on my arms stand to attention, shapes flicker at the periphery of my vision and the air crackles with the whispered conversations of the dead. Whether they're imagined or real, it's an amazing place to visit, but I wouldn't be able to live here. A few months of this and I'd be fit for Bedlam.

I've been exploring the city, either with Joe – he runs a small electrical repairs shop on a part-time basis, so has plenty of free time on his hands – or by myself. I use cabs, buses and the Tube more often than not, searching for shades of the dead among the detritus of the living.

I didn't always believe in an afterlife. In truth, I'm still not convinced. But I'm open to the possibility of it now, and have been since I attracted my own coterie of other-worldly spirits.

My ghosts follow me everywhere, four men, one woman and a nine-year-old girl, haunting my every waking step, standing guard while I sleep, ever vigilant, spitefully waiting for a chance to catch me unawares and shock me. I know they're probably delusional projections. The six are shades of people I knew, whose deaths darkened the corridors of my mind. The spectral figures are almost certainly products of a guilty subconscious. But I wanted them to be real. I *needed* them to be real. So I opened myself up to the possibility that there's a life after death, and I've been searching for proof of that ever since. The quest for answers has helped keep me sane. Or as sane as someone who sees ghosts can be!

All of my novels focus on where ghosts come from, how they form, why they exist. In my first three I looked at how souls could be bound to this realm by magical or spiritual forces. This time I want to take a more scientific approach. I've pretty much exhausted the mystical angles, at least for the time being. Time to travel down another route in search of something that might explain how and why *my* ghosts came to haunt me, that might provide me with the means to banish them from my line of sight, back to whatever dark holes the army of the dead rest up in.

I really am vague about the plot. That wasn't a lie. I know I'm going to focus on spontaneous human combustion – because it lets me explore the concept that ghosts might be the result of a violent, unnatural death – but I'm not sure where I want to go with it. I'm relying heavily on research for inspiration and direction. Right now I have no idea where it's going to lead me.

We meet Pierre Vallance in his local Starbucks. At first we chat about the States. I've noticed that lots of people here like to discuss America with me when they hear my accent. The media keeps telling us that the US has lost its standing as the world's foremost superpower, that China, India and Russia are taking over, but from what I've experienced in my travels, America is still the place that everyone wants to talk about.

When Pierre's had his fix of Stateside tittle-tattle, he tells us about his life as a sceptical medium. Pierre has heard voices all his life. He doesn't believe in ghosts, but became a medium so that he could explore (and exploit) his talent. Over time he came to the conclusion that his brain acted as an amplifier for electromagnetic signals which the people close to him were transmitting.

'When people think, their brains generate waves,' he explains, sipping an espresso. 'I somehow pick up on those signals and convert them into voices.'

'You mean you can read minds?' Joe asks, squinting nervously — I guess we all have dark secrets we want to hide from the world at large.

Pierre shrugs. 'To an extent. I always explain to my clients that I'm using science to help reveal the workings of their subconscious, but many choose to ignore me. They'd rather believe in an afterlife and ghosts whispering through me. And since the customer's always right, I don't argue with them too strenuously.'

I come away from our meeting intrigued. If Pierre can transform brain waves into voices, maybe there are others who can turn them into visions or physical objects. In such a world, almost anything is possible. That gives me a whole universe of ideas to play with.

I breeze through the next week, plot lines clicking together neatly, my muse trilling like a diva. To my surprise, I enjoy working with Joe. Although I willingly took him on as an assistant, I wasn't convinced it was the right move, and I thought I'd have to cut him loose sooner rather than later. But he's been a real asset. Without forcing me, he's got me talking more than I have in years. Usually I grunt when people ask me questions, instinctively cautious around strangers and even warier of those who try to get close to me, but with Joe I've started stringing whole sentences together. I'm not sure what it is about him. I just like the guy. He brings out a lighter, warmer part of me, a part I thought I'd lost a long time ago.

To reward him for helping me connect with my positive vibes, I tell Joe where my story has been leading me. The book is going to be a supernatural thriller. My central character dies of spontaneous human combustion, then returns as a ghost and embarks on a quest to unearth the truth behind his demise.

'A ghost out for revenge,' Joe beams. 'I like it!'

Trying to decide on locations, I check out the infamous Whitechapel area, haunt of Jack the Ripper. It's as eerie now as it must have been back then. I'd love to set my book there, but I'm worried that readers might dismiss it as a Ripper cash-in.

Brixton appeals to me more. You come up out of the Tube to find street preachers set among hawkers and homeless people trying to flog copies of the *Big Issue*. A dark atmosphere. Brixton Market feels like something out of a horror film, maze-like, roofed-over, claustrophobic. I could have my ghostly hero burst into flames outside the Tube station, in front of a preacher.

I look around and imagine a burning man stumbling through the market, women screaming, men trying to extinguish the fire, the stench of scorched flesh. I grin ghoulishly. Sometimes this job requires me to explore the sickest of scenarios. That's why it's so much fun!

To afford me a different taste of London, Joe has arranged a night out on the river. One of his friends is holding a party on a boat. There'll be a meal and a disco, and the boat will sail up and down the Thames into the early hours of the morning. I'm not keen on parties, and at first I gave Joe the brush-off. But he persisted, said I'd been working hard and that it would be good for me to let my hair down. In the end I agreed just to shut him up.

I'm shaving when my cell phone (they call them mobiles here) rings. It's Joe. 'You're gonna kill me,' he groans. 'I can't make it. My mam took ill. I'm catching the next train to Newcastle.'

'Is it serious?' I ask, concerned.

'Hopefully not. Mam's had a couple of bad turns these last few years and seen them off. She'll probably be fine, but I need to be with her, just in case.'

'Of course. I understand completely. It's not a problem.'

'I don't know when I'll be back,' he says.

'Don't rush on my account,' I tell him.

'Will you still meet up with John Meyher?' Joe asks. Meyher's an expert in the field of spontaneous human combustion. He doesn't give many interviews, but Joe pulled a few strings.

'Of course,' I tell him. 'Unless you'd rather I wait until you're back?'

'No need to do that,' he says, but he sounds pleased that I offered. 'What about tonight? Will you go to the party?'

'I'll probably give it a miss. I don't know any of your friends.'

'So introduce yourself to them.'

'Maybe. I'll see how I feel. I might just pop out for dinner and a walk instead.'

'Don't be a miserable old sod,' Joe growls. 'Go!' He hangs up on me.

I sit on the edge of the bed rubbing the smooth half of my face, considering the night ahead. Missing the party doesn't concern me, but I liked the idea of sailing along the Thames in the dark. I decide to go. Even if I don't mingle, I can have a few drinks, sit on deck, enjoy the fresh air and the sights. I might pick up some ideas.

I finish shaving. Slap on aftershave and deodorant. I sit half-naked by the TV for an hour, flicking through the channels. Then I dress and head out.

I avoid the grander hotels when I travel, but I don't like roughing it either. The Royal Munster is typical of my hotel of choice, old and faded, situated close to Earls Court, anonymous among the scores of other hotels in the area. Dusty doormen and bellboys, family-friendly, favoured by tourists rather than business executives.

The doorman is a white-haired guy in his sixties who tips his hat to customers and addresses them with exaggerated formality. I've told him to call me Ed, but he only nods and smiles, then hits me with a hearty 'Mr Sieveking, sir!' His name's Fred, but he prefers Mr Lloyd.

'Nice night to be heading out, Mr Sieveking,' he wheezes, hailing a cab.

'Care to join me, Mr Lloyd?'

He chuckles. 'I would if I was off duty. I'd take you to see people you could use in your books. I know a man in the Queen's Guard who puts mustard on everything he eats. And there's a . . .'

He rattles on for a few minutes, but I make no move to halt him. I like listening to Fred. He's one of the world's great liars, full of outrageous stories.

He pauses to catch his breath and I make my excuses. 'Have to be loving and leaving you, Mr Lloyd,' I say, slipping him a tip.

'Maybe I'll catch you on the way back,' he says.

'Only if you're a late bird,' I laugh.

The taxi driver heads for the Chelsea Embankment when I tell him where I'm going, then it's a quick journey parallel to the river and we're at the Victoria Embankment about ten minutes later. I stroll down the gangplank to the deck, where a pretty stewardess in a revealing naval uniform welcomes the guests. She asks for my name, checks her list, hands me a whistle, a paper hat and party poppers. She says I can have my picture taken with her kissing my cheek, for a reasonable rate. I refuse politely. I'm a camera-shy guy. I prefer not to be photographed even when giving interviews, which annoys reporters. My agent often argues with me about it, but I don't want shots of me to be freely circulated.

The meal doesn't start for another hour, so I make my way to the bar and order a beer. I don't want to drink too much, not on a boat, or I'll be throwing up all night. Alcohol and boats don't mix. I learnt that lesson the hard way on a cruise of the African coast many years ago.

I'm surrounded by young party animals, all of whom seem to be in select groups. A couple of teenagers waylay me and ask who I am, what I do, how I know the birthday girl. I explain my connection to Joe, but they don't know him. My job description draws more of a response.

31

'A writer!' they hoot, impressed. One says, 'I always wanted to be a writer. Do you make much money?'

I spend a quarter of an hour trying to convince them that my books don't sell by the millions. They don't accept it. They insist that I must be fabulously well-to-do, on a par with Stephen King, even though they've never heard of me. Finally I concede that yes, I'm stinking rich, and yes, I wrote *The Exorcist*. With that settled, they roll away to tell their friends about me, with the unexpected result that hours later, long after I've forgotten about them, an irate gentleman jabs an angry finger into my chest and grunts, 'You didn't write *The Exorcist*. That bloke Blatty did. You're a fraud.'

Dinner's a simple affair — mashed potatoes and sausages, some unsavoury-looking carrots, cheap wine. The other guests go at it with conviction. Maybe I'm fussy because I'm getting on in years. The birthday girl is celebrating her twenty-first, and most of her friends fall into the same age bracket. It's been a long time since I saw twenty-one.

As the paper plates are collected and disposed of, the tables are removed and the dance floor opens up. The DJ hasn't taken up his post yet, but someone sticks on a track and the more avid revellers writhe to the beat. I stand watching the dancers before it strikes me that this is a sign of seedy middle age – enviously ogling scantily clad girls while they strut their funky stuff – and I scuttle away in search of a refill.

I prop up the bar for a couple of hours, eavesdropping on the conversation of strangers. Most people ignore me, but at one point a girl with a blond bob shows interest. She can't be more than twenty, way too young for a man with a receding hairline, but the beers have stripped me of a decade and I'm thinking about what it would be like to take her back to the Royal Munster for a night of merry debauchery.

That's when I'm accused of fraud by the testy William Peter

Blatty fan. In the ensuing embarrassing silence, my pretty admirer coughs, says she ought to be mingling more, wishes me well and hastily takes her leave.

Ordering another beer, I decide I've had enough of the bar and head for the deck. The fresh air revives me. I stand alone at the stern and study the trail of churning water we leave in our wake. Leaning across, I peer towards the bow, which is packed.

A couple emerge up the stairs and glare at me. I think they want the stern to themselves. Too bad. I'm not moving. Grumbling softly, they stand with their backs to me, making out. A few more stagger up over the next half-hour, but the area remains relatively clear, emptying when the DJ plays a popular number, slowly half-filling as tired legs force temporary retreats from the action.

I'm not a dancer. I keep a vigil on the riverbanks instead, casting a curious eye over a variety of buildings, old and new, decrepit and abandoned, or simply closed for the night, trying to find ways to incorporate them into the slowly forming plot of the novel. There are plenty of recognizable landmarks nestled in among the mix, the Tower of London, the Globe, Tate Modern, the Oxo tower, but I don't want to use any of those — too well known.

My ghosts share the deck with me, glittering lightly against the backdrop of the night sky. Two of them are floating over the Thames, treading air as if it was the most natural thing in the world. They ignore the sights, their eyes, as ever, trained on me. The thin bald man with a sharp beard drifts through me, resulting in a momentary chill. I could recall his name if I wanted – I'll never forget their names – but I don't. I try not to dwell on their identities. It reminds me of my past and why they haunt me.

As we pass the London Eye and the historic Houses of Parliament, I glance at the buildings across the way and notice a hospital. I ask a young man for its name. 'St Thomas's,' he says, staring at me as if I'm mad for asking.

The hospital interests me. I could use it in my book. Perhaps my central character rematerializes there. It's a logical spot for a ghost to turn up. I picture the scene as his eyes emerge from an ethereal fog, opening for the first time since his death. He gazes around, wondering where the hell he is. When he realizes it's a hospital, he relaxes. He remembers burning in Brixton and assumes he's been brought here to recover. Digging out my notebook (it goes everywhere with me), I jot down ideas.

Calmly he tries turning — can't — looks down at his body — there's nothing there!!! Tries to scream — can't — no lungs! — fades away again.

I like it. Later he re-forms, and this time he has a body and knows something is seriously wrong, although he doesn't yet accept that he's dead.

While I'm working on plot lines, a woman comes up the stairs and steps to the rail, close to where I'm standing. She perches her wine glass on the rail, fingers lightly cupping the stem, and stares off into space. I study her out of the corner of my eye. Older than most of the guests, mid to late twenties. Light auburn hair, straight cut, pageboy fashion, long at the back. Slender build, tightly clad in a stunning black dress which reveals plenty of leg but little cleavage. Her fingernails have been painted silver and she wears soft silver tights. There's some sort of silver glitter around her eyes too, so the lids sparkle every time she blinks.

I'm paying attention to her because she's the first unaccompanied female I've seen up here. The rest have been with boyfriends. Although I've been concentrating on work, I now remember why Joe pressed me to come to the party – to unwind and have fun – and turn my thoughts to chat-up lines. I was never good at this kind of thing. I'm not a natural charmer.

Women are sometimes attracted to me because of the curt, moody front I present to the world, but I usually struggle if I'm the one who has to do the chasing.

While I'm pondering my approach, destiny lends a hand. The woman sighs and rolls her head from side to side. Her hand twitches while she's not looking and she inadvertently knocks her wine glass overboard. She gasps, dives after it, misses. As it sails over the side, I lean across, fingers outstretched. I almost grab it – if I was the hero in one of my books, I'd catch it – but it eludes me, plummets downwards and vanishes into the dark water of the Thames.

'Oh dear,' the woman says as I pull myself back from the rail.

'Sorry,' I smile.

'Not your fault,' she assures me, and glances around semi-guiltily. 'Do you think the crew saw?'

'I doubt it.'

'Maybe I should offer to pay for it just the same.'

I laugh lightly. 'I'm sure it happens all the time. A hazard of river life. Yours won't be the only glass lost to the tide tonight.'

She relaxes and leans against the rail. 'I suppose you're right. I always panic when I break something. It's the way I was brought up.' She speaks in soft, measured tones. 'Are you American?' she asks.

'Yes.'

'Which part?'

'I've travelled around a lot, but I live in Montana now.'

'I've never been to Montana. It's somewhere I always meant to visit.'

'You should. It's spectacular.' We're standing, elbows to the rail, facing one another. She gives me a speculative once-over. I hold my gaze steady.

'Are you a friend of Shar's?' she asks.

'Shar?' I echo blankly. Then I remember the birthday girl. 'No. I'm a FOAF.'

'A foaf?' She blinks, and her eyelids glitter silver confusion.

'FOAF — friend of a friend.'

'Oh.' She giggles. 'I thought you meant you were in the forces.'

There's a moment of nice silence.

'I'm a friend of Joe's,' I explain, not wanting to let the silence develop. 'Joe Rickard?'

She shakes her head. 'I know hardly anyone here. I'm a client of Shar's. She works in a beauty salon.' She drums her fingernails on the rail, then holds them up in the air and waves. 'Ta-da!'

'Did Shar paint those?' I ask.

'No. But she gave me the manicure.' She studies her nails and frowns. 'You don't think I went a bit heavy on the silver, do you? I thought it would look good under disco lights, but out here in the open . . .'

I shrug. I like the way they look, but if I said so it'd sound lame, like I was hitting on her. Which I *am*, but I don't want to be obvious about it.

'I'm sorry I came,' she says, lowering her voice. 'Shar invited me, but she invited lots of her clients and I'm about the only one who turned up. I think I was supposed to give her a card and a big tip and make my excuses.'

There's another pause, during which we smile awkwardly at each other and try thinking of things to say. This time she breaks it by holding out a hand. 'Deleena Emerson.'

'Ed Sieveking,' I respond, touching my hand to hers. 'Pleased to meet you.' As our hands part I say, '*Deleena?* I haven't heard that name before. Where does it come from?'

'It's not a real name,' Deleena says. 'Just something my mother thought up.'

'It's nice. I like it.'

'Me too,' she says, and blushes sweetly. 'Ed Sieveking,' she murmurs, running the backs of her fingernails down her left cheek, as if trying to wipe the rosy glow away. 'Did you know there's a writer called Edward Sieveking?'

I stare at her, momentarily thrown. 'What?'

'A horror writer. Worth checking out if you like that sort of thing.'

I'm caught off guard. I'm not used to strangers recognizing my name, unless it's at a convention. Deleena stares at me uncertainly as I gawp at her. I think about saying nothing, letting the moment pass. For some ridiculous reason I'm almost ashamed to admit to my identity. But then I take a deep breath and squeeze it out. '*I'm* Edward Sieveking. The writer.'

'No,' she frowns, suspecting a joke.

'Yes,' I grin, gaining in confidence.

'*You* wrote *Soul Vultures*?' The disbelief – as if no mere mortal could have been responsible for such a wonderful book – makes me preen like a peacock.

'Yes,' I drawl. 'And *Nights of Fear* and *Summer's Shades*. I used to write under a pseudonym . . .'

'. . . E.S. King!' she finishes, whooping with delight. 'That's how I discovered *Summer's Shades*. I mistook it for a Stephen King book. When I realized it wasn't, I decided I might as well buy it anyway, since there was nothing else I was interested in.' She covers her mouth with a hand. 'Oh, what an awful thing to say! Like I only bought your book because I was desperate.'

'That's OK,' I laugh. 'I'll take any sale I can get.' Licking my lips, I fish blatantly for a compliment. 'Did you like it?'

'I bought the other two, didn't I?' she replies impishly. 'Actually, I wasn't *too* keen on *Shades* – I think it's your weakest – but it interested me enough to make me pick up *Nights of Fear*, then *Soul Vultures* when it came out.' She studies me again. 'This is weird. I've met plenty of writers at parties and functions but I've never bumped into one of my favourites by accident. And to think I was regretting coming.'

'You don't regret it any more?' I smile.

'No,' she says. 'I'm only sorry I didn't know in advance that you'd be here. I could have brought my books to be signed.'

'Maybe I can sign them for you another time,' I suggest.

'Maybe,' she agrees, eyes half-slit as she considers that.

We talk about my books and what it's like to be a writer. As much as I love discussing my work, I try steering the conversation on to other topics a couple of times, afraid she'll think I'm in love with myself. But she won't have it. She asks about sales and royalties, how long it takes to write a novel, how I research my stories. She's dismayed when she learns how little I make.

'That's terrible!' she cries, resting a sympathetic hand on mine. The heat almost moulds the flesh of my palm to the rail. 'I knew you weren't on the best-seller lists but I'd no idea your sales were that poor.'

'They're not *that* bad,' I demur. 'Those are actually pretty good figures. And sales have picked up a lot this last year or two.'

'Still,' she mutters, 'how can you afford to write full-time?'

'My parents left me an inheritance,' I lie, as I always do whenever that question is asked. 'And I was in business – computers – before striking out as an author. I've enough set by to see me through the lean years. Besides, I can live frugally when I have to. Money isn't everything.'

'Nice to see someone dedicated to his craft,' she says.

'I don't know about dedication,' I respond modestly. 'I'm just stubborn. I know I'm not the world's greatest writer – not even its greatest horror writer – but I'm determined to prove that I can make it, even if my books are lacklustre, thrill-free affairs, as one critic cruelly put it.'

'But they're not!' she exclaims, tightening her fingers over my knuckles, which melt with ecstasy at the pressure. 'You're a wonderful writer.'

'Oh stop.' I grimace, and lay my free hand over hers. 'How'd you like to become my agent?'

'What's the starting salary?'

'Nothing.'

'I'll take it.'

We laugh in chorus and my fingers link with hers. Deleena looks down at our hands and her laughter subsides. I half-unhook my fingers from hers. If she takes her hand away now, the moment will be spoiled and I'm sure she'll find an excuse to leave. But to my delight she lets it lie where it is and gazes up at the underbelly of a bridge as we pass.

We discuss her life. She works in the City for a private banking firm. Not the most interesting of jobs, she says, but the pay's good and so are the perks — trips abroad three or four times a year, regular hours, plenty of promotion opportunities.

Deleena left school at sixteen and 'arsed about for a couple of years' before marrying an older gentleman a week after her eighteenth birthday. 'It was a mistake. I didn't love him, didn't even really like him. But he was a man of the world, he had a good CD collection, he was –'

'You married a man for his CDs?' I interrupt.

'Taste in music is very important,' she asserts. 'I could never get involved with anyone who listens to the Eagles or Rod Stewart.'

'What about Dire Straits and Bob Dylan?' I ask nervously.

'Dylan's a legend. Dire Straits . . .' She makes a so-so gesture.

'Acceptable?'

'Just about.'

'Phew.' I pretend to wipe sweat from my brow.

The marriage lasted eight months. 'I hated him by the end,

which was wrong, because I was the one who forced him to get married. I sat down with him a few years ago and we managed to put things straight. We're good friends now.'

After the divorce, she ran home to her parents to sort out her head. Her mother convinced her to finish her education, which she did, earning three A levels at night class, then graduating with honours in business studies at university. She spent a couple of years in Europe brushing up on her languages – she speaks six and is working on Chinese – and fell into banking more by chance than design. Upon her return to London she went to work for one of the major banks, before being head-hunted by her current employer four years ago.

Piecing together her chronology as it unfolds, I realize she's older than I thought. When I ask delicately about her age, she laughs, taps her nose and says she won't see thirty again.

I quiz her about current boyfriends. Nobody serious. There was a guy called Mark who she met while travelling across Europe. They were together for a few years. Only brief flings since then.

Then it's my turn to spill the beans. I tell her a bit about my early life, how I was born in Chicago, moved to Seattle when I was six, then to Detroit when I was ten, when my father got a job there, back when they still made cars. I gloss over my pre-writing career, like I do when giving interviews, saying I worked in a variety of job across the States. I move on quickly to my more recent travels, the countries I've visited over the last few years.

Given all the travelling, she's convinced I have a girl in every port. I swear that isn't true and pretend my modest sex life is a choice. 'Sex by itself is nothing special,' I insist. 'It's not enough for bodies to touch — hearts and minds have to touch too.'

She stares at me silently, solemnly, then explodes into laughter. 'Bullshitter!'

'What?' I react with wounded innocence, but my smile gives me away.

'How many girls have you sweet-talked into bed with that one?' she jeers.

'Not as many as I'd like,' I admit.

'No wonder. The sixties are a long time gone, flower boy. Get with the programme.'

'So educate me,' I encourage her. 'What am I saying wrong?'

'Everything. Ditch the lines. You don't need them. Be yourself.'

'OK.' I chance it. 'Despite the gruff front, I'm a quiet, introspective guy. One might even say shy, if one was so inclined. I was married once but that went wrong and it hurt. I haven't committed to anyone since. I often think I'm not meant for love, that I'm destined to be alone.'

'Nobody's destined for loneliness,' she disagrees. 'People choose it or they don't. No one's saddled with it.'

I could argue that one with her, but I shrug diplomatically and mutter, 'Maybe.'

The serious turn in our conversation doesn't drain the night of its pleasure, but it sets us reflecting and we don't say much afterwards, just stand, hands joined, listening to the sounds of the disco, staring out over the flowing water of the darkly entrancing Thames.

THREE

Deleena refuses to give me her phone number – she never gives it out to people she's just met, even if they *are* 'fabulously wonderful writers' – but she takes mine and promises to call sometime soon. I don't get to sleep until nearly three in the morning, thinking about her, replaying our conversation inside my head.

A ringing phone startles me. The ghost of the girl is in my face when I jerk awake, hissing silently at me. I ignore her and glance quickly at my watch — I've been asleep less than half an hour. Sitting up, I grab my cell, shake the worst of the wooziness from my head and answer.

'Did I wake you?' Deleena asks.

'Yes,' I yawn.

'I can call later if you'd like.'

'No,' I say quickly. 'Don't hang up.'

There's a long pause. Finally Deleena says, 'I had a good time tonight.'

'Me too.'

'I hope I didn't come across like a groupie. It was only when I got home that I realized how many questions I'd asked about your books. I wanted to ring and say sorry. I was hoping to catch you before you went to bed.'

'Please,' I chuckle. 'You don't have to apologize for fawning over me.'

'I wouldn't have said I was *fawning*,' she mutters.

'Well you were,' I smirk.

Running a hand through my hair, I discover a long piece of purple paper stuck to my scalp. Peeling it off, I ask Deleena if she'd like to meet for breakfast or lunch.

'I can't. I start work early, and I only get to do lunch if it's with a client. Every other day I'm stuck at my desk till closing time.'

'I thought you said you worked regular hours.'

'Regularly long,' she laughs. 'How about meeting up around eight?'

'Great. Where?'

'The National Film Theatre? They're showing a season of eighties horror features. I think *Killer Party* is playing tonight. I know you love slasher flicks, so I thought we could –'

'What gave you that idea?' I interrupt, then recall that *Summer's Shades* features a protagonist who is hooked on gory films.

'You *don't* like horror?' Deleena asks, taken aback.

'Not really, apart from the classics like *The Omen*, *Hellraiser*, *The Exorcist*.'

'But *Summer's Shades* . . . ?'

'My characters aren't me, Deleena.'

'But it's so convincing. *Shades* reads like it was written by somebody truly in love with the genre.'

I laugh. 'Trust me, it wasn't!'

'You aren't a horror buff?'

'Uh-uh.'

'Thank heaven for that,' she sighs. 'I can't stand horror films. I love to read nasty stuff but I can't bear to watch it.'

—'You only suggested the film to keep me happy?' I ask cockily.

'Don't crow,' she warns. 'You don't know my phone number.

If I disconnect and don't call back, you'll be trotting around London on your tod.'

'What's a tod?'

'Don't change the subject,' she snaps.

'OK. Horror films are out. What does that leave?'

She hesitates. 'A meal?'

'Anywhere particular?' She mentions a small restaurant in the West End. I agree to that, then ask, 'And after?'

'Let's wait and see,' she responds. 'Maybe I'll have had enough of you and will want to go home early.'

'Or maybe you'll want to take me home with you,' I whisper cheekily.

A pause. It lengthens. Just when I'm about to ask if she's still there, she whispers back, 'Maybe.' And hangs up.

The next two nights are delicious. We dine by candlelight in snug restaurants, chatting easily, laughing freely. I'm at ease around her, even more so than I am with Joe. I feel like a different, less complicated and reserved person.

Later we go for slow walks around Piccadilly Circus, bustling with young, loud tourists as it always is, no matter what time of the day you visit. The Mall, the wide road running along St James's Park, quiet at night, peaceful, Buck Palace glittering at the end of it like a fairy princess's palace. Through the lovingly maintained expanse of Hyde Park and down by the casually meandering Thames, the green heart and dark blue soul of this grand old dame of a city.

Sometimes we stroll hand in hand, other times with our arms around each other. We talk softly about our past and future, hopes and dreams, disappointments and failures. I don't tell her everything about myself, but I spill more than I have to anyone else recently. Details from my youth, my difficult teens in Detroit, how my parents died (mother of cancer when I was

44

sixteen, father of what I hope was an accidental overdose two years later), some of my marital woes, how few friends I have, what a quiet guy I am.

She works my past out of me effortlessly, charmingly. And I do the same with her, learning of her equally difficult teenage years, the time she spent in rehab, her fractured relationship with her parents, the way she retreated from the world after she split from her husband.

For all our talking and sharing, we don't kiss. At the end of each night I expect her to offer her lips, but she doesn't. A quick peck on the cheek and that's it, she hops into a cab and slips away. I'm confused but pleased — it's nice to be on the slow burn. I'm sure there will be kissing and more later, but for the time being I'm content to talk and walk, getting to know her, letting her get to know me.

Joe returns to London. We meet at a café in Soho in the early afternoon. We order drinks and sit outside, baking in the severe July sun. Joe looks tired and drawn. His mother pulled through but the doctor told him it's only a matter of weeks before she succumbs to a fatal stroke.

'I knew she was close to the end,' he says, wrapped up tightly even though everybody else is in shorts and T-shirts, 'but to have it confirmed . . . to be taken aside and told . . .' He shakes his head. The glass trembles in his hand.

'You should have stayed with her.'

'No,' he says, tugging miserably at his beard. 'Two of my sisters have moved in with her and I've got a brother three doors down. I'd be in the way. I might miss the finale, but that's not such a bad thing. I'm not sure I want to see her when . . . when she . . .' He comes to a halt. I glance down at the plastic table, ashamed to think of how great a time I've been having while Joe's been up north preparing for death. 'My brother told me a

45

good one,' Joe mutters, managing a thin smile.

I groan. Joe loves terrible jokes. I almost tell him not to bother me, but I know he wants to distract himself from thoughts of his mother. 'Go on,' I growl.

'Sunday. Monday. Tuesday. Wednesday. Thursday. Friday. Saturday.' He pauses, then sighs wistfully. 'Those were the days.'

I chuckle despite myself. 'That's one of your worst ever.'

'So why are you laughing?'

'Damned if I know.'

We grin at one another, Joe managing to put the darkness of the last few days behind him for the time being.

'So what have you been up to?' he asks.

'Nothing much,' I lie.

'No developments on the plot front?'

'To be honest, I haven't paid a lot of attention to the book. I was waiting for you to return.' He perks up when he hears that. 'Also, I've been seeing someone.' He waits for me to elaborate. 'A woman.'

He laughs. 'I didn't think it was a man.'

'I met her at the boat party.'

'Shar's?' he interjects excitedly. 'You went?'

'Yes.'

'And you pulled?'

'I did.'

'Artful bastard,' he snorts, looking more like his old self. 'Didn't take you long to muscle in on the action. What's her name?'

'Deleena Emerson. She works for a private bank in the City.'

I tell him a bit about Deleena, our nights together, how she looks in a black dress, a few morsels about her background. Joe smirks like a shark as I describe her long legs, soft hair and sparkling eyes.

46

'Tasty,' he purrs. 'Does she have a sister?'

'She's an only child.'

'Pity.' He taps the table admonishingly. 'But I'm not impressed with the way you've let it affect your work. I'm all for romance, but it shouldn't interfere with your writing. What happened to your meeting with John Meyher? Did you go?'

'I postponed it in the end. I wanted you be there, given that you were the one who set it up. He said his diary was open and to simply give him a few hours' notice before dropping by.'

Joe wags a finger at me. 'Can't leave you alone for a minute,' he scolds, then digs out his cell phone and slides it across the table. 'Try and arrange something for this afternoon.'

'But you're tired, Joe. Let's wait until –'

'No waiting,' he insists. 'When I return to work I'll be stuck in that bloody shop for most of the week, repairing toasters and microwave ovens. I've got an excuse not to go in today – I'm still on leave – but if we don't go and see him now, I'll be too busy to come.'

'OK.' I pick up the phone and dial.

'You know the number off by heart?' Joe asks.

'I have an almost perfect memory for numbers.'

'You're a man of hidden depths,' he grins.

'You have no idea,' I mutter.

Meyher's wife answers and says that her husband's out but will be back in the afternoon. I check their address with her – numbers stick in my brain but nothing else – and schedule the meeting for four o'clock.

'We're on?' Joe asks as I hand back his cell.

'Four.'

'Excellent.' He drinks up and accompanies me to my hotel, where he steals a nap on the couch while I wash and dress. He's exhausted. I know how he feels. When my mother was dying, I rarely squeezed in more than a few hours of sleep a night. I'd

47

like to leave him slumbering but he'd hate me if I went without him, so I shake him awake, ply him with coffee, then off we set in a cab hailed by the redoubtable Mr Lloyd.

John Meyher lives in Roehampton, a quiet, nicely maintained suburb in south-west London, very different to the city I've been getting to know, with more of a small-town feel. The air is actually halfway breathable out here. I like it. If I was to live in London, I'd choose somewhere like this.

John is pruning in a small garden in front of his house when we arrive. He's a large man, heavy and tall, thinning grey hair. He welcomes us with a warm smile and takes us inside for the obligatory British cup of tea and a lot of talk about spontaneous human combustion. John's an expert. He doesn't give many interviews. Like most SHC theorists, he's had to deal with ridicule and official denial over the years. He says it's worn him down. But when he sees how eager we are to learn, he comes alive and talks quickly and eagerly.

After a brief history lesson and a swift but comprehensive overview of current trains of thought, John shows us photos of SHC victims, large piles of ash sitting on floors in the middle of kitchens, bedrooms or living rooms. In some a stray hand or foot rests nearby, as if sliced off prior to burning. A pipe lies in the middle of one pile, tobacco spilling out of it on to the human remains.

John points out the surrounding areas, drawing our attention to the fact that although some of the walls and floors are spotted with soot, the floorboards aren't burnt through and the furniture stands unharmed.

'Do you know the kind of heat required to reduce a human body to ash?' he asks. 'It's in excess of nine hundred degrees Celsius. In a crematorium they use giant furnaces and pumps to generate the heat. Assuming you could start a fire that intense in an ordinary house, how could it incinerate a living human and do no other damage to the room in which they died?'

'How do officials explain it?' I ask.

'They don't,' John snorts. 'They just ignore it.'

'And you?' I press. 'What do you think happens?'

'They burn from within. Even scientists opposed to the concept of SHC accept that possibility. Internal gases can build up and ignite. But an explosion like that should hurl shreds of the victim about, not just leave the odd cleanly amputated hand or foot. It's like these people generated a pillar of fire that spread from the centre outwards, and the only bits to survive were the limbs outside the pillar's circumference. I don't know how that can happen. Nobody does. It defies all known physical laws.'

I gaze at a photograph where a hand lies next to a mound of ashes. I think about what John has told us. I put it together with what I already had in mind coming into this meeting. And I start to smile.

After our interview with John, we head to a pub – the Minotaur – and I down a couple of glasses of rum, my tipple of choice. Wine with a meal, beer if I fancy a casual drink, rum when I want to enjoy my liquor. I'm buzzing. John was the last significant link in the chain. With what he told me, I'll soon be ready to write.

Joe waits for me to explain myself. I catch his eye and grin, lifting my third glass of rum in salute. Joe scowls, half amused, half annoyed.

'Sorry,' I chuckle. 'I know I'm acting like an ass, but this ties everything together. I've been picking away at the strands of this story for a year, and today it finally fell fully formed into my lap. I don't have all the twists and turns worked out yet, but the core is there.'

Joe leans forward. 'Can you tell me, or is it still a secret?'

I stare at my hands and collect my thoughts. 'Remember

Pierre Vallance telling us how he can convert mental waves into voices?'

'Yeah.'

'If that's true, and if you could convert the waves into images or objects, it would mean reality is subjective. Some people would have the power to change the world with their thoughts — as an example, if one of them imagined a unicorn or an alien, they could bring it into being.'

Joe tugs at his beard. 'You think?'

'Why not? If reality can be physically what we make of it, then someone like Vallance – but more powerful – could play God. Now, let's say a guy with that power drops a match. He panics and imagines himself going up in flames. Only, due to his ability to reshape reality, he doesn't just imagine himself catching fire, he unwittingly makes it –'

'Actually happen,' Joe interrupts.

'You got it. And because he's panicking, the flames don't act the natural way — they do what his fevered imagination tells them to do and burn through him like a pillar of unbelievably hot fire.'

I sit back, more pieces of the novel clicking together as I speak. 'If a person is unaware of their power and accidentally taps into it and burns to death, that's a tragedy. But if someone *is* aware of what they can do, and uses their talent to target other people . . . Hell, that's murder, prime material for an Ed Sieveking novel.' I raise my glass, finish off the last of my rum, then tell Joe to drink up. 'We can't sit around boozing all day. We've got a book to write!'

FOUR

I meet with Deleena most nights. Sometimes we dine together or pop into a bar for a drink, but often we just stroll, taking London's warren of streets at random, seeing where the night leads us. I feel like a prince when she's by my side. All is good with the world. Even my ghosts pull back, as if repelled by the warmth I'm feeling inside. For the first time in years I find my waking hours more than just bearable at best, as they've been ever since the ghosts entered my life — with Deleena, they're a pleasure.

Deleena seems to be a creature of the shadows. She favours dimly lit spots. She has sensitive eyes, which is why she prefers small, romantic restaurants to those which are harshly illuminated. That suits me fine. It means I'm discovering new sides of her every time we meet. A mole on her left shoulder when her bra strap slips. A freckle on her right ear which was previously hidden by her hair. A slightly discoloured tooth.

I occasionally worry that her beauty might crumble if I ever see her in strong, direct, sustained light, that she'll be revealed as a hideous hag, hiding behind a veil of paint and make-up. But of course that's nonsense. I see enough of her, even in the shadows, to know it's no mask.

She loves books, and though our tastes are similar, they differ in many ways too. For instance, her favourite novel is

The Alchemist. I always dismissed that as a feel-good piece of New Age hokum, but she argues its case convincingly and has started to win me over.

One night she brings the book with her and reads out some of her favourite extracts to me while perched on a stone bench in Trafalgar Square. I listen to her with a warm smile, dreamily studying her lips as they softly open and close while forming the words. If Paulo Coelho himself happened to be passing and offered to stop her and treat me to a personal recitation, I'd scowl and tell him in my best British bobby impression, 'Move along, sir. Move along.'

Since we spend much of our time discussing books, I start telling Deleena about the new novel that I'm working on. I hadn't meant to share the details with her. Normally I don't reveal anything about my work during the formative stages. The first anyone usually sees of an Ed Sieveking story is when I send a third or fourth draft to my agent. But it seems natural to involve her in my thought processes, to bounce ideas off her as I do off Joe.

As close as we've become, at the same time I feel somehow strangely distant from Deleena. Our dates have been chaste affairs. We haven't even kissed. Twelve nights of wining and dining, exploring the streets, baring our souls, and we haven't touched lips. Does that mean she simply wants me as a friend? I'm not sure. Sometimes she looks at me like she wants to pledge herself to me on the spot. Other times I catch something melancholic in her expression and feel sure that she's about to cut me off with her next words, tell me she never wants to see me again. She confuses me. Maybe that confusion is part of her appeal.

She can be miserly with her time too. She'll often leave early, maybe before the end of a meal or not long after we've set off on a walk, offering one feeble excuse or another, leaving me to stare longingly after her and brood on what might have been. On those nights I try to walk off my frustration and tune her out of my thoughts, but the less time she spends with me, the more I lust after her.

I like to think I'm a good judge of character – a writer needs to be – but with Deleena I just don't know. There are moments when I feel incredibly close to her, then she'll blink and it's like I don't know her at all.

Joe can't help as he hasn't met her yet. I'm keen to introduce them but they keep missing one another. Joe has cried off a couple of times when customers have made after-hours demands of him. Deleena had to work late another evening. We were meant to get together last Sunday for a barbecue, but first Joe got called away and then Deleena rang to say old friends had dropped by unannounced. If I didn't believe that we live in a universe of chance, I'd swear destiny was working to keep them apart.

I've been grinding away on the plot of the book, trying to figure out why my lead character was killed. It can't be random. The story is crying out for a reason that will drive the narrative forward, but I can't decide what it should be. One evening, surrounded by a sea of notes in my hotel room, I mention to Joe that I've come to a block, and in a moment of genius he provides me with the answer.

'The killer works for an agency,' Joe says. 'They eliminate people with powers like theirs, people who won't work for them, who they see as a threat. Our main guy is spotted. They check him out, decide they can't use him, and kill him.'

'Then he comes back as a ghost and makes them eat a hundred unholy pillars of fire when he tracks them down,' I enthuse, thumping Joe's back.

'Know what?' I mutter a few minutes later, having scribbled

down the idea and played with it a bit. 'You just earned yourself a credit in the book.'

Joe's eyes widen. 'You're gonna put my name on the cover?'

'No,' I laugh. 'But how about a creative consultant nod on the title page?'

'Are you serious?' Joe whoops.

'Of course I'll have to cut you in for a percentage of the profits as well.'

'Aw, Ed, there's no need to . . .'

'I insist. How does five per cent sound?'

'Why not ten?' Joe responds immediately.

'Let's stick with five,' I chuckle.

'This calls for a toast,' Joe beams and rushes to the minibar.

'I can't believe how generous I've become,' I note wryly as Joe pours a rum for me. 'If you'd told me a few weeks ago that I'd be offering to share credit with somebody, I'd have said you were crazy.'

'Having second thoughts?' Joe asks nervously.

'No,' I smile. 'I'll hold true to my word. Do you want it in writing?'

'Don't be stupid. I trust you.'

I finish off the rum and pour myself a second miniature bottle. I take this one slowly. I don't want to drink myself into a stupor before nightfall.

'Maybe I'll include Deleena in the credits too,' I murmur.

'Why?' Joe frowns. 'She hasn't injected any ideas.'

'True, but we have her to thank for my generosity of spirit. If I wasn't falling in love, I doubt I'd be so willing to involve you in the creative process.'

Joe drops his gaze. 'You're falling in love with her?' he asks quietly.

'I guess. Hell, I don't know, maybe it's the rum. Cheers.'

'Cheers,' Joe says, but soberly.

'What's up?' I ask.

'Nothing. It's just . . . when am I going to meet her? It's been more than two weeks and you haven't let me see her.'

'Is it my fault you've been fixing fridges, TV sets and God alone knows what else every time I try to introduce you?'

'No, but . . .' He shrugs. 'I've spoken to a few of my friends who were at Shar's party, and nobody knows her. I've been wondering why I haven't bumped into her before. From the way you describe her, she's hard to miss.'

'She is,' I sigh, day-dreaming of Deleena in the black dress she wore when we first met. 'But it's not odd that your friends don't know her. She's a client of Shar's. She didn't know anyone on the boat. That's why we hooked up — we were the only two who were alone.'

'Still, you have to bring her to see me, Ed. For all I know, she's one of the ugly sisters.'

'Up yours,' I retort, and Joe laughs.

I pour a third shot of rum and ponder my good fortune. A book that's shaping up nicely. A relationship with a beautiful lady who brings out the best in me. And a good friend. It's a far cry from my usual lonely, passionless life. For years I've limped along, nursing grudges, bitter at the world for what it did to me, haunted by my ghosts, desperately searching for proof that the spirits are real, that I'm not insane, struggling to hold on to whatever thin slivers of sanity I can claim to be in possession of. Now I can see light for the first time in ages. Maybe love will cure me of my ills and banish the spectre of the ghosts. If they're the product of a disturbed mind, perhaps all I need to make them go away is to find the happiness that I was sure I'd always be denied.

I'm not sure what I've done to merit this good fortune, but I'm determined to appreciate it for as long as it lasts, and if the fates are kind, who knows, it might just last for ever.

Another night in the company of the delectable Deleena. She takes me to a busy little restaurant overlooking the Thames. I tell her about my conversation with Joe. She laughs and says to bring him along any time. I propose heading out to the countryside for a weekend away, all three of us, but she isn't warm on that idea.

'Work's even busier than usual. I could be summoned without notice any day, even a Saturday or Sunday. I don't fancy having to cut short a break and drive all the way back.'

'I thought slavery had been abolished,' I scowl. 'Surely you can ask for a Sunday off?'

'Of course I can. But there's a post opening up shortly and I'm in with a chance of bagging it. That would mean more income, more security and –' she leans over to playfully stroke my nose – 'longer holidays. Three of us are in the running and we've been working flat out to impress our lords and masters. A plea for personal time now and I might as well forfeit. So, sorry, but . . .' She shrugs prettily.

We move on to the subject of the book and I tell her how it's progressing.

'Have you interviewed any more mediums?' she asks.

'Not this week.'

'Did you look up Etienne?' She's referring to Etienne Anders, a medium she recommended.

'I rang her a few times. She was engaged once and I got her voicemail the other times. I hate leaving messages, so I hung up.'

'Do you still have her card?' Deleena presses, and I nod. 'You should ring her. I told her you'd get in touch. She's really good, Ed. I've been to lots of mediums over the years and she's the only one who genuinely impressed me.'

'I'll contact her, I promise, but at the moment I'm exploring other angles. If you want, I can cancel a few things, swing by tomorrow.'

'No,' she smiles, laying a hand on mine. 'You don't have to go out of your way on my account. I'm trying to help, not interfere. Just hold on to the card and . . .' As her eyes wander, she freezes. Her hand goes limp and slides away. Following the direction of her gaze, I spot a table of five middle-aged men, boisterously pulling crabs apart. Deleena is focused on a man to our left, long grey hair tied back in a ponytail, a heavy tan, immaculately dressed.

'Something wrong?' I ask.

'No,' she gasps, but now she's leaning over, using me to block the man's view of her if he happens to look across.

'Who is he and why are you hiding from him?' I murmur.

'Someone I know and don't want to meet.' She removes her napkin from her lap. 'Do you mind if we leave now? I know we haven't finished, but . . .'

'That's OK.' I signal the waiter for the check, keeping my body between Deleena and the mystery man. Once I've paid, I rise carefully, let her tuck in behind me and head for the exit, shielding her all the way, asking no questions, trying not to stare at the table of strangers as we pass.

I picked up a knife as we were standing. I didn't let Deleena see. I keep it held by my side, ready to sweep it up defensively if we're threatened, old habits kicking in automatically. Nobody living sees me palm the knife, but the ghosts spot it and press forward, leering, sensing blood. They'd love it if things went bad. I imagine it's what they long for more than anything else in the world.

But this time the ghosts are disappointed. The man doesn't spot Deleena. Once outside, she slips around the side of the restaurant and stands staring across the river, arms crossed, shivering. I say nothing, waiting for her to tell me what's going on, calmly pocketing the knife. Part of me wishes I'd been given a chance to use it. That part misses the old days. It wants them back.

'This looks bad, doesn't it?' Deleena croaks.

'An ex-boyfriend?' I guess.

'God, no, nothing like that. Bond Gardiner? Never!' She looks up at me. 'Does that name mean anything to you?' I think for a minute and shake my head. 'He's . . . well, I guess there's no other way to put it. He's a gangster.'

I frown. 'What does he have to do with you?'

'He wanted to open an account with my bank. My superiors rejected his request, but I was charged with breaking the bad news to him. He lost his temper and said some vicious things, stopping just short of open threats. He sent a card the next day apologizing for his outburst, but still . . .'

'You don't want to talk to the scary gangster again.'

'Right.'

We share a smile. I'm relieved it's nothing serious. There's a lot I don't know about Deleena. All sorts of dark thoughts had been flitting through my mind. The ghosts look sullen. They start to drift into the background again. My power over them is growing. I almost turn and flip them the finger, but then I'd have to explain that to Deleena.

'Where now?' I ask.

She shrugs. 'Grab a cab? Head up the West End and catch a late film?'

'I'd rather go for a walk.'

'OK.'

I'm staring at her, pressed against the wall of the restaurant. She looks so young in the shadows. Beautiful. I reach out and brush her hair from her eyes, then run a finger down her cheek and over her chin.

Deleena stares back, lifting her head slightly, lips thinning into almost invisible lines. This is the first time I've made an advance. I'm not pushing for sex – I don't want our first time to be out in the open, against a damp wall – just a kiss. Normally I wouldn't feel nervous, but with Deleena I'm petrified. If she turns her head away, where does that leave us?

I lean forward slowly, lips opening, giving her plenty of time to object. She doesn't move. I press my lips softly to hers, hold a moment, withdraw and gaze into her eyes, searching for encouragement.

Deleena parts her lips, edges forward, stops. 'Ed . . . I know you've been patient. I know we haven't discussed this. I know you must be wondering what I'm up to.'

'That's OK,' I whisper.

'I want to.' The briefest, shakiest of grins. 'But in my own time. Don't rush me, Ed, please?'

'I won't.' I steal another short kiss. 'I'm in no hurry.'

'It's OK if we just kiss?' she asks.

'We don't even have to do that,' I tell her.

'I don't mind kissing,' she says, and now she's smiling. 'Just go easy with the wandering hands.'

'I'll be the perfect gentleman,' I swear, taking her into my arms as she stands on her toes and embraces me, opening her mouth, exploring my lower lip with hers, tugging at it teasingly with her teeth, then allowing her lips to slide over mine, sealing the kiss.

We stand in the shadows, joined. I let my hands move down to the base of her spine, but no further. She presses closer into me. Through her warm tongue and lips I detect the brisk beat of her pounding heart.

'Deleena,' I moan, but before I can say any more, she silences me with another kiss and soon I'm lost. Words become meaningless. The ghosts are forgotten. There's only me, the night and her.

FIVE

I've been sleeping quite well since I started seeing Deleena but I know tonight's going to be a bad one. Back in my hotel room, I dig the knife from the restaurant out of my pocket and study it solemnly. I'm amazed by how quickly the old instincts kicked in. If we had been attacked, I'd already played out various scenarios in my mind's eye, plotted my defensive strokes and our route of escape. The knife isn't the sharpest or sturdiest, but I'd automatically accounted for that. In my hands it would have been an adequate weapon.

I remember other nights and other knives. Drunken nights when I wept like a baby and held the tip of a knife before one of my eyes, wanting to drive it through my eyeball and deep into my brain, the ghosts egging me on, silently urging me to follow through and join them in their shady sub-world.

They press closer towards me now, eagerly searching for any chink that they might be able to manipulate to their advantage. It doesn't matter if they're not real, if they're only projections of my inner turmoil. At times like this they present an all-too-real threat. They look so hateful. An observer who could see them would think I was a victim, a sympathetic figure under attack from malevolent forces.

I know better. I deserve my ghosts. They're entitled to their spite.

I lay the knife aside and sigh. 'Knock yourselves out,' I tell the disappointed spirits, then I start to get ready for bed and the nightmares that I'm sure will find and torment me.

Joe and I have been driving around, looking for places I might be able to use in the book. I'm keen on the back streets which spread out from the oddly named Elephant and Castle. Very centrally located, yet many of the shabby old houses look like they're stuck in the past. The area has a grim, eerie feel to it. I take notes of street names, parks, schools, shops, deserted buildings.

Joe is behind the wheel. He's moodier than usual, hasn't said much. Finally, once we've wound up the scouting mission and have crossed the river, he says, 'Do you think you can use any of those places in the book?'

'Probably. I like the Elephant and Castle. Any idea where the name comes from?' Joe grunts negatively and takes a sharp, aggressive left turn. I study him curiously. 'How's your mother?' I ask.

'Fine.'

'And work?'

'Same old.' He looks across at me. 'What's with the questions?'

'You seem out of sorts.'

He grunts again, then slows and finds a place to pull over. For a couple of minutes he doesn't say anything, and nor do I. In the end, he sighs. 'You're gonna hate me. I shouldn't say anything. I wasn't going to and I still don't know if I should.'

'What's up, Joe?' I ask, worried now.

'I wasn't prying,' he says 'I wasn't poking my nose in. I just . . . You remember I told you I'd been asking my friends about Deleena?'

That wasn't what I'd been anticipating. I thought he'd

been digging around in my past. I let out my breath and nod, relieved.

'I went to see Shar's boyfriend last night,' Joe says. 'He has an old VCR that was on the fritz. I asked Shar about Deleena. I was curious.'

'Uh-huh.' I'm not sure what's coming, but at least it has nothing to do with my past.

Joe hesitates, then comes out with it. 'Shar doesn't know her.'

I digest the information, then seek clarification. 'Shar doesn't know Deleena?'

'She doesn't have a Deleena Emerson on her books. None of her clients even has a name *like* Deleena Emerson.'

'Did you describe Deleena to her? Maybe she uses another name when –'

'How could I describe her?' he cuts in. 'I've never seen her.'

'Oh. Right.' I stare at the dashboard, bewildered.

'I should have kept my mouth shut,' Joe mumbles.

'No. You were right to tell me.'

'What will . . . ?'

'Please. No questions. Just leave it with me.'

'OK.' He taps the steering wheel. 'You want to hang out here a while or go back to the hotel?'

'Back to the hotel.' I smile humourlessly. 'I've got a date to prepare for.'

We meet in a pizza house. Deleena is a woman of varied tastes. A Michelin-starred restaurant one night, Burger King the next. I order a ham and mushroom pizza, Deleena opts for pepperoni. A bottle of house white.

I've been keeping conversation to a minimum. Deleena senses something wrong but pretends that all is normal. She tells me about her day at work and how much she enjoyed last night – we went to a beer festival and drank from massive wooden pitchers – and makes suggestions for tomorrow. I respond with sniffs and shrugs, waiting for her to get frustrated and force the issue.

'OK,' she finally says, laying down her knife and fork. 'What have I done?'

I finish the slice of pizza I was working on and wash it down with a mouthful of wine before replying. 'I know that you've been lying to me.' Deleena stiffens but says nothing. 'Shar doesn't know you. You're not one of her clients.'

She rocks forwards and backwards, face neutral, hands on the table, fingers at rest. 'You can leave now if you want,' she offers. 'I'll take care of the bill.'

'I'm going nowhere until you explain.'

'Why bother?' she says. 'If I've lied once, I'll probably lie to you again. The wise thing would be to walk away, delete my number from your phone and hang up if you ever hear from me again.'

'I thought about that. A week ago I might have. But now . . .' I want to reach across and shake answers from her, but I settle for a glare. 'Is Deleena even your real name?'

'No,' she says coolly. 'It's Andeanna. I *am* a client of Shar's — that much is true. Check with her. She'll recognize the name this time.'

'Why feed me an alias?'

'I'm sure you can guess. It's not especially complicated.'

'You're married?' I ask, and she nods. That simple gesture almost drives me from the table and out of her life. Only her expression of utter misery holds me. 'Do you love him?'

'Christ, Ed!' She laughs blackly.

'Do you love *me*?'

She's shaking now. Can't look me in the eye. Slides her hands under the table so I can't see them trembling. 'It's not as simple as that,' she croaks. 'There are things you don't know.'

'So tell me.'

She raises her head. Tears are welling in her eyes. I ignore them and focus on her lips, reading the words as they form, alert for lies. 'You remember that man we ran into? Bond Gardiner?'

'He's your husband?'

'No. Emerson is my maiden name. My married name is Menderes. My husband is –'

'Mikis Menderes,' I interrupt, one jump ahead of her.

She blinks, taken aback. 'You know him?'

'Mikis Menderes, aka the Turk.'

'You know who he is? *What* he is?'

'I've read about him in the papers,' I lie

'He makes the papers in the States?' she frowns.

'No,' I correct myself, quickly tweaking my story. 'I read about him here, on one of my previous trips to the UK.'

'Then you know why I've been so afraid to get close to you,' she says. 'Why my heart beat with terror the first time we kissed. Why I didn't want to let things go any further. You know why you should walk away and never look back. Because if Mikis finds out about us . . . if he even suspects . . .'

She can't continue, and I can't think of anything to get her started again. We sit, staring at one another, until a waiter checks to see if we're finished. I nod, and he asks if we'd like anything for dessert. 'No thank you,' I mumble, then pay up and escort Deleena – *Andeanna*, Mrs Menderes, wife of one of London's most notorious gangsters – outside into the uncertainty of the sultry, menacing night.

PART TWO

SIX

It's amazing how quickly one's impression of a place can change. Last week I was in love with London, its architecture and layout, its people, its aura. Now the buildings look old and crumbling. The people have grey, pinched faces. It feels like a city of the lost.

Three days have passed. No word from *Andeanna*. I still can't accustom myself to her new name. I should be working on forgetting both, wiping them from my memory. Deleena, Andeanna, what's the difference? She's poison no matter what she calls herself. A married woman who lied. Worse, a married gangster's woman. What if the Turk's henchman had seen us that night in the restaurant? What if he'd caught us kissing and run to tell his boss?

I'm furious that she sucked me in like that. I can protect myself when I have to. Mikis Menderes doesn't frighten me. But unaware of the risk, I would have been taken by surprise and left to the mercy of a man who had no cause to show me any.

She should have told me. If she'd been married to an ordinary guy, I might have been able to accept the lie. But my life was on the line and I never knew. She treated me with contempt and I don't want anything to do with a woman who plays games like that. I should blow this city, set the book elsewhere, turn my back on London without a farewell glance.

Except . . .

I feel her lips on mine every time I close my eyes. I haven't fallen in love often in my life, but whenever I have, I've fallen hard. If I could be logical about it, I'd take the view that I don't know Andeanna well enough to claim that I love her. But I know what I feel. She has me hooked. How can I leave her behind when my heart aches with every step I take without her?

Two more days pass. My ghosts are having a whale of a time. My misery has given them a new lease of life, so to speak. They circle me like sharks, darting at me when I least expect it, clawing at my face with their insubstantial fingers, mocking me, mutely urging me to end it all, to join them in their shady realm and take what I have coming for what I did in the past.

I tried immersing myself in the book, but I couldn't concentrate, and not just because of the hyperactive spirits. I'd be sitting over a pile of notes with Joe – he's been compassionately tight-lipped, never mentioning Deleena – and my mind would wander. I'd think how like a ghost she's become, gone from my life, never to return, irreclaimable, uncontactable. Except she *isn't* dead and she *can* be tracked down. I could take her in my arms again and . . .

I told Joe I needed a few days to myself. He said to ring when I felt like it and not to spare a thought for him in the meantime. I took to the countryside, chose a direction at random and drove west, into territory that was all virgin to me — I've rarely been outside London on any of my trips to the UK. It was difficult driving – the ghosts kept wrapping themselves in front of my eyes, obscuring my vision – but having to focus on the road helped take my mind off my troubles. I wound up in far-flung Devon, which I spent yesterday exploring, clambering over moors, pushing myself physically, ignoring my ghosts, trying to forget about Andeanna.

I tossed and turned in the back of my rented car the first night, the ghosts writhing around me, half in and half out of the car's structure. Then I booked into a cottage that has been converted into a B&B. I slept sweetly, exhausted after my hard day, and didn't dream of Andeanna. There was even a moment when I woke when she wasn't in my thoughts. Then the memories returned. I groaned, rolled over and started planning another day of harsh, demanding exercise.

That was when my phone rang. I wasn't going to answer, but nerves got the better of me and I lunged for it, only to discover it wasn't Andeanna. It was Jonathan Wood, my agent. He was in London and wanted to arrange some meetings with prospective publishers. *Soul Vultures* is being reprinted here, and a couple of editors have been in touch, wanting to know what I'm working on next. I asked to be excused from the negotiations, but Jonathan was adamant. He doesn't get over to England often (he's in town drumming up business for another of his clients) and he said it would be crazy to miss such a golden opportunity.

Returning to London was the last thing I wanted, but professional hunger got the better of me. I was loath to waste all those years of hard work, especially over a woman who would probably laugh with vixen delight if she found out how deeply she'd cut me. 'OK,' I sighed. 'Let's meet this evening and you can tell me more about it.'

So I'm back. Evening has come and gone. I met Jonathan in the bar of his hotel, and we passed a pleasant few hours discussing the re-release of *Soul Vultures*, and my new work, which I told him would be called *Pillars of Fire* or *Spirit of the Fire*. I promised to toss together a summary to present to the editors in the morning.

The ghosts have been sluggish since I got back. They feed on negative energy. When my mood improved – when work distracted me from my dark thoughts – they lost a lot of their power and had to settle back into their familiar holding pattern.

I rang Joe on my way back to the Royal Munster but got his voicemail. I left a message, then settled down to work. Joe calls an hour later when I'm in the middle of a wild oasis of notes. I growl into the mouthpiece, 'Get over here. I need you.'

'Is this about the book or . . .?' he asks diplomatically.

'The book.'

'I'll be with you in a flash.'

I tell Joe about my morning meetings. He wants to come with me, but I say that isn't a good idea. I haven't told Jonathan about my partner and I'm not sure how he'll react. The longer we wait, the fewer objections he can make. I explain all this to Joe, but I can see he's disappointed. I'll make it up to him later, take him on tour with me, let him sit in on interviews, stuff like that.

We work until four in the morning, fine-tuning our mass of ideas, putting them in order, searching for a nice, neat way to sum up the plot. Finally I groan, push the pile of notes away and hold up the three-page plot outline, the fruit of all our endeavours, as if it was the Holy Grail.

'What about typing it up?' Joe asks.

'Screw that.' I stand and yawn. 'It'll do as it is.'

'Are you sure?'

'Yes.' Rubbing my eyelids, I ask Joe if he wants to sleep on the couch instead of making the long trek home.

'That's OK,' he says. 'I'll head back to the flat. I find it hard to sleep if I'm not in my own bed. But do you mind if I treat myself to a nightcap?'

'Help yourself,' I tell him, heading for the bedroom. 'But if you get arrested for drink-driving, don't blame me.'

In the morning I find that all the notes have been tidied away and nine sheets of A4 paper rest on top of my laptop

— the word-processed plot outline and two copies. There's a note from Joe. *Thought we should type it up all the same. Hope you don't mind. Let me know how you get on. Good luck!!!*

The meetings go well. Both editors claim to be fans of my previous work, are intrigued by the plot of the new book and want to see more. I had American editors on my other books, but Jonathan thinks I should go with a Brit this time, seeing as how the story is set in London. He claps my back just before we part, tells me this could be the start of something big, then heads for the airport to catch a flight to France, leaving me behind to dream.

I spend the next week coming up with characters and exploring plot angles. I try not to think about Andeanna, but it's hard. I can forget her for brief spells but she's never far from my thoughts. All it takes is a moment of quiet reflection or a glimpse of an attractive woman and I'm off, recalling the lines of her face, the curves of her body, the sparkle of her eyes. I wish I wasn't this weak, this open, but it's an old flaw of mine.

Joe thinks I should call her. I told him the truth a few days ago, though I didn't mention that she was married to a gangster. At first he agreed that I'd done the right thing giving her the elbow, but now he's not sure. He says I'm tearing myself apart agonizing over her.

I think about phoning her, but I don't know how to start the conversation.

'Hi, Andeanna, how's the Turk?'

'Hi, Andeanna, or is it Deleena today?'

'Hello, Mrs Menderes, this is the man whose heart you broke.'

Forget it!

To distract myself, I concentrate on *Spirit of the Fire* (I've decided on the title), and jot down descriptive paragraphs of

71

what the characters look like. I also start seriously mapping out the parts of London that I plan to use in the book. I wander the metropolis, notebook in hand, searching for creepy buildings and alleys. At first I explored by day, but I've switched to nights. My ghost should be a creature of the darkness, only able to brave the streets when the sun goes down. More atmospheric that way.

Because I'm out late and sleeping in, I skip the first two calls on Wednesday. I wake when the phone rings, but ignore it, and only answer shortly after midday when it rings for the third time.

'Where the hell have you been?' Jonathan roars.

'Sleeping,' I yawn.

'I've been ringing all morning,' he exaggerates.

'Sorry. I was dead to the world. Didn't hear.'

'You've got a great life,' he grumbles. Then adds brightly, 'Guess what I just sold?'

'Not *Spirit of the Fire*?' I snap, coming fully awake.

'Bet your skinny sleeping ass I have,' he laughs. 'Even on holiday, basking by a swimming pool in southern France, I push deals through for my ungrateful stable of would-be superstars.'

One of the editors phoned him yesterday with an offer. Jonathan batted terms back and forth, and this morning a deal was agreed subject to my approval, the first time a book of mine has been bought on the strength of a synopsis.

I tell Jonathan he's the world's best agent and promise to treat him to dinner in a restaurant of his choice the next time we meet. As soon as I'm off the phone, I punch the air with delight and grin stupidly. Then I call Joe to share the news. I get his voicemail, which frustrates me. I try leaving a message, but the words mix awkwardly on my tongue and I wind up mumbling something incoherent.

I stand in the middle of the room, mind whirling, then sit

down, breathe deeply and wonder who else I could call — I *have* to share the news. Forgetting all of my anger and suspicion, I dial the number of the one person apart from Joe who might care. It rings on and on. I'm about to hang up when suddenly there's an answer. 'Hello?' *Her* voice, hesitant, maybe scared, as if she thinks I might be calling to curse her out.

My mouth goes dry. 'Delee– I mean, Andeanna? It's me. Ed.'

There's a long silence. I feel my heart tightening. I think something in it will fade away for ever if she hangs up or cuts me dead with a withering wisecrack.

'Ed,' she finally murmurs, warm as sunlight. 'Hi.'

'Hi,' I reply softly.

And we take it from there.

SEVEN

We meet in a beer garden, find a table and sit down with two glasses of their finest brew. Andeanna is dressed in green, another of her high-collar, high-hem numbers. She sips from her glass. Her fingers are damp when she lets go. She runs them over the back of her neck and smiles. 'Hot,' she says.

'Yes.' I smile self-consciously and murmur, 'I've sold my book.'

She frowns. 'What book?'

'*Spirit of the Fire*. My agent –'

'Ed!' she squeals, and lunges across the table to hug me. 'That's wonderful! Who bought it? How much did you make? Have you started writing it? How can they buy a book that isn't written? What if you change your mind or get stuck?'

I take her questions one at a time, loosening up while I answer, and by the end of the explanations we're almost back to where we were before Andeanna dropped her bombshell. She touches my hands with her fingertips when she wants to make a point, stroking my knuckles unconsciously. For a while we chat about work, my trip to Devon, what she's been up to. I'd like to go on like this for ever but I can't. The elephant in the room has to be addressed.

'We need to talk about Mikis Menderes.'

Andeanna sighs but doesn't drop her gaze. 'I know.'

74

'I've been thinking about him constantly since we had our little disagreement.' She smiles at the understatement. 'It wasn't the lie that maddened me so much. It's what could have happened if he'd found out. I don't know Menderes –'

'Call him the Turk,' she interrupts. 'Everyone else does.'

'– but I know his reputation. He wouldn't have shrugged and made light of it if Bond Gardiner had seen us together, would he?'

'No,' she says. 'He'd have torn into me, then gone after you.'

'And if he caught up with me?'

She shrugs. 'A beating. Maybe worse. Mikis is a dangerous man.'

'That's what infuriated me. It looked to me like you were playing games, toying with me, setting me up for –'

'No,' she begs. 'Don't think that. Please, Ed.'

'I don't,' I sigh. Then, leaning across the table, 'I love you, Andeanna.'

Her eyes widen. 'No,' she whispers.

'I love you,' I repeat, louder this time. A couple at a nearby table glance at us and smile. 'I love you –' I lower my voice – 'and I don't care who you're married to. I'll take my chances with the Turk if you love me too.'

'It's not that simple,' she says miserably. 'You're a writer. Before that you sold computers. You can't defend yourself against Mikis or Bond.'

'I can deal with the Turk,' I grunt.

'How?' she asks sceptically.

'I'm a black belt in karate,' I joke.

She raises an eyebrow, but I don't blink. Finally she grimaces. 'Where does this leave us, Ed?'

'That's down to you. Do you love me?'

On the wings of a long, trembling breath, she says, 'Yes.'

I take her hands and squeeze. 'Tell me about your marriage.'

75

Her story unfolds over the course of the night. She keeps jumping between the present and the past, so I have to concentrate to piece it together. She was young when she married Mikis Menderes. It was a shotgun wedding — she was pregnant with their son, Gregory, now a grown man in his twenties. (That caught me off guard. It means she's quite a lot older than I originally guessed. But that's OK, I like older women.)

It was an unhappy union from the start. She knew going in that it would be. Mikis was unpleasant even when they were dating. She endured the mild abuse in the beginning because he was older than her, he was a gangster, it was a thrill to be with him. Later, when he learnt of the pregnancy, she had no choice. He insisted she keep the baby and marry him. If she'd had her parents to turn to, she might have defied him, but they'd disowned her when she hooked up with Menderes, and she didn't dare approach them.

'He wouldn't let me wear white at the wedding,' she says, her eyes a pair of dark, bitter mirrors. 'I wanted to, even though I was five months pregnant, but he said white was for virgins, not whores. He called me a whore even though he was marrying me. He made me dress in red. It was a beautiful gown, but . . .'

Mikis has no respect for her, no love, no compassion. She's his wife, the mother of his only son, so she wants for nothing — the finest clothes and jewellery are hers for the asking. But no kind words, no fond caresses, no gentle gestures. He's proud of her – he takes her with him when he wants to impress, shows her off like a prize dog – but jealous too. He regularly accuses her of flirting with men and beats her for it. He hits her for a variety of reasons – speaking back, not making a fuss of him, sometimes just for looking at him askance – but more often than not because he believes she's considering infidelity.

'He's obsessed with the idea,' she hisses. 'He makes me

mingle when he takes me to parties, forces me to talk with his associates or friends, to make him look good, so they go away saying what a charming wife old Mikis has. But then he attacks me for coming on to them. He accuses me of flaunting myself.' She sniffs. 'I've learnt not to argue. I stand and take it. It's easier that way. Once, I threw his accusations back in his face, said I'd fucked one of the guys I'd been talking with. I thought that might shut him up.

'I spent three weeks in hospital recovering. He's normally careful when he hits me, focuses on my shoulders, arms, breasts.' She touches the high collar of her dress. 'It's why I cover up so much, to hide the bruises. But that time he lost control and almost killed me. Since then I've taken my punishment without complaint.'

I would ask why she's stuck by him instead of fleeing, except I already know the answer — you don't run from men like Mikis Menderes. He'd hunt her, find her, kill her. Besides, he's been her whole life since they married. I'm sure she has no friends or allies of her own. Who could she turn to for help?

'Does he ever go after the men he accuses you of flirting with?' I ask.

'No,' she snorts. 'He knows I've never betrayed him. He just likes to act as if I have. He's betrayed me plenty, though, and he doesn't bother to hide it. He's had so many women. He taunts me with them when he's bored, phones them when he knows I'm listening, comes home with their lipstick all over him, moans their names while he's fucking me, tells me how much better they are.'

'Why doesn't he divorce you and marry one of his other women?' I snarl.

'He doesn't believe in divorce. I don't think he'd marry again, even if I died. He's in love with the idea of family.'

'What does your son think? Does he stand by and —'

'Greygo?' she interrupts with a smile. 'That's what we call him. Mikis insisted on naming him Gregory, but he has trouble pronouncing it.' She shakes her head. 'He doesn't know. Mikis never hits me in front of Greygo, and has threatened terrible things if I turn informer. He won't have his son thinking ill of him.'

She says that the beatings aren't the worst. The worst is when he makes love to her. Menderes believes that it's a wife's duty to satisfy her husband's every need. Even though he spends most of his nights with other women – hence her nocturnal freedom – he works in three or four 'shafting sessions' a month with his wife. He's horrible in bed and has grown more so with the passing years.

'In the early days our lovemaking was a comfort. He could be kind towards me. There were nights when he'd make slow, gentle love, then lie beside me and talk softly. I used to tell myself that things were taking a turn for the better. Now I haven't even got that false hope. He comes into my room and –'

'Please,' I stop her. 'I don't want to know. Imagining's awful enough. If I have to listen to a blow-by-blow account . . .'

'Of course.' She looks away. 'I don't want to bother you with my problems. I'm sorry. I shouldn't be waffling on like this.'

'That's not what I meant.' I take her chin gently between my fingers and turn her face back towards me. 'I want to listen. I want you to be open with me. I just can't stomach a graphic description. I'm not sure I could control myself.'

She sneers automatically. 'What could *you* do about it, Ed? Track down Mikis and whack him over the head with your laptop?'

'Maybe,' I deadpan. 'Or I could throw copies of my books at him until he begs for mercy.'

We share a smile. 'This is crazy,' she notes. 'There's nothing funny about Mikis or what he does to me.'

78

'I know,' I chortle, 'but I can't stop grinning.'

'Me neither. Let's order more beer. I feel like getting tipsy.'

The mood lightens after that, and even though Andeanna carries on describing her trials, the sting has gone from her tone and she talks blithely, as if about somebody else. She finds the humour in her situation. Mikis accused her of coming on to one of his uncles once, an elderly, incontinent, wheelchair-bound man. When she took driving lessons, he didn't trust her instructor, so he made one of his men accompany her and sit in the back seat, even during the test. And then, of course, he accused her of seducing her minder.

I think, if dawn could be put off for a week, we'd still be here talking about the Turk and his abuse of her. But the beer garden closes at midnight, and although we intend finding somewhere else to cuddle up, our legs turn to jelly when we stand and realize how much we've drunk.

'I can't handle a nightclub,' Andeanna says. Her face and neck are flushed from the beer. Knowing the truth about her, I think she looks more beautiful than ever. It's incredible, having endured what she's had to, that she's held on to her looks and spirit. Most women would have crumpled years ago in her place.

'We could get a cab and drive around for a while,' I suggest.

'Would you mind if we left things as they are?' she asks. 'I'd rather head home and get my head down. It's been a long night.'

'No problem. I feel the same way.'

Our smiles fade as we stare at one another.

'What now, Mr Sieveking?' Andeanna asks.

'We catch some shut-eye.'

'I mean tomorrow and the next day and –'

'I know what you mean.' Leaning forward, I kiss her. 'I won't run away,' I whisper when we break.

'What about Mikis?'

'He doesn't matter. If you loved him, that would be different. But I won't let a monster come between us.'

'If he finds out . . .' She leaves the unspoken threat hanging
in the air.

'Are you worried about what he might do?' I ask, and she
nods silently. 'Will your fear drive us apart?'

'I don't want it to, but . . .'

I kiss her again. 'A simple yes or no. Do you want to stop
seeing me?'

A long pause, then the softest of answers. 'No.'

'So we carry on, whatever the risks, and take it one day – one
night – at a time. To hell with Mikis Menderes.'

'If you're sure . . .'

'I am.'

'Then so am I,' she says with a kiss, and our destiny is sealed.

Now that we've declared our love and reconciled ourselves to an
uncertain future, I expect the physical side of our relationship
to explode into passionate life. I'm not sure how to react when
a week passes and it doesn't. I understand Andeanna's initial
sexual hesitancy, but now there should be nothing to come
between us. I know about the Turk. We've made a commit-
ment to each other. So what's holding her back? Our petting
has increased and her fingers roam more freely, but whenever I
make heavy advances, she tacitly diverts me.

When I ask about it, she shrugs and says she wants to take
things slowly. 'This is a big step,' she mutters, nuzzling my
neck. 'I've become conditioned to the demands of sex. I'm
used to surrendering my body, not giving it freely. I want it
to be special between us, not like it is with Mikis. Will you be
patient?'

I say that of course I will, but it's frustrating. I can feel the desire in her, the sexual longing. She wants me as much as I want her. So again I wonder — what's holding her back?

I try not to let my personal life interfere with *Spirit of the Fire*, which is chugging along nicely. I've been devoting a lot of time to the science side of the book and I've got a good idea of how to blend it with the horror elements. Soon I'll be ready to start.

Jonathan gets in touch to say he's in the process of finalizing the contract, but it might still take a few weeks. He's not going to rush them — he'll use the time to scout around for an American publisher. He asks if I'm free to return to the States if needed. I say I'll let him know, then discuss it with Andeanna. I mention the possibility of her accompanying me, but she vetoes the idea. There's no way the Turk would let her travel to America without him.

'But go if you must,' she urges. 'I don't want to hold you here. If your work takes you away, I won't interfere.'

'Don't say things like that,' I scowl. 'You know I won't leave you.'

'I know,' she smiles. 'But I don't want you thinking that you *can't*. It won't crush me if you call it quits. I'll survive. I'm quite accomplished at surviving.'

Though Andeanna rules out a trip to the States, Joe would love to go. I've told Jonathan about my partner, and while he isn't keen on the idea of a collaborator, he's accepted my decision to involve Joe and is preparing a contract for him. I told Joe he shouldn't sign if he doesn't want to, and I urged him to seek legal advice, but I don't think he paid any attention. He's so excited at the thought of being involved, he'd sign away all rights if a deal to that effect was placed before him.

I'm paging through a monstrously thick book about unusual deaths when my phone rings. It's Andeanna. 'Guess what?'

'Surprise me.'

'Mikis has been called away on business. He'll be gone for three days. I have the house to myself.'

I lay the book aside. 'What about bodyguards? I thought he didn't leave you alone at home.'

'He doesn't. A guy called Axel Nelke is guarding me. But things aren't so hot between Axel and his wife. He could do with some extra time at home with her. I told him I wouldn't tell Mikis if he didn't.' She lowers her voice and does a pretty good Mae West impression. 'So why don't cha come up and *see* me some time?'

'I can't,' I reply solemnly.

'Why not?' she asks, perturbed.

'I don't have your address.'

'Funny guy,' she drawls, and tells me where she lives, describing the quickest route from my hotel. I jot down directions, grab my keys and hurry downstairs, not bothering to change my clothes.

The Menderes mansion lies tucked off the main road in the northern suburbs of London, hidden behind a scattering of trees. The electrified gate opens as I approach and closes smoothly behind me. It's a short drive to the house, where Andeanna waits on the steps of the front porch. Rolling down the window, I ask where I should park.

'Here is fine,' she says, so I cut the engine and step out. She glides down the steps to greet me, wraps her arms around me and buries me in a long, eager kiss. It's a kiss I'm in no hurry to break, but then I catch a glimpse of a security camera overhead.

'You have CCTV?' I snap.

'Of course,' she says.

I stare at the camera, feeling my stomach drop.

'But you don't have to worry about it,' she smirks.

'How come?' I frown.

'I sneaked in and switched off the record function.'

'Won't somebody notice that when they check?'

'Don't worry,' she smiles. 'I'll turn it back on when you leave. I do this every time I slip in and out. It's second nature now.'

I grunt uneasily. I trust her, but the camera sets me on edge all the same and I start thinking about other things that could go wrong. 'What about the staff?' I ask.

'All gone,' she says, tugging me up the steps. 'Mikis can't tolerate servants. He employs the slimmest of crews and gets them in and out as swiftly as possible. The maids, cleaners and gardeners come in the morning and are gone by early afternoon.'

'Who does the cooking?' I ask.

'Me. Except when we have guests. Then Mikis hires caterers. But when it's just us, he keeps the help at arm's length. That's one of the reasons I feel so lonely. I have to stay in all day with bodyguards who never talk with me. I don't know how I'd survive if I wasn't able to slip out at night and mix with real people.'

'Does the Turk know about your nightly escapades?'

She shakes her head. 'He doesn't think I could be so bold. He believes I'm locked away all the time.'

'Don't your guards tell him?'

'I retire early every night – I always have done, so there's no call for them to be suspicious – then disable the CCTV and sneak out.'

'You'll be caught eventually,' I warn her.

She laughs. 'Not as long as there's sport on the telly for them to watch.'

Taking my hand, Andeanna leads the way inside. She's nervous, and so am I. Regardless of her guarantees, I can't shake the thought from my head that this is the Turk's stronghold. I expect him to burst in on us at any moment.

Andeanna takes me on a tour of the house. I feel edgy, and it's not just the feeling you get when you enter somebody's home without the owner's permission. There's a chill in the air. The rooms are larger than normal. Sounds echo through them. And there's a . . . I don't know if I can describe it . . . a solemnity to the atmosphere. This feels like a house of mourning. Even my ghosts look sombre.

Each room is a hall of garish wonders. Crystal chandeliers, mounted heads of lions and deer, banisters studded with jewels, paintings by artists whose names are familiar even to me, leopard-skin rugs adorning the hearths, lots of marble and gold leaf. It's been a long time since I visited such a monument to lavish, vulgar taste.

'You don't like it,' Andeanna notes.

'No, it's lovely, I . . .'

'Don't lie,' she laughs. 'I hate the place too. It's Mikis's dream home, not mine. He took control of the plans. He even designed *my* bedroom and makes me keep it the way he wants.'

'That's a room I'd like to see,' I mumble artlessly.

Andeanna looks at me without saying a word, then turns on her heel and marches upstairs. I follow silently, eyes glued to her shapely calves as she climbs the stairs ahead of me. At the top she takes a left and escorts me to a room at the end of the corridor. Another huge chamber, soft blue wallpaper, billowing curtains, antique dressing table, walk-in wardrobe and an en suite bathroom. A four-poster bed occupies a full quarter of the floor. Several framed wedding photos of Andeanna and Mikis adorn the walls. She's hardly aged at all.

While Andeanna stands just within the doorway, I stroll to the dressing table and study the few personal artefacts scattered across it — brushes, a compact, hair pins. A photo album rests next to a powder box. I pick it up and flick through. Snapshots of Andeanna and her son. He's young in most of them, but there's a recent shot of him near the back. He's shaved his hair off and the glow of his scalp creates a halo-like impression. 'Gregory?' I ask.

'Greygo. Yes.' She comes over and stares at the smiling young man.

'Handsome,' I note.

'*He* thinks so,' she laughs, 'but that bald head's awful! He's an actor. Very talented, and that's not just his mother talking, the critics have often said so too.'

'Have I seen him in anything?'

'I doubt it. He prefers the stage to movies or the telly, and he likes to take small, interesting character roles. That's why he shaved his head — he wears a lot of wigs, darting from one play to another.'

My eyes flick from the photo to Andeanna. 'He favours you.'

'Yes,' she says proudly. 'He inherited my finer characteristics and hardly any of Mikis's lesser features. It drove Mikis mad. He hated the fact that his son looked more like me than him. I used to lie and tell him that Greygo has his eyes and mouth. Over the years he's come to believe that. But it isn't true. He's mine.'

Her fingers brush across her son's face, then she takes the album from me and closes it. 'Mikis insisted on a blood test. When Greygo didn't look like him, he dragged us to our doctor to make sure he was the father. If there'd been even a shadow of a doubt, we would have wound up at the bottom of the Thames. Mikis isn't the sort who'd bring up another man's child, or allow him to live.'

'Where is Greygo?' I ask.

'On tour with a rep company. He spends a lot of time on the road. I think he finds it easier that way.'

'What do you mean?'

She sighs. 'Greygo loves his father, and it's reciprocal, but he

85

knows he's a disappointment. Mikis wanted his son to follow in his footsteps, but Greygo fell in love with acting when he was a child. Mikis tried to dissuade him, but Greygo was adamant. When Mikis refused to support him, he won a scholarship to RADA. Any other parent would have been bursting with pride – do you know how hard it is to get into RADA? – but Mikis went into depression. I think he was worried because so many actors are gay — at least that's the myth. He was afraid Greygo might go pink. To a man like Mikis, there's nothing worse than a gay son.'

She's babbling because she's nervous. I gently bring her back to the point I was trying to make. 'So we're alone,' I remark.

She nods tensely. 'Yes.' Then, trembling, she offers her lips. Our kiss is brief. When we separate, she looks troubled. 'I know you've been patient, and I know how hard it's been. I don't want to keep you hanging in suspense, but I . . .'

'It's OK,' I tell her.

'There are things I haven't told you, things . . .' I silence her with a kiss, but she's determined to say her piece. 'Mikis forces me to submit to gynaecological tests. My doctor is one of his oldest friends. She answers directly to him.' I stare at her, understanding at last why she's been keeping me at arm's length. 'He springs her on me without warning. Sometimes months pass between examinations. Then she'll test me three times in a week.' Andeanna looks up, tears forming. 'She's a godawful bitch and thorough as the devil. No matter what precautions we took, I couldn't be sure that she wouldn't find a trace of you. That's why . . .'

'Oh God,' I groan, embracing her. 'You should have told me. If I'd known . . . Christ, I wouldn't . . . I'd never have . . .'

'I want to give myself to you,' she cries. 'I want to be with you properly, but if she found out and told Mikis . . .'

'It's OK,' I whisper, kissing her forehead. 'I can wait.'

She sniffs. 'There's no *wait*. I love you, but I won't risk my life for you. If we could run away – if I thought he couldn't find us – I'd light out in an instant. I'd give it all up, this house, the lifestyle, everything. Even Greygo. I love you that much. But he'd find us. He'd kill us.'

'Not if we killed him first.' It's barely a whisper.

She giggles. 'Right. With copies of *Soul Vultures*.'

'I'm serious. With a gun. A knife. Mikis Menderes is human. He can be killed. I could –'

'Stop,' she smiles. 'It's cute – no, not cute, volunteering to kill a man can't be *cute* – but you're being silly. You're a writer, not a thug. You couldn't kill anyone and I don't expect you to, so quit with the macho crap. It doesn't become you.'

'And if it wasn't crap? If I could really kill him?'

She pinches the love handles I've developed over the last few years. 'Stop.'

'OK.' I force a smile. 'I won't kill your husband.'

She laughs, then grows serious and steps back. 'Now that you know. Now that you realize how impossible it is. Do you want to go on seeing me?' She stares at the floor. 'I'll understand if you don't. Our only hope is if Mikis drops dead of a heart attack or if one of his rivals eliminates him. I don't think that will happen. Although he's older than either of us, he's fit as a fiddle, and he leads a charmed life. He may live to be a hundred.'

'Andeanna.' She looks up, hopeful, fearful. 'I love you. Nothing can change that. If I can't have it all, I'll take whatever I can.'

'You don't mind?' She sounds doubtful.

'Of course I mind! Being with you and not having you tears me to pieces. But it's better than not being with you at all. Just to see you, to talk with you, to hold and kiss you . . .' I stop when I feel a lump in my throat. I haven't cried (except when drunk and pitiful) since I was a kid, and I don't want to embarrass myself by starting now.

'Oh, Ed,' she sobs, and throws herself on me. I hold her and whisper and tell her everything's fine, the sex doesn't matter, simply having her with me like this is enough.

Eventually Andeanna pushes herself away, grabs tissues from the table and wipes around her eyes, then sits and applies make-up. I watch, amused. She notices my grin in the mirror and lowers her head. 'Force of habit,' she mutters, then stands and clears her throat. 'There *are* things we can do, if we're careful.'

'What are you talking about?'

She blushes and whispers something beneath her breath.

'I can't hear you,' I tell her.

She looks at me straight, defiant this time, and with a twinkle in her eye. 'I could give you a handjob.'

I laugh out loud at the unexpected proposal.

'What?' Andeanna snaps, pretending to be offended. 'I'll have you know I have very skilled hands.'

'I'm sure you do,' I smirk.

She wriggles her fingers. 'Kings would offer fortunes for a few quick jerks from me.'

I explode in a fit of giggles, and I can't recall the last time that ever happened to me. 'Stop!' I gasp, clutching my sides.

'Well, I'm glad I can make you laugh, even if I can't satisfy your carnal desires,' Andeanna sniffs, then flexes her fingers at me again. As I chuckle, she gets up, grabs hold of me and pulls me down on to the bed. We wrestle with each other, playfully. She tickles me. I kiss her and start to slide a hand up between her legs, drawing a delighted squeal. I stop before she pushes me away, respecting the boundaries the Turk has forced on her.

After a while she falls still and rests her head on my shoulder. 'I'm sorry,' she murmurs. 'I want you more than anything else in the world. I want to give myself to you. Not being able to . . .'

'Don't let it get you down,' I tell her, kissing the top of her head, running my hands through her hair, relishing even this much contact, content to have to stop here. 'Our time will come. Things will work out.'

'You really think so?' she asks sceptically.

'Sure,' I sigh. 'It happens in fairy tales all the time, and you're as beautiful as any fairy-tale princess, so . . .'

'Bullshitter,' she says, pinching me lovingly. Then we hold each other tight, smiling, kissing, letting our warm breath mingle. If I was to be truthful with her, I'd have to admit that I don't know if I can settle for a chaste relationship in the long term. But for the time being, it doesn't matter. She has me and I have her. That's enough. For now.

EIGHT

A pattern develops over the next fortnight. Days spent working on the book with Joe, time moving with all the speed of a slug. Nights devoted to Andeanna, hours slipping away like minutes.

I can't stop thinking about Andeanna, the Turk, the pressures he brings to bear on her, the restricted nature of our relationship. I fantasize about killing him, catching him alone and cutting the bastard down. But Andeanna told me that his bodyguards are always with him, except when he's at home. I'd have a crack at him there if not for her. She'd be with him. If she saw me kill him, she might hate me, even though it would mean her freedom. I can't risk that.

I try to lose myself in work. Joe and I have come up with a name for our central character — Don Sanders. In the book, when Don comes back to life, he sets out to find answers to explain his return. If you want to learn more about life after death, you track down people who deal with the dead. So Joe and I set off on a trail of fortune-tellers and clairvoyants. I've got the names and addresses of many reputable mediums – including Andeanna's friend Etienne Anders – but I don't pursue them. Instead, imagining ourselves in Sanders's shoes, we turn to the internet for leads, and our search engine results lead us from one merry fraud to another.

In other research, I discover that spontaneous human

combustion isn't confined to humans. There are reports of animals, furniture, books, all sorts of objects bursting into flames. I'm not sure how to work that into the novel, so I'll just neglect to mention it. What the readers aren't told can't confuse them!

Andeanna agrees to spend an evening with Joe and me. We've nothing special planned – meet at a pub, go for a meal – but it'll be nice to get them together at last. We're due to meet at a quarter to eight. Joe and I arrive a few minutes early, order drinks and find a table in clear view of the door. Joe has dressed smartly and even came equipped with a tie. I told him not to be so formal, but he insisted on looking his best. 'I feel like a father waiting to grant approval of his son's fiancée,' he said.

Eight comes and goes. No sign of Andeanna. I don't worry. She's a woman, so I hardly expect her to be on time. But when nine o'clock ticks by, I'm sweating. She can't have got the pub wrong – we've been here before – but maybe we got our times mixed up. I ring her cell phone, but it's switched off.

Joe's mood darkens before mine. He was telling loads of terrible jokes earlier, but they've dried up and he's tight-lipped now. Even though he doesn't know her, he guesses the truth before I do — she isn't coming. He doesn't say anything, but I can see by the way he keeps looking around that he's embarrassed. Finally, with ten o'clock looming, I try her cell again, then give up. 'She's blanked us.'

Joe sighs with relief at having the truth out in the open. 'Maybe she was delayed,' he says diplomatically. 'Traffic. A puncture. An accident.'

'No. She stood us up. She's gone out of her way to avoid meeting you. I don't know why, but she has. She told me she'd be here tonight, but I don't think she ever meant to come.'

'Why would she be anxious to avoid me?' Joe asks, startled.

I frown, considering it. 'Maybe you know her. She said

her maiden name was Emerson, but maybe she lied. Hell, Andeanna might an alias too. It wouldn't be the first false name she's given me.'

Joe tugs at his beard. 'You really think I might know her?'

I shrug. 'Probably not. Maybe you're right — she could have been delayed.'

'Sure.' Joe beams encouragingly. 'She'll most likely ring any minute now and clear things up. We'll be laughing about this by the end of the night.'

'Yes,' I say, not believing it for a second.

I down more rum than I should. Joe looks on worriedly and suggests it might be for the best if we drink up and leave. My nasty streak coming to the fore, as it sometimes does when I drink too much, I sneer at his worries and tell him to lighten up. I urge him to take off his stifling shirt. When that suggestion upsets him – maybe he thinks I want to mock his scars – I make a bullying grab for the top buttons. He loses patience and storms out, saying I can follow if I want, or stay and rot.

'Fuck him,' I growl, tossing back another shot of rum. Then I forget about Joe. Andeanna's treachery consumes my thoughts. I've started thinking of things I could do to hurt her – maybe call Mikis and drop a few hints about his wife's indiscretions – when I spot a girl staring at me. 'Help you?' I snap.

She turns away and says something to the two girls with her. All three glance at me, giggle and return to their drinks. I keep watch on the one who first caught my eye. She doesn't look more than eighteen or nineteen, dark blond hair, lots of make-up. She has nothing in common with Andeanna except her gender, but I convince myself otherwise and pretend she's my beloved's spitting image.

I wait until one of the trio heads for the toilet, then slide over and take her seat. As the others start to object, I raise my hands, smooth as silk now that I'm half-steamed. 'It's

OK, ladies, I'm not stopping, I'd just like to apologize for my rudeness earlier.' I smile broadly, and the pretty young blonde smiles back.

'Are you American?' she asks.

'Yes.'

'New York?'

'No, but I know the city well.'

'I have a brother in New York,' she informs me. 'I'm going over for a visit next month.'

Her friend returns and I swiftly vacate her seat. 'Would any of you care for a drink?' I ask. They all place an order and I shuffle off to the bar. Handing out the cocktails when I get back, I murmur as sexily as I can, 'My name's Ed. Could I have yours?'

After checking with her friends, who give her the nod to show they think it's OK to speak with the tall American, the blonde tells me her name is Louise Maloret and she's from Kent but is currently living in Roehampton, studying to be a teacher. The address rings a bell and I recall John Meyher. Excited by the coincidence, I tell her I was out her way recently. When she asks why, I let her have it. 'Research. I'm a writer. Ed Sieveking. You may have heard of me?' I don't grow discouraged when she says that she hasn't. Instead I say I'm big in the States. 'Your brother's probably read my books.'

A fourth chair soon materializes – nothing's too much for a famous American author! – and it isn't long before I'm spinning yarns that would make Pinocchio blush. Stephen King? Sure I know him. Have they read his latest novel? They haven't? Oh, they should. I'm mentioned in it. 'A character's reading one of my books,' I chuckle modestly. 'I'll have to return the favour, keep Steve happy.'

They're more interested in movie stars than writers. I tell them that two of my books are being adapted, and of course then I have to name all the actors who've been linked with the imaginary films.

The girls drag me to a nightclub when the pub closes. After a couple of painful numbers on the dance floor, I hurry to the toilet and throw up. I feel better after that, and better still when someone in the next cubicle offers me some Charlie at a good price. I don't normally do drugs, but the spirit of the night takes me, and by the time I track down Louise, I'm wide-eyed and jerking convulsively to the beat. This time, when we get on the dance floor, there's no stopping me. I hold Louise captive for most of the night, a true party animal.

Later on I find myself locking lips with the girl in a niche near the cloakroom. I don't know how we got here — the last hour or so is a blank. Between kisses I suggest we slip back to the Royal Munster. After some hesitation – she doesn't want me thinking she's easy – she agrees, but first goes to tell her friends where I'm taking her. I start to feel guilty while I'm waiting for her to return, thinking about Andeanna. Another shot of rum helps drive the guilt away.

In my room I throw Louise on to the bed and practically rip off her clothes. She stops me as I'm pulling down my trousers, panting like a horny dog. 'Hold on a sec.' Rising, she empties the contents of her purse and finds a cache of condoms. Tearing one open, she tells me to put it on.

'Anything to please,' I mumble, sliding it over my erection.

'You speak funny,' she laughs, then turns off the light.

Sex is swift. As I thrust blindly into her, I moan, 'Andeanna!' Louise overlooks the slip and yells my name out loud. I clutch her tightly and grind into her, lips pulled back over my teeth, sweating like crazy from the mix of sex, drink and cocaine. It isn't long before I climax with a groaning shudder, porn-star style. Louise lets rip with a considerate fake groan.

In the aftermath she peels off the condom and wraps it up

neatly in a tissue. 'You'd better keep this,' she says. 'Safer that way.'

'What do you mean?' I pant, needing a glass of water but not trusting my legs to support me if I get up.

'You're a famous writer,' she giggles. 'I could slip in some seed and hit you with a paternity suit.'

'Christ! Is that what they teach you in university these days?'

'No. It's what my mum taught me.'

We fall asleep chuckling.

Louise is already up when I wake with a hangover that isn't as bad as I thought it would be. She bounces around in the buff, examining the hotel room. She tells me about her digs, the students she shares with, the awful state of the kitchen, their landlord from hell. Typical student troubles.

After breakfast we shower, dress, swap numbers and kiss goodbye. Louise says I don't have to call her if I don't want to. I say that I will but I don't mean it. By her relieved smirk, I know she knows it's a lie, so I don't feel guilty.

I also don't feel guilty for what I've done. I should – I've betrayed the woman I pledged my heart to – but I don't. Thinking about that after Louise has left, and the normal night of fun we shared, I realize it's because life with Andeanna is so *ab*normal. Why should I feel guilty for cheating on a married woman who can offer me nothing but kisses?

I love Andeanna, and I think she could love me if the circumstances were different, but right now we aren't a good match. She's trapped and I can't help her break out of the prison of the Turk's making. One of us needs to stand up big and break this off before we destroy ourselves.

I'm going home to Montana.

*

Joe's face drops when I tell him I'm quitting London. 'What about the book?' he splutters.

I shrug. 'I'll work on it from home. I'll keep in touch with you. It shouldn't make much of a difference now that we've put in most of the legwork. I can work better in Montana. Fewer distractions.'

'You mean Andeanna,' he says quietly. 'Is she the reason you're going back?'

I see no point in lying. 'Yes.'

'Have you told her?' he asks.

I shake my head.

'Are you going to?'

'I don't know,' I sigh. 'I'd like to see her one last time, but I haven't been able to contact her. I'm booked to fly out early tomorrow, so it –'

'Tomorrow! Why so soon? Jesus, Ed, I know you've been unhappy, but running away like this . . . Are you sure it's a good idea?'

'I'd have gone today except I wanted to talk with you first and clear the air. I acted like a dick the other night.'

'Forget it. We all do stupid things when we're drunk.' Joe sits back and looks around at the cases I've packed, one for my clothes, two for the notes, maps and research material. 'You're really going,' he says glumly.

'Afraid so.'

He sighs. 'I'm not too surprised. I sensed things weren't working between you and Andeanna.' He thinks for a minute, then says, 'I could go see her if you want, take a message, give her your address.'

'Why bother?' I scowl.

'It isn't nice to slip away without saying farewell. Besides, I'd like to meet this beauty you've been bragging about.'

I squint suspiciously. 'You're not thinking of making a move on her when I'm out of the way, are you?'

'Certainly not!' he howls. 'Ed, how can you even think such a –'

'Joking,' I smile.

'That wasn't funny,' he sniffs.

'Sure it was,' I chuckle, then shake my head fondly. I'll miss Joe. My smile fades. Maybe as much as I'll miss Andeanna.

I almost don't phone her. As day turns to night, I argue the decision with myself. She's the one who broke our appointment. If she cared, she'd call. But what if I've misjudged her? Maybe she did have an accident. What if she's been in a crash or a fire or . . .

Eventually, knowing I won't be able to rest easy if I don't attempt to make contact, I try her cell phone again. This time it rings. I disconnect before she can answer. I'm shaking. What will I say? Should I be cruel or compassionate? I'm not experienced in scenes of this nature. Finally I hit redial and let the conversation take its own course.

'Hello?' Her voice is low, trembling, pained.

'It's me.'

A long silence. 'I didn't think you were going to call.' She sounds like she's been crying.

'I almost didn't. I'm leaving tomorrow, going home to Montana.'

'Oh,' she says emotionlessly.

'Is that all you can say?' I snap.

She sighs. 'I'm tired, Ed.'

'What sort of an answer is that? For Christ's sake, I'm leaving! You'll never see me again, and all you can say –'

There's a click. Staring at the phone, I realize she's cut me off. My initial reaction is to hurl it away and let her go hang.

Then I consider the way she spoke, the tremble in her voice. Something's wrong. Redialling, I walk to the window and gaze out at the quiet road, letting the calm of the external world wash through me. 'I'm sorry,' I mutter when she answers. 'I didn't mean to get angry. I'm upset. Not thinking straight.'

'That makes two of us,' she half laughs, then chokes back a sob. 'Are you really leaving?'

'Unless you can convince me to stay.'

'I don't want you to go,' she says in a monotone. 'But as for convincing you . . .' I sense her shrugging. 'I can't think of anything to say that would keep you.'

'Why did you stand me up?'

'It's a long story.'

'Has it got something to do with Joe?'

'Joe?' She sounds confused.

'You're avoiding him. Every time I set up a meeting, you . . .'

Sardonic laughter cuts me short. 'It has nothing to do with *Joe*,' she sneers. 'Your friend was the last thing on my mind.'

'So why didn't you show?'

She pauses, then whispers, 'I love you.' That's followed by tears. 'I have to hang up now.'

'Andeanna! No!'

'Goodbye, Ed. I'll read your new book when it comes out. I'm sure it will be –'

'I'm coming to see you.'

'No!' she gasps. 'You mustn't, it isn't safe.'

'I don't care. I'm coming.'

'I won't let you in. I'll keep the gate locked. I'll summon Mikis.'

'That won't stop me. I'm not leaving until I find out what happened. If I have to go through the Turk to get to you, I will.'

She moans, then sniffles. 'You're being a damn fool, but OK, come if you must. Wait until you see the gate open and a car leaving. Axel's on duty tonight. I think I can persuade him to pop out, like when you came before. But if he won't go – if you don't see a car pulling out – promise me you won't come in.'

'I can't. I've got to see you.'

'If you don't promise, I'll be gone when you get here.'

I rest the phone against my forehead, then lower it and answer in as controlled a tone as possible, 'OK. I promise.'

'If you break your word, it's over between us.'

'You know me better than that.'

'Yes. I do. See you soon. I hope.'

I park fifty yards from the turn-off to the mansion. It's a clear night. I can't fail to spot any exiting vehicles from here. Switching off the lights and crouching low, I keep vigil.

An hour passes. Two. Three. Patience has always been one of my virtues. I've sometimes spent a week shadowing people, sitting quietly in hotel rooms or cars, watching, waiting. I was never nervous then, but I am now. My hands are shaking.

Finally, close to one in the morning, the gates open and a car emerges. I throw myself sideways before the driver completes his turn. He passes by moments later, picking up speed, engine loud in the still of the night. I give it half a minute, then sit up and make the call.

'Ed?' Andeanna answers on the first ring, breathless.

'A car just passed. Axel?'

'Yes. He should be gone twenty, maybe thirty minutes.'

'Have you turned off the CCTV?'

'No. I'll delete the footage from the hard drive later. There isn't time to go fiddling with it now.'

I don't like the sound of that, but I have to trust her.

'You want me to drive in or walk?' I ask.

'Drive and park round back.'

'What about getting out again?'

'I've spent the last few hours in the music room, listening to classical records. You can hide when Axel returns. I'll take him in there. He won't hear you leave.'

Again, I don't like it. I think it would be less risky if I left the car where it is, but I don't want to start an argument, in case she changes her mind and forbids me entry. So I go with her call and hope she knows what she's doing.

The gates are opening again when I reach them. I glide through, take a sharp left at the end of the driveway, then a right around the building. Once I'm parked in the shadows, I leave the keys in the ignition and look for Andeanna. She isn't here, but one of the doors is open.

I enter a huge, cool pantry. I expected Andeanna to meet me, but she's nowhere to be seen. I pad cautiously through the pantry and kitchen, not turning on any lights, finding my way through the darkness by touch. When I reach the door to the main hall, which is brightly lit, I take stock of the situation.

This feels wrong. Why hasn't Andeanna come to greet me? For all I know, the Turk is lying in wait beyond this door, about to spring a trap. One more step could be my last. It's not too late to retreat. Unless guards have closed in behind me, the route is clear. I could crash through the gates, hit the road at full speed and slow for nothing. To push ahead is suicidal.

My ghosts sense my uncertainty and press close around me, making spitting gestures, shrieking silently, doing their best to unnerve me and force me back.

Thinking of Andeanna and the fear in her voice, I ignore the ghosts, turn a deaf ear to reason and advance.

The hall is clear. No Mikis Menderes. No Bond Gardiner. No armed guards. Just emptiness and silence.

'Andeanna?' Her name echoes back. I move to the foot of

the stairs, determined to go no further unless she returns my call. 'Andeanna?' When she doesn't answer, I start up, ignoring my vow to myself. The ghosts dart around me, doing their best to freak me out. They're loving this, more animated than they've been in a long time.

There are footsteps behind me. I turn quickly, hand reaching for a gun which isn't there, then relax when I spot Andeanna emerging out of the gloom of a dining room.

'Sorry,' she says, stopping in the doorway, hands crossed nervously over her abdomen. 'I was watching for Axel, afraid he might forget something and return.'

'You startled me,' I smile, stepping down towards her, through the phalanx of scowling ghosts. 'I thought . . .' I come to a halt. Andeanna hasn't moved into the light, but now that I'm closer, I can see more clearly. Her face is a mess. Bruises on her cheeks and forehead. Split lips. Black, puffy eyelids. 'Jesus,' I whisper.

'Pretty, isn't it?' A hand sneaks to her left cheek and one of the larger bruises. 'Nothing broken, thank God. None of the cuts needed stitches. I'll be OK in a week or two.' A thin smile. 'Maybe three.'

'The Turk?' I ask, and she nods. 'He knows about us?'

'No. I'd be dead if he did.'

'Then why . . .?'

'Come here,' she says, backing up. I follow reluctantly. When I get there, she's reclining on a couch. She pats the space beside her. As I sit, she lays a hand on my knee and leans forward to kiss me. Winces and stops. 'Sorry. It hurts.'

She slips into silence. I study her, appalled. I'm glad it's dark. The shadows mask the worst of the damage.

'I wanted to ring you but I couldn't. Yesterday I was in no shape to talk – you should see the state of my ribs – and today I was penned in by guards. It was lucky you rang when you did — Axel was in the toilet. I was about to call you. Strange, the timing. Maybe we're telepathic.'

'Why did he do it?' I snarl.

'A poem.'

'*What?*'

'I'd booked in to see Etienne before meeting with you and Joe,' she explains. 'Etienne Anders, the mystic I told you about?'

'What does she have to do with this?'

'She read my fortune.' Andeanna's cracked smile tears at my heart. 'She predicted wonderful times, happiness, companionship. She doesn't know who my husband is, but she's always been able to sense my sadness. This was the first time she'd made such promises. She said there was a new man in my life and he'd care for me, love me if I let him, and everything would work itself out.'

'Wise woman,' I remark, managing a sickly grin.

'I came home on a high,' she continues. 'I practically floated in the door and started getting ready. I wanted to make a good impression on Joe. In the middle of shaving my legs, I put my razor aside and jotted down the beginning of a silly poem that popped into my head.

> 'My lover's kiss is like a drill,
> His heart supplies its power.
> Resistance he is quick to kill,
> And my love he devours.'

She pulls a face. 'Woeful, isn't it?'

'I've heard worse,' I smile. 'But not often.'

Her expression twists. 'I was working on the second verse when Mikis sneaked up on me. Before I could stop him, he'd ripped the poem away. He lost his head. Screamed and demanded to know the name of my lover. I told him it was about him, something I'd made up for fun, remembering our early days together, but he wouldn't listen. It infuriated him. He . . .' She points vaguely to her face.

'I'll kill him,' I growl.

'Don't start that again.'

'He did all this because of a fucking *poem*?'

'That's Mikis. It would have been worse if I'd finished it. I was going to mention your name in the third or fourth verse, intending to give it to you later.'

'The bastard.' I wish I had him here, where I could lay my hands on him.

'I don't know,' she sighs. 'His suspicions were justified this time. The poem *was* about an actual lover. I convinced him in the end that it wasn't – he beat me so badly, he was sure I was telling the truth, that I couldn't lie in the face of such a thrashing – but, to be fair, I brought this on myself.'

That's a point I could debate sourly, but I don't. Instead I get to my feet and say firmly, 'Come on.'

'Where?' she asks, alarmed.

'We're leaving. I'm taking you with me. If we can't book you on to my flight to Montana, we'll take the next one. Pack what you can't live without and don't forget your passport.'

She shakes her head. 'Sit down. We're not going anywhere.'

'We are,' I insist. 'I'm not leaving you here in the hands of that son of a bitch. I can hide you, arrange fake papers. We'll change our names and move on. He won't find us. And if he does, he'll regret it. You'll be safe with me, Andeanna. I swear, on all that's sacred, I'll protect you.'

She stares at me, taken aback. 'I think you mean it,' she murmurs.

'Bet the Crown Jewels I do.' I grin and offer her my hand. 'Let's go.'

She reaches towards me. Stops. 'No,' she whispers. 'I can't.'

'You can!' I shout, and she flinches. Lowering my voice, I kneel beside her. 'Is it because you're afraid?'

'Partly,' she says, starting to cry. The ghosts pull sad faces and wipe crocodile tears away. I don't let them distract me. 'But even if I wanted to leave, I'm in no shape to go on the run. Just walking around the house is an effort.'

'We'll manage. We can hire a wheelchair. Hell, I'll carry you if I have to.'

She touches my lips to silence me. 'You're thinking crooked. How will we cover our tracks if I'm confined to a wheelchair or slung over your shoulder? People will notice us. Mikis will track down those people and find out where we went. It isn't possible, not now, not tonight.'

Those last four words fill me with hope. 'But you *will* come?' I ask, seizing her hands. 'Soon, when you're able?'

She nods hesitantly. 'I think so. Mikis has hurt me before, but never like this. I really thought he was going to kill me. Do you know what went through my mind?' I look at her questioningly. 'I wished I'd let you fuck me.' She blushes behind the clouds of dark purple bruises. 'That was my only regret. I was sorry I hadn't made the most of you when I had the chance. That was when I realized how much I love you and how I can't go on without you.'

'Andeanna,' I groan.

She strokes my chin and kisses me. This time she doesn't wince. 'We'll make plans,' she says. 'We have time. Mikis hates me, but that can work in our favour. I don't think he'll come to see me any time soon. The guards are a problem, but I can ring you when the chance arises. Maybe you can find sleeping pills and slip them to me. I often cook for the guards, so I could –'

'Greygo! Where are you?'

We swivel as if on springs. Through the door we see a man standing in the hall, hands on hips, looking up the stairs. My first thought is that it's the Turk, and I welcome the intrusion, but then Andeanna hisses, 'Axel!'

Whether he hears her or just senses our presence, the guard turns and spots us. Frowning, he starts forward. 'Who's there?' he asks, squinting into the darkness.

I have maybe four or five seconds before he's upon us. Reacting calmly, as I did in the restaurant when I thought we might be attacked, I look for a weapon. There are vases on a shelf, but they're small, fragile, useless.

Andeanna stiffens. 'If he sees us, it's over. He'll tell Mikis. He'll . . .'

The guard reaches the doorway and stops. 'Who's there?' he barks. 'Greygo? Are you with a woman?'

While my eyes search for something to defend myself with, Andeanna stands and walks towards the guard. 'Hello, Axel. Greygo's not here. Can I help?'

'What the fuck?' the guard mutters, staring at Andeanna. He takes a step back and stumbles over a telephone cable which hasn't been tacked to the wall. *That's* my weapon.

Leaping to my feet, I dart past Andeanna, lowering my head as I charge. The guard's eyes flicker towards me, but then, even though he must know I'm a threat, they return to Andeanna. Taking advantage of his confusion, I barrel into him and knock him flat to the floor. The air explodes out of him in a huff. His hand goes for his gun, but I'm too fast. Grasping his wrist, I elbow him between the eyes with my free arm.

As Axel's head snaps backwards, I drag him to the door, grab the telephone cable, loop it round his throat, take firm hold of the cord with both hands, dig my right knee into the small of his back and pull. The guard's eyes bulge as the cable cuts into the flesh of his throat. He slaps at my hands and jerks at the noose. No good. The loop tightens. He's at my mercy. And I have none.

Andeanna screams as the guard's legs thrash. The stench of released faeces hits the air. His hands claw at mine, nails scratching my lower arms. His tongue sticks out obscenely. His teeth grind down on it, drawing blood, then peel apart as he seeks the elusive breath which might restore his vitality.

The ghosts writhe with delight and applaud grotesquely. This is what they want, me shedding my respectable charade, giving in to my baser instincts, damning myself. They think that violence will unhinge my senses and leave me vulnerable, in their clutches. They might be right, but I can't let that stop me.

I concentrate on the cable, driving my knee down into Axel's back, pinning him to the floor, making sure my sweaty fingers don't slip, not letting myself forget that he has a gun and needs only the slightest opportunity to reverse our situations.

Wicked choking sounds. His palms slap flatly on the floor. His body goes limp as he passes out. If I release him now, he'll revive in the morning, bruised, maybe mute for a few days, but alive. I want to free him. I don't enjoy killing. But he's seen us together. He'd tell the Turk. It's us or him.

I relax my grip on the cable, let the loop loosen, wipe my hands on the thighs of my trousers, take hold of the cable again. I maintain the pressure for a long minute before letting go and stepping away from the corpse.

Andeanna approaches, hands clasped as if in prayer, finger-tips to her lips. She walks around the lifeless body, then stares at me, terrified. 'You killed him,' she whispers.

'I had to.' She stares at my hands, which are only trembling slightly. I'd like to talk her through this, but there isn't time. The guard wasn't calling her name. He was looking for her son. 'Where's Greygo?' I ask.

'You strangled him,' she says, ignoring me, captivated by the corpse.

'He called for Greygo. Is your son here?'

'You killed him. Just throttled him until . . .'

I raise a hand to slap her, then think of her bruises and lower it. Grasping her shoulders, I shake her lightly. 'Andeanna!' Her eyes snap into focus and fix on mine. 'Is Greygo here?'

She considers the question carefully before replying. 'No.'

'Then why was the guard calling his name?'

She frowns. Her gaze darts towards the body, but I step in front of her, blocking her view, forcing her to concentrate. She shakes her head. 'I'm not sure. I didn't think he was home. But I've been in the music room all night. Maybe . . .'

'We have to check.' I turn to the guard and search for his gun, which I find strapped to his side in a sleek leather holster.

Andeanna gasps when she sees me holding the pistol. 'No! I won't let you harm Greygo. He's my son. You're not going to –'

'This is for protection only. I might club him over the head with the butt if I have to, but I won't shoot him.'

'If you kill my child . . .'

'I know. Now let's go see if we can find him.'

I help her up the stairs. Her legs are weak and she has to lean on me much of the way. Watching someone die is never easy. Watching someone being murdered is harder still. I'd let her rest if I could, but if her son's upstairs he has to be neutralized. If we're lucky, he'll be sleeping and we can lock him in his room. If luck's against us, I'll try to knock him out. I don't want to hurt him. I know that Andeanna would never forgive me if I did.

I ask her to call his name when we reach the landing. Her first attempt is a brittle croak. Swallowing, she tries again. 'Greygo.' No answer. 'Greygo! Are you here?' The silence is absolute.

'His room,' I whisper. She leads the way, walking stiffly, and pauses by the door, unwilling to open it. Pushing past her, I turn the handle and slide into a cool, dark room. The curtains are open. The bed's unoccupied. Nobody home. 'Where else could he be?'

'I don't think he's here. He'd have checked in with me if he'd come back.'

'But if he was here, where would he be?'

She shrugs. 'The pool room, maybe.'

We proceed cautiously. Andeanna observes me silently. I don't know what she's thinking, but I doubt it's anything positive. The ghosts are still cavorting madly, as if dancing on hot coals. This is the most excitement they've had in years. They're eager for more. Even the little girl is bloodthirsty, wanting to see me kill again, condemning myself to more guilt, suffering and madness.

The lights are on in the pool room but nobody's present. I sniff the air for traces of aftershave or smoke. Nothing. Only chalk dust.

'He isn't here,' Andeanna says with relief.

'Are there any other rooms where . . . ?'

She shakes her head firmly. 'He isn't home.'

'You're certain?'

She nods. 'We can check if his car's in the garage, but I know it won't be. We'd have run into him by now if he was here.'

She's probably right, but I make her take me to the garage all the same. It's empty. No Greygo. We're alone.

Back in the dining room, I study the sprawled guard and consider my next move. No blood, which is good. He's tall, but not heavily built. Shouldn't be too hard to carry. 'We have to wrap him up,' I tell Andeanna, frisking him for keys, his wallet, rings and chains. 'Do you have any rubber blankets?'

'I don't know,' Andeanna replies, staring at the cord around his throat, the ugly red line of death carved into his flesh.

'If you haven't, we'll use a couple of ordinary blankets covered with plastic bags.' I gently unwrap the telephone cable from around his neck. Tracing it to the phone in the hallway, I check for a dial tone and find one. That means I just have to wipe the cable with a cloth and stick it back against the wall.

'We need to work quickly,' I tell Andeanna as I return to the dining room. 'Once we have him wrapped, I'll get my car, bundle him into the trunk and . . .' I stop. 'Where's *his* car? Why didn't we hear him pulling back into the drive?' Andeanna looks blank. 'He drove out of here but he didn't drive back. We'd have heard him. Why did he return so soon, on foot?'

She shakes her head. I reach out to grab her shoulders again, but she pulls away. 'Don't touch me!' she snarls.

'OK.' I lower my hands. 'You don't have to fear me. I'll give you all the space you need. But don't freak out on me. We have to hold it together.'

'You killed him.'

'Yes,' I sigh. 'But that isn't the issue. Where the hell is his car?' It comes out louder than I intended.

Andeanna blinks. 'Axel drives an old Skoda. It sometimes stalls. It must have quit on him on the way to the shops. That's why he called for Greygo — he hoped he was here, to help push the car.'

'We have to find it. We'll use it to get rid of the body, then dump it. That will be safer than taking him in my car. Then we can —'

'You killed him,' Andeanna interrupts.

'Are we back to that?' I groan.

'You killed him coldly, calmly, like it was no big thing, as if it wasn't the first time you'd done it.' Her voice is steady. I stare at her wordlessly while she circles me as she earlier circled the corpse, eyes pinning me to the spot. The ghosts circle with her, swaying and cooing. 'I saw Mikis kill a man once. Fourteen years ago, in Blackpool. He attacked us. He had a knife. Mikis disarmed him, took the knife and kept stabbing until he was dead.'

'Andeanna. We don't have time for this.'

She ignores me. 'Mikis didn't panic. I'm sure he'd been in that sort of situation before. He knew what to do. But even so, he didn't react as icily as you. He was shaking. He took my hand and ran, then stopped and cursed — he'd dropped the knife and had to go back to get it. In our hotel room he downed half a bottle of vodka before the shakes subsided. He looked like hell.'

She stops. I cross my arms, resigned, and wait for the inevitable question.

'*You* don't look like hell, Ed. You dispatched — yes, *dispatched* him as if you were tearing open an envelope. And now here you are, cool, composed, casually talking about how to get rid of the body.'

'I have to. If we don't –'

'Earlier,' she barks. 'When you were trying to convince me to leave with you. You said you could protect me.'

I nod wearily. 'Yes.'

'You didn't sell computers before you were a writer, did you?'

'No.'

She steps up close. 'What *did* you do, Ed?'

I consider a variety of lies, then dismiss them all. It's time for the truth. 'I killed people,' I tell her, then add emotionlessly, to make sure we understand each other completely, 'I was an assassin.'

PART THREE

NINE

I find Axel Nelke's Skoda less than half a mile past the gate, parked in the shade of a tree. I check both sides of the street for signs of life. Observing none, I pull on an old pair of the Turk's driving gloves which Andeanna found for me – I don't want to leave any fingerprints – open the driver's door, sit in and try to start it up, anticipating problems.

The engine kicks into life immediately. I let it turn over for a few seconds, then complete a U-turn and head for the mansion, where Andeanna is waiting with Nelke inside the front door. He's wrapped in dark sheets and black plastic bags. We dragged him there after I'd taken off his trousers and cleaned him up, so that his death stench wouldn't foul up the air of the car.

I leave the engine running – I don't want to risk not being able to restart it – and duck inside. Andeanna is pale-faced. We haven't said much since I told her of my true past. I will explain everything, but not while there's work to be done. It's better to operate in silence and save the biography for later.

'Where will you take him?' Andeanna asks.

'I haven't decided. Any suggestions?' I'm not being sarcastic.

She shakes her head hopelessly. 'I don't know.'

I flash her a confident smile, trying to put her at ease. 'Don't worry. I'll sort it out.' She nods, but there's no warmth or thanks in the gesture, merely a cool acknowledgement that she trusts me to handle things. 'Can you drive?' I ask.

She frowns. 'Of course. I passed my test years ago.'

'I mean can you drive *now*? Are your nerves up to it?'

'Oh.' She looks at the bagged body and gulps. 'Why do you need a driver?'

'My car,' I explain patiently. 'Somebody has to drive it back to the Royal Munster. If you can't, I'll have to call Joe.'

'No,' she says quickly. 'I don't want to involve anyone else. I'll do it. It won't be easy, but I'll manage.'

'The keys are in the ignition. There's a car park beneath the hotel. Get a cab back here, but get it to drop you nearby, not at the house.'

'What about the keys? How will I return them to you?'

'Leave them under the seat. Don't lock the door.'

'But someone could steal it.'

A time like this and she's worried about motor theft! 'Let them,' I snap. 'It's a rental. It doesn't matter. And don't forget to wipe the CCTV hard drive when you get back.'

'God, yes. I'd forgotten.' She glances at the bag again. 'Will you come back when you're finished?'

'You're fucking joking, aren't you?' She blinks, stung by my sharp tone, and I sigh. 'We won't be able to see one another for a while. I doubt the Turk will connect his guard's disappearance with you, but let's not take any chances. I want you to phone him when you return. Tell him Axel took a call and bailed. Act annoyed. Let the Turk worry about it after that.'

I pick up the body by the shoulders. Andeanna takes the legs. I expect her to struggle with the weight, but she must be stronger than she looks, as she carries it with ease. We heave Nelke's corpse outside and into the trunk. I'm about to close it when I stop and take out the jack, the bag of tools and the spare tyre, which I lump into the back seat. This way, if I get a puncture and have to stop by the side of the road, I needn't open the trunk, baring the body bag to the eyes of curious passers-by.

I gaze at the mansion, wondering if I've forgotten anything. I quickly go over the events of the night. Phone cable in place. Floor cleaned. No garments left behind. Fingerprints wiped clean. I could go back and deal personally with the CCTV, but I'm keen to be out of here ASAP. I'll leave that to Andeanna, hope she doesn't forget again or screw it up.

'I'll keep out of London for a few days,' I tell her. 'It's best I don't ring while I'm gone. Will you call me on my cell – my mobile – three days from now, if you're sure it's safe?'

'Yes.'

Hard to tell if she means it. 'Andeanna.' She looks at me, slightly unfocused. 'I love you.'

'Yes.'

'You'll call me when I get back?'

'Sure.'

'I had to kill him. It was for us. If he –'

'Just go, Ed. Do whatever you have to. I don't want to discuss it. I'll call you. Maybe not in three days, maybe not for a week, but eventually, when I've got my head around what happened tonight.'

I want to kiss her, one last kiss in case things go to hell and I never see her again. But I'm sure she'd pull away from me if I tried.

I run through the checklist. Body bagged and trunked. Nelke's personal effects in a small plastic bag on the passenger seat. His gun tucked into the waist of my trousers — I'll slide it under the seat and hold on to it until I've got rid of the body. Andeanna's been told what to do. I'm not sure she won't crack when I leave – she looks composed now, but once she has time to dwell on the last hour, who knows how she'll react – but I have to trust her.

'See you soon,' I mutter.

'Soon,' she agrees, and turns back into the house.

Getting into the car, closing the door, I face the driveway with the calm of a professional, blank the ghoulishly giggling ghosts who have spread across the back seat like revellers on their way to a party, switch on the air-con and go.

I'm not familiar with this country's road network, but I've done a lot of driving around London, so I know enough to head north for the nearest freeway (they call them motorways here). On the M25, I circle west and south until I hit the road to a town called Southampton. It's quiet at this time of the day. If I wasn't afraid of being stopped, I'd floor the accelerator. But a run-in with the police is the last thing I want, so I keep within the speed limit.

I turn off before Southampton, into a gas station to fill up. I don't want to stop, in case the car dies, but the tank is almost empty. I'm not sure what I'll do if I can't restart the engine. I think about my options as I'm filling up. Push it out of the way, hire or steal another car, transfer the body? Just leave the corpse in the car and run, hope my face isn't captured on CCTV?

Thankfully it's not a bridge I have to cross. The engine kicks in smoothly when I get back in and turn the key – the gods seem to be on my side – and I carry on. I continue in a westerly direction. I came this way when I visited Devon, so it seems as sensible a place as any to bolt for now.

I stop off at a services restaurant an hour later. Park the car, leave the body in the trunk, pocket the gloves, go and order a full English breakfast. I find a window with a view of the car and eat in glum silence.

Next I explore a newsagent's beside the restaurant and pick

up a map and a booklet on the local area. I spend a long time leafing through both, searching for a quiet village or town on the coast. When I find one that fits the criteria, I head off, leaving the map open on the seat beside me so that I can check directions. (Nelke must have been old-school because he didn't have satnav. I suppose, given the car's age, I should be grateful even for the air-con.)

I take my time, not wanting to arrive too early. I drive up and down the coast, enjoying the scenery, listening to the radio, forcing myself to slip into tourist mode, so that I don't stand out and draw attention. I don't make for the town until eleven. I'm pleased with my choice when I arrive — a sleepy place, yet busy enough for nobody to take any notice of a stranger. It's littered with B&B signs, but I make for a hotel on the outskirts.

The girl at the registration desk pays no interest as I sign in, only smiles mechanically and wishes me a nice stay. Leaving the car parked in the nearby lot, I retire to my bedroom, undress and fall asleep as soon as I'm under the covers. I sleep dreamlessly, until four in the afternoon, when my alarm goes off.

After I'm done on the toilet, I study myself in the bathroom mirror, silently, thoughtfully, not liking what I see but glad of it at the same time. I thought I'd left the killing behind, but now I'm back in the middle of bloodshed and it's like I've never been away. Already I can see that ice-cold look I've been trying to work out of my repertoire. It's scary how swiftly the past can catch up with you.

The ghosts don't like my calm expression. They thought I'd be more shaken. They stare at me sullenly, their hopes that I'd suffer a mental breakdown fading away swiftly, exposed as wishful thinking on their part. I cracked before under the pressure and guilt, but this time it's different. This time I have the love of a good woman to fight for. That helps me hold my shape.

I take dinner in my room, then go for a walk. I visit a couple of pubs and fall into conversation with crusty old-timers. I let them bore me with their tales and pretend to be interested. When they ask, I tell them I'm in the computer business, but on holiday, taking things easy, doctor's orders. I enquire about boats and if it's possible to rent one and take it out by myself. An old guy called Jock asks if I have experience. I've sailed solo before – I'm fine on the sea as long as I'm sober – and it doesn't take long to convince him that I'm a confident skipper. I tell him I want something easy to handle, between eighteen and twenty-five feet.

'Well,' he drawls, 'I know a man who might let you have a wee gem of a boat for a day or two, assuming the price is right.'

Jock takes me to see his friend, Peter, and we spend the tail-end of the evening on the bay, where I prove I can handle the patched-up, weather-beaten boat. A deal is struck over drinks in a pub, and I agree to leave my car keys as collateral before setting sail each day.

After another consultation with the map and booklet, I drive to a town half an hour away – in case anyone is tracking my credit cards – and withdraw cash from an ATM. The next morning I head to the quay, buying a bale of rope along the way. I give Peter his money and the keys, then hit the waves. I'd like to take the body out and dump it today, but I want to cast an eye over the terrain first. I check that the boat is equipped with binoculars, then set off up the coastline.

I putter along, keeping close to the shore, faking an interest in the countryside. In reality I'm clocking houses, scanning roads, searching for an isolated area, out of view of land, where nobody will see what I'm up to. I discover the ideal place before midday. Cliffs shade the stretch of water, there are no nearby houses, the only road is shielded from the bay by a forest.

Happy with my choice, I move on and devote the rest of the

day to rest. I drift with the currents and watch fish flitting by, drop anchor in a secluded spot and pop in for a swim, naked as an eel. Later, I moor and enjoy a slap-up lunch in a pub. I get back about six, track down Peter, agree to take the yacht out again tomorrow, and collect my keys.

I catch a few hours of sleep at the hotel, then head out late, having asked the clerk about the local nightlife. I drive to the quay, where I park and leave my car. I find a pub, have a couple of pints, return to the car and sit in darkness until I'm sure I'm alone. Getting out, I pop the trunk, extricate the wrapped corpse, toss him over my shoulder and take him to the boat, where I stash him, covered in burlap sacks and the rope I bought yesterday. I don't like leaving the body on the boat overnight, worried in case Peter pops back for some reason, but this is better than trying to move it in the morning, when people are at large.

I'm back at the hotel by two, asleep five minutes later, and again I sleep like an innocent child.

Up early. I hurry to the boat. Peter isn't around, so I leave the keys and cash with one of his friends, then ease out on to the bay and retrace yesterday's route. I pull in to load up with stones from a rocky beach before heading for the drop-off point.

Once I'm in place, I unwrap the body and attach the stones with the rope. As the boat drifts, I raise the binoculars and study the coastline. When I'm sure it's safe, I haul up the body and position it by the side of the deck. One last check, then I bend over and send Axel Nelke to a watery grave, sparing him neither a prayer nor a curse. His personal belongings follow, except for his gun, which I've left under the seat in the car. I'm holding on to that, in case I need it later. I scan the coast again – clear – then head out into the Channel, where I idle away the rest of the day, shedding the sheets and plastic bags as I go, in different places.

With night drawing in, I meet up with Peter, make sure he got the money and thank him for the loan of the boat. He tries persuading me to stay another day, but I say that I have to move on. I buy him a couple of whiskies, then trudge back to the hotel, where I shower the scent of salt out of my hair.

I'm anxious to return to London, but it's late. Better to leave it until morning. Too many bad things can happen in the dark.

The hotel's Wi-Fi is no good to me, since my laptop's in London and I don't own a smartphone, but there's a small business centre. I go online before I check out and investigate long-term parking options in London. I want to keep things straightforward, so I settle on the car park at Heathrow. I can see from their site that there's a twenty-five-day parking rate, so nobody should bother with the car for a month, by which time I'll hopefully be long gone.

I also research shopping malls and choose WestQuay in Southampton, since it's on my way back. When I get there after an uneventful drive – I've had far more luck with the Skoda than poor Axel Nelke – I buy a suitcase, a wide-brimmed hat and dark sunglasses, a pack of Handi Wipes, new shoes and a jacket. I remove all the labels on my way to the car and dump them. Slip on the shoes, stick the case in the trunk, lay the rest of the gear on the passenger seat, and I'm set.

With the help of the map I make Heathrow early in the afternoon, collect my ticket at the barrier and find a quiet parking spot. Opening the wipes, I quickly clean inside the car, wheel, handles, switches, anywhere I might have touched. I've worn gloves all the time, but I'm paranoid, worried that I maybe took them off for a few seconds at some point and forgot about it. When it comes to prints, you can't be too cautious, not in this day and age.

Pulling on the hat, glasses and jacket, I get out – carefully wiping the side of the door and the outside handle as I go – and pull the suitcase out of the trunk, again taking the time to erase any prints as I close it.

I think about taking the keys with me, but I don't want to be caught with them on my person, so I open the driver's door and stash them under the dashboard, leaving the door unlocked. Not the best way to dispose of a car, but it will suffice. If I need to, I can collect it later and lose it for good. Right now, I just want rid of the damn thing.

I also leave the gun under the seat. I considered ditching it en route, but figured it might be useful to have a weapon where I can lay hands on it if things get messy.

Taking off the gloves and pocketing them, I lug the case to the bus stop, acting as if it's packed with clothes, in case an eagle-eyed guard happens to be watching and thinks it strange that someone would park in long-term without a suitcase. This makes me look like just another tourist heading off to catch a flight to the sun.

After a short wait, a bus takes me from the car park to the terminal. I keep the hat and glasses on the whole way, and my head down, all too conscious of the British predilection for CCTV — they have security cameras everywhere in this most watchful of countries. I wander around the airport a while, then catch the Tube into central London.

It's crazy, returning like this. I should have paid someone to fetch my passport from the hotel – you can always find a willing gopher at an airport, backpackers who are happy to ask no questions if you flash enough cash – then caught the first flight out. But I can't run, not while there's hope that Andeanna still loves me.

I think about her all the way in, staring down at my hands, wondering what the future holds in store for us.

I have to change lines at Hammersmith. I get off and cross

the platform to the District Line. As a train approaches, my attention is drawn to a man and his son. The boy can't be more than four or five. He's white-faced and crying — he seems to be scared of the incoming train. As his father tries to comfort him, the boy throws up.

Feeling sorry for the child, I glance aside, wanting to afford the pair some privacy. As my head turns, I catch sight of someone rushing towards me. Before I can react, a man throws himself at me, hands waving furiously, eyes wide, mouth opened in a grotesque grimace.

Instinct kicks in and I jerk away from my mad-looking assailant. My left heel catches and I start to topple backwards, on to the track, in front of the incoming train. It's slowing down, but won't be able to stop before it smashes into me. My arms flail as I try to regain my balance, but I can tell it's too late. I'm done for.

Then, as I'm falling, a lost cause, a station guard grabs my arm and wheels me back on to my feet. 'Easy, sir,' he chuckles, as if it's no big thing, as if he hasn't just saved my life. 'Don't want to give the boy any more of a fright, do we?'

'Thank you,' I gasp, heart pounding, legs trembling as the train screeches past. I extend a hand, but the guard has already moved on. He doesn't have time to shake hands with stupid Americans who can't obey the simplest and most repeated of orders on the underground — stand away from the edge of the platform.

I look around, searching for the man who almost sent me reeling to my doom. He's in front of me, glaring. Axel Nelke's ghost.

'Didn't take you long to make your presence known,' I mutter, glaring back at the real or imagined ghost as it's surrounded by the other shades, all seven bunching together to subject me to their combined blistering gaze. How happy the rest would have been if Axel's sneaky ploy had worked! Though I think there would have been an element of jealousy there too. The six of them have spent the last several years trying to drive me mad or shock me at a critical moment, to no avail. How small would they have felt if Nelke had swaggered on to the scene and got rid of me at the first attempt?

'Better luck next time,' I sneer, then board the train and head for home.

Back in my room, I drop the jacket, shoes, hat, glasses and gloves into the suitcase – I'll get rid of it later – and head for the shower, where I soak for twenty minutes, then dry off and lie naked on the bed, staring at the ceiling.

The phone rings as I'm scratching an elbow. Not my cell, which I've kept switched off the entire time I was away. The room phone. I stare at it suspiciously. Andeanna? Surely it's too soon for her to be calling.

'Hello?' I answer cautiously.

'*Ed?*'

I breathe easily. 'Hi, Joe. How's tricks?'

'You son of a bitch!' He shouts down the line at me for a full minute. I hold the phone away from my ear, letting him blow off steam. When he pauses for breath, I ask if he's finished. 'Finished? I'm only getting started! I was worried sick. I thought you'd been in an accident. I rang the hospitals and police to find out if –'

'What did you say to the police?' I interrupt sharply.

'Nothing much. I just asked if they could tell me if you'd been in a car crash or anything like that.'

'Did you file a missing-person report?'

'I was tempted to.'

'But you didn't?' Relaxing a little.

'No,' he grumbles. 'I thought it might have something to do with Andeanna.'

Wise little Joe. 'Did you ring her?' I ask, trying to sound casual.

'I don't have her number. I looked in the directory but she isn't listed and you never told me the name of her husband.'

'Just as well. I can imagine you phoning to ask if his wife's lover was OK.'

'Please!' Joe snaps. 'Credit me with some common sense.'

'I credit you with a lot more than that.' I claim that I did leave on account of Andeanna, that I went to see her and we had a blazing row, after which I stormed out of London in a huff, not thinking about Joe, the book or anything else, even forgetting about my flight home. 'I should have called,' I admit humbly. 'It was wrong to leave you hanging. But my thoughts were all over the place. I just drove, slept in the car and ate when hunger dictated.'

'Is it really over?' Joe asks.

'I don't know. I'll wait for her to ring. If she doesn't . . .'

Joe says he came to the hotel the morning of my scheduled return to America, to see me off. Thinking he'd missed me, he hurried to the airport, but there was no sign of me and I hadn't checked in. When the flight took off and I failed to show at the hotel, he started to worry.

'Where'd you go?' he asks.

'I'm not really sure,' I lie, trying to picture a map of the British Isles. 'I wandered randomly. I passed Birmingham on my way back, so I guess I must have gone north.'

'You should have taken me with you,' he says. 'I could have introduced you to my family. Some of them don't believe I'm working with you on the book. They think I'm making it up.'

Talk turns to *Spirit of the Fire* and my future plans. Joe wants to know if I'm still going back to the States. I tell him I'm not sure.

'And the book?' he presses.

'I can't focus on that now. I'm going to leave it for a while. Later, when I'm thinking straight, I'll tackle it again.'

'OK,' Joe sighs. 'If that's the way you want it.'

'It's not what I want, but I'm in no state of mind to deal with all the complications of a novel. We'll get round to it, I promise. I just don't know when.'

He asks if I'd like him to come over. I tell him I'm a mess, tired, confused. I say I'll ring in a day or two and we'll meet up, sit down and discuss the matter over a bottle of wine, but for now I just want to be on my own. He wishes me well, makes me promise not to flee the city again, then hangs up and leaves me sitting naked on the edge of the bed. After a few minutes I switch on my cell phone and stare at it glumly, waiting for Andeanna to call, yearning to hear her voice, but dreading what she might have to say.

TEN

No word from Andeanna by the time I fall asleep. I spend all of the next day waiting. After an early dinner, I clutch my cell phone and sit by the window watching the twilight. As the sky darkens, I don't move. I could see my ghosts in the glass if I looked up, but I keep my sights trained on the street below.

I'm so sure Andeanna isn't going to ring that when the cell finally goes off in my hand, I drop it with shock. Cursing, I dive after it and answer curtly, 'Yes?'

'It's me.'

I move to the bed, relaxing. 'Hi.'

'Are you back in London?' Andeanna asks.

'Yes.'

'How did things go?' Trying to sound blasé.

'All sorted. What have I missed?'

'Mikis is up in arms. He thinks Axel has betrayed him, that he fled ahead of a planned hit on the house. His people are scouring London. He even took my guards away to concentrate on the search.'

'He doesn't suspect you?'

'No. He bought my lie, hook, line and sinker.'

Her choice of phrase puts me in mind of Axel Nelke. I try not to linger on the image of him floating at the bottom of the sea, fish stripping his bones bare.

'We have to meet,' Andeanna says.

'Not at your place,' I reply promptly.

A sick laugh. 'No. Somewhere neutral, where we can talk freely.'

'A park?'

She thinks about it. 'Yes. St James's. Outside Inn the Park — it's a restaurant.'

'I know it. Tomorrow?'

'No. Tonight.'

'*Tonight?*' I glance out of the window at the darkness and rain.

'Tonight or never,' she says, then hangs up.

This smells of a trap, meeting in the open on a dark, wet night. Few people will be out at this hour, in this weather. Easy for the Turk and his men to ambush me. But I have to trust her. I've nothing to cling to if I don't.

The streets are mostly deserted and the cab makes swift progress. When I get out, I pass no more than four people in the park. Andeanna is alone when I spot her, seated close to the pond, sheltered by a petite umbrella. No sign of lurking conspirators. But there wouldn't be, not if they know who I am and what I used to do. If she's told the Turk about me, he'll have had time to research my past. He'll know better than to underestimate me.

As my stomach tightens, I stride to where Andeanna is seated. She looks up, meets my gaze briefly, then looks away. Her face has healed, though there are still bruises around her left cheek. I wipe the bench clear and sit a foot away from her, holding my umbrella high above my head. There's a long, uncomfortable silence. Finally, without looking at me, she asks what I did with Axel. I give her a condensed version of the story, leaving out names and places.

'Very clever,' she notes numbly when I finish.

I shrug. 'Getting rid of a body isn't so difficult. If you don't panic, the chances of someone catching you are slim. Dump it at sea, drop it down a well, bury it in a forest. It's the people who start trying to chop it up or dissolve it in acid who come unstuck.'

'I've been thinking about what you said. About being an assassin.' At last her head turns and she stares at me. 'Was it true?'

'Yes.'

She flinches. 'You killed people for money?'

'I did.'

'How many?'

I shake my head a fraction and glance at the ghosts which have followed me everywhere all these years, Nelke now nestled comfortably among them. 'You don't want to know.'

'*How many?*' she presses.

'Half a dozen,' I reply stiffly. (I actually only killed five of them for money. One was for revenge. But this isn't the time to slip that in.)

'Did you just kill bad people?'

I don't answer.

'Tell me you didn't kill women and children, Ed.'

My gaze snakes to the slim young girl. She was an accident. I didn't mean to hurt her. But that's no excuse. 'I killed who I was paid to,' I mutter.

'How could you murder for money?' she gasps.

'It was business. If I hadn't taken the contracts, someone else would have. I was only a tool in the hands of the real assassins.'

'Bullshit,' she hisses. '*You* killed. Blaming others is –'

'The truth,' I cut in. 'My victims were marked for death. I couldn't have saved them. The world is full of greedy, vicious scum prepared to slit a few throats if the price is right.'

Her face crinkles. 'But why were you one of them? Why

involve yourself in such distasteful affairs? You're intelligent, gifted, wealthy.'

'Where do you think the money came from?' I counter.

'You mentioned an inheritance . . .'

'I lied. I made a fortune killing people and I've been living off the profits. My books could never have been written otherwise. I'd have been tied to some lousy job, struggling to keep afloat.'

She opens her mouth to object. Closes it and shakes her head. 'I thought I knew you, Ed.'

'You do.'

'No. The man I fell for was kind, gentle, loving.'

'That's who I am, who I've become.'

'But you're a killer!' she shouts, then immediately glances around to make sure nobody has heard.

'I *was*,' I correct her. 'That's in the past. Six years dead and buried.'

'Until Axel,' she sniffs.

'Which was for *you*,' I remind her.

'I don't know what to make of you,' she sighs. 'The way you talk about what you've done . . . You show no remorse.'

I hold in a bitter laugh. 'You don't know shit,' I grunt. 'There were nights when I sat alone in the dark, a gun pressed to my head, hating myself, trying to work up the courage to end it all. But there's only so much self-hatred you can take. If you don't pull that trigger – and in the end I couldn't – you have to accept what you've done and find a way to live with it.'

The rain starts coming down heavily. Andeanna draws her legs in under her small umbrella. Reaching across, I take hers and force mine into her hands. She doesn't shy away when our fingers meet. 'Tell me how it started,' she whispers.

'It's a long story,' I warn her.

'We have plenty of time.'

'OK. Remember that night on the boat, when I told you I was married once?'

She has to think back. Then she recalls our first meeting and nods.

'Well, it started for real when I met Belinda Darnier – my wife – but I have to go back further than that, to when I was in the army . . .'

I enlisted about a year after my father died, eager to put the difficulties of my teens behind me and see more of the world. I'd have made a good soldier. I enjoyed being part of a finely tuned system of command, where everyone knew his place and all worked for the good of the whole.

I wasn't a withdrawn, softly spoken figure in those days. I was a good-natured young man, mixed freely, got on well with others. Awkward around women – I was never a natural charmer – but fine with the guys.

My closest friends were Bill Phelps, at twenty-three the oldest of the recruits. Abe Lambourne, quiet and studious, but a wild man when he'd had too much to drink. And Lars Liljegren, Lily Lars, a born joker. We were no Musketeers, but we were tight.

Bill's twenty-fourth birthday fell on a weekend when we all had passes out of the compound. We drank until we fell into a stupor on Friday, spent Saturday recovering, launched back into action that night.

There were two cadets we despised, Simon Dale and Parson McNally. They were widely loathed, more loyal to our commanding officers than to the rest of us. That pair would rat you out without a second thought, just to get a salute from a sergeant.

Lily Lars was itching with devilment. Dale and McNally were sitting at a table near ours, drinking light beers, acting like a pair of generals. He wanted to shake them up. He started plotting ways to get under their skin, and cooked up a plan with Abe. Bill and I were in on it. If any of us had been sober, we'd have stopped him, but we were all drunk.

Lars had brought a handgun to impress the ladies. It was loaded with blanks. Lars and Abe faked an argument. They yelled at one another, then exchanged blows. Lurching to their feet, they thrashed around the bar. Bill and I followed, pretending to be concerned, pushing customers out of their way.

As they stumbled towards Dale and McNally's table, Lars drew his gun. People screamed and ducked. Not the arrogant cadets. They glared at the grappling pair, waiting coolly for the fuss to die down. Abe darted away from Lars, towards Dale and McNally. He deliberately slipped as Lars took aim, exposing Dale. As Dale's face registered the first flickers of fear, Lars fired twice. Dale shrieked and threw his hands over his face. McNally also yelled and rolled away, terrified. Lars's scheme had worked to perfection.

Lars and Abe collapsed laughing. Bill and I laughed too. When Dale realized he'd been made a fool of, his face darkened. Getting to his feet, he ran a hand through his cropped hair, furiously studied the howling pair in front of him, then took a knife from a strap on his left thigh, stepped forward, took hold of Abe's nose, jerked upwards to expose his throat and lashed the blade across the soft flesh.

As a surprised-looking Abe fell, spraying blood, Dale went after Lars. Bill hauled him to the ground. I got hold of Dale's arm and bit into it. Lars was too shocked to join in. He was staring at Abe, who was jerking feebly in his death throes.

As we grappled with Dale, McNally jumped us. He may have been coming to the aid of his partner, or he might have been trying to assist us. Nobody would ever know, because as he rushed in, he ran on to the knife, which drove into his chest an inch or so below his heart.

The sight of his dying friend brought Dale to a halt. The fight drained from him and he slumped to the floor, covering his eyes with an arm. Lars, Bill and I didn't look away. We watched the two men die, stunned by how our world had turned so fatal so swiftly.

Parson McNally's death was declared an accident. Simon Dale was charged with the murder of Abe, but the judge took Lars's provocation into account and handed down a soft sentence. He was free within two years. That disgusted me then and it still does. Dale deserved to suffer a lot more than he did.

The rest of us had disgraced the army and we knew what we had to do. Our resignations were accepted without question and we were released within days of each other. Ashamed of the part we'd played in Abe's death, we went our separate ways and I haven't seen Bill or Lars since.

I stop and study the violent splashes of rain on the pond. Andeanna stares at me silently. Her hand rests on my knee. It must have crept there while I was speaking. 'It wasn't your fault,' she says. 'You didn't mean for anyone to get hurt.'

'I know,' I sigh. 'But I let it happen, so I have to share the blame. There's no getting away from that.'

Andeanna's fingers squeeze my knee sympathetically, then slide away as she asks what happened next. Glad to be moving on, I tell her of the next couple of years, my withdrawal into myself, the drinking binges, the fits of rage, the short spells in prison, usually for creating a nuisance and destruction of public property. I wandered aimlessly, trying to lose myself in foreign lands where my guilt couldn't haunt me.

I ran into one of my old instructors, Carter Phell, in a bar in Mexico. I thought it was coincidence, but I soon learnt that he'd tracked me down. He got me to take a long, hard look at myself and helped me realize how pathetic and self-pitying I'd become. He weaned me off the booze and steered me straight. Once I'd sobered up, Carter revealed his motive for rescuing me. He'd moved into the business of recruiting assassins, and thought I'd be a perfect addition to the team.

'A growing market, is it?' Andeanna asks sarcastically.

'Yes, actually,' I murmur. 'Professional killers are always in demand, but hiring one is a complicated procedure. A well-connected, trustworthy middleman can charge what he likes. Carter died last year and left an estate in excess of eight million dollars.'

'How much of that did he make from you?' Andeanna enquires.

'Not as much as he'd planned,' I mutter, and return to Mexico.

I turned Carter down. He accepted my rejection and we parted on good terms. He gave me a contact number and said the offer stood indefinitely. I threw away the piece of paper, but not before glancing at the number. Not before my brain had a chance to store it away with all the other phone numbers in my memory bank.

Over the coming years, I saw more of the world than I'd ever dreamt of. Africa, Asia, South America, Europe. I wandered at whim, staying in hostels or sleeping rough, hitching rides, dodging fares on public transport. It was during those years that I first began to write. I kept a diary, in which I jotted down my experiences and thoughts. That developed into longer descriptions of the places I visited and the people I met. It never struck me that I might make a living as a wordsmith. It was just a way to pass the time.

In Seattle, everything changed when I ran into Belinda Darnier.

Belinda should have been out of my league. She was beautiful and exotic, and moved in the sorts of circles I normally would have had no access to. But I'd recently struck lucky at the racetrack and was living the temporary high life.

'I used to like the occasional flutter,' I tell Andeanna. 'In Seattle I won on an accumulator, almost fifty thousand dollars. That brought me into Belinda's world – we met at an art launch. She liked the fact that I was awkward. I'd never had much experience of women or money, and while most of her acquaintances viewed me with disdain, Belinda was amused. She let me wine and dine her for a couple of weeks. I was an entertaining aside – a bit of rough, as you say over here.'

'Sounds like I have a lot in common with her,' Andeanna sniffs, and I detect a hint of jealousy in the way her eyes narrow.

'Belinda was beautiful, but not as beautiful as you,' I whisper.

'Forget the compliments and get on with the story,' Andeanna huffs, but she can't hide a quick, pleased smile.

It was an incredible fortnight. Top hotels, fine restaurants and champagne every night, amazing sex, not a dull moment between rising and falling asleep. I was sure it wouldn't last – once the money ran out, I couldn't hold her interest – but that was fine. I was determined to enjoy the ride and let her go without a whimper when it ended. I figured even a small slice of a woman like Belinda Darnier was more than I had any right to hope for. I was looking forward to savouring the memories.

Belinda loved casinos. She was a born gambler, though she only bet with other people's money. My luck from the track followed me when she took me along. I won a further twenty thousand on roulette and blackjack, which kept Belinda sweet for an extra week. I spent money wildly, tossing fifty-dollar tips to cab drivers, splashing out on clothes, watches, wine, blowing my stash as lavishly as I could. I even went on a short cocaine binge, which wasn't my style, but Belinda had told me not to be a prude.

One night, high on coke, I told Belinda about my past,

how I got kicked out of the army, my hatred for Simon Dale, Carter Phell's obscene offer. Her interest in me skyrocketed. She wanted to know the going rate for an assassination, how Phell trained his men, the sort of people a killer would have to deal with. She regarded me with renewed respect, as if I was a celebrity. In the face of such a response, my ego soared. I couldn't answer her questions fast enough.

In three weeks the money was gone. I expected Belinda to go too, but to my shock, she hung on. She kept threatening to leave, but didn't. I was stunned but ecstatic. I'd been planning a trip to Australia, but cancelled it, got a job, rented an apartment and kept my fingers crossed.

A couple of weeks became a month, and Belinda suggested giving up her pad and moving in with me. 'While we're at it,' she added with a mischievous smile, 'we might as well get married too. If you'll have me.'

'How romantic,' Andeanna says, and her annoyed look tickles me. I have to hold back the laughter and remind myself that this isn't the time to be chuckling.

I could only nod numbly at Belinda's unexpected proposal and wonder if I was dreaming as she arranged the wedding. It was a quick registry service, just a few of her friends in attendance, but I felt like a man who'd won the lottery. That day was one of the happiest of my life. It still is, even given all that followed.

For a long time I was sure I'd wake up one morning and she'd be gone, but as the weeks ticked by, I came to believe that she was into me for the long haul. I couldn't imagine what I'd done to merit such good fortune, and I didn't care. She had made herself mine. That was all that mattered.

A short while later, Belinda began complaining of headaches. She was tired and irritable most days. I told her to see a doctor, but she wouldn't. Eventually, when her condition didn't improve, she agreed to seek medical advice.

I came home from work early that day, but she wasn't there. Night closed in — still no sign. I tried calling her doctor, but his phone was engaged. Finally, as I was growing frantic, the door opened and an ashen-faced Belinda walked in. She staggered past me as if I didn't exist, poured herself a huge vodka, downed it in one. Then she stared at me with wide, frightened eyes and said, 'Cancer.'

And she collapsed into tears.

'Oh, Ed,' Andeanna sighs. 'I'm sorry. You should have told me before. I never –'

'Save the tears until you've heard the rest,' I snort.

It was tragic and awful. It felt like the end of the world. I had a hard time getting specifics out of Belinda – she broke down every time she started to explain – and it wasn't until I discussed it with her doctor that I learnt how serious it was.

'It's a rare form of cancer,' he explained plainly. 'It's in her brain. By rights she should be dead already, but luck's on her side and it's spreading slowly. But it will kill her soon unless treated.'

'It *can* be treated?' I asked, sensing hope.

'Yes,' he said hesitantly. 'Surgery is out of the question, but there's a new procedure involving an advanced form of radio-surgery. There's no guarantee it would work – it's still at an experimental stage – but she'd stand a chance.'

'When do we start?' I asked.

'It isn't that simple. As I said, it's experimental. Her insurance won't cover it.'

'I'll make up the difference,' I promised.

He grimaced. 'I'm talking about a *serious* shortfall. Just to be accepted, you'd need three hundred thousand dollars.' I gawped at him, unable to even contemplate such an amount. 'I

136

wouldn't mention this procedure to most clients,' he continued, 'but I know Belinda had some wealthy boyfriends over the years. I'm guessing she must have stored away jewellery and cash. If she can raise the money, and if we can enrol her on the programme within the next few weeks, she might pull through. Otherwise . . .'

Sitting down with Belinda later, I told her what the doctor had said, and she laughed sickly. 'I haven't been as frugal as he thinks. I don't have much set aside. We might as well start looking at coffins.'

Refusing to abandon hope, I made her list everything of value that she owned, added my meagre possessions to it and rounded it up to the nearest thousand. Belinda was worth more than she'd thought, but we still came in two hundred and forty thousand short of the sign-up fee.

I spent the next days desperately angling for money. Tapped old friends – no joy – then hit the loan sharks. I knew that no one would advance me such a huge lump sum, so I intended borrowing smaller amounts from several lenders. A cunning plan, but I wasn't the first to think of it, and the sharks weren't fooled. The first two deals went without a hitch, but when I hit the third, alarm bells rang and I wound up having to immediately pay back the money I'd borrowed. There should have been harsh reprimands, but when they found out why I'd been trying to play them for suckers, they took pity on me and let me off with a beating.

I was back where I'd been at the start of the week, facing the prospect of Belinda's slow, painful death. That's when the crazy schemes started. I could rob a bank. Run drugs. Kidnap a millionaire's child. Train a gun on the doctors with the miracle machine and force them to treat her.

Belinda listened to my wild plans with a sad smile. She'd shake her head every so often, tell me I was insane, then let me carry on plotting. It wasn't long before I hit on the idea of calling Carter Phell. Belinda didn't dismiss that one as she had the others. She didn't jump at it, but her lips pursed, her eyes went distant and she leant back thoughtfully. Seizing hope, I ran with the idea, barely aware of what I was saying.

'I could get him to advance us the money. Training shouldn't take more than a few months, maybe less. A couple of early hits will cover the next crop of invoices. After that, we can take it a treatment and a hit at a time.'

'You're not a killer,' she whispered.

'I could be. For you.'

'I couldn't ask it of you. There must be another way.'

But of course there wasn't, and over the next seventy-two hours I *convinced* her to let me give it a go.

I had reservations – I wouldn't have been human if I hadn't – but I called the number Carter had given me. He was surprised to hear from me, but agreed to fly in for a meeting. I didn't tell him about Belinda, just said I needed the money badly. He agreed to forward me an advance. I gave it to Belinda, then went into training.

'As simple as that?' Andeanna asks sceptically.

I nod. 'I didn't have time to waste and Carter wasn't a man to drag his feet. Neither of us knew if I'd be able to kill — that's something you only learn when you come to the crunch. Carter had trained men before who'd backed out when it came time to strike. He said he'd bear no grudges if I couldn't go through with it and would give me as long as I needed to pay back the advance.'

'Nice guy,' Andeanna grunts.

'Not nice,' I correct her. 'Professional.'

Training was laborious. Two months with virtually no rest, no chance to see Belinda. I kept in contact by phone. She'd been accepted on to the programme and treatment had commenced.

Her doctors were pleased with how she was responding.

My apprenticeship was gruelling, physically and mentally exhausting. Endless drills, dismantling and putting together every known make of gun, learning how to turn ordinary objects into weapons, how to shadow people, how to plan a hit, how to arrange transport in and out of countries. But I took to it with the ease Carter had predicted. He had a keen eye for potential.

By the end of my training, I still didn't know if I could kill. Doubt had set in. I went to visit Belinda. She looked drained but healthy. Her doctors were hopeful, though it would be months before they'd know if the cancer had been whipped.

I told her of my fears. I didn't want to kill. Wasn't sure I could. She took me in her arms and said she expected nothing of me. She said it was a terrible thing to ask, so she wasn't going to. If I could find it within myself, she would be grateful to me for ever. If I couldn't, she wouldn't hold it against me. Either way, she'd go on loving me to the end, be it sooner or later.

Her calm resignation decided me. She was battling bravely and with dignity for her life. If I could swing the battle her way, I would, no matter what the cost to myself. I rang Carter that afternoon and told him I was in. A few days later, I was given my first assignment, a businessman in Germany. I flew in, shadowed him, slipped into the apartment he shared with a mistress one night when she wasn't there, drowned him in the bath, making it look like an accident. I was on a plane out in the morning, home with Belinda by nightfall.

'How did it feel?' Andeanna croaks.

I pause. 'Honestly? It was exciting. Terrible, but thrilling. I came away on a high. Later, I felt empty, wretched. I didn't cry, but for three weeks I lived in a nightmarish fugue, replaying the hit over and over, unable to put it behind me.'

Although I don't mention it to Andeanna, not wanting to

reveal the complete picture of my fragile mental state, that was when the first of my ghosts appeared. He materialized as I was sitting in a bar, drowning my sorrows. Walked through a wall and hurled himself at me, cawing wordlessly. I fell from my stool and screamed with terror, shocking everyone else in the bar. Fled into the night, the ghost trailing behind, wrapping himself around me, seeking revenge. I finally curled up in a ball in an alley, shut my eyes and rocked myself to sleep. I told myself I was hallucinating, that the ghost was a by-product of the drink, but when I woke in the morning, he was still there.

I went crazy again. I lashed out at the spectre, trying to make it go away. I didn't think it was a real ghost. I was sure I was insane, that the phantom was my subconscious way of punishing myself. I made appointments with psychiatrists, then broke them. Telling someone about my ghost would necessitate unburdening myself fully, explaining about the hit. I wasn't able to do that, so I had to deal with my demons on my own.

I survived by putting Belinda's needs first. She had regressed. She told me the doctors wanted to move up a level, but that would require more money. I'd have to continue killing or Belinda would die.

I thought the first would be the worst, that I'd grow accustomed to murder and take the subsequent assignments in my stride.

I was wrong.

Second time, Carter sent me to kill a woman, a reporter who'd been waging war on major drug cartels. I begged him to give it to someone else, but he said hit men couldn't afford sensitivity. If I turned the hit down, he wouldn't offer me another.

I tracked her for a week. From a technical point of view, it was a fascinating exercise. The authorities knew she'd been targeted, and an armed guard travelled with her everywhere. I treated it like a game of chess. I was able to distance myself emotionally until the time of the actual execution. But when I outwitted her guards and the moment came to pull the trigger . . .

I shudder at the memory. Instead of taking my shot, I hesitated, which gave her time to beg for her life. If she'd stopped at that, I might have crumbled and let her go, but she made the mistake of breaking for freedom. Acting on instinct, I fired. Hit her low in the back. Brought her down but didn't kill her. As she lay there like a wounded crab, gasping, sobbing, begging for mercy, I had to walk across and fire directly into her face, finishing her off.

'Please,' Andeanna interrupts with a trembling wave of her hand. 'Spare me the details. You're a sick son of a bitch. I don't want to know how you killed them.'

She gets to her feet. I gently pull her down. 'I'm almost finished,' I promise. 'You have to hear me out.'

'I don't want to.'

'I know. But you must.'

She stares at me, then nods. I continue, quicker now, rushing to the finale.

I sank into depression after killing the journalist. I hated myself. I hated Carter Phell. I hated Belinda. I tried to leave her and drink myself to death. We'd both die young and horribly. It would be simpler than way. More humane.

I got as far as the airport. My feet wouldn't take me any further. Try as I might, the lure of Belinda was too strong. I slunk back to her, ashamed of myself for almost deserting her. I accepted another assignment and went about it mechanically, listlessly, professionally.

The third hit went without a hitch. A gangster, deserving of death. Not that it made much difference to me. Innocent or guilty, what did it matter? I'd abandoned morality and given myself over to the darkness. At least I thought I had.

The fourth hit broke me. A minor Russian politician who had made too many enemies. The locals didn't dare tackle him by themselves – he had powerful allies – so they hired me. As with my first hit, I had to make it look like an accident. But after ten days of trailing him, I realized he was too closely guarded at home and work. It took another week to figure it out. He owned a villa in the mountains and went there most weekends. The road climbed steeply. A sharp drop if you went over the side.

I didn't hit him on the way up. Instead I chose my spot and settled in, rifle trained on the road, until late Sunday evening, when he started back. He was alone in his BMW – or so I thought – sandwiched between two other cars. I sighted on a rear wheel, waited for the ideal moment, then fired. The tyre exploded, the car veered off the road, down the cliff. I returned to my hotel.

The next day, waiting for a taxi to take me to the airport, I saw his photo in one of the papers. There was a photo of a girl too. I asked the guy behind the counter to translate the headline – *Family Horror! Two Die In Tragic Crash!* – then paid him to read out some of the article for me. The mark *hadn't* been alone. His nine-year-old daughter was asleep on the rear seat. Killed along with her father.

That was the end. It didn't matter what happened with Belinda. I couldn't go through something like that again. I was out of the game. I told Carter and he accepted my decision. Paid me the money I had coming. No hard feelings.

Belinda didn't argue with me. She was a tower of strength. Told me I could cry on her shoulder if I wanted, but I still couldn't find tears within myself. I felt nothing but self-loathing. I spent the days numbly studying the faces of my five ghosts, especially the young girl I'd inadvertently killed, as they swept around me in a hateful whirlwind, silently trying to break my mind, drive me to suicide or nudge me towards having a fatal accident.

I was in the process of withdrawing completely from the world, waiting for the visions to break me, at my lowest ebb, when I had an unexpected visitor. A face from the past. And that was how I learnt the brutal, crushing truth about how low I had actually fallen.

Belinda had gone away for another treatment. I was asleep, dreaming of the people I'd killed, unable to escape them even when I retired at the end of the day. An alien click brought me snapping back to my senses. I awoke facing up into the barrel of a revolver. A man said, 'It won't trouble me in the slightest if I have to use this, so I'd keep still as a corpse if I was you.'

I didn't recognize the voice. It was only when he stepped back and switched on the lamp that I realized who it was.

'*Simon Dale?*' I gasped.

'Wait,' Andeanna interrupts. 'The guy who killed your friend in the army?'

'Yes.'

'What the hell was *he* doing there?'

'I'm coming to that.'

I thought I was still dreaming. Then Dale fired and the pillow where my head had been resting exploded in a shower of feathers. I knew then that this was real.

'That bullet was meant for *you*,' Dale said, grinning viciously.

To my surprise, I wasn't afraid. Dying didn't bother me. In many ways it would have been a relief. The ghosts pressed in eagerly, faces alight at the prospect of my execution. 'Is this personal or business?' I asked.

'A little of both,' Dale replied.

'Did Carter set you after me?'

Dale shook his head. 'He doesn't know about this.' Pulling

out a chair, he sat and made himself comfortable. 'Did you ever try to find out what happened to me after I got out of prison?'

'No. I didn't give a fuck. You don't matter to me.'

'I do now,' he chuckled. 'Carter recruited me.'

'So you're still in the assassination business,' I noted bitterly.

Dale's smile dropped. His gun didn't. 'Wise guy,' he snarled.

'*Bored* guy,' I said. 'If you're going to kill me, get it over with.'

'But I'm not going to kill you,' Dale said softly. 'I've been paid to, but for once I'm going to renege on a deal. It'll be more fun this way.'

My eyes narrowed. 'What the hell are you talking about?'

'A woman came to see me.' He lowered his gun, but I made no move to attack him. 'She knew about the bad blood between us. Asked if I'd accept a lower rate than usual for the privilege of bumping you off. I'm not sure how she found out about me. I guess through Carter. I have a feeling she tracked him down, seduced him, humped him senseless and got him to talk when he'd spent his load and was feeling groovy. You know what guys are like — please us in bed and we'll tell you how many times we wipe our ass after we shit.'

'Who was she?' I asked hoarsely, knowing already but hoping – praying – he'd prove me wrong.

'I thought it was a trap,' he smirked. 'I checked up on her. Found out she was a scam artist with a taste for exotic risks. Her latest scheme was a doozy. She'd convinced some sap that she was dying of cancer. Hired a fake doctor to fool him. Persuaded her distraught husband – yes, the dumb bastard only went and married her – to become an assassin. Took the money he earned, said it was for treatment, then squirrelled it away. When he lost his nerve and *retired*, she came to me.'

'No,' I moaned softly, pointlessly.

'I wasn't going to accept the hit,' Dale went on. 'I try not to mix business with pleasure. But then I had an idea.' He got up and crossed to the door. Paused and looked back. 'What if I accepted, but instead of killing you, I told you the truth? You and your asshole friends fucked up my life, Severs —'

'That's my real name,' I interject. 'Brad Severs.'

'Very American,' Andeanna says drolly.

'— and now it's time to return the favour,' I continue in Dale's voice. 'Killing you is too easy. This is far sweeter. Say hi to the missus from me.' He winked and slipped away, leaving me to suffocate in the coils of the vile, inhuman truth.

There's a long silence. I'm thinking about that night. Andeanna is putting all the pieces of my story together. 'It was a set-up?' she finally asks.

'A beauty,' I whisper, staring dead ahead at the pond, through the misty shapes of my ever-vigilant ghosts. 'She planned it all in advance, once she found out about my secret past. Fake cancer, make a fortune by tricking me into becoming an assassin, use Dale to get rid of me when I was of no more interest to her.'

'There must have been easier ways for her to make money,' Andeanna objects.

'Sure. But the cash was secondary. She got off on the danger. The game. The thrill. That's what she lived for.'

Andeanna gulps. 'Did you kill her?'

I close my eyes. My head aches. I wish I had something to drink.

'I tracked her down the next day. Found her sharing her *doctor's* apartment. They were fucking in the living room when I arrived. I kicked in the door, put a bullet through her boyfriend's forehead —' my eyes open and I gaze at the angry-looking shade to the far right of the six ghosts — 'then took aim at Belinda.'

She didn't plead for mercy. Just sat on the couch, naked,

145

covered in her dead lover's blood, staring at me with eyes as cold as diamonds. There were so many things I wanted to say, but nothing would come out. Eventually I told her to wash, get dressed and take me to the money. 'No need,' she replied without missing a beat. 'It's here.'

It was in a safe, ready cash, eight hundred and twenty thousand dollars, not just the fees I'd been paid, but funds she'd squeezed from other suckers too. The price of my soul, plus a bonus. I emptied it all into a large plastic bag, then tried to kill her.

I couldn't. For all that she'd done, part of me still loved her and I wasn't able to finish her off. At the same time I couldn't just walk away and leave her. She had to be punished. Binding her tight, I fetched a knife from the kitchen and went to work on her face.

'Ed!' Andeanna gasps, hands flying to her mouth.

'She had to pay,' I croak. 'I carved her up until I was sure she couldn't be stitched back together again. I had to neutralize her, so she'd never be able to play another guy like she'd played me.'

Andeanna stares at me. To fill the silence, I complete my tale.

Leaving a wailing, ruined Belinda behind, I walked away with the money. For more than a year I lived in a daze, contemplating suicide, tormented by ghosts and memories of the past. (I still don't mention the ghosts to Andeanna. We don't need to go there.) But I didn't have the strength to kill myself, and gradually my will to live returned. Fear of what I'd assumed to be my inner ghosts turned to interest when I considered the possibility that they might be external, supernatural phantoms. I embarked on a quest to prove that ghosts were real, hoping that if I could do that, I could find a way to deal with my own half-dozen. As I played around with all sorts of crazy ideas, I began to write short stories, thinking I might find the truth through fiction. In time I moved on to write *Nights of Fear*.

'And the rest is history,' I conclude blithely.

'And Belinda?' Andeanna asks.

I smile bleakly. 'She changed her name and went to work for Simon Dale.'

Andeanna's jaw drops. '*What?*'

I shrug. 'Intrigue and killing are what she excelled at. Once she recovered, she approached Dale and offered her services. Told him how much more he could be making if he ditched Carter and set up on his own, with her running things behind the scenes. I'm sure he was wary of her, but he gave her a chance, she made the most of it and they're still together. Doing very nicely from what I hear.'

'You're something else,' Andeanna laughs. 'Christ!'

The rain has eased, but Andeanna hasn't lowered her umbrella. She holds it at an angle, shielding her face from me, thinking. I want to know what's going through her mind and whether we have a future together now that she knows the truth about me, but I hold my tongue and wait.

'Would you have told me?' she asks in the end. 'If Axel hadn't stumbled in on us, and we'd run away together, would you have come clean?'

'I don't know.'

'That's not good enough,' she growls.

'It's the truth. My past was a closed book. I never intended reopening it. Then again, I never thought I'd fall in love again. I'd have carried on lying to begin with, but whether I would have continued . . . I honestly don't know.'

Another long silence. Then she says, 'I don't think I can love you. You killed people. I understand that it's not black and white, and I want to accept you, but you murdered for money. I could never forget that.'

'Then go back to your husband,' I respond harshly.

Her gaze drops. 'I don't know if I can do that either. You're part of my life. You killed for *me*. I can't cut you out and pretend you never happened.'

'What do you want?' I snarl, growing exasperated. 'Just tell me. If you want me to stay, I'll stay. If you want me to go, I'll go. It's your call.'

'Ed,' she says, shaking her head, tears falling. I wait for her to continue, but she doesn't.

'Is that it? *Ed?*'

'Yes,' she sobs, rising. 'I have to think about this. I need time alone, to work out where I stand.'

'What if I'm gone by then? I'm not going to stick around for ever, waiting for you to make up your mind. You want me or you don't, it's as simple as that.'

'No,' she disagrees. 'I want you but I might not be able to have you.' She turns to leave.

'Andeanna,' I call. She stops and waits but doesn't look back. 'Now that you know about me, you know what I'm capable of. I can eliminate the Turk. If he's the only obstacle between us, he can be removed.'

She starts to turn towards me, then shakes her head and scurries away, leaving me alone on the bench in the dark.

ELEVEN

My ghosts are my only company over the next couple of days and nights, keeping the same silent vigil they've maintained these past six years. I don't know why they can't make noise. If they're creatures of my own creation, there's no reason why I shouldn't be capable of providing them with voices as well as faces. If they're real, in the course of my research I've encountered plenty of other spirits that have no trouble causing a ruckus.

Axel Nelke has settled in swiftly. Apart from his first sly attack on the Tube platform, he hasn't attempted to unnerve me, slotting into the cluster of ghosts as if he's been one of the gang for years. I'm guessing (if they're real) that they have some means of communicating with each other, or else they just react instinctively when they come back from the dead.

I truly thought I'd left the killing behind, that nothing could drive me to murder again. I hoped I might one day be able to atone for my crimes, that the ghosts would see I'd repented, forgive me and move on — or that I'd forgive myself and disperse them if they were inner projections. But I was deluding myself. The killer is still alive and hungry within me. Part of me rejoiced when I killed Axel Nelke. Part of me had been waiting longingly for another chance to lash out and taste blood. And that dark, dreadful, needful part of me wants to do it again.

When my cell phone rings in the middle of the night, I spring awake, lean over and answer instantly, 'Andeanna.'

A startled pause. 'How did you know it was me?'

'Who else would be ringing –' I check my watch – 'at four in the morning?'

'One of your other mistresses,' she teases.

'They never ring before nine,' I joke, sitting up in the darkness, joyous that she's called, but terrified too. What if she says she never wants to see me again?

'I've missed you,' she sighs.

'Does that mean . . . ?' I ask hopefully.

'That I want to be with you? Yes.'

My heart glows hot. 'I love you,' I croak.

'I love you too,' she replies simply, wonderfully.

'So. What now?' I ask.

She doesn't answer straight away. Maybe she has no answer. Or maybe she's just reluctant to voice it. Then, in a morose tone which might be funny under other circumstances, she says, 'We have to kill Mikis, don't we?'

'If we want to be together, yes.'

'We couldn't just run away?'

'We'd always be looking over our shoulders, worrying, wondering. Fear would destroy us.'

'He's Greygo's father,' she says.

'He's a worthless son of a bitch,' I retaliate. 'Your son is the only one who'll miss him. Apart from maybe a couple of his favourite whores.'

She sighs. 'We won't get away with it. His men are loyal, especially Bond. They'd come after us.'

'Not if we do it right.'

A long, *long* silence follows. Then, 'Tell me how.'

And our sinister pact is sealed.

Killing Mikis Menderes is relatively easy. Making sure the finger of blame doesn't point at Andeanna is the hard part. His men won't rest until they've flushed out the assassin and his employer. They'll suspect everyone, starting with her and her son, since they have the most to gain.

'Not me,' she snorts. 'Mikis has willed everything to Greygo. I get nothing.'

'That's good,' I mutter. 'But it's not enough. We need to divert their attention. Make it look like an accident or throw them a scapegoat.'

'How do we do that?'

'I don't know. I'll have to think about it.'

When she hangs up, I head for the shower, where I can think more clearly under the rush of flowing water. The basic frame of a plan comes to me almost immediately. Before anything else, I need to acquire a gun. That might have been a problem previously, but Axel Nelke's pistol is waiting for me at Heathrow. I smile grimly at how I obeyed my instinct to leave it in the car. Part of me must have guessed this was where things were heading. I was thinking further ahead than I realized when I held on to the gun.

Stepping out of the shower, I dry myself, then dress, slip a thin pair of gloves into the pockets of my jacket and catch the Tube to Heathrow. This time I stay well clear of the platform edges on the way.

I buy a hat and sunglasses in a shop at the airport, put them on in a restroom, then catch a bus to the car park. In the lot, having pulled on the gloves, I stumble around for a while, acting lost in case the Turk's people have tracked down the car and set a team on watch. Spotting nobody suspicious, I stop and open the unlocked driver's door, digging into my pocket first and pretending to produce a set of keys. I get in.

The air is stale and the seat is cold. I keep my hands on the wheel, staring ahead as if in deep contemplation. After a minute, my left hand sneaks down the side of the seat. My fingers touch cool metal. I drag it forward, hook a finger through the trigger guard and hoist it up. I glance down to make sure the safety's on, then jam it inside my jacket.

If there were people around, I'd make a show of starting the engine and letting it cut out, curse as I left the car, pretend to go off in search of a mechanic. But I'm alone, so I simply step out, walk away, get the bus to the terminal then the Tube back to the Royal Munster, where I store the gun in my safe.

Weapon secured, I sit down with a pen and writing pad and work on my plan. I jot down names – mine, Andeanna's, Axel Nelke's, the Turk's, Bond Gardiner's – and draw lines between them. I need to point the finger of blame at Nelke. Killing the Turk with Nelke's gun will be a good start, but the gun then has to fall into Bond Gardiner's hands, so he can trace it back to the missing guard. I can't post it to him or leave it at the scene of the crime. He won't accept Nelke as the villain of the piece if I frame him clumsily. There has to be a legitimate way of tying him to the hit . . .

I smile tightly as the answer hits me. I add a new word to the page, in capitals — *ASSASSIN*. I operated anonymously when I was in the game, but others weren't so modest. Some signed their work like an artist. If I could drag one of those into the scheme, I'd have an excuse to leave behind incriminating evidence. Gardiner could trace that to the assassin, then the gun through the assassin to Nelke.

I wouldn't under normal circumstances think of double-crossing a hired killer – far too dangerous – but I have a man in mind who fits the criteria perfectly, who not only signs his kills but has a score to settle with the Turk. On top of that, he's a man I'd love to drop in the shit. There are still a lot of details to iron out, but I can feel the plan taking firmer shape. It's only a matter of time before the tumblers of death click fatally into place.

In the afternoon, my thoughts turn to Joe. The plot I'm hatching is far from foolproof, and I don't want him getting sucked in if things go wrong. I have to sever the link between us. It won't be pleasant, but it's for his own good.

He answers brightly when I call. 'Hi, Ed. What's up?'

'Joe,' I reply tonelessly, 'we have a problem.'

'What sort of problem?'

'My agent told my editor about our partnership and she kicked up a stink. The publishers are afraid of getting caught in the middle of a legal war if we fall out with one another.'

'That's crazy,' Joe grunts.

'I know. But I'm just the writer. My opinion doesn't count.'

Joe laughs. 'Tell them to send me a contract. I'll sign whatever they want.'

'Jonathan suggested that, but they didn't bite. They say it's a straight-up Ed Sieveking book or the deal's off.'

Joe's sigh pains me, but there's worse to come and I steel myself against it. 'I guess that leaves me out in the cold,' he says, trying not to sound disappointed. 'Still, the most I hoped for when we began was a mention, so I can't be too upset.'

'Actually, that's not possible either.'

'Why not?' he asks, bewildered.

'Jonathan wants to exclude you entirely. He wants me to say I did all the research and planning by myself. He thinks that if I mention you in the book or in interviews, you could stake a claim to royalties. I went ballistic at first, but the more I thought about it, the more I came round to his way of thinking.' Stunned silence greets that last statement. 'Joe? Are you there?'

'I'm here,' he says weakly.

'I mean, it's not as if you contributed substantial ideas,' I rush on. 'You certainly helped, and it's a shame we can't acknowledge that, but you only had the barest creative input, right?'

'Sure,' he answers shakily.

'I'd hate it if this got to court. You'd hate that too, wouldn't you?'

'I guess,' he says. He sounds dazed.

'So you'll sign away all claims to the book?'

'Sign away? But I never made any in the first place. How can I –'

'We'll send you a form,' I cut in. 'A disclaimer. Once you've put your name to it, we can meet up again, share a few drinks and laugh about it all.'

'You mean . . .' He clears his throat. 'You don't want to see me until the form's been signed?'

'It's not that I don't *want* to see you. I *can't*. It'll be for the best if we keep out of each other's way until the book's been in the shops a while.'

'What if we don't talk about the book?'

'Sorry, Joe. Lawyer's orders. I've worked a long time for this break. You don't want to wreck it for me, do you?'

'Of course not.'

'So!' I boom hollowly. 'I'm glad that's out of the way. It's a pain, but I guess that's part of the price of success.'

'Yeah,' Joe says sickly.

'Of course,' I chuckle, 'after all this fuss, the book probably won't sell shit.'

'No,' Joe disagrees. 'It's going to be a great book. I'm sure it'll be a hit.'

I wince. This would be easier if he lost his rag and cursed the hell out of me. 'I'll let you go,' I say, jovial to the end.

'I'll send you an advance copy of the book when it's ready, no matter what those bastards say.'

'That would be nice.'

'See you around?'

'Sure, Ed.'

And that's the end of my friendship with Joe.

When Andeanna calls, I tell her we have to meet. She suggests Trafalgar Square, one of our favourite spots when we were courting innocently, so I head over at the agreed time. The square is teeming with tourists, even at this late hour. Everyone's making the most of the clear sky and warm breeze. This could be one of the last sweet nights of the summer, and nobody wants to waste it.

Andeanna is sitting by a fountain. She kisses my cheek when I sit beside her. She looks more composed than last time. Her face has healed cleanly.

'You look good,' I compliment her.

'I know,' she laughs. 'It's crazy. I've been a mess since we met in the park. But this morning I woke up and felt light, giddy, free. It's bizarre.'

'It's because you made up your mind and committed yourself to killing him. You know you're in this to the end. Your choice has been lifted from you, so you feel unburdened.'

'Hark at Mr Freud,' she smiles. 'How did you get to be so wise?'

'I've seen this kind of reaction before.'

'I'm following a trend?' she shrieks mock-hysterically.

'Yes,' I smirk. 'First comes the vow — "I'll kill him, no question about it." Then confusion — "I can't kill him! He's my husband! But I must! But I can't!"'

'Stop,' she giggles.

'Then comes acceptance — "I'll kill him. No big deal. Oh, look at the state of those nails. I need a manicure."'

Andeanna glances at her hands and blushes. 'Incredible. I've got an appointment booked for the morning.'

'I should write a book about it,' I say drily. '*How to Murder a Loved One.*'

'That should be *How to Murder a* Not So *Loved One.*'

'I stand corrected.'

It feels wonderful to be here with her, to look into her eyes and find no trace of fear, doubt or hatred. She loves and accepts me, and I know she'll never again ask about my past or how I could have done such awful things. We've reached an understanding.

'I hate the thought of killing Mikis,' she says, her smile fading. 'For all his faults, he always provided for me, and he's Greygo's father.'

'I know.'

'But three into two won't go,' she sighs. 'We can't carry on as we have been. He'd find out eventually and kill us. I can't get a divorce. He'd chase me if I ran. We can't wait for him to die of natural causes — he could live for decades. So it's this or nothing.'

'And I can't settle for nothing.'

'Me neither,' she agrees, taking my hand. 'But it has to be swift, as painless as possible. I don't want you choking him like you choked poor Axel.'

'It'll be clean. A bullet through the brain.'

She nods grimly. 'You can get a gun?'

'I already have one — Nelke's.'

Her eyes narrow. 'Won't they be able to trace that to him from powder or bullet grooves or something like that?'

'They're meant to. I want them thinking that Nelke set up the Turk.'

'*Axel?* Why would he?'

'I don't have a motive, but I don't think we need one. Mikis suspects Axel of betraying him, right?'

'Yes, but Mikis always suspects the worst of people.'

'So this time he was right,' I snort. 'It's the perfect set-up. Mikis has already cast Axel Nelke as a traitor. Bond and the others will be looking for someone to hang. If we throw them the hook of Nelke, they'll snap at it gratefully, so long as we don't make it look too much like a frame.'

'So you'll kill Mikis with Axel's gun, then leave it by the body?'

'That won't work. If Axel was smart enough to slip back into London unseen and carry out a hit, he'd be smart enough not to incriminate himself. If we'd acted swiftly, while we still had his body, we could have arranged a car crash and accounted for him that way — the gun would have been found in the wreckage and Bond would have put two and two together. Since it's too late for that, we have to give them someone else.'

A couple of Japanese tourists sit down close to us. I remain seated a while, so it won't look like we've been frightened away, then rise and take Andeanna on a stroll around the square, speaking softly out of the side of my mouth. 'Assume Nelke's alive and wants to kill the Turk. He can't do it by himself while all the Turk's men are scouring London for him. So how does he go about it?'

'He gets someone else to do it,' Andeanna answers promptly.

'Right. But he can't risk hiring a thug who'll make a meal of the job. He needs a professional. Also, since Mikis is well known and his death is going to create merry hell, it has to be someone who won't be put off by the measure of the assignment. Your average assassin, if there is such a thing, won't go after the likes of Mikis Menderes unless his employer is even more powerful. If we could pin this on one of the Turk's rivals,

157

it would be plain sailing. But we only have Nelke, so he'll have to be the one who hires the assassin.'

'Could Axel afford that?' Andeanna asks.

'He could if he'd been skimming from the Turk,' I chuckle darkly. 'And you can bet Gardiner will draw those sorts of conclusions by himself, without hard evidence. But we need more than financial incentive. We need someone with another reason for accepting this particular hit.'

'I don't understand.'

'No professional would accept money from a guy as insignificant as Axel Nelke to take out someone as well connected as the Turk, unless it was personal.' We stop by one of the lions at the base of Nelson's column and I murmur, 'Does the name Sebastian Dash mean anything to you?'

'No.'

'He's an assassin. He's worked for the Turk in the past. Last time, something went wrong and the Turk refused to pay. They parted on bad terms.'

'So we pay Dash to kill Mikis, then pretend to Bond that Axel put him up to it?'

'No. Dash wouldn't accept the hit. He doesn't like the Turk, but he's not dumb enough to let that cloud his judgement.'

'Then what good is he to us?'

'We don't need to directly involve Dash. We only need to point the finger of blame at him. When the Turk turns up dead and Dash's signature is found, Bond Gardiner and the others will assume the worst.'

Andeanna looks blank. 'Signature?'

'When Dash kills, he usually unties the lace on the victim's left shoe. If we can get him to London, so that he can be seen by people who'll recognize him, then connect him to Nelke's gun, I can kill the Turk and fake Dash's signature.'

She isn't convinced. 'What if Bond tracks down Dash and learns that he didn't do it?'

'How? By asking politely?'

'Bond could torture him.'

I shake my head. 'You don't fuck around with men like Sebastian Dash. If Gardiner catches up with Dash, he'll execute from a distance, not risk taking him alive. Not that I expect him to get that chance — when Dash learns that he's been framed, he'll go to ground.'

'You don't think he'll try to find out who set him up?'

'How will he trace us? All roads will lead to Axel Nelke, and nobody's ever going to find *him*.'

'And Axel's gun? How will we pin that on Dash?'

'They might be able to identify the gun from the bullet. After the hit, I'll head out to Heathrow, where Nelke's car is parked, slide the gun under the front seat and leave it there. If they can ID the bullet, I'll retrieve the gun and dispose of it. If they *can't* link the bullet to the gun, I'll break into Nelke's car. A couple of weeks after the murder, I'll return to the car park with a crowbar, smash in the side window and –'

'How likely is that?' she interrupts. 'Bond will know something's wrong if the car with the gun in it *just happens* to be broken into.'

'Hear me out. Nelke obviously liked music, because there was a top-of-the-range CD player in the car. I'll rip that out and break into other cars as well. There's CCTV in the car park, so I'll have to get in and out in a hurry. The police probably won't find the gun, since they won't be looking for it. But they *will* trace the car back to Nelke and try to contact him, to inform him about the robbery. One of Gardiner's men will take a message, retrieve the car, find the gun, and there you have it.'

She ponders the plan. 'Why would the gun be in Axel's car?'

she asks. 'If Dash was the killer, wouldn't he have got rid of the weapon?'

'Sometimes your employer slips you a piece, then takes it back after the hit to dispose of. The break-in and plant *are* too neat, but this wouldn't be the first time a plan was undone by the meddling of amateurs. Gardiner will buy it.'

'And if he doesn't?' she asks.

I shrug. 'I can't make guarantees. I could simply kill the Turk and walk away, but if his murder isn't solved, you'll always be a suspect. What happens six months or a year from now when we move in together? People will wonder when we met and where I was the night the Turk was killed. But if the hit is considered a closed case, we're in the clear. If you can think of another way to frame Nelke, great, I'm all ears.'

'You know I can't,' she pouts, then asks, 'How will we set up Dash?'

I smile, pleased by her sharpness. 'I haven't worked that out yet. We have to come up with a pretext. Ideally we'd fake a message from Nelke and supply Dash with a bogus target, but that won't work.'

'Why not?'

'Dash wouldn't accept an assignment without doing his homework. He'd want to know who Nelke was, if he was reliable, how he was going to pay.'

'So how do we lure him in?'

'I don't know,' I groan. 'Maybe pretend to be one of his other employers. I know people in England who've used him in the past. I'll try to get a sample of their handwriting – Dash insists that correspondence be handwritten – so that I can forge a note asking him to fly in for a job. If I can convince him to come, I'll put him up in a safe house, then leave another note instructing him to wait, with a promise to slip him a weapon later.'

Andeanna turns away from me and strolls ahead. I follow patiently, waiting for her to work through whatever's troubling her. Finally she looks back. 'If Mikis asked Dash to do a job for him, would he?'

'Mikis wouldn't hire Sebastian Dash. I told you they parted inamicably.'

'But might Mikis want to make things right between them again?'

I think it over. 'Possibly. Business is business, and Dash is one of the best in his profession.'

'So if Mikis offered him a job,' she pushes, 'would Dash feel compelled to accept?'

'Maybe. The Turk would take it as an insult if he extended the hand of friendship and Dash blanked him.'

Andeanna stops. She's trembling, but with excitement, not fear. 'I can fake Mikis's handwriting. I learnt to copy it years ago. If *I* wrote to Dash, pretending to be Mikis . . .'

I stare at her, stunned by the simplicity of her plan.

'Would it work?' she asks.

'It . . . Andeanna . . . I . . .'

Unable to find the words, I wrap my arms around her and kiss her hotly. A kiss of pure delight. A kiss of promised death.

We find a quiet café. Taking a table at the rear, we order cappuccinos and fall into a mumbled conversation. After a while, I take out my writing pad and pen and we experiment with notes to Dash.

'We can't make outright mention of the hit,' I mutter as I scribble. 'Dash demands handwritten letters from his clients, to use against them if they try to shaft him. But they must be ambiguous, so they won't tip anyone off if they go astray in the post.'

I finish my first draft and hand it to Andeanna. *My wife has*

*been cheating on me. I'm not happy. I want to discuss it with you.
I have lodgings set aside for you. If you can spare the time, please
move in, make yourself comfortable and wait. I'll be in touch. Mikis
Menderes.*

'We'll include your address, as well as that of the safe house,'
I tell her.

'Mikis's middle name is Theopolous,' Andeanna says. 'He
always uses it when signing his name.'

'OK. That's an easy adjustment. What about the rest?'

She reads it through a second time. 'We should take out
my wife. Mikis refers to me as his *woman*. And I don't think
he'd say I'd been cheating on him. He'd be more likely to say
something like I'd been seen with another man. And . . .'

We go over it a few more times. Finally Andeanna is satisfied
and reads it out softly, mimicking Mikis's accent. '*My woman
has been seen on the arm of another man. Not happy. Want to talk
with you about it. Lodgings set aside for you. If you're agreeable,
move in and wait. I will be in touch.*'

'You're sure he'd be this curt?' I ask.

'That's a novel as far as Mikis's letters go.'

Smiling, I turn over the sheet of paper and write on the
back.

'What are you doing now?' Andeanna asks.

'Adding the name of Dash's contact, a woman in Switzerland.
She's the person you need to send the letter to.'

'*Me?*' Andeanna reacts with alarm. 'I thought you were
going to send it.'

I shake my head. 'The letter needs to be written on the
Turk's own stationery and posted locally. It will be safer if you
do it.'

Andeanna looks uncertain, but she nods and takes the note,
folding it in half and tucking it away in her purse. 'What about
fingerprints?'

'Wear gloves at all stages, before you pick up the paper, before you touch the pen. Make sure it's a self-sealing envelope, so you don't have to lick the flap.'

'When should I send it?'

'As soon as we sort out a safe house.'

'How long will it take him to respond?'

'That depends on where he is and what his schedule's like. We haven't stressed a time frame, so he'll know we aren't in a rush, but he won't want to keep the Turk waiting too long. I'd guess a few weeks. If it goes beyond that, I'll head out to Heathrow and move the car, so the security guards don't take an interest in it.'

'If Dash doesn't accept? How will . . .' She stops, eyes widening. 'What if he calls Mikis?'

'He won't. The note says to move in and wait. It doesn't say anything about direct contact. Where instructions aren't provided, Dash won't substitute his own.'

She doesn't look convinced. 'What about the safe house?'

'I'll visit estate agents tomorrow, tell them my name's Axel Nelke, that I need somewhere secluded for the next few months. I'll pay with cash.'

'What about proof of identity? Credit checks? References?'

'Cash buys discretion. Not everywhere, but you can always find people who are prepared to waive the rules if the price is right. I'll avoid the chains, hit independent agents, spin them some story about being in the middle of a messy divorce and not wanting to leave a paper trail. As long as I'm paying up front, it shouldn't be a problem.'

'Can you afford that?' Andeanna asks.

'Haven't you heard? I'm hooking up with a wealthy widow-in-the-making.'

Andeanna waves a finger under my nose. 'That isn't funny. Besides, like I told you, everything goes to Greygo.'

163

'That's OK,' I grin. 'We can kill Greygo too.' Her expression flattens. 'I'm joking. You know I don't care about money. We'll get by.'

She takes my hand and squeezes. 'I'm scared, Ed.'

'You should be. This is a scary business. But it will all work out in the end.' I lean forward to kiss her, and whisper, 'Trust me.'

TWELVE

The next few days fly by. I alter my appearance slightly before hitting the estate agents, combing my hair a different way, pencilling in an array of freckles across the bridge of my nose, purchasing a cheap pair of glasses, along with a second-hand suit which is too short in the legs and sleeves. I print up business cards with Nelke's name, a fake address and the number of a second cell phone, which I buy, and I'm ready to go.

It's more difficult than I'd anticipated. The agents here don't seem to be as open to bribes as those in America. Or else they don't believe my divorce story and think I'm trying to set them up for a sting. But finally I find a dapper little man who bills himself as James Biesty Esq., who sympathizes with my predicament and says he has the perfect place for me, a small house that has been on his books for months with not even a sniff of an offer. The owner lives abroad, has a string of other properties which are making regular returns. He'll be none the wiser about our 'little arrangement'.

'What's good for the goose is good for the gander,' Mr Biesty chuckles, and I smile as if I have a clue what he's talking about.

We drive out to the property to give it the once-over. It's a bit run-down, and backs on to a busy railway line, but that doesn't bother me. I thought I'd have to rent a flat, but a house is even better, so I'm delighted. I barter James down – I think that's expected, even on a shady deal like this one – then return to the office to arrange payment. I pay for the first three months up front. James agrees to issue a refund if there are complications and I have to vacate prematurely, but as no receipt is proffered, I have only his word for that. I think he's probably good for it, but I'm not bothered either way. If everything works out, Mr Biesty Esq. will be more than welcome to his profit.

Once the keys are mine, I tell Andeanna to send the letter. Then the waiting begins.

I spend a couple of days rattling around the rented house, cleaning and airing it. The radiators run off an oil tank, which I have filled. I check all the lights and replace those that have blown. I don't try to hook up the telephone. Instead I buy another cell and leave it there, fully charged, with credit on it. I also buy a bed, chairs, some other bits and pieces, and have the furniture delivered. I pay for everything with cash.

When the house has been arranged to my satisfaction, I scout the neighbourhood, making notes of shops and super-markets, which I later type up and leave lying on the kitchen table for Dash, along with spending money and a map of the area. After that, I sit back and ring the cell twice a day, waiting for him to answer.

I try getting back into *Spirit of the Fire*, but the real-world intrigue proves too distracting. Instead I go for long walks, taking in museums and art galleries, and read a lot of books, old thrillers mostly.

I wish I could call Joe. The time would pass quicker with him around to crack dumb jokes and accompany me on my tours. But I'm determined not to involve him, not with things balanced the way they are.

Two weeks drag by. I go back to Heathrow to move the car. I park it elsewhere for a couple of nights, in a lot with no CCTV or security guards, then return it to the airport.

Another week ticks past. Autumn is sweeping the city. Leaves turn orange and brown. Dark clouds move in to stay, although it doesn't rain much. The nights draw in. The temperature dips. I invest in some sweaters and return to the house to heat it up and set the timer to come on at regular intervals. I also recharge the phone while I'm there.

Finally, almost a month after we posted the letter, I call the cell phone one day and a man answers. 'Hello?'

'Good morning. Is Antonia there?'

'I'm afraid you have the wrong number.'

'Sorry to trouble you.'

'No trouble at all.'

Game on!

Dash has to be seen. It's no good bringing him all the way over to be our fall guy if we leave him sitting indoors, hidden from those who can identify him. At the same time, we don't want to place him in a situation where he might run into the Turk or his men. Andeanna recommends a small pub called the Purple Platypus. It's on the Turk's turf (they call it a manor here, a phrase I add to my lexicon in case I ever return to work on my book), but he fell out with the landlord years ago and shuns it these days.

We send a second letter to the assassin. *Glad you could make it. We must meet to discuss terms. It's a private matter. Only you and I must know about it. Be at the Purple Platypus between seven and nine every night this week and I will make contact.*

I'm sure Dash will be recognized in the pub. I'm just as sure he'll reject any overtures from the locals. He keeps his head down when he's on a job. By Friday, word will have spread that he's in town. Come Saturday morning, the Turk will be dead, his left shoelace left untied, and the gossipmongers will have tried and convicted Dash by midday.

It has to be Friday, because that's when the Turk is throwing a dinner party for several of his more legitimate colleagues — bankers, stockbrokers and so on. He hosts the house parties three or four times a year. On such occasions he dispenses with his regular guards, not wanting to alarm any of his associates who might not know about his seedier business interests. If the timing hadn't been so perfect, we would have made other arrangements, but with Dash arriving shortly before a gilt-edged opportunity, we'd be crazy to waste it.

I spend the days before Friday worrying about the hit. The Turk might not stay on after the party. Or he might invite some of his guests to spend the night at the mansion. Or . . .

To distract myself, I stake out the Purple Platypus on Thursday and take note of Sebastian Dash entering and leaving as scheduled. He looks a little longer in the tooth and greyer at the temples than the last time our paths crossed, but still in excellent shape. The sight of him stirs up bitter feelings, and any tinge of regret I might have felt at involving him evaporates in a mist of melancholy memories.

Friday finally dawns. I spend the morning rehearsing, mentally putting myself through my paces, trying to ensure the margin of error is as narrow as possible. I dismantle the gun then put it back together, as I have done several times since retrieving it from Nelke's car. I'm also packing a hunting knife in case the gun misfires.

I haven't heard from Andeanna since Wednesday — the Turk or one of his men must have been with her last night. I want to call her to make sure everything's OK, but that would be foolish. I have to trust that the dinner party is going ahead and that the Turk will be alone afterwards. Except, of course, for Andeanna.

I'd rather she wasn't present. We discussed it. She could have spent the night with one of her friends, or gone to visit

Greygo — he's on tour in the Midlands. But the Turk likes to have his wife by his side at business functions. It might have seemed suspicious if she'd cried off. Andeanna suggested I slug her unconscious and make it look like she walked in on the killer. The trouble is, assassins don't knock out people who get in their way. They kill them.

We've settled on alcohol. Andeanna occasionally over-indulges and blacks out. The Turk's crew know this and won't link it with his murder. We hope.

Six o'clock passes. Seven. Eight. Dash should be sitting in the Purple Platypus now, patient as the Sphinx. This could be his last night of freedom, perhaps his last of life, but I feel nothing for him. Nine. Ten.

Time to move.

I drive north and park close to the gates of the mansion. Lights off. Head down. No nerves now. Totally focused on the job. A killing machine, all doubts and fears forgotten.

The first guests leave shortly after eleven, early birds. Then nobody until half twelve, when the rest trickle out.

I wait an hour after the last car, to be absolutely sure. The Turk normally sends the caterers home before the meal starts (he likes to serve up the food himself), but sometimes they stay to clean. I don't want to run into them if they're still there.

Two o'clock. No signs of life. Sliding out of the car, I cross the street, hop the wall and hurry towards the mansion, avoid-ing the driveway, ready to drop to the ground at the slightest hint of human life.

I circle the house. No unexpected cars or vans. I glance nervously at the CCTV cameras. Andeanna was supposed to disable the system earlier, while the caterers were setting up. If she did her job, Bond Gardiner and the others will assume that someone on the team was in league with the assassin, maybe even that one of the members of staff was the killer in disguise. But if she forgot about it, or made a mistake, I'm screwed.

I slip up to the back door and slam it open. Andeanna suggested leaving it unlocked, but it will look better if it's been forced. The Turk usually doesn't think to set the alarm after a party — he gets careless when he's had a few drinks. If he's broken with habit, our plan is dead in the water.

No siren. The plan lives on.

I advance through the dark rooms into the main hall, then pad up the stairs. I pause on the landing and check the gun. Ready to shoot. All I need is a target.

A door opens. I drop and swivel, raising the gun automatically. I almost fire, but catch myself in time. Thank God I do — it's Andeanna, a bottle of vodka clutched in her hands, looking wretched.

'We mustn't do it,' she groans, staggering towards me. I clutch her before she topples down the stairs. 'He's my . . . they'll know . . . we can't . . .'

I silence her with a kiss, tasting vodka on her lips. She's sobbing when we part, but doesn't repeat her plea for clemency.

'You're supposed to be unconscious,' I chide her.

'I soon will be,' she sniffs, shaking the bottle. 'I drank all through dinner. Mikis sent me to my room in disgrace. I'll have hell to face tomorrow. He'll . . .' She stops. 'Oh. I forgot. There won't be a tomorrow for Mikis.'

'But there will be for us,' I smile, kissing her again. 'Did you remember to disable the CCTV?'

'Of course.'

I kiss her a third and final time. 'In that case we're sweet. Go back to your room. Finish your bottle. Sleep.'

'Maybe I should come . . .' She trails off even before I start shaking my head.

'Let's stick to the plan. The less you see or know, the better.'

'Will I phone you in the morning?'

'No!' I'm angry now. 'No contact. Play the part of the grieving widow and play it damn well. I'll catch the Eurostar to Paris on Tuesday. You stay here, bury Mikis, tend to the formalities, then follow me in a few months. We'll meet, *fall in love*, everyone will say how romantic it is and no one will ever suspect.'

She forces a smile. 'I knew all that. It's the vodka. I never could handle hard liquor. I get weepy.'

'That's OK. I understand. Now — bed.'

She nods and kisses my cheek, a fleeting brush of her lips, then slides back into her room and closes the door softly. Clicking back into killer mode, I clear my thoughts of Andeanna and Paris, and focus on the present, the Turk and the gun.

I push on.

I know where Mikis's room is — Andeanna included it in the tour the last time I roamed the corridors of this house. I halt at the door and press an ear to the wood. I hear light snoring. I turn the handle and enter.

It's a shrine to masculinity. Photographs of beautiful women adorn the walls, every one a romantic conquest. Shots of Mikis fill the space between his lovers, most from when he was a young man in his prime, in the Turkish football strip, stooping from a polo horse with a mallet, clinging to the side of a mountain, in a gym with his bare chest glistening as he hoists weights high above his head.

And there, on the bed, is the legend himself, the lady-killer, the wife-beater, Mikis Menderes, aka the Turk.

I should shoot him while he sleeps. But I can't. If it was business, sure. But this is personal. It wouldn't feel right.

I position myself at the foot of the bed, grab his ankle through the covers and tug sharply. The Turk comes awake with a startled grunt. He spots me. Confusion floods his expression, then anger, but not panic. He glares at me, and I know he knows that he's finished.

'Who the fuck are you?' he asks.

'Call me Ed.'

'Who sent you?'

I don't answer.

'You gonna kill me?'

I don't answer.

'Fucking dummy. Can I light a cigarette?'

'No.'

'Aw, c'mon, surely you won't deny a –'

'It's for Andeanna.'

His expression crumples, and I realize that this is what I want, this is why I woke him. I need to see guilt wash over the bastard's face. I want him to know that he's paying for the way he abused his wife.

'*Andeanna?*' he croaks. 'What the fuck does she have to do with –'

My finger jerks. The gun kicks once, twice, a third time. Mikis Menderes's face evaporates. The wall behind the bed blossoms with the bloody remains of his thoughts, memories and personality. His body shudders grotesquely, then goes still for ever.

I lower the gun and study the havoc of my making. There can be no doubt that he's dead, but I start forward to check all the same. Then I stop, thinking of blood on the carpet, and footprints. I turn towards the door and hurry from the room.

I'm at the top of the stairs before I remember the laces.

Grimacing, I retrace my steps and look for shoes. I find a closet full of them, and extract a pair. I tie the laces on the right shoe, leave those on the left undone, then lay them on the floor by the bed. The police will think they were put there by the Turk. They'll leave them as they are, along with the other items in the room. They won't notice the laces, but the Turk's henchmen will.

Dash's signature successfully forged, I make my exit. The plan has a long way yet to run. Things could still unravel spectacularly. But I've got a feeling they won't. The hit went perfectly. I'm certain that fate is on our side. I could whistle as I trot down the stairs, out via the kitchen, through the trees, over the wall and back to the car. But I don't. It wouldn't be professional.

THIRTEEN

Sleep is an impossibility, so I don't even try, and instead of returning to the Royal Munster to brood, I spend the night driving around London, listening to the radio, flicking between stations, humming along to corny ballads, listening with interest to people who phone in with their problems, love stories or tales of the city night.

In the early hours, I park close to a bagel shop on Brick Lane. I wolf down a salmon and cream-cheese bagel, then order another, which I munch slowly. When I've washed down the last of the crumbs with coffee, I make for the restroom and check my appearance in the mirror. A little wild about the eyes, but that's the only sign that all isn't well.

I return to the hotel, shower, bag my clothes for incineration and pull on fresh jeans, a shirt and a sweater. It's too early to hit Heathrow, so I sit on the end of the bed and flick through a magazine. But the words mean nothing. My thoughts return to the Turk's room, how he collapsed when I killed him, the last look on his face, how the gun kicked in my hand.

I catch the Tube to the airport in the morning rush. It's full of surly commuters. A pregnant woman boards at Acton Town. Nobody offers her a seat. I want to give her mine but I dare not do anything that might attract attention.

Axel Nelke's car is even colder than before. I get in and stick the gun under the seat. I take the keys and lock the door this time when I leave, so if I have to break in a few weeks from now, I won't be smashing the window of an unlocked vehicle.

Back in central London, I go for a stroll by the Thames and find a quiet spot on a bridge, where I drop the car keys and my gloves into the river. The true and final end of the unfortunate Axel Nelke. After that I head to the Royal Munster and bed.

The murder of Mikis Menderes is major news. He was well known to the media, and they pick over his bones with predictable zeal. I ignore the hoopla, not bothering with the newspaper articles, catching only a couple of items on TV. The police have no firm suspects but are 'pursuing definite lines of enquiry', which means they haven't a clue who killed him. No sign of Andeanna, which is good, although there are clips of a pale-faced Greygo pushing through the hordes of reporters outside their house and blanking questions.

I'm tempted to call Andeanna, to check that she's OK. But it's best to let sleeping dogs lie and look ahead to Paris. It will be months before she can slip away and be with me. I'll have to get used to the loneliness.

I've made arrangements to check out of the hotel on Tuesday. I plan to work on *Spirit of the Fire* in Paris. I call Jonathan to inform him of my change of address. He's alarmed when I tell him I haven't started writing, but relaxes when I state my intention to complete the book within a few months.

Monday passes with surprising speed. I'm so busy packing clothes, organizing my notes and checking my travel plans that before I know it I'm undressing for bed and falling asleep to dream of Paris, Andeanna and our new life together.

Hotel account paid in full. Bags in order. Nothing left in the room. Train ticket tucked securely into my money belt, along with my passport and credit cards. A spare pair of socks and a toothbrush in my travel bag in case I get delayed. A book. A map of Paris. The name and address of my new hotel.

Adieu!

I'm catching the Eurostar from St Pancras. Rather than drag all three of my bags with me, I send the pair filled with notes and books as registered baggage — they'll follow on after I've travelled, which means another trip to the train station in Paris to collect them, but I'm going to have plenty of time on my hands over there, so I don't mind.

Before checking in and passing through security, I stroll around the shops, but nothing catches my interest. There's still almost an hour before I board — not having been on the Eurostar before, I allowed plenty of time. To distract myself, I buy a newspaper and scan it while sipping a cup of coffee. The front page reveals some kind of royal scoop and the next six are devoted to the same story. Bored, I flick ahead. A few pages further on, I find an article devoted to the Mikis Menderes murder.

It's trashily written, but that's what I'm in the mood for. Having skimmed the first couple of lurid paragraphs, I settle back, intending to take my time chuckling wryly through the rest of it. But something has unsettled me. It's one of the pictures, a black-and-white photo of the Turk and Andeanna. They're seated at a large table, smiling for the camera. The Turk holds a fat cigar. Andeanna is sporting a tiara, which has slipped slightly.

Why am I disturbed by the photo? There's nothing glaringly unusual about it. The Turk looks smug, as he did in most photos that he posed for. Andeanna is smiling in a sad way, which was often the case. It's only when I read the caption that I focus in on what I'd subconsciously clocked first time round. It says simply, *Mikis Menderes and his late wife.*

I blink dumbly and read it again, then a third time.

Late?

Hands trembling, I speed through the rest of the article until I find it, eight paragraphs down.

While it's hard to muster any sympathy for Mikis Menderes, he does seem to have genuinely suffered when his young wife perished in a car crash. His beautiful bride burnt to death and the grief-stricken gangster vowed never to remarry. True to his word, he never took another wife, although he has been linked with many glamorous women over the years.

I read the sickening paragraph again and again, unable to tear my eyes away. My train is called, but I don't respond. I'm rooted to the chair, the paper glued to my hands, eyes sliding from the photo to the words to the photo to the words to . . .

More calls for my train, but I pay them no heed. I'm off in a world of my own. A world of love and promises. Of Andeanna and the Turk. Of contradictory truths and looming madness. A world of shades.

PART FOUR

FOURTEEN

Eventually life returns to my limbs. Paper grasped in one sweaty hand, I stumble through the station to the taxi rank and tell a cabbie to drive me back to the Royal Munster. They're surprised to see me return, but not half as surprised as I am. I mumble a story about a friend being taken seriously ill. The receptionist is genuinely concerned. When she realizes I've returned without my bags, she says she'll arrange for their retrieval. I mutter a subdued thank-you.

In my new room, I sink on to the bed and stare at the photograph in the paper. *Burnt to death*. I clutch it close the entire night, even as I drift in and out of sleep over the course of the long, dark, crazy hours. The ghosts revel in my sickening bewilderment. They wrap themselves around me and coil and uncoil like snakes whenever my eyes flicker open.

In the morning, I order breakfast and eat mechanically, forcing down the food. After that I phone Andeanna, even though it's dangerous, hoping the call will clear up the confusion. But the number has been disconnected. I want to try the house, but if the paper got it wrong (it must have) and Andeanna is alive and well (she must be), then ringing the mansion could be the biggest mistake of my life.

I pace the room to get the blood flowing to my brain. There has to be a logical explanation. The journalist might have been misinformed. Perhaps the article was a huge screw-up. I need to check other sources.

If it's not a mistake, maybe it's a smokescreen. Andeanna might not have wanted to face the press. Perhaps she faked a rumour that she died years ago, so reporters wouldn't come bothering her.

No. No matter how hysterical I might be, I can see that I'm clutching at straws with that one. You can't turn around, pretend to be dead and expect the press to buy it.

What if Andeanna was the Turk's second wife? Maybe he was married before, and the paper mixed up the photographs. Or what if she was never married to him in the first place?

I pause in the middle of my pacing. Maybe Andeanna was only a mistress. I scan the photo again. It looks like the woman I know, but the similarity might be what drew Menderes to her.

I whip out my pad and pen and jot down *Deleena Emerson*. That could be her true name. Maybe the woman I initially fell for was the real deal, and Andeanna Menderes is the fake.

Relief floods my system. For a mad, unhinged period, I thought I'd fallen in love with a ghost. I knew it was lunacy, but I couldn't see any other explanation. Now I know better. Andeanna/Deleena is flesh and blood, like anybody else, but with some hidden, twisted agenda of her own. I hope she truly loves me, that she wasn't acting just to trick me into killing the Turk. I could forgive her anything if she loves me. But whatever her motives, she's real, she exists, she's alive.

And I'm going to find her.

By the weekend, I don't know what to think. Was she real, a ghost, an impostor, a figment of my imagination? I can't even hazard a guess.

I've spent the last three days in the library. It hasn't been easy, especially with the ghosts continually taunting me, seeking to distract and further disorient me, but I forced myself to focus. First I worked through this week's papers and magazines, reading every published article about Mikis Menderes. I learnt more about the man than I ever cared to. There was plenty about Andeanna, too. She was born to a decent family. Her father was a successful accountant, her mother – *Deleena Moore, née Emerson* – a housewife and amateur actress. Andeanna was a bright student with a promising future, but fell in love with Menderes and married him shortly after her eighteenth birthday, against the wishes of her parents. She was a dutiful wife who raised their son and had nothing to do with the Turk's business affairs. She died one month short of her twenty-seventh birthday.

Twenty-seven. I recall how young I thought she was when we first met. I had her pegged for twenty-something. Later she convinced me that she was in her early forties, which is the age she would be. If she was alive.

There were photos of the Turk with some of his lovers. None could pass for his wife's double. I went back further and found snaps of his old flames, but no one who looked like Andeanna.

Maybe one of the Turk's foes found a doppelgänger, briefed her on Andeanna's past and set her up to frame me. But why go to such lunatic lengths? There are far easier ways to kill a man. It makes no sense. Unless . . .

Unless *I* was another Sebastian Dash. Perhaps the Turk's enemy was on the inside and needed a fall guy. That would explain how Andeanna was able to get in and out of the mansion. She might have been working for Bond Gardiner or one of the Turk's other trusted aides, someone who had to distance themselves from the murder, by weaving as complex a web as possible.

So many theories, each more warped than the one before.

I groan and push myself away from the photos, the papers, the computer, and head back to the hotel. On the way, I find myself digging out my phone and dialling Joe's number. I get his voicemail. As much as I hate leaving messages, I croak, 'It's Ed. I need to talk. Please call me or come to the hotel. It's important.'

It's wrong to involve Joe. However perilous the situation was before, it's ten times as likely to end in disaster now. But I need someone to bounce ideas off, a friend to steer me straight. I'm going crazy on my own. Literally.

In my room, I ignore the notes and photocopies which have consumed my last few days and nights, and instead of poring over them, I sit by the window and stare at the sky. For once, the ghosts leave me alone. I doubt they feel sorry for me. They probably just want to give me some quiet time, to soften me up, before launching a fresh offensive.

A couple of hours later, I haven't moved. I'm chewing on my fingernails when someone knocks on the door. I cross the room suspiciously and open the door a crack. For a split second I think it's Andeanna, and my hopes flare. Then my eyes focus and it's just Joe, looking bemused. 'You rang, m'lord?'

'Thanks for coming.' I let him in.

Joe stares around at the mess. 'Is everything OK?'

'No,' I choke. 'Everything's fucking horrible.'

It's insanity, but I tell him the whole story, about my past, Andeanna, the Turk, Axel Nelke, Sebastian Dash, the murder. I tell him things that I didn't even tell the fake Andeanna, talking for the first time ever about my ghosts. Joe listens silently, asking no questions, though his eyes flicker nervously when I describe my ever-present shades. At the end, exhausted, I trickle to a halt and await his response.

Without saying anything, he walks to the bathroom. He's in there ten minutes. When he returns, his face is damp, pearls of water glistening on his moustache and beard. He shakes his head and says, 'Was that the truth, Ed?'

'You think I'd make up something that crazy?'

'You're a writer. Crazy plots are your life. Maybe this is a new idea for a book and you're testing it out on me to see how –'

'It's true,' I stop him. 'Every word. No bullshit.'

He sinks into a chair. 'You killed people.'

'Yes.'

'That crap about not having my name associated with the book — was that to keep me out of this, to keep me safe?'

'Yes.'

'Thanks,' he says drily.

'I couldn't involve you. If something went wrong and you'd been sucked in . . .'

'So why involve me now?'

'I had nobody else to turn to,' I answer honestly.

'Hah!' Joe grins.

'You can leave if you want. You don't have to stay.'

'After the story you've spun? I couldn't walk away from a mystery like this, as you well know, you manipulative bastard.'

'Do you hate me?'

'Yes.' He jumps to his feet. 'But we'll get into that another time. First we have to figure out what's going on. Show me your notes. Maybe there's something you've missed. That is why you asked me over here, isn't it?'

'Yes,' I say, shamefaced.

'Then let's not dilly-dally, as the actress said to the bishop.' He strides to the nearest stack of papers then glances back at me. 'If it's any comfort, I'd have called for help too in your shoes.'

'Thanks,' I smile.

'But that doesn't mean it's right,' he growls. 'It just means I'm as dumb and selfish as you.'

With midnight approaching, we break for a coffee. Joe is as confused by now as I am. He favours the impostor theory, but proposes a new twist on who might have put her up to it. 'Maybe there was no middleman. What if this was personal, her looking to get even with Menderes? Let's say she was his mistress and he pissed her off. She finds out who you really are and –'

'How?' I interrupt. 'I don't advertise it in the biography on my website.'

'People have a way of discovering things when they go looking for answers,' he says. 'She learns the truth about you and cons you into falling in love with her and killing Menderes, having passed herself off as his dead wife to make sure the shit couldn't rebound and stick to her.'

'But she looks so much like the woman in the photos,' I mutter.

'Maybe they were related,' Joe says, then his face lights up. 'Maybe that's it! A younger sister or daughter who wanted to kill Menderes for the way he treated his wife when she was alive.'

'The papers said she was an only child, and they didn't mention any children apart from Gregory.'

'Every family has secrets, Ed. Maybe she had another kid when she was too young to wed. The daughter grows up, finds out that Menderes used to bully her mother, comes looking for revenge.'

'You're stretching, Joe.'

'Sometimes the truth is so weird, you have to stand on your toes and reach at full stretch to touch it.'

'Very poetic,' I commend him.

'You don't buy it?'

I sigh. 'It's thin.'

Joe thinks again. 'There's another explanation,' he says softly. 'She might have been . . .' He stops and pulls a face.

'A ghost?' I finish for him. Joe nods glumly and looks away. 'No,' I whisper. 'Ghosts aren't real.'

Joe gawps at me. 'How can you say that, having just told me about your own private posse?'

I chuckle sickly. 'Just because I see them, it doesn't mean they're real.'

'You think you're crazy?' Joe asks.

'I don't want to be,' I mutter. 'That's why I went down the investigative road in the first place, to try to prove they were real, that there is an afterlife, that the shades of the dead can come back. That seemed preferable to accepting the fact that I'd lost my mind.'

'Now you'd rather be mad?' Joe sniffs.

I shrug. 'No. But having searched for proof for so long without finding any, I can't believe that it would drop into my lap in such astonishing fashion. Besides, even if my ghosts are real, Andeanna was different. She was flesh and blood, not a phantom. Other people saw her.'

'*I* never saw her,' Joe reminds me.

'Waiters saw her, cab drivers, Axel Nelke.'

Joe squints. 'Maybe she found a way to come back from the dead and take physical shape, like the guy in *Spirit of the Fire*.'

I laugh harshly. 'Don't be stupid.'

'Hey, it's *your* theory,' he retorts. 'We know that Andeanna Menderes burnt to death. What if she was a victim of spontaneous human combustion? She dies traumatically, her spirit can't rest, she returns in a new body, seeking revenge on the husband she hated . . .'

'That was a plot device,' I growl. 'I treated it seriously because when you write, you have to make the world of the story seem as real as possible. But I know what's real and what's not. If you can't tell the difference, maybe you should –'

'Hold on,' Joe interrupts hotly. 'I never saw this dream lover of yours. For all I know, she never existed and you're completely gone in the head. You say that waiters and taxi drivers saw her, but maybe you imagined them as well. Hell, maybe *I'm* not real. You could be sitting here arguing with yourself and . . .' He grinds to a halt and scratches an ear. 'I lost the run of that, didn't I?'

'You were going good until you tried to write yourself off,' I smile.

'But you get my point. Logically I should disregard everything you say and call in the men in the white coats. But you're my friend. I'd rather believe in a ghost than denounce you as a lunatic.'

'You're right,' I sigh. 'Sorry for snapping. Truth is, I'm not so sure of my sanity. That's why I want to keep things as level as possible. If I head down crazy paths, I don't know where I'll end up.'

'OK,' Joe says. 'I'll lay off the ghost angle. But can I ask you one more thing before I let it lie?'

'What?'

'Did you . . .' His cheeks redden. 'Did you have sex with her?'

I silently count to ten before replying. 'Why do you want to know?'

'Your ghosts are silent, ineffective, insubstantial things, but that doesn't mean that every wandering spirit must be. I think a more advanced ghost could pass for human in all sorts of ways, fake the look, scent, maybe even the feel of a person. But in the most intimate of couplings, when it's just the two of you, everything's been laid bare and you're exploring every last inch of your lover's body? I can't imagine a phantasm managing to be *that* convincing.'

I think of my asexual relationship with Andeanna. The lines she fed me about the Turk and her gynaecologist. How I never even saw her naked.

I call it a night.

FIFTEEN

I ask Joe to find out everything he can about Andeanna Menderes, her background, family, associates. I tell him to track down distant relatives, old friends, anyone who was close to her. Try to find people who might have known the *new* version of her.

'Start with that beautician, Shar, who was celebrating her birthday the night we met,' I advise him. 'Talk to your friends who were at the party. Take a photo of Andeanna with you, show it round and ask if anyone remembers seeing a woman who looked like that.'

While Joe is exploring the Andeanna angle, I check out Dash's safe house. It looks deserted. No car in the drive. Curtains open. I should stake it out for a day or two to be safe, but I don't feel like wasting time, so I slip around back and let myself in with the spare set of keys which I kept.

I move cautiously through the rooms. No clear signs that Dash has been here – the bed is stripped, the chairs stacked neatly against the walls, the heating turned off – but there's a slab of cheese by the bread bin that wasn't there before, and a can of beans in a cupboard under the sink. Peculiar of Dash to leave behind even these slight reminders of his stay. Maybe he left in a panic.

From the safe house I make my way north, where I spend

the next three days doing the rounds of every seedy-looking pub and club, making contact with low-level gangsters. I call myself Edgar Sanders and pretend to be a journalist doing a piece about Mikis Menderes. I buy drinks for anyone who'll chat with me. Many are eager to add to the Menderes legend and be associated with him in some small way, so most talk with me freely.

They tell me all sorts of juicy stories, how Mikis drove out into the countryside every once in a while to chop the heads off sheep, the time he ate the prize poodle of someone who was slow to repay a loan, his incredible sex drive. ('He once had twelve women on the go at the same time,' a pickpocket called Ernie tells me. 'That's what I call a dirty dozen!') Entertaining tales, but nothing about who killed him or why he might have been executed.

Finally, in the Star and Anchor, a grim, grey place that's at odds with its name, I run into a member of Bond Gardiner's gang, a youthful but grey-haired man called John Horan, who shoots a mean game of pool. After letting him thrash me a couple of times, I ask if he's heard any strange stories about how the Turk was killed.

'What sort of stories?' John snaps warily.

'I heard it was suicide and someone made it look like an assassination to big up the Turk's legend.'

'Bullshit.'

'I guessed as much,' I sigh. 'I mean, how can you trust a guy who builds a conspiracy theory out of a pair of shoes? I should have known he was –'

'What's that about shoes?' John interrupts.

'Some crazy shit about Menderes's laces. I shouldn't even have –'

'Go on,' John says tightly.

'Well, this guy said he knew a journalist who works for *The*

Times, and *he* said he saw a pair of shoes in a photo and the lace on one of them wasn't tied.'

'So?' John sniffs, eyeing me beadily.

'According to him, it's something people do when they kill themselves, if they don't want to leave a note. They tie the lace on one shoe but not the other. It's a way of letting people know it wasn't an accident.'

John laughs, at ease again. 'That's the dumbest thing I've heard all week.'

'Yes,' I chuckle ruefully. 'But I figured I might as well ask.'

'You should be careful,' John warns me. 'Loose talk like that can earn you a slap round here. If I was you, I'd keep shit about laces to myself.'

And after that, I do, since I know by his reaction that the laces were noted. I'm not sure what happened to Dash, whether he escaped or was taken down, but that's unimportant. It's enough to know that Bond and his men have swallowed the bait. I can forget about Dash and focus on hunting for the ghostlike Andeanna.

Joe hasn't discovered a secret sister or daughter. He's done a remarkable job of assembling a family tree, filling half a scrapbook with names, dates of birth, photographs and details. I go through the photos several times, with a magnifying glass, but none of Andeanna's relatives is close enough in looks or age to pass for the woman I knew and loved.

'I called several of them,' Joe says, 'pretending to be a reporter, asking about her past, her life with the Turk. Most were happy to talk about her, but nobody had much contact with her after she married Menderes.'

'What about friends?'

'Plenty from the past, but not a one from her London years. It seems like the Turk kept her locked away from everybody.'

I flick through the pages, admiring Joe's research skills, then thumb back to the first page and the photos of Andeanna's parents. Her mother died nine years ago. Her father is alive and living alone. 'Did you check if Deleena Emerson had any other children?'

'There's no record of it,' Joe replies.

'But did you ask?'

He shakes his head. 'It's not the sort of thing you can say to strangers. I asked if Andeanna had brothers or sisters and they all said she didn't.'

'What about her father?'

'He wouldn't speak to me. He doesn't discuss his daughter.'

'If anyone knows, it would be him.'

'True. But if he doesn't want to talk about it . . .'

'He'll talk,' I grunt.

Joe squints at me. 'Ed, you wouldn't . . . I mean, you aren't going to do anything illegal, are you? I don't want to be part of –'

'Don't worry,' I stop him. 'Violence isn't my style.'

Joe snorts. 'This from an assassin?'

'Ex-assassin,' I grin bleakly. 'But even back then I didn't rough anyone up. I killed, I didn't torture.'

'Interesting distinction,' Joe mutters, but pushes the point no further. 'There was one other thing.'

'Yes?'

'Andeanna's death. You know how the police say she veered off the road and crashed, the car burst into flames and she couldn't get out?'

'What about it?'

'There were no on-hand witnesses, but a few drivers in the distance saw the car careen down the bank. One of them, Marian Fitzgerald, said she saw flames in the car *before* it hit the trees and exploded.'

'So?'

'The forensic guys who examined the wreckage couldn't explain why the car left the road in the first place. Given the Marian Fitzgerald evidence, I got to thinking that maybe . . .' He stalls.

'Go on,' I quietly urge him.

'Could it have been SHC?'

'I thought we'd dismissed that theory,' I snap impatiently.

He shrugs. 'I know there's probably nothing to it. I was tossing out wild ideas the first time I brought this up. But when I read the report, it made me wonder. I started thinking about something you'd said, about how the impostor had known you were an assassin.'

'People knew,' I mutter. 'Not many, but a few. One of them must have told Andeanna or whoever hired her to con me.'

'More than likely,' Joe says. 'But if we admit the possibility that she might be a ghost — I'm only saying *might*, don't lose your temper!'

'Go on,' I sigh wearily.

'If she spontaneously combusted and came back as a ghost,' Joe continues, 'maybe she was drawn to you by the research you were doing. Your mind was fixated on the subject. She might have been able to tap into that. Or . . . hell, Ed, I know this is a long shot, but maybe *you* brought her back to life.'

'What are you talking about?' I gawp.

'If Pierre Vallance has the power to channel mental waves and convert them into voices, maybe *you* have a similar talent. Maybe you unwittingly gave form to Andeanna, the way you gave limited form to your other ghosts. She dies horribly, some residue of her circles the streets of London all these years, you hit town, her spirit gravitates towards you, you somehow give her back her body, she seizes her opportunity and uses you to take revenge on the man she hated.'

I consider Joe's crazy proposal. Because he's my friend and I know he means well, I treat it seriously. 'What was the state of her corpse when they found it?'

Joe checks his notes. 'Burnt beyond recognition.'

'It hadn't been reduced to ash?'

'No.'

I smile thinly. 'There you are.'

'But SHC victims don't always burn away entirely,' Joe presses. 'And even if she didn't die of that, maybe you gave form to her spirit regardless. We should bear it in mind. If we can't find a plausible explanation – if there isn't a lookalike – we'll have to explore other angles, won't we?'

'I suppose,' I mutter, too tired to argue.

'I'm not being obtuse,' Joe says. 'I'm not confusing the world of the book we were working on with the real world. But if we eliminate all other possibilities and only this remains . . .'

'Then I'll investigate it. But I won't have to. Because she wasn't a ghost.'

Saying it firmly, wanting to mean it. But not one hundred per cent positive. My gaze flickers to the seven supernatural shades in the room with us, and I wonder if Joe has hit on the answer to the riddle I've been picking at all these years. If I'm not crazy . . . if my ghosts are more than just the product of a deluded mind . . . then maybe I have the ability to give shape to disconnected spirits. Perhaps I've subconsciously brought about my own haunting. If that's the case, and these seven ghosts gain their power from something in me, why *shouldn't* I be able to go even further and create a physical body for another?

Andrew Moore lives in Birmingham. He's a loner who rarely entertains visitors. I make the long drive up early on Friday morning, locate the house, then call him from my car. I don't go with the Edgar Sanders approach, since Joe has already tried the faux-journalist gambit.

'Andrew Moore. How may I help you?'

'Good afternoon, Mr Moore. My name is Edward Sieveking. I'm a novelist, doing some research. I'd like to meet you, if –'

'What's this about?' he snaps. 'Are you a reporter?'

'No, Mr Moore, I'm an author. I write books.'

'What sort of books?'

'Fiction. Horror, mostly.'

He pauses. 'What's your interest in me, Mr Sieveking?'

'I'd like to talk with you about a new book I'm working on.'

'Is it about Mikis Menderes?'

'Not directly, no.'

'But he's the reason you want to talk to me?'

'Yes,' I confess. 'But mostly I want to ask about your daughter.'

'My apologies, Mr Sieveking, but I have nothing to say about either of those people.'

'But –'

'Good day, Mr Sieveking. Good luck with your book.' He hangs up. I wait ten minutes before ringing again. Despite the delay, he's waiting for the call and answers on the second ring with a curt, 'Mr Sieveking?'

'Please, just give me a chance to –'

'My no *means* no.'

End of conversation. When I ring a third time, he doesn't answer. I wait half an hour before trying again — no luck. Leaving the car, I march to the front door and ring the bell. It takes him a while to appear. When he does, the curtain covering the side window swishes aside and I glimpse a pair of angry eyes. 'Sieveking?' he snaps, dispensing with the formalities.

'I only want a few minutes of your time, Mr Moore.'

'Leave now or I'll call the police.'

'That would be unwise,' I caution him. 'If the police question me, I'll have to tell them why I'm here, and if word of what I've discovered leaks to the press, this place will be swarming with reporters.'

'What are you talking about?' he growls.

'I'm talking about your daughter and the role she may have played in the death of Mikis Menderes.'

The curtain slides back into place and the door is thrown open. Andrew Moore is a big man, broad and straight-backed despite his age, with a commanding face. 'My daughter died nearly twenty years ago. She had nothing to do with that bastard's death. Now get the hell out of here before –'

'I'm not here to waste your time,' I interrupt. 'I drove up from London to speak with you in person. Give me five minutes. If I don't grab your interest, I'll leave voluntarily and I won't pester you again.'

Moore glares at me, then takes a step to one side and waves me in. He points me towards an immaculately maintained living room, an old man's room filled with mementos and photographs of his life. I don't expect to find any of Andeanna, the daughter he cut off, but to my surprise there are several from her youth, set proudly next to pictures of his wife.

We sit down and he asks if I'd like anything to drink. 'I'd rather get straight to my reason for coming,' I tell him.

'Good,' he nods, pleased by my directness.

I show him a hazy photograph of Andeanna, one from the archives. I've blanked out the faces of the other people. 'Your daughter?' I ask.

He reaches for a pair of glasses and studies the photo. 'It's a poor shot, but yes, it's her.'

'That picture was taken a month before Menderes's death,' I lie.

He shrugs. 'Then it's not Andeanna.'

'But they look alike, don't they?' I press.

'What of it?' he says.

'This woman was seen with Menderes during the weeks prior to his death. She may have been living with him.'

Andrew starts to look interested. 'Do the police think she killed him?'

'They don't know. She vanished. Can't be found.'

He processes that, then says, 'Why come to me? Because she's similar in appearance to my dead daughter?'

'And because she called herself Deleena Emerson.'

He flinches. 'That was my wife's name.' He gazes at the photograph again, his wrinkled hands trembling slightly. 'I've read nothing about this in the papers.'

'My brother-in-law works for the Metropolitan Police. He knows I'm fascinated by ghost stories. He was the one who told me.'

'*Ghost stories?*' Moore echoes.

'A woman who looks like your daughter and uses the name of your dead wife enters Mikis Menderes's life, and within a couple of months he's been killed. It sounds like something a horror writer might concoct. My brother-in-law thought I might be amused by the idea.'

The old man's face darkens. 'There was nothing *amusing* about Mikis Menderes.'

'You didn't approve of him?' I ask glibly.

'Nothing to approve of,' Moore says. 'He was a pimp, a thief, a bully and a paedophile.' He leans forward, undisguised hatred in his expression. 'Do you know how old Andeanna was when he first laid his filthy paws on her? Seventeen! A child who should have had nothing on her mind except homework and teenage boys. Seventeen years old and he made a slut of her. *That* was Mikis Menderes.'

'Didn't you try to stop her seeing him?'

'It was too late!' he roars. 'We only found out when she came sobbing to us, telling us she was pregnant. We offered to help her raise the baby here, where we could love and care for it, but she insisted on returning to London. She said the child needed a father and she swore that she loved Menderes.'

Tears of remorse and regret flood Moore's cheeks. I'd like to walk away and let the past lie, but I can't. I have to know the truth about Andeanna. 'The child,' I say softly. 'Was that Gregory?' He nods. 'Did she have any other children?'

'No.'

'What about you and your wife?'

'Andeanna was our one and only.' Moore wipes tears from his cheeks and grimaces. 'Menderes's death has raked up the past. I'm not normally this fragile.'

'I'd like that drink if the offer's still valid,' I murmur. 'A cup of tea would be great if it's going.'

'Of course.' He gratefully heads for the comfort of the kitchen, pausing only to ask if I take milk and sugar. I pass the time studying photos of Andeanna on the walls. Even as a teenager she was beautiful. I can see why the Turk fell for her, although what she saw in a beast like him escapes me.

Moore looks more composed when he returns and hands me a steaming cup of tea. 'Can I ask why you're interested in this, Mr Sieveking?'

'When my brother-in-law jokingly mentioned the possibility of a ghost in the Turk's life, I was intrigued. I meant to take the germ of the idea and run with a story about a gangster whose dead wife returns from beyond the grave. But then I heard that the police think the woman with the Turk might have mimicked your daughter's looks to attract him and set him up for assassination.'

Moore grunts. 'It would be poetic justice if it was true.'

He glances at me shrewdly. 'But again I must ask, why come to me? *I* didn't hire a woman to masquerade as Andeanna, if that's what you're thinking.'

'No,' I smile. 'I'm trying to get an angle on your daughter, what she was like, what kind of a marriage she had. If someone impersonated her, she must have done a lot of research. I'm trying to get inside that woman's mind, to figure out how she ticks and nail her down if she exists.'

'I don't understand.'

'If someone *did* use a ringer for your daughter to get at the Turk,' I explain, 'and if I can track down the pair of them and expose them, I can forget about the horror story and write a straight-up account.'

'I see.' His smile turns icy. 'You're looking to exploit my dead daughter.'

I scowl. 'If Andeanna *was* indirectly instrumental in destroying the man who stole her childhood, you'd like to know, wouldn't you?'

He scratches an ear. 'I suppose. But won't the police tell me?'

'They're not actively pursuing the lead. To be blunt, they're glad Menderes is dead. They're not too concerned about finding the person who killed him.'

Moore studies me in silence, then chuckles drily. 'I don't know why, but I like you, Mr Sieveking. Go ahead. Tell me what you want to know.'

I start with some background questions, confirming things that Joe turned up. Then I ask if anyone plugged Andrew for information on his daughter during the last few years. 'No,' he says. 'I never discuss Andeanna, except with Gregory.'

'Greygo?' I frown.

The old man smiles. 'Menderes's legacy. The fool gave his son a name he couldn't pronounce, then made everyone use the abbreviated version. To me, he will always be Gregory.'

'He comes here?'

'Yes. He used to visit a lot when he was younger, eager to learn about his dead mother. He clicked instantly with Deleena, both of them being actors and having so much in common, but it took me a while to warm to him. I grew to love him over time. He helped me get through the long nights when Deleena died. Now he only drops by occasionally, but he rings often. He's a good boy.'

'You talk about Andeanna with him?'

Andrew nods. 'He was ten when his mother died. He never really got to know her. To learn about her history, he came to Deleena and me.'

I mull that over. Could Gregory Menderes have been behind the execution? The fake Andeanna told me that Greygo loved his father, but if Menderes Junior had put the woman up to the deceit, she would say that. Maybe this is a case of a greedy, neglected son doing away with his cruel, wealthy father.

'Did Gregory like the Turk?' I ask.

Andrew grimaces. 'He adored him. Menderes used to hit Andeanna, but he never raised a finger to his son. I don't have much good to say about that man, even now that he's dead, but he was a first-rate father. Gregory loved him unreservedly.'

'What about the family business? Will Gregory get involved now that –'

'No,' Andrew cuts in. 'He never wanted anything to do with that. As an adult he refused to let Menderes give him money. He was determined to make his own way in the world.' The old man puffs up with pride. 'Did you know that he won a scholarship to RADA?'

'Yes.' I remember Andeanna – or whoever she was – mentioning it. 'That's a big thing here, isn't it?'

'If you're an actor, RADA's the best,' Andrew beams. 'Deleena was over the moon when she heard. We all were. Except for Menderes.'

'Did it get nasty?' I ask, clutching at straws. 'Did he threaten to disinherit Greygo or cut him off?'

'No.' Andrew smiles begrudgingly. 'As I said, he was a great father. He grumbled about Gregory's choice of profession but never let it drive a wedge between them. He even forced himself to go and watch Gregory on stage a few times. The boy's a natural, and I'm not saying that because he's my grandson. So versatile, able to take on any part and make it his own. He could be a star, but he turns down the movies and TV shows he gets offered. Menderes was always baffled by that. He couldn't understand that Gregory only hungers for roles that will stretch him as an actor. He doesn't care about fame or money.'

So much for the conspiring son theory. I suppose, given the complex nature of this mystery, the solution was never going to be that simple.

'Who else stood to benefit from the Turk's death?' I ask.

Andrew snorts. 'I don't know and couldn't care less.'

'Did you have any contact with Andeanna after her marriage? I know you and your wife disowned her, but did you keep tabs on her? Do you know if she had any close friends in London?'

There's a long pause. Finally he sighs. 'She kept in touch with Deleena. Not right away – we both despised her to begin with, and rebuffed her efforts to re-establish contact – but after a few years Deleena's resolve melted and the pair of them began talking again. I didn't learn of their conversations until Gregory was eight. I found Deleena sobbing in the kitchen one day, clutching a photo of a boy at a birthday party. When I asked why she was crying, the truth came gushing out.

'I was furious. I made her call Andeanna so that I could

tell her to sever all ties with her mother.' He smiles wryly. 'Of course once I got on the phone, *I* burst into tears and spent the better part of an hour catching up on all the years that I'd missed.'

Andrew falls silent, thinking about his daughter and the painful past. I grant him a few minutes of inward reflection, then touch his left knee. 'Did you speak to her much after that?'

'Not as often as I would have liked,' he sighs. 'It was difficult. She'd changed. She was a live spark when she left home, afraid of nothing. Now she was scared and lonely, terrified of Menderes, captive to his demeaning whims.'

'Why didn't she leave him?' I ask angrily, although I already know — she was afraid the Turk would follow and kill her.

'We asked her to,' Andrew assures me. 'I told her there was a place for her here, that I'd protect her from the monster, but he'd broken her spirit. And there was Gregory to consider. The boy worshipped Menderes, and she feared losing his love if she separated them.

'We saw her a few times before the end,' Andrew says quietly. 'She came three times in the months before she died. Twice she stayed overnight. Once she stayed a whole weekend.'

'That must have been nice,' I remark.

Andrew nods, but he looks troubled. 'She didn't come just to see *us*.' He stops, and glances around nervously. 'This next bit,' he croaks. 'You must swear never to repeat it.'

I lean forward, fingers clenching with anticipation. 'OK.'

'Swear it!' he hisses.

I stare at him solemnly. 'I swear.'

There's no reason why he should trust me, but he chooses to, I think because he *wants* to tell someone about it, has wanted to for a long time.

'She was seeing someone,' he says in the barest of whispers.

My heart quickens. 'Who?'

Andrew shakes his head. 'She wouldn't say. It was a secret.

Maybe she told Deleena, but I don't think so.'

'Was she having an affair?'

'I don't know. She wouldn't talk about it. All I know is that she came here three times, used this house as a base and met someone in private. She'd slip out when she thought we were asleep, return early before we got up. We didn't ask any questions. We hoped she was going to pluck up the courage to leave Menderes. But she never got the chance, because a few weeks later . . .'

Tears bring him to a halt. He's said all that he can. To press him further would be heartless. It would also be meaningless, because I've uncovered the truth that I knew must be hidden somewhere.

There was a lover. Someone who has flown a flag for Andeanna all these years, waiting for a chance to avenge her. I use the word *avenge*, because something Joe said comes back to me and makes sense in light of this new information. He spoke of a witness to the crash who'd seen flames in the car *before* it hit the trees.

I put it together while Andrew weeps. Andeanna Menderes had a lover. A few weeks after their final romantic tryst, she perished in a fatal car wreck, even though there was nothing wrong with the car, no ice or oil slick on the road, no reason for her to swerve down a bank and crash. Add that to the report of flames in the car before it exploded, and everything clicks neatly into place.

Mikis Menderes murdered his wife.

The Turk found out she was cheating. Enraged, he killed her and made it look like an accident. Years later, her lover gets around to wreaking revenge and plots the Turk's downfall, hiring a lookalike to drag me into his scheme, confident that his ghostly middlewoman will ensure there's no way to link the crime back to him.

I have my motive. Now all I need is to find the vengeful lover and the woman who manipulated me. Then I'll show them how I deal with people who think they can fuck with my head and heart, and blithely set me up for a fall. I carry seven ghosts around with me wherever I go, the shades of those I've killed.

There's plenty of room for two more.

SIXTEEN

Back in London, I tell Joe about my meeting with Andrew Moore and my theory. He isn't convinced. How does Andeanna's lover know she was killed, assuming that she was? Why would he wait so long for revenge? Why not simply shoot Menderes himself? Legitimate questions, but I don't waste time on them. I'll squeeze the answers out of the guilty pair before I kill them.

I ask Joe to focus on the months leading up to the original Andeanna's death, to scour the clippings for photos of her and the Turk, and note who's with them. Given the tight leash he kept her on, I doubt she'd have strayed far beyond their immediate circle of friends in search of a lover. I'm betting her mystery man was one of the Turk's crew, or a close business associate. I want as complete a list of his contacts for those months as possible. Joe doubts he'll be able to find out much, but says he'll see what he can come up with.

The following morning, I resume my investigations as Edgar Sanders and return to Menderes's turf in north London. Life has gone on as normal since he died. Bond Gardiner assumed control of the Turk's business interests even before the funeral. Nobody challenged him. The locals are satisfied with Gardiner. He runs things calmly, efficiently, the same as before. They appreciate the continuity.

Many of the people I approach have already heard about the journalist from the States and are eager to be part of the book. They talk freely about the Turk, happy to share their incriminating stories now that he's dead. They're careful not to say anything that I might be able to use against Gardiner or his men, but it's open season on Mikis Menderes.

A lot of them boast about the Turk's love life, but no one gives any hint that his wife was disloyal. They say she was a charming lady, a perfect mother, but none of them knew her personally. I ask if she had friends who could tell me more about her, but she seems to have kept to herself and didn't say much in company. Her friends were Menderes's friends.

I keep asking questions about Andeanna, determined to worm my way into her sad, solitary world. Finally, on a dark, wet Wednesday, a man in a pub called the King's Battalion taps my shoulder and asks if I'd care to have a drink with his mates. Glancing towards the back of the pub where he was sitting, I spy a table of middle-aged, neatly dressed men. Bond Gardiner is among them. With a tight feeling in my stomach, I head over and, at a nod from Gardiner, take a seat.

I stare around the table. Hard men, cold eyes. Gardiner stands out, even though he's dressed the same and looks no tougher. It's the charged air around him, the space the others afford him. 'Know who I am?' he grunts.

'Yes.'

He smiles thinly. 'I hear you're a writer.'

'Trying to be.'

'Writing a book.'

'I hope to. I've never written one before. I'm not sure how it will go.'

'American?' he asks.

'Yes. Montana. It's up near Canada.'

Gardiner is holding a book of matches and plays with them

while he speaks, flicking open the lid and running his thumb over the phosphorus heads. 'Tell me, Mr Sanders, what's a Yank doing in London, investigating Mikis Menderes? Don't you have gangsters where you come from?'

'One or two,' I chuckle. 'But I was over here freelancing. Then the Turk –'

'Mr Menderes,' Gardiner corrects me.

'Excuse me. Then Mr Menderes was killed. I set out to write an article about him, but the more I learnt, the more fascinated I became.'

Gardiner carries on playing with the matches. 'Will it do him justice,' he asks softly, 'or are you out to dish the dirt?'

I shrug. 'I'm not going to pretend he was some kind of Robin Hood, but I don't want to demonize him either. I want to explore behind the mask, chart how he got started, why he chose a life of crime, how his work conflicted with his home life. I want to show how a modern gangster lives, how those close to him cope, whether his challenges and problems are the same as any ordinary Joe's.'

'I'll tell you what,' one of the others barks. 'Ordinary blokes don't have to cope with having their brains blown out by some bastard of an assassin while they're home in bed!'

They all murmur angrily.

'You haven't found out who killed him, have you?' Gardiner asks.

'No.'

'You'll let us know if you do, won't you?'

'Sure. I'll send you a copy of the book before it's published. You can proofread it for me.'

Gardiner laughs and the mood lightens. 'Tell me what you've found out.'

'All of it?'

'Just the good bits.'

I recount some of the more fanciful tales I've collected in the course of my investigations. Gardiner and his men listen silently at first, but soon interject with stories of their own. They discuss jobs the Turk pulled, boasting of those that were a success and delighting over those that went awry, as if it was all a game without real consequences.

I ask the questions I imagine a journalist would ask, verifying names and dates. I jot down a few details in my writing pad, to make it look like I mean to use this. After a while I steer talk round to Andeanna. 'What was his wife like?'

'A looker,' a pug-nosed man called Harold says.

'A lady,' Gardiner corrects him.

'A looker of a lady,' a guy called Larry laughs.

'She was young when they married, wasn't she?'

Gardiner taps the table warningly. 'If you want us to talk about that child-bride shit and how he was a dirty old lech, you can go fuck your –'

'No,' I interrupt. 'That's not it. I'm just saying that even though she was young when she died, she was *very* young when they got married, so they had quite a long time together. I want to stress how much value Menderes placed on family and his marriage vows. I know he had other women, but he was loyal to her in his way. She was at the centre of his world and he was careful to shield her from the darker areas of his work. I want to show his more compassionate side.'

'Compassionate?' Larry snorts. 'The only compassion Mikis ever . . .'

An angry glance from his boss shuts him up. 'You're right, Sanders,' Gardiner says. 'Mikis was a provider. He doted on Andeanna and Greygo and was always there for them.'

'Yeah,' Larry says meekly. 'He loved her.'

The rest of the gang mutter their consent.

'Do you know how the two of them met?' I ask.

'Now there's a story!' Gardiner beams, and proceeds to tell me the cinema tale, how Andeanna was sitting behind the Turk at a premiere and kept on talking until he turned round and told her to shut up. In reply she dumped a bucket of popcorn over his head. I've heard the story before, several times, but I pretend it's new to me and laugh in all the right places.

At the end, I frown and clear my throat. 'I've heard rumours,' I begin. 'I don't want to upset you, but some people have said that Menderes used to hit her.'

Gardiner's smile vanishes. 'Who told you that?'

'Various people.'

'*Who?*' He leans across the table menacingly.

I shake my head. 'I can't reveal my sources.'

'I'll tear the fuckers to pieces for spreading lies like that,' he vows.

'It's not true?'

'Of course not! If you mention that in your book, I'll have your bollocks for marbles.' I blink at the blatant viciousness of the threat. 'Mikis wasn't perfect, but he wasn't a wife-beater. Ask anyone who knew him, they'll tell you the same.'

'OK,' I mutter. 'I only brought it up because –'

'Shut it,' Gardiner growls.

'Fine, whatever.' I stare at the table and fidget, like I'd been meaning to say something else but have thought better of it.

'What?' Gardiner snaps.

'Nothing. Just . . . No. Forget about it.'

'Say what you were going to.'

'It was just more gossip. Don't worry, I won't –'

'Spit it out, or so help me . . .' He starts to get to his feet.

'I'll call for help if you attack!' I yelp, pulling away from him, acting as if the very thought of taking a punch fills me with terror.

Gardiner curses, then controls himself, sits and gestures for me to take my place. After a few carefully judged seconds I join him at the table again, faking wariness. 'Tell me what you've heard,' Gardiner says stiffly.

'I haven't repeated this to anyone, and I won't,' I tell him. 'I wouldn't even say it to you, except I know how close you and Menderes were.' I let a few seconds drag by, then come out with the query I've spent the better part of a week building up to. 'I heard that Andeanna Menderes was having an affair.'

A vein pulses in Gardiner's forehead, but he says nothing. The other men around the table look disbelieving.

'That's bullshit,' Larry says.

'What else have you heard?' Gardiner growls.

'Nothing,' I mutter.

'What. Else.'

I stare at his colleagues, then look to Gardiner questioningly. With a curt wave of a hand he dismisses them. Once they're out of earshot, I slide into the chair next to Gardiner and address him in a veiled whisper. 'I think she had a lover, that Menderes found out and killed her, then staged the car accident.'

Gardiner's jaw tightens. 'Who told you this?'

'Nobody, not directly. I pieced the theory together from various accounts.'

'It's a theory you should forget as soon as fucking possible,' he snarls.

'I can't.'

He stares at me with flat eyes. 'You don't know what I could do to you if you got on the wrong side of me.'

'Of course I do,' I retort, not dropping my gaze. 'But I've got to be able to verify or dismiss the theory. I'll go on searching until I'm sure.'

'You've about one minute left to live,' he says. 'Any last requests?'

'Just tell me the truth,' I plead. 'If I'm wrong, look me in the eye and say so. I'll take your word for it. If I'm right, confirm it. Either way, the story can stop here. No need for anything that might come back to haunt you. You can get rid of me with the truth.'

'You expect me to believe you'd keep it to yourself?' he sneers.

'I'd have to. There's no evidence linking Menderes to his wife's death. There aren't even any rumours that he killed her. This is a theory of my own invention. If I was dumb enough to include it in the book, I'd be torn apart by Menderes's lawyers. You can't come out and openly accuse a man of murdering his wife, not without at least some shred of proof. It would be a great hook for the book if I could substantiate it, but without substantiation no publisher would touch it.'

'And you expect *me* to give you the proof you need?' Gardiner sniffs.

'It can be off the record,' I say softly. 'Not for the book, just for me. It sounds crazy, and I don't expect you to understand, but this has taken over my life. It was only a story in the beginning. Now it's more. I can't use anything you say – without a witness, you could claim in court that you didn't tell me shit – but I need to *know*. For my own sake.'

Gardiner squints at me. I'm not what he expected. He makes a sudden growling noise and tells me to stand. He frisks me, searching for a hidden recorder. When he's satisfied that I'm clean, we sit down and he leans in close. 'You're right.'

I shudder involuntarily. 'She had a lover?'

'Yes.'

'Menderes knew?'

'He found them together,' Gardiner says. 'He was away on business. He returned early, caught them fucking, lost his rag and killed them. I helped him arrange Andeanna's *accident* and I disposed of the other body.'

That's not what I wanted to hear – a dead lover can't exact revenge – but it's way more than I'd hoped to learn. I can't believe Gardiner is telling me this. My head is spinning. To have so much information dropped into my lap so suddenly . . .

'Who was he?' I ask.

'You don't need to know.'

'Yes I fucking do.'

Gardiner lays a hand on my arm and squeezes hard. 'No you fucking don't.'

'OK,' I mutter. He squeezes tighter until I sigh and repeat it. '*OK*.'

Releasing my arm, Gardiner returns to his book of matches and begins playing with it again. 'Mikis had a savage temper. He vented it on Andeanna. He loved her but he couldn't help himself. He was jealous as the devil, even when he didn't need to be. When he found her in bed with . . .' He breathes through his nostrils like a dragon. 'He didn't mean to kill her, but he lost control. We did a good job of covering it up. Nobody ever questioned it. I stopped worrying years ago. Just goes to show, you can never drop your guard.'

'Can I ask something else?' He nods warily. 'Why tell me this?'

Gardiner smiles terribly. 'Because you asked.'

'No, seriously. It would have been a lot easier to scare me off or silence me. Hell, you could have just kept your mouth shut. Why come clean after so many years, when you didn't have to?'

Gardiner considers that, then sighs. 'I've done a lot of bad shit in my time, but that's the one thing that keeps me awake nights, that I wish I could take back. I guess I've wanted to confess for a long time, and you're as good a confessor as any.'

'Because you trust me to keep it to myself?'

He grins bleakly. 'Because I can get to you any time I like. You even dream of repeating any of this, you'll be an easy man to kill.'

He's wrong on that score, but I don't correct him. Instead I reflect on what he told me. It's confusing. I was right about Andeanna being murdered, but her lover was killed too. Does this mean her death wasn't connected to the Turk's, that I've unravelled a mystery that has nothing to do with the one I set out to expose?

'Happy now?' Gardiner asks.

'I'd be a lot happier if you'd tell me the name of her lover.'

'We all want things we can't have.' He puts the matches away. 'I'll say this much — he was someone we couldn't afford to kill. If the truth had trickled out, it would have been cata-strophic. Make of that what you want, but keep your theories to yourself. And know this — your enquiry ends here. If you've gathered enough material to write a book, go ahead. If not, tough. You don't have the freedom of the city any more. I want you off my manor.'

'OK. I've got what I was after anyway.'

Almost true. I need the name of the lover too, to make sure he's dead, to check if he left behind a son or other relative who might have engineered the plot to kill Menderes. But I won't find it proceeding the way I have been. Gardiner is the end of the line as far as open enquiries go. With one exception.

'There's one more person I'd like to interview before I quit — Gregory.'

'What do you want to speak to him for?' Gardiner asks.

'Human interest. People will want to know how his father's death affected him, what their relationship was like, if he knew about Menderes's secret life and loved him regardless.'

The truth is, I want to know if he can recall any of his dead mother's friends who maybe dropped by when his father was away on business.

'Greygo has shunned the press,' Gardiner says. 'I doubt he'll agree to meet you.'

'But if he does, can I speak with him?'

Gardiner considers it, then shrugs. 'Sure. But he's the last. And if you mention anything about what I told you . . .'

'I won't.'

Gardiner grunts. 'In that case, there's just one more thing.'

'What?'

He grips my right leg above the knee and stares into my eyes, his expression bleak. I wonder if I've misjudged the situation, if he's going to take me out back and shoot me to ensure my silence. Then he smirks and says, 'Can I have a signed copy of the book when it comes out?'

SEVENTEEN

Back at the Royal Munster, I tell Joe about my extraordinary meeting. He can't believe Gardiner was so forthcoming. 'How come he opened up to you? He thinks you're a journalist. I'd have thought someone in his position wouldn't trust a journalist with the time, never mind admit to being an accomplice to murder.'

'It was . . . strange,' I agree, for want of a better word. 'He said he wanted to confess, and maybe that was partly true, but I think he was also worried about me stirring up interest among his associates. He had to stop me asking questions and taking this further. That meant coming clean or killing me. I guess telling me the truth was less of a hassle.'

'Maybe he knows something about the Andeanna impostor,' Joe suggests. 'He's profited most through Menderes's death. Maybe *he* arranged the set-up.'

'I considered that. But Gardiner was set to take over anyway when the Turk retired. Everyone says they were like brothers. I don't think he was involved.'

Joe shrugs. 'So, where next?'

'It's time I paid Greygo a visit. He might be able to give us the name of Andeanna's lover.'

'Andeanna's *dead* lover,' Joe corrects me.

'Alive, dead . . .' I grimace. 'It doesn't seem like there's much of a difference any more.'

Gregory Menderes doesn't want to talk. I have his number – picked it up during the course of my investigations – but he's heard about me, the book I'm meant to be writing, and once I identify myself, he hangs up every time I ring, sets the phone to voicemail if I persist.

Joe suggests waiting outside the mansion, but I don't want to chase after him like an ignorant paparazzo. Instead, I leave him be for a while and kick my heels around the Royal Munster, thinking about Andeanna and all that I've learnt about her, trying to piece the various links of the mystery together.

I phone Greygo the following Wednesday and he cuts me off. When I call again and get directed to voicemail, I leave a message. 'I've uncovered some alarming secrets about your mother. If you don't meet with me, I'll have to publish them unapproved and uncorroborated. I don't want to do a smear piece, but if you leave me no choice, I will.'

A couple of minutes later the phone rings. 'If you're bull-shitting me, you'll regret it.' Greygo has a strong Cockney accent, nothing like his father or mother. At least not the mother *I* knew.

'I'm not bullshitting you,' I assure him. 'I wouldn't bother you if it wasn't important. I've spoken with your grandfather, so I know how much –'

'Andrew?' he interrupts, surprised.

'I interviewed him in Birmingham. He told me about –'

'Andrew let you in?' Greygo interrupts again. 'He answered your questions?'

'Yes. I've also been in contact with Bond Gardiner and others who knew your parents. I want to paint as complete a picture of your father's life as I can.'

'That's why you're ringing? To get my opinion of him?'

'No. At first, yes, that was all. Now there's more. I learnt something yesterday that changes everything. This is personal, maybe nothing to do with the book. It's about your mother.'

Greygo is silent. Finally, when I think he's going to cut me off, he snaps, 'Do you know where I live?'

All too fucking well!

'Yes.'

'Can you meet me this afternoon, two o'clock?'

'I can.'

'There'll be guards. Come alone. You have two minutes to impress me, so start with the big revelation.'

'Thank . . .' He hangs up. '. . . you,' I finish, and grin victoriously.

I call Joe to let him know of the development. He's worried – he talks about stepping into the lion's den – and asks if he should call the police if I haven't contacted him by evening. I tell him not to bother, just dial a good undertaker. He doesn't laugh. He wasn't meant to. I was being serious.

It's weird returning to the Menderes mansion, feigning unfamiliarity. I'm met at the gate by an armed guard who makes me leave my car outside and walk up the drive ahead of him to the front steps, where I'm subjected to a body search by two of his colleagues. If Bond Gardiner was thorough, these guys are absolute, and stop just short of a rectal probe.

Gregory Menderes, known to one and all as Greygo, awaits inside, seated in one of the mansion's smaller rooms, a leather-lined study. He's behind a desk. A thin layer of stubble crowns his shaven head. He's dressed in a white suit. His face is darkly tanned. He doesn't offer to shake hands.

'Sit down,' he growls.

Even though the room is dimly lit, I can see his mother in his features. He looks a lot like her, same nose, mouth and eyes, although his are a soulful blue where hers were a vibrant

218

green. The memory of Andeanna – *my* Andeanna – brings a lump to my throat.

'Get on with it,' he orders briskly, and I cough the lump away.

'Your mother was murdered.'

Greygo stares at me coldly. 'Is that it?' he asks. I've no answer to that. I can only nod dumbly, stunned by his nonchalant reaction. 'I don't know who filled your head with such nonsense, but they were wrong. If that's all you came to tell me, this meeting is at an end.' I stare at him wordlessly. 'That's your cue to leave, Mr Sanders.'

Finding my tongue, I splutter, 'You don't understand. It was your father. He killed her.'

'Ridiculous,' Greygo snorts. 'My father loved my mother.'

'Sure,' I sneer. 'He loved her so much, he knocked the shit out of her every time she looked sideways at another man.'

Greygo's eyes narrow to slits. 'Did my grandfather tell you that?'

'Yes. But he wasn't the only one.'

The Menderes heir nods slowly. 'They tried to hide it from me. They thought I didn't know. But children always . . .' He snaps back to attention. 'That's neither here nor there. My father didn't kill my mother, no matter how many times he hit her. Now, if that's all, I'm a busy –'

'She had a lover,' I bark, determined to make an impact. He says nothing, but I can tell by the way he fidgets that I've got to him. 'Your father killed them. He arranged the crash to look like an accident and had Bond Gardiner dispose of her lover's body.'

Greygo lifts one of his hands and chews a fingernail. 'Since Bond is the only person in the world who could have told you that story, I assume you picked it up from him?'

'I can't reveal my sources,' I reply weakly.

Greygo smiles thinly. 'It couldn't have been anybody else. I'm shocked that he confided in you. He never told anyone about this, not even me. He thinks I don't know, and I'm happy to let him go on thinking that.'

'You mean you *knew* about the murders?'

'I know about *a* murder,' he corrects me. 'Axel Nelke's.'

My face grows ashen.

'That was the name of her lover,' Gregyo continues. 'The man my father murdered when he caught them betraying him.'

I'm glad I'm sitting down. All the strength has drained from me. I feel like a sack of moon rock.

'Are you all right?' Greygo asks, something close to concern in his tone.

'Nelke,' I gasp.

'Do you want a glass of water? Some fresh air?'

I wave away his offers. 'Did . . . one of your father's body-guards . . . go missing shortly before his death?' I wheeze.

'What?'

'I heard that one of your father's men disappeared. That he might be a suspect.'

Greygo frowns. 'I haven't heard anything like that. I don't keep a close tab on everything that happens, but I'd have been informed of something that important.'

'No guards have gone missing?'

'No.'

I reflect on what that means, but my mind is a blank, and if there are conclusions to be drawn, I can't draw them.

'This Axel Nelke that your father killed,' I croak, staring at the smirking ghost in the room who went by that name before I strangled him with a telephone cable not too far from where I'm sitting now. 'Describe him.'

Greygo laughs. 'I was ten years old. All adults looked the same.'

The ghost of Axel Nelke cackles silently and flips me the finger.

'Did he have any children?' I ask.

'I don't think so. He was single when he and my mother . . .' He grimaces.

'I don't understand this,' I moan as Nelke's ghost presses closer, puckering up his lips as if he's going to kiss me, then snapping at me with his fog-like fangs. 'It's like a nightmare, and the more I try to wake up, the further into it I slip.'

Greygo stares at me uncomprehendingly. After a while he stands and starts for the door. Afraid that he plans to summon the guards, I lurch to my feet and block his way. As he takes a sharp step back, I raise my hands to show I mean no harm. 'I know how strangely I'm behaving. I'm sorry. This is the first book I've written. It's stressing me out like you wouldn't believe.'

'Then drop it,' Greygo says drily.

'Maybe I will,' I sigh, pretending that's an option. 'It just seems to get crazier the further I run with it.'

Keeping a wary eye on me, Greygo sits and points towards my chair. Once I'm seated, he asks why I reacted that way to the name of Axel Nelke. Thinking quickly, ignoring the ghost of the man in question as it tries to distract me, I start talking.

'I began this book shortly after your father's death. At first I meant to tell his story in a traditional fashion. Then a man calling himself Axel Nelke told me that Mikis Menderes had been seen with a woman the spitting image of your mother in the weeks prior to his death, and that she'd vanished afterwards. That fascinated me and led me to . . .'

I stop. Greygo's face has misted over and he's smiling benignly. He gets up, heads for the door and beckons me to follow. Outside, he dismisses the guards and leads me on a tour of the mansion, although he doesn't talk about the rooms, just glides through them, touching the walls and furniture as he goes.

'Bond Gardiner lied to you about my mother,' he says as we mount the stairs. 'He wanted to misdirect you. This is what really happened.

'My mother enjoyed a short affair towards the end of her life, with Axel Nelke, one of her guards. My father suspected from the start. They had a couple of close calls, which should have been warning enough, but they persisted. Things came to a tragic but predictable head. He killed Nelke, I'm not sure how, though I think he strangled him.'

I flinch at that. Nelke's ghost raises his chin and smugly points to the mark around his neck. 'And your mother?' I ask.

'He gave her one hell of a beating, I'm sure, but he loved her and would never – *could* never – have killed her.'

'But Gardiner said –'

'Mr Sanders,' he tuts, 'do you think I'd have shared this house with my father all these years if he'd murdered my mother?'

'If you didn't know about it . . .' I mutter.

'But I have known, for five years or more. Nobody murdered my mother.' He pauses. We're outside one of the guest bedrooms. The corridor is long and empty. Nevertheless, he lowers his voice and says, 'She killed herself.'

He starts walking again. After a moment of horrid pause, I hurry after him, catch him by his right arm and spin him round so he's facing me. I'm not surprised to see tears in his eyes. 'It was *suicide*?' I hiss.

'Yes. My father killed Axel Nelke. Bond got rid of the body. My mother lost her will to live. A few weeks later she went out driving, took a sharp turn off the road and deliberately rammed her car into a tree. Obviously that makes me feel sick every time I think about it, and yes, I blamed my father to an extent. I wish he'd been gentler with her, more understanding, as he was with me. But *she* made the decision to give up. My father suffered when he lost her, more than he ever admitted. Hating him would have served no viable purpose.'

I take in this latest twist, mind reeling. 'A witness said there were flames in the car before it crashed.'

'There couldn't have been. It was suicide.'

'You can't know that for sure,' I disagree. 'Nobody was in the car with her. You want it to be suicide, so you don't have to blame your father.'

'It's not a theory,' he replies softly. 'It's the truth.'

'How can you know?' I huff. 'Only one person really knows, and she's . . .'

'. . . dead,' he finishes calmly. 'But the dead can talk, and this came straight from the horse's mouth.'

'What the hell are you talking about?'

Greygo looks me calmly in the eye. 'Do you believe in ghosts, Mr Sanders?'

I take a step away from him and glance at the seven shades huddled around me. I expect them to snicker and mock me, as Nelke's ghost has been doing, but they only stare at me accusingly, still and serious. I almost run, for some reason afraid of what Gregory Menderes has to tell me, but I'm compelled to hear him out. I have to know the truth, or at least *his* version of it.

'This used to be a haunted house,' Greygo says. 'People have often asked me what it's like to lose your mother at such a young age. I've never been able to tell them, because until recently, I hadn't truly lost her.'

He starts to walk again. I trail after him, listening numbly. The ghosts follow in a line, like mourners at a funeral, Nelke slipping into place among them, the sad little girl at the head of the procession.

'Her spirit came to me the night of her death,' Greygo says.

'I awoke to darkness, scared, somehow certain that my mother was dead, only to find her by my bed. She didn't speak, but in my head I heard her telling me it was OK, I had nothing to fear, she wasn't going to leave me. I fell back into a deep sleep. When my father came to break the news to me in the morning, I took it serenely, knowing she wasn't really gone.

'She's been patrolling the halls of this house ever since. Always at night. It's hard to describe her. She looks real, like when she was alive, but at the same time there's something insubstantial about her.'

'This is madness,' I croak.

Greygo shrugs. We've come to Andeanna's room. He stands in the doorway, gazing in. 'My father kept this room as she left it. She spent much of her time here, seated in her favourite chair or lying on the bed.' He closes the door gently, lovingly. 'I don't know if anyone else saw her. Our servants sensed something – so many refused to work nights that eventually we employed them only in the day – but I never heard them discussing her. I think my father knew. I suspect that's why he never married again.'

'And Axel Nelke?' I ask sceptically. 'Does he hang out here too?'

'No.' Greygo frowns. 'It's only ever been my mother. I don't know who the person you spoke with could have been, how he knew about her or why he told you what he did. Where did you meet him?'

I open my mouth to answer, then shut it sharply. What can I tell him, that I met Nelke *here*? That I also met with his dead mother? Oh, and by the way, I'm the guy who killed his father, but it's OK, I did it because Andeanna told me to?

'Show me your mother,' I say instead, challenging him to back up his wild story with proof.

Greygo's face softens. 'She doesn't come any more. Not

since my father died. I like to think she was waiting for him, that they're together now and have moved on to a better place.'

'Very romantic,' I scoff. 'Or perhaps she was hanging around to see him die. Maybe she was waiting for revenge. Maybe *she* set up his murder.' Greygo stares at me as if I'm mad. Maybe I am. Right now I don't know where this world stops and all the other worlds begin. I've criticized Joe for jumping to phantastical conclusions, but now I find myself leaping higher than he ever did. 'An eye for an eye, a life for a life. Perhaps she found a way to materialize outside of this house. Maybe she hired the assassin who . . .'

Gregory Menderes bursts out laughing. 'That's insane.'

'You're the one who claims to have lived with a ghost,' I remind him.

'A ghost, yes, the shade of a woman who died of extreme unhappiness. Not some zombie who arranges assassinations. Besides, as I said, my father didn't kill her, so there was no call for revenge.'

'You're back to that again. How do you *know*? How can you stand here and claim to –'

'Does the name Etienne Anders mean anything to you?' he cuts in.

I'm about to tell him it doesn't, when I recall the mystic the fake Andeanna encouraged me to see when I was researching *Spirit of the Fire*. 'Yes,' I say cautiously.

'Do you know how to contact her?'

'I have her number.'

'Arrange a meeting. Tell her I sent you. Ask her to put you in touch.'

'*In touch?*' Now it's my turn to stare at him as if he's the mad one. 'In touch with who?'

He smiles thinly. 'If you can't figure that out, you're not half the detective you think you are.' He offers his hand, and in a daze I take it. 'Good day, Mr Sanders. I should show you to the door, but I'd like to be alone for a while. I'm sure you understand.'

'But the ghost . . . your mother . . . the truth . . .'

'Etienne can explain better than I can,' he promises. 'You wouldn't believe me if I told you. Go see her. Call me when you're finished, if you like, though I don't think you'll need to.' He nods curtly, wheels away and heads back to his study.

I stand on the landing, brain cranking creakily. Then, with the ghosts following, still in a sombre line, I shakily make my way down the stairs and stumble away from the house of madness and death, into the shadowy mysteries beyond.

EIGHTEEN

I dial Etienne Anders's number while sitting in my car. My hands tremble so much that it takes several efforts to press the right buttons. Finally I hit the correct combination, her phone rings six times then cuts to voicemail. I leave my name and number and ask her to call me as soon as she can.

My heart is pounding and my thoughts are circling faster and faster, like goldfish on speed. If Gregory Menderes has told me the truth, and the mystic can prove it, then I fell in love with a ghost, one who was able to pass herself off as a member of the living. If that's the case, life as I knew it just ceased to exist. How can I trust anything in a world where ghosts can walk among us and not be known for what they truly are?

I never believed that ghosts might be real. All the years of research were mainly an attempt to keep madness at bay. The search for supernatural proof was a way of evading what I felt sure was an undeniable truth, that my ghosts were nothing more than evidence that I had suffered a mental breakdown. I didn't think there was a God, or life after death. If I was wrong . . . if Andeanna was the proof that I'd been sceptically seeking . . . then everything has changed. On the one hand, that thrills me. On the other, it terrifies me, as every belief I once held true will have to be re-evaluated. I'll have to try to make sense of the world all over again.

I think back to the storyline of *Spirit of the Fire*. I'd started to feel far removed from the novel, as if it was some leftover relic from an earlier life. Now I find myself running through the plot again. Was I closer to the truth than I thought? Could my bumbling efforts to weave together a decent ghost story have nudged me over some unseen edge, into a very real, supernatural corner of the world? Did I inadvertently invite the ghost of Andeanna Menderes into my life, bring her into being or open a door through which her spirit could slip and physically form?

Joe rings while I'm considering the impossible. He wants to know how my meeting with Greygo went. I lie and say I learnt nothing new, then tell him I'll be in touch in a few days, that I'm chasing up leads. Not wanting to expose Joe to the labyrinthine terrors of this mad new world. Not wanting to drag him down into the darkness with me, where the dead can catch hold of you and do as they wish.

Hours tick by. I try not to think about Andeanna and Axel Nelke. I fail.

Finally my cell rings again. I answer hoarsely, 'Hello?'

'Edgar Sanders?' a woman asks.

'Yes.'

'Etienne Anders. Sorry it took so long to get back to you, love. It's been a hectic day.'

'No problem. Thanks for returning my call.'

There's an awkward silence. She's waiting for me to say something but I don't known how to begin. When she realizes I'm stuck, she comes to my rescue. 'Were you looking to have your fortune read?'

'No, I . . .' Want her to materialize the spirit of the dead woman I fell in love with? Unpick the lock of a mystery that defies description? 'Gregory Menderes told me I should call.'

'Greygo?' I sense her smile. 'He used to be one of my

favourites, bless him, though I haven't seen much of him lately. How is he? I heard about his father and sent a condolence card.'

'He's good. He . . .' I go for it. 'I rang about his mother, Andeanna.'

'Oh?' Cautious now.

'I'm writing a book. There are things I want to learn about her. Greygo told me to get in touch with you. He said you knew more about it than he did.'

'I don't think so, love,' she replies. 'I've channelled for Greygo a few times, but I don't . . . Do you know what channelling is?'

'That's when a mystic acts as a conduit for the dead.'

'Yes. I let them speak through me. Well, I channelled for Greygo, but I didn't hear what was said. Sometimes a spirit takes over and tunes me out, so that it can converse with its loved one in private.'

'But he told me to phone you,' I bleat.

She makes a soft sucking sound with her teeth and lips. 'Do you mind if I call you back, love? I'd like to check with Greygo before taking this further. Not that I don't trust you, but you've got to be careful, haven't you?'

'Sure. But if you can't get through to him, will you let me know? I don't want to sit around like a fool all night.'

'Will do, love. Hold tight. I won't be long.'

I think about our short conversation while I wait. A channeller. Is this how Greygo learnt about his mother's death? I've visited lots of mediums over the years. Most were blatant charlatans. A few left me wondering if there might be something to them, but not even the best could provide concrete proof that they were in touch with the dead. None could answer a direct question to my satisfaction, in a way that proved beyond doubt that they could communicate with spirits.

Etienne is back within ten minutes. 'Sorry about the delay, love. I got chatting to Greygo about his father. He's awfully upset. They still don't know who did it. I told him he should come in and try making contact. His father might be able to shed light on the subject.'

That's a twist I hadn't taken into account — the ghost of Mikis Menderes returning to point the finger at me. Even surrounded by madness, my self-protective drive kicks in and I ask how Greygo reacted to her suggestion.

'He pooh-poohed it. He wants to get over his father's death, not wallow in it. I understand that. It's better not to rush these things. The dead can wait, that's for certain.'

'What about me? Did he OK our meeting?'

'He was ambivalent. He regretted telling you about his secrets, but given the fact that he had, he agreed that you might as well learn the rest, seeing as how you know so much already.'

'When can you see me?'

'Right now's fine. Do you have a pen? I'll give you directions.'

Etienne Anders operates from a small apartment in a block of flats in the East End. She lives elsewhere, she tells me as I make myself comfortable in a cramped living room, but never reveals her home address, even to her most trusted clients. 'One of my quirks, love. I'm full of them.'

She's a middle-aged woman with straggly grey-brown hair which she doesn't take care of. Light brown skin. Her striking cheekbones make me think she might have been a looker once, but now her face is dark with wrinkles and moles. She walks with a stoop, her left shoulder hanging lower than her right. She wears crisp white gloves but otherwise is dressed casually, baggy jeans and a faded sweater with a picture of Bob Marley sprayed across the front.

'I look a fright, don't I?' she laughs, collapsing into a soft, springy chair. 'I don't normally, but this has been a long day.

I'm usually finished by now. I'm no nightbird, love. In bed by ten more often than not.' She glances at a digital clock hanging on the wall above my head, and sighs. 'But not tonight. Let's crack on, shall we?' Taking my hands, she looks at me directly. 'I won't feed you a load of guff, love. If customers come to be charmed and amused, I charm and amuse them. But I can turn on the real stuff when asked.'

'You can speak to the dead?' I ask dubiously.

'Not *to* them, love. *With* them. I can't contact anyone who doesn't want to be contacted, or find someone who doesn't want to be found. I open up my mind and invite them in. If they come, they come. If they don't, they don't. If Andeanna wants to speak with you, she will. If she doesn't . . .' Etienne shrugs.

'I understand.'

'Good.' Settling back, not letting go of my hands, she closes her eyes. 'Ever been to one of these before?'

'Quite a few, actually.'

'Then you know the routine. Keep still, say nothing, don't disturb me. It might take a while. There's nothing either of us can do to speed things up.'

She takes deep breaths and relaxes. Her head is soon tossing from left to right and her lips move, forming barely intelligible words. At one point she cries out, a young boy's voice, and I fear I'm going to be stuck with a whimpering child, but the youth's voice fades and she resumes her search.

My ghosts drift around her as she rolls her head, making crude gestures, mocking the both of us, as they often have at seances. If she could truly do what she claims, surely she'd be aware of the seven malevolent spirits in the room. The fact that she isn't disheartens me, and I ready myself for the usual mumbo-jumbo that I get fed by those of her ilk.

Five or six minutes later, Etienne Anders stops squirming

and sits up, eyes still closed, lips spreading in a suitably ghostly smile. 'Hello, Ed,' she says, only it isn't her voice. It's Andeanna's.

I freeze. Whatever I'd been expecting, it wasn't this. A moaning approximation of her voice, perhaps, at best. But this is the real thing, the voice of the woman I met on the boat, the woman who seduced me and had me dispose of the Turk. The voice of a ghost.

'Who are you?' I croak. 'Is this a recording?'

'Don't be silly, Ed.' I see now that the smile is Andeanna's as well. A warm but worried smile, like the one she flashed the first time we kissed. 'You know it's me.'

I lean forward, fingers digging into the mystic's. 'I want to hear you say it.'

'I'm Andeanna Menderes,' she sighs, 'but I called myself Deleena Emerson the night we met at Shar's party.'

'You died,' I whisper. 'Years ago. You're dead.'

'Yes, Ed. I know.'

'But you were real!' I shout. 'I touched you. Kissed you. We made love.'

'No,' she corrects me. 'We couldn't. I would have, if I'd been able, but there are limits.'

'Who sets them?' I croak, but she only smiles and shakes her head.

'How have you been?' she asks, as if we'd parted the day before.

'How do you fucking think?' I snarl, no longer seeing Etienne Anders, no longer doubting, chatting with Andeanna the same way I did when she was alive. When I *thought* she was alive. All the doubts blown away. Adjusting with surprising ease to the resettlement of my axis of reality.

'I've kept track of you as best I could,' Andeanna says as my ghosts drift into the background, sullen, disappointed, and also confused-looking. 'I've been with you much of the time. I tried letting you know I was present, but I don't have that power any longer. If you hadn't come here, we could never have spoken with each other again. That's why I told you about Etienne. I didn't know what was going to happen when Mikis died, but I guessed it might be like this. I didn't want to leave without explaining.'

I feel tears building, but I blink them back. 'Explain that you made a fool of me? That you used and discarded me? That you forced me to kill your ex-husband, promising it would make you mine, knowing it would only drive us apart?'

'I'm sorry,' she mutters, dropping her head with shame. 'There was no other way. I had to have him killed. Just like he killed me.'

I push my anger aside and concentrate on this immediate part of the puzzle. 'The Turk killed you?' I ask, and she nods. 'But Greygo said –'

'Greygo started coming here when he was nineteen,' she interrupts. 'I'd been with him since I died, as your ghosts are always with you, but that wasn't enough. He'd only known me as a child knows. He yearned to learn more about me. He did the rounds of mystics and seers, longing to talk with me and hear me tell him that I loved him. Etienne was the only one I could speak through. She's special, the way you are. You both have connections to the dead which most of the living lack.

'Greygo had harboured suspicions for a long time. Mikis was careful never to let his secret slip, but sometimes he'd drink too much, moan my name in his sleep and beg forgiveness. Greygo wondered what his father had to feel guilty about.

'It took him a long time to build up to the question.' The mystic's face lifts, filled with Andeanna's pride. '*Did my father kill you?* It almost destroyed him as he asked it. I meant to tell him the truth and turn him against the monster who took my life. But there was so much fear in his eyes, fear that I'd say yes . . .' Her face clouds over. 'As much as I hated Mikis, I loved Greygo and couldn't bear to destroy him. I made up a suicide story, mixing in enough truth to explain Mikis's guilt. It hurt Greygo, but not as much as the truth would have.'

'And killing his father — don't you think that hurt?'

'Of course,' she sighs, 'but I had no choice. I had to kill Mikis. I couldn't know peace until I did.'

'Tell me how you did it,' I whisper. 'Tell me how you assumed human form and tracked me down.'

Etienne shrugs, exactly the way Andeanna used to when I asked a question she couldn't answer. 'I don't know.'

'Bullshit,' I snarl.

'The truth,' she says gently. 'This is the real world, Ed, not one of your books. There aren't answers to every question. For years I was a bodiless entity, haunting the mansion. I glimpsed fellow spirits from time to time, but I had no way of communicating with them. I was alone, and lonely, but at least there was Greygo. I watched him grow up. I was there when he brought his first date home. I kept an eye on him and spoke to him, even though he couldn't hear me.

'One night I felt myself changing. *Forming*. I was terrified. I didn't know what was happening. I was feeling things again, smelling, hearing, seeing. After the initial shock, it was wonderful. But now that I was solid – visible – I had to leave before I was seen. So I grabbed some of Greygo's clothes and fled.

'I wandered the city, bones and flesh strengthening while I walked, and if you think that was painless, you couldn't be more wrong. I was cold and scared, in agony. Then, when the sun rose, I disintegrated like a vampire. Sunlight always undid me. That's why I never met you in the day, always late in the evening when the sun's power was fading.

'I re-formed the next night, in the place where I'd come

234

apart. Naked and defenceless, I hid, only coming out when the city was asleep. I returned to the mansion and raided my old room. I sold jewellery – my own, items that Mikis had held on to, so I didn't feel bad for stealing it – and set myself up in a small apartment, where I retired each night before dawn, so that I could rematerialize somewhere familiar and safe the next evening.

'Shortly after that, my thoughts turned to revenge.' Her expression hardens. I'm amazed by how much of Andeanna there is in the mystic's face. It's as if she's taken over Etienne Anders from the inside, making the medium's features her own, moulding them to mirror hers. 'I wasn't driven by hatred. Killing Mikis was just something I had to do. Without know-ing *how* I'd re-formed, I knew instinctively *why* — to make Mikis pay.'

'How did you know?' I ask.

'I just did. It's . . .' She grins sickly. 'It's a dead thing. You'd have to die and come back like I did to understand.'

'I'm not *that* eager to find out,' I deadpan, and for a few seconds we smile at one another the way we used to, like it's a big joke.

'Anyway,' she says, 'I knew I couldn't kill Mikis by myself. I didn't have murder in me. I had to find somebody else.'

'Which is where I came in,' I growl, and she nods glumly. 'Why me?'

'Pure misfortune,' she sighs.

'Don't lie. You tracked me down and tricked me into an affair. You used me like a puppet.'

'No.' She shakes her head vehemently. 'It wasn't like that. I know that's how it looks, but I swear on all that's sacred, on *Greygo*, I didn't set out to trap you.'

'I don't believe you,' I mutter.

A pained expression crosses her face. 'I was at that boat

party by chance,' she says. 'I crashed a lot of parties. Given who and what I was, I couldn't mingle with those who'd known me when I was alive. I'd fall in with groups on their way to a party, pretend to be human for a few hours, slip away like Cinderella before the break of day.

'The only thing I had on my mind that night was fun. Like so many other nights, that proved elusive, which is why I wound up on deck, to brood about the cruel twist of fate that had placed me there. Then I found myself next to *you*.' Although the mystic's eyes don't open, the lids fix on me as if the spirit of Andeanna sees through the thin layers of flesh. 'I knew instantly that you were a man of violence. I saw your ghosts and sensed their hatred of you. I knocked the glass overboard to start a conversation with you, and . . . you know the rest.'

'I thought I did. But why don't you tell me how it really was? It was never about love. You saw me as a tool from the start, didn't you, a way to kill Mikis?'

She sighs. 'My interest was wholly mercenary that first night. But that changed as we spent more time together. I forgot what I was. I fell in love with you. It was crazy, and it messed up everything, but I couldn't help myself. When I was with you, I *was* real, alive, desperate for love. That wasn't a sham, Ed. I couldn't have faked those emotions.'

'You're lying.'

'I'm not!' she cries. 'Listen to me. *Hear* me. I know you hate me, and you've every right to, but don't turn your ears against the truth. I love you, Ed, and if you ever loved me the way you claimed, you'd know in your heart that I'm not lying.'

The terrible thing is — I do.

'What about Axel Nelke?' I ask, anxious to steer talk away from love.

She stares through her closed eyelids, disappointed by my

236

reaction, then shrugs. 'Axel was my lover. Mikis killed him. What more do you want to know?'

'The guard I killed. You said he was Axel Nelke.'

'I lied. When you saw through my first disguise – Deleena Emerson – I knew I had to make my next seem as genuine as possible. I had to tell you as much of the truth as I dared. If I'd invented a name for my fictitious bodyguard, you might have sensed the lie. I felt safe using Axel's name. I knew I wouldn't blurt out the wrong surname by mistake, or tell you he had red hair then turn round later and say he was blond.'

'But the man I killed . . .'

'A guard. I don't know his name. There was one on duty most nights. They usually knocked off at ten or eleven if Mikis and Greygo weren't home.'

'You didn't set me up to kill him?'

'Of course not. I wanted Mikis's head, nobody else's. I don't know why the guard returned when he did.'

Is she telling the truth? I don't know. If I could see her eyes, I'd have a better idea. 'Greygo hadn't heard of a guard going missing,' I note.

She smiles bitterly. 'Greygo didn't want to know about Mikis's business, so he was kept in the dark whenever possible. If he'd been home around that time, he would have noticed that the guard had disappeared. Since he was absent, Mikis saw no reason to share the troubling news with him.'

'Why did you invite me there?' I ask, reluctant to let it drop. 'What was with the battered face? Was that faked?'

'Self-inflicted,' she mumbles. 'By then I'd fallen in love with you. On the boat, I thought I might be able to hire you to kill Mikis. But I now knew that whatever you'd done in the past, you weren't a killer any more. Yet you remained my best hope. I thought you could be encouraged to kill. So I used your love for me to turn you against Mikis.'

'Then you did manipulate me!' I shout.

'Yes and no,' she sniffs.

'You can't have it both ways, Andeanna.'

'But I did,' she protests. 'I loved you, Ed — that was real. But I had to kill Mikis. My first priority, my very reason for existing, was to make Mikis pay. So, yes, I used you. But I didn't fake love to win you over.

'My plan was for you to see that Mikis had hurt me, lose your temper and target him. Afterwards I'd have told you the truth. Or if, as I suspected, I faded away when Mikis was dead, I'd try to contact you via Etienne, as I'm doing now. Then the guard turned up, you killed him and a new plan formed. You revealed the truth about your past, you asked to eliminate Mikis, you dreamt up the assassin angle. I didn't want that – it was complicated, and it implicated you too deeply – but I was powerless to turn you from your path.'

'You could have told me the truth,' I contradict her.

A wan smile flickers across her lips. 'That I was a ghost? A shade of the night? Would you have believed me?'

'Probably not,' I mutter. 'But if you'd let me see your form unravel one night . . .'

'I considered that,' she says. 'But if I'd let you see me for what I truly was, I didn't think you'd be able to love me any more. I was worried I'd scare you off.'

'It takes a lot to scare me,' I grunt.

'Don't I know it,' she grins. Then she tickles my left wrist with one of her fingers. 'If it's any consolation, I did what I could to protect you. I lied to suit my purposes, but also to suit yours. I could have betrayed you to Bond, planted evidence to condemn you. But I wanted you to escape.'

'Very thoughtful of you,' I snap.

Silence descends. I mull over what Andeanna has told me. It's too insane to be true. I want to reject it out of hand. But what's the alternative? Andeanna Menderes was murdered twenty years ago — fact. I fell in love with a woman who shares her looks — fact. I have it on good authority that the woman's ghost has roamed the halls of her home since her death — fact. That woman is now speaking to me through a medium — fact.

Too many facts to ignore. When there's no sane answer, a man must accept the insane. As impossible as it is, as crazy as it sounds, the truth is undeniable. 'I fell in love with a ghost,' I groan.

'Yes.' Andeanna smiles sadly. 'And a ghost fell in love with you.'

Incredibly, my mood is lifting. The truth has been revealed. It's an awful, twisted truth, but now I can begin to deal with it. It won't be easy, but I don't have to chase around wildly any longer, pursuing false threads, driving myself mental in search of an answer.

'It's asking a lot,' Andeanna murmurs, 'but do you think you can forgive me?'

'I don't know,' I reply. 'This has thrown my world out of whack. I don't know what I feel for you, or what I'll feel a week from now, a month, a year. If I said I could, I'd be lying.'

'That's fair,' she nods.

'I was always fair with you,' I note pointedly.

'And I wasn't with you,' she agrees.

'So.' I settle back, studying the face of the channelling mystic. 'Where do we go from here?'

'Our separate ways,' she answers promptly.

I feel a strange pang of regret. Even after all she put me through, I still love her, and the thought of parting for ever fills me with dread. 'Can't we . . . isn't there some way we can . . . ?'

'No,' she says softly. 'I have to move on. Mikis's death released me. I'm being called. There's another world or dimension where I'm supposed to be. I have to go. I *want* to go. I think I'll enjoy it.'

I feel something running down my cheeks. At first I think spiders have dropped from the ceiling. But as I blink, I realize they're only tears.

'Can't you come back?' I weep, managing a weak smile to show I know how dumb my request is. 'On a weekend pass, perhaps?'

'I doubt they have those where I'm going,' Andeanna giggles. 'But if they do, I'll apply for one.'

I wipe my right sleeve across my cheeks, careful not to break contact with the medium, wishing the tears had held off for a while, so that I could focus on Andeanna's face, clearer than ever in the features of Etienne Anders.

Andeanna puts her lips to my cheek and removes a tear with the tip of her tongue. I moan, and she draws back from me, her smile fading. 'I have to go now. Etienne can't maintain this link indefinitely.'

'Just a few more . . .' I begin, but she shakes her head slowly.

'Before I leave,' she says, 'can I make a final request?'

'Sure,' I reply, fresh tears falling.

'One last kiss, Ed?'

'I could never refuse a lady,' I laugh brokenly.

'But promise you won't tell Etienne.' She smirks. 'I don't want her thinking we took advantage of her body.'

'I'll never tell anyone about tonight,' I vow.

'Not even Joe?'

'I'll fill him in on the essentials. No more. He deserves to know the truth – he guessed it before I did – but I won't discuss it in depth with him. I couldn't.'

'I'll go with the kiss, Ed,' she says, leaning forward. 'No prolonged goodbyes. One last kiss and – puff – I'm fairy dust.'

'I love you, Andeanna,' I cry.

'I love you too,' she whispers, then thrusts her lips against mine, devouring them with a hunger born of impending finality. I clutch her to me, holding her as close as I can, our fingers linked, tears splashing down my face, wishing I could vanish into her lips and make her journey with her, praying that one day I can follow and taste her sweet flesh again.

Then it's over. I feel it before we break, the way she goes limp, the fluttering of her eyelashes against my cheek, the diminishing action of her lips. Slowly I let her go, and she sinks back in her chair, Andeanna no more, just Etienne Anders, medium, channeller, bridge between worlds.

'Goodbye,' I whisper. And maybe it's an echo, or my imagination, or wishful thinking, but it seems to me that the air shimmers and the faintest voice carries to me on the lightest of breezes.

'*Goodbye, Ed.*'

Then she's gone. It's over. And although I feel wretched, I feel wonderful too, because I've been touched by the miraculous and I know that no matter how lonely I get, I'll never be truly alone again. Our loved ones don't leave us. They just move out of sight for a while, and wait . . . in the shades.

PART FIVE

NINETEEN

I'm ready to transfer all of my savings across to Etienne Anders, but she only laughs when I mention a fee and says the first time is free. I protest vehemently, but she's adamant. She says the joy in my expression is payment enough and suggests I make a charitable donation if I feel strongly about it.

'It went well, didn't it?' she notes as I dry my face with a fistful of tissues. 'I could tell you were miserable. Your pain was dragging behind you like an anchor. Now I see plain sails blowing in a soft wind.'

'A nice turn of phrase,' I compliment her.

'Guff like that is my forte, love,' she grins. 'But it did help, didn't it? You got through to her?'

'Yes.' I lower the damp tissues and beam.

'She must have been very special, judging by the effect she has on the men in her life. Greygo bawled like a baby the first time he made contact.'

'I wouldn't say I was *bawling*, exactly,' I grunt.

'Of course you wouldn't,' she laughs. 'Men like to act tough. But a man never truly fools a woman, not if he lives to be a hundred.'

She invites me to stay for a cup of tea, but I'd rather be alone. I want to replay my conversation with Andeanna, commit every last word and nuance to memory. Etienne escorts me to the front door and tells me to come again any time. I know I won't be returning, but I thank her and promise to deal with her exclusively in future if I have need of a medium.

Then I depart, heading out into the night and the rest of my life.

I drive back slowly to the hotel through the misting London rain. I think I'll leave this city soon. It holds too many memories. I'll visit again one day, check out the restaurants and pubs that Andeanna and I frequented, take a boat ride down the Thames and reminisce about the wine glass that started it all, but for the moment I want to get far away and unwind. Maybe somewhere tropical, where I can relax on a beach, go for long swims and dream of Andeanna. *Spirit of the Fire* will have to wait. I'll call Jonathan in the morning and tell him to cancel the contract. I might trickle back to it a year or two from now, or to some other story, or maybe I won't. Maybe I'm done writing. Why chase wonders in print when you've experienced them first-hand in real life?

I smile in my rear-view mirror at the glowering ghosts. I hold nothing against them. I feel sorry for the seven shades, seeing them for what they truly are, trapped, tormented souls. Now that I know they're real, I can look for some way to release them, to set them free from their earthly chains, so they can follow Andeanna's spirit into whatever lies beyond. My priority to this point has been proving my sanity. Now that I no longer doubt the stability of my mind, I can focus on helping those I've unwittingly tied to this physical realm.

The cheerful hotel doorman, Fred Lloyd, is sheltering from the rain inside the foyer. I wave to him as I drive past, but he doesn't see me. I must ask if he knows any good beaches. I'm sure he'd be able to make some interesting suggestions.

The underground car park is quiet. Strong yellow lights

press back the gloomy shadows, and the smell of gasoline is subtler than usual, which means the floors have been washed recently. I pull into an empty spot and slide out of my car. A sky-blue BMW slots into a space a little further up and a tall man gets out. He sees me approaching and nods politely. 'Evening.'

'Good evening,' I reply, only barely glancing at him as I pass, mind dancing, marvelling at what the night has brought.

When the man steps up behind me and trips me, I think it's an accident. I get ready to wave away his apology with a laugh. Then he shoves me to the ground and hurls himself on top of me.

My first thought — he's a mugger. Then — no, he's driving a BMW. I don't waste any more time considering it. He has me pinned, but not securely. My right hand is free. Making a blade of my fingers, I drive them back over my shoulder and connect with his cheekbone. My nails cut into his flesh and slice up towards his eye. He jerks back a fraction. I throw him off and elbow him aside.

While my assailant flounders, I leap to my feet and turn to kick him if he draws a gun or a knife. But he's just cowering, patting the scratch on his cheek, wincing like a child.

'Who are you?' I snap, nudging his lower legs to attract his attention.

'Fuck off!' he shouts, kicking back.

'Tell me who you are or I'll –'

'That's enough, Mr Sieveking,' a voice says behind me.

I don't turn and gawp. I know better than that. Instead I swivel to my right, meaning to dive behind the nearest car for cover. A bullet spits up the floor in front of me.

'I won't miss with the next. Hands behind your head, Mr Sieveking, then drop to your knees.' Grimacing with disgust, I do as he orders. The decoy gets to his feet and steps forward, meaning to let me have a fist or knee in the face. 'There's no call for that, Officer Langbein.'

'You said my name!' the officer yaps.

'It doesn't matter. He won't be telling anyone.'

Langbein glares at me, fingers flexing by his sides, but stays where he is.

'Fetch the chloroform, Alan,' the man with the gun says, and Langbein shuffles off to the BMW. 'We're going to put you to sleep for a while, Mr Sieveking. I'd wish you pleasant dreams, but we both know it's only nightmares for you from here on in.'

'Who the fuck are you?' I ask, expecting no reply.

'You'll see soon enough,' he purrs.

Langbein returns with a small bottle, which he opens and tips into a cloth. A dark stain spreads from the centre.

'I'm sure you'll hold your breath and feign unconsciousness,' the man behind me says, 'but I won't lower my guard until I'm sure you're out.'

'If money's an issue . . .'

'It isn't.'

'Care to tell me what is?'

'Soon, Mr Sieveking, soon.'

Langbein jams the handkerchief over my mouth and nose and holds it in place, clasping the back of my head with his other hand to stop me pulling away.

As the fumes set my senses spinning, the man with the gun steps in front of me, revealing his face. It's a calculated move, designed to make me gasp and draw in the noxious fumes more quickly. The last thing I hear before blacking out is my captor murmuring, 'Night-night, *Severs*.' And the last thing I see through watery tears is the distorted face of Sebastian Dash as he bends over me and laughs.

Then it's just blackness.

Consciousness returns slowly. At first I think I'm safe in bed. I wonder why it's so dark, why the bed is rocking and what the strange growling noise is. As my brain clicks into place, I recall the grinning face of Sebastian Dash, and moments later everything is clear.

I'm gagged and my hands are tied behind my back. I try rotating my fingers, in search of the slightest slack, but Dash knows his knots as well as I do. We learnt from the same teachers. I'll go on testing the ropes – nothing ventured, nothing gained – but Dash isn't the sort who lets a fish wriggle free once it's hooked.

I'm in the locked trunk of a moving car. I've no idea how much time has passed since I was knocked out. I don't even begin to guess where he's taking me.

As well as the rope around my hands, another binds my ankles. They're linked by a third length, further limiting my movements. There's also a long, thin noose around my neck, connected to the other ropes. It tightens when I struggle. I'm certain Dash has rigged it so it won't choke me to death – he wants me alive until he's had time to play with me – but it could cut off my oxygen supply long enough to force another blackout.

While I seek a weakness in the ropes, I probe the puzzle of how I've fallen prey to Sebastian Dash. He must not have fled when the Turk was killed. He hung around, despite the danger, to search for the person who framed him. He couldn't do that personally while Bond Gardiner and his crew were hunting him. So he must have had help — the decoy, Alan Langbein. Dash probably recruited him to do the legwork, ask questions, stake out pubs. Langbein must have heard about the journalist who was writing a book, checked up on me, maybe followed me and took photos.

I've only myself to blame for this. I should have been more careful. I never looked for a tail. I thought Dash was out of the equation. I fucked up, plain and simple, and now I'm going to pay with my life.

I go on working at the knots and plotting ways out of this mess — I'll head-butt him in the stomach when he opens the trunk, spit in his eye, maybe latch on to his nose and bite. But I know it's hopeless. Hollywood heroes blast their way out of tight spots like this week in, week out, but that's not how it works in reality. When your arms and legs are tied, and there's a rope around your throat, and you're languishing in the trunk of a killer's car, you're finished, roll credits.

My ghosts know it's the end of me. They're crouched close around. I can sense them, even though I can't see clearly, crowing with laughter, knowing their time of release is far closer than I believed it was. They don't need my help to escape the pull of this world. A bullet through my brain, courtesy of Sebastian Dash, and all their worries are behind them. Their ordeal is almost over. Mine, on the other hand, is just beginning. Where do the souls of the guilty go when they cast off their mortal coil? Nowhere good, I'm guessing.

The car slows and takes a left. By the bumping that follows, I figure we've left the main road. Heading somewhere nice and quiet.

Finally the car draws to a stop and I hear the driver getting out. No further sounds, meaning one of them is either still in the car or hasn't made the journey. A key is inserted into the lock of the trunk and it swings open. My captor nimbly steps back out of the way, in case I've managed to work myself free of the ropes.

Although it's brighter outside than in the trunk, it's a dark night and it takes my eyes a few moments to adjust and focus on Sebastian Dash, gun in hand. I glare at him, filled with loathing. He chuckles at my foul expression, makes sure I'm still tied tight, then leans forward to remove my gag. 'It's been a long time, Brad.' I don't reply. 'You've put on a bit of weight, but it suits you.' Silence. He sighs theatrically. 'Are you sour because of Antonia?'

'Fuck you,' I snarl.

'Ah. He talks.' Dash laughs bitingly, then squats and locks gazes. 'You made the biggest mistake of your life involving me in this shit,' he says coldly. 'Did you think I wouldn't come looking for the son of a bitch who set me up?' He waits for me to answer. I let him go on waiting. 'What drove you to this madness, Brad? You've hated me a long time, but you weren't dumb enough to come after me when you could have maybe taken me, when you were sharp and in shape, so I assumed you never would. I thought our quarrel was behind us.'

'It's not a quarrel,' I retort.

'No?' His smile returns. 'What, then? A vendetta?' I don't answer. 'No matter. We'll find out soon enough. It will all come out in the wash.' Standing, he raises a cell phone – *my* phone – and dials one-handed. When he connects, he says, 'Are you ready?' A pause. 'Alone?' Another pause. 'If you pull anything stupid, the deal's off and you'll never know.' A long pause, then he grunts, hits disconnect and dials a new number. 'He's there. He says he's alone and unarmed. Remember what I told you. If it feels wrong . . .' Dash listens, grunts again, hangs up.

'What's going down?' I ask.

'You are,' he smirks. Then he slams shut the roof of the trunk and plunges me back into darkness.

When the roof lifts again, Alan Langbein is standing beside Sebastian Dash. The two men haul me out of the trunk, Dash wisely taking my head in case I lash out with my bound feet. They drop me to the floor. We're in an oak-surrounded glade.

As I roll on to my back, I spot a third figure behind the others — Bond Gardiner.

'This is the man you claim killed Mikis?' Gardiner rumbles.

'Ed Sieveking, the one and only,' Dash agrees.

'He told me his name was Edgar Sanders, that he was writing a book.'

Dash laughs. 'That might not have been total bullshit. This is the *famous* Ed Sieveking. Surely you've read about his critically acclaimed work in the *Times* or the *Guardian*? Modern classics like *Nights of Fear* and *Winter's Shades*.'

'*Summer's Shades*,' I correct him automatically.

'A regular on the best-seller lists,' Dash presses on. 'The most successful horror writer of his generation.'

Gardiner grunts. 'I'm not much of a reader.'

'I've never heard of him either,' Langbein frowns. 'And I read a lot of horror. Are you sure he's a best-seller?'

Dash rolls his eyes. 'I was taking the piss, Alan. This poor fucker couldn't even give away copies of his lame potboilers, could you, Brad?'

'Fuck you,' I grunt.

'With a limited vocabulary like that, one hardly need wonder why,' Dash grins, then addresses Gardiner again. 'I didn't expect you to recognize his pen name. I bet you know this one, though — Elland Severin.'

Gardiner's eyes widen. 'The assassin?'

'Bingo.'

'But he retired years ago.'

'And swapped his gun for a typewriter — or is it a computer, Brad?'

'A computer,' I sniff.

'Why do you keep calling him Brad?' Gardiner asks.

'That was his original name, Brad Severs, the name he went by in the army. We go back, Brad and me. Recruits together.

He knew me as Simon Dale. Didn't have much time for me or my buddy, Parson McNally. A couple of his friends wound us up. There was a fight. Parson and one of Brad's compadres didn't walk away from it. I went to prison, Brad went free. A few years later we were hired by Carter Phell, though neither of us knew about the other. A woman brought us together. The beautiful Belinda Darnier — now the savagely scarred Antonia Smith.

'I paid Brad back for the mess he made of my life,' Dash continues. 'But I was merciful. I could have killed him, but I didn't. I thought that was the end of our feud. Obviously he had other ideas.'

'How's *Belinda* these days?' I sneer.

'Wealthy. Not as pretty as she used to be, though plastic surgery took care of the worst of the damage. She'll flip for joy when I tell her about this. She always wanted me to finish you off. She would have hired somebody else, except I told her I didn't think –'

Bond Gardiner coughs, cutting Dash short. 'I didn't come here to listen to you settle old scores. I don't know what the deal is between you two, and to be honest, I don't give a fuck. All I want to know is who killed Mikis and why.'

'Brad did!' Dash booms.

'Is that true?' Gardiner asks me.

'Yes,' I sigh.

Gardiner's shoulders sag. 'Why?'

'Too long a story. Can't you just accept my confession and leave it at that?'

'No!' he barks, then eyes Dash. 'Do you know why he did it?'

Dash shakes his head. 'I haven't a clue.'

'Tell them what they want to know,' Langbein growls, kicking my left thigh.

'Might as well, Brad,' Dash says. 'We aren't leaving till you do. I'm no sadist, but you know I can get nasty when I must, and hot-headed Alan here was born to dominate, weren't you, Alan?'

'Too fucking true,' Langbein laughs. He's acting tough, trying not to appear out of his depth, but I can tell he's new to this. I catch a quick look between Dash and Gardiner. I know what it means and take slight comfort in the knowledge that I won't be the only one joining the ranks of the dead today.

I see no point in playing out the hand to the last. I'd like to think I wouldn't crack under duress, but everybody does. There's only so much pain anyone can withstand before the tongue starts working by itself. I'd rather go out with my dignity intact than wind up whimpering beneath the feet and fists of Alan Langbein. Besides, this way I can hold back the details I'd rather not reveal, such as Joe's involvement. 'It started on a boat,' I begin, and take it from there.

It's a long, convoluted story, even condensed, and the sun is rising by the time I finish. I tell them about my initial meeting with Andeanna, the name she gave, falling in love, learning her true identity, killing the guard, getting rid of the body, plotting to kill the Turk, finding the newspaper while I was waiting for my train, meeting with Andrew Moore, Gardiner, Greygo and the psychic. They listen in silence, bar a few hissed curses from Dash when I describe how I set him up.

There's a long pause when I finish. I've regaled them with a story that each of the trio will carry to his grave. When they've forgotten my name, and maybe even their own, they'll remember Andeanna's and recall this tale of supernatural love, murder and deceit.

Dash finally breaks the silence. 'The crazy bastard's telling the truth.'

'No,' Gardiner says. 'He *thinks* he is, but he isn't. He can't be.'

Dash chuckles. 'You don't believe in ghosts?'

'No.'

'How about you, Alan?'

Langbein shakes his head. 'This is too fucked to be true. He's mad as a hatter. We'll be doing him a favour when we kill him.'

Dash has been leaning against the car. Now he steps away from it and turns slowly, gazing around at the dawn shadows. 'Are your ghosts here with us?'

I glance at the shades of those I've killed, standing in a line in front of me, sketched against the morning landscape, faces alight with expectation, but otherwise calm now that the end has come, waiting patiently, feeling no need to mock me in my final moments. 'Yes.'

'Where are they?'

I nod as much as I can. 'Over there.'

Dash squints. For long seconds he says nothing. Finally, disappointed, 'Nope. Can't see them.'

'Nobody can. Only me.'

'Maybe they're just in your head.'

'Maybe,' I smile, knowing that that isn't so.

He faces me, his expression oddly compassionate. 'I sometimes dream of the people I've killed, and those are never easy nights. To face them every day when you're awake . . .' He shudders, then glances at Gardiner. 'Heard enough? I don't want to stick around any longer than we have to.'

Gardiner looks uncertain. My story has shaken him. He regards me warily, as if I'm contagious. 'This isn't right,' he mutters.

'You don't believe him?' Dash asks.

'He's told us all he can, but there's more to it. Someone set him up, just as *he* set *you* up. It couldn't have been a ghost.'

'Whatever,' Dash shrugs. 'I've cleared my name and exposed

the lunatic who framed me. If you want to chase it further, that's your business.'

'Let's do it!' Langbein hoots. 'Let's spill this fucker's guts!'

Dash and Gardiner share an amused smile. How can Langbein not see what's coming? I almost feel like warning him. If he wasn't such a dick, maybe I would. But anyone who'll kick a man when he's down doesn't deserve fair warning.

'What do you say?' Dash asks Gardiner. 'Are we done or not?'

Gardiner nods reluctantly. 'I guess we are.'

'We're squared? You'll spread the word that I didn't kill Menderes?'

'Yeah.'

'Sweet.' Dash grins, raises his gun and fires twice.

Two bullets shatter Alan Langbein's breastbone and make jagged red-white shards of his chest. He slams against the car, arms flying out Christ-like. Blood coughs from his mouth, spews over the ground in front of him, then he sinks to the floor, limp, broken, dead.

'Alas, poor Alan. I knew him, Horatio,' Dash deadpans.

'Show a bit of respect for the dead,' Gardiner scowls.

'You agreed to it,' Dash defends himself. 'I wouldn't have cared if he'd lived – he couldn't touch me – but you'd have been a marked man. It was only a matter of time before he came looking for a pay-off. Men like Langbein get greedy.'

'I know,' Gardiner says, 'but I don't like it. Killing a cop's a messy business.'

'Not this way,' Dash disagrees. 'It'll look like they shot each other. We don't have to worry about dumping the bodies or having them traced back to us. It's the perfect solution.'

'You don't think they'll tie Langbein or Sieveking to Mikis?'

'Why should they? Alan wasn't working on the Menderes case, and Ed is just a writer. They'll wonder what it was about, turn over a lot of stones in an attempt to find out, but if we keep our mouths shut, who's to know but you and me?'

'Andeanna,' I answer quietly.

The two men stare at me, Dash contemptuously, Gardiner uneasily.

'All right,' Dash smirks. 'Apart from the ghost.'

'Whoever set him up,' Gardiner says. 'I can't slip away like you. I have to stay and deal with the fallout.'

Dash shrugs. 'We've all got our crosses to bear. I doubt it will go any further than this, but it's your problem if it does. All I want to know is, are we done with Brad? Is it time to kiss the sweet prince good night?'

Gardiner thinks about it. 'Yes,' he says, and starts towards Langbein's cooling body.

'What are you doing?' Dash asks, the slightest hint of tension in his voice.

'Getting Langbein's gun,' Gardiner says without slowing. 'We've got to make it look like they shot each other, right?'

'I can fetch it,' Dash says quickly, taking a defensive step to his left.

Gardiner looks over his shoulder, notes Dash's stance and turns, hands spread flat by his sides. 'This is very simple,' he growls, 'so I'll only say it once. This sack of shit killed Mikis Menderes. Mikis was like my brother. I swore revenge and I'm gonna make good on that vow. If you have an issue with that, our relationship is about to take a very serious turn for the worse.'

I see Dash weighing up his options, deciding whether or not he can trust Bond Gardiner with a gun. For a moment it looks like he's going to object, and my heart leaps with the slightest tinge of hope — if these two start taking potshots at one another, I might walk away from this yet. Then Dash smiles. 'Be my guest,' he says magnanimously, and there goes my future.

Gardiner makes his way to the sprawled body of Alan Langbein, pulls on a pair of thin plastic gloves, uses a nearby twig to swish back the corpse's jacket and prizes the dead officer's gun from its holster. Dash watches warily.

Gardiner slips up behind me. I listen with resigned dread as he approaches, marking every step. I don't fear death, but now that it's upon me, I can't say that I welcome it either. The thought of entering the vast abyss fills me with fear. I know that Andeanna is waiting for me, but maybe I'll have to pay for my crimes. Perhaps my ghosts will attack my spirit, keep us separate, subject me to an eternity of torment.

Gardiner towers above me. Turning my head, ignoring the rope about my throat, I watch as he cocks the pistol, then lays the tip of the barrel to my temple. I want to shut my eyes and wait for the end in darkness, but I can't. My eyelids won't work. I'm forced to bear witness to my own death.

'Hey!' Dash snaps. I flinch, anticipating gunfire, but Gardiner's finger relaxes and he looks questioningly at Dash. 'You can't do it like that.'

'Why not?'

'It's supposed to look like they killed each other,' Dash says, exasperated, hurrying over. 'How's he meant to have shot Alan with a bullet plugged through his skull at point-blank range?'

Gardiner scowls. 'Sorry. I wasn't thinking.'

'No,' Dash agrees. 'You weren't.'

He glares at me, then tucks his gun away and bends. 'Grab his feet,' he tells Gardiner. 'We don't want to leave tracks.'

They haul me away from Langbein and stand me up. I immediately drop to the floor. I'm not going to make it easy for the bastards.

'Get up,' Dash snarls.

'Fuck you.'

'Hold him up for me,' Gardiner says to Dash.

'The fuck I will,' Dash snorts.

Gardiner smiles. 'Still don't trust me?'

'It's not that. Bullets can ricochet. The best marksman can miss. If you think I'm going to stand next to him while you take aim, you've got a fucking screw loose.'

'OK.' Gardiner kneels beside me. 'Sieveking.'

'Gardiner,' I reply politely, grinning in spite of everything.

'You made a good impression on me in the pub. I confided in you because I thought you were a man of honour. Now you've made a fool of me. I don't like that. I want to take you back to my manor and let the boys play with you, put you through the kind of hell you don't even want to imagine. But Dash is right — killing you here, making it look like Langbein's work, is the simplest solution for all concerned, yourself included.'

'You want me to stand and take it like a man?' I sneer.

'If you don't, I'll pump a bullet through each of your knees, bundle you into the trunk and let you suffer the ride back to London, where the real pain will begin.'

I consider my options. A few more hours of life in exchange for a shitload of suffering. Not an attractive proposition. Of course, as long as I'm alive, there's a chance I might escape. Gardiner could crash, or be pulled over by the police. The odds would be against me, but . . .

No. One look at Gardiner's face and I know he doesn't make mistakes. All I'd have to look forward to would be the shattered knees and torture. It isn't worth it. My number's up. 'Get on with it,' I growl, and let them drag me to my feet.

While Gardiner retreats, measuring his paces as if fighting a duel, Dash studies me. 'This isn't what I wanted, Brad. You forced my hand. I couldn't let you —'

'Go fuck yourself,' I cut in brusquely.

Dash frowns. 'Anyone ever mention that chip on your shoulder?'

'I'm ready,' Gardiner says. He's standing sideways to us, right arm levelled in front of him, left arm bent slightly behind his back.

'So long,' Dash says, patting my cheek. 'It was fun while it lasted. I'll give your love to Antonia. Give mine to the ghosts.'

He steps away. He hasn't taken more than two strides when Bond Gardiner fires. My eyes snap shut and my stomach goes cold. I wait for the pain, but there isn't any. I don't dare hope he's missed, so I assume my nerve endings are slow to react. But then someone groans and it isn't me.

Opening my eyes, I spot Sebastian Dash lying on the ground in a pool of blood, his stomach ripped open, gazing crookedly at the mess bulging out of the shredded gap with a look of agonized confusion. 'What the fuck?' he gasps, sticking a couple of fingers into the cavity to make sure it's real.

Gardiner advances, never lowering his arm, ready to fire again if Dash goes for his gun. I stand rooted, as stunned as Dash. The assassin looks up. His eyes are wide, appealing for answers. 'You shot me. I think I'm –'

A torrent of blood gushes up his throat and out of his mouth. Gardiner steps back quickly to avoid getting his shoes splashed. Dash seems to snap back to life at that, and scrabbles for his gun. He prizes it free of its holster, but his fingers are slow, and wet with blood. He doesn't stand a chance.

Gardiner puts two more bullets through Dash's ribcage. The gun drops limply from the assassin's hand and he sinks into the grass, face white, body shuddering. He's suffering a more painful death than Langbein. I can't say I'm sorry, though I don't exactly rejoice, knowing that a similar fate is surely in store for me.

Dash tries to staunch the flow of blood, but even in his distressed state he knows it's a hopeless task. Giving up, he lets his head flop back and stares at the sky. An almost serene look passes over his face as he whispers, 'Antonia.'

Then he's dead, and it's my turn.

Bond Gardiner casts a cold eye over me.

'Why?' I ask quietly.

The gangster's head cocks to the left. 'I had to.'

'*Why?*'

He wipes the gun clean, strides across the glade and sticks it in Langbein's hand, then he pats down the officer and finds a Swiss army knife. He extends the longest blade and steps up behind me. I tense, expecting him to slit my throat, but instead he sets to work on the ropes. Within seconds I'm free, my extremities tingling as blood flows back into them.

'If I hadn't killed Dash,' Gardiner says, snapping the knife shut and pocketing it, 'I'd have had to kill you. And I didn't want to do that.'

I limp forward, rubbing my hands together, half afraid I'm dreaming. 'You're going to spare me?'

'Not *going to*,' he corrects me. 'I *have* spared you. You're free. Get the fuck out of here before I change my mind.'

In a daze I start away, thinking he'll grab Dash's gun and shoot me in the back. When I reach the edge of the clearing and he still hasn't fired, I stop and slowly, against my better instincts, turn. My ghosts are howling silently, spitefully. If they could give voice to their fury, they'd probably be screaming, 'Not fair!' I ignore them and study Bond Gardiner. He's standing over Dash's body, staring down with an unreadable expression.

I return and take up a position to Gardiner's left. He doesn't notice me at first. When he does, his features darken. 'I told you to go.'

'I can't, not until you tell me what's going on.'

He sighs, then nods sombrely. He turns away from Sebastian

Dash and moves to the far side of the car, where he doesn't have to look at the corpses. I follow, lean against the hood of the engine next to him, and wait while he produces a book of matches and starts playing with it, the way he did in the pub. 'You really believe it was Andeanna's ghost you fell in love with?' he asks.

'I know that it was.'

'You accepted everything she told you through the mystic?'

'Yes.'

'You're a fool,' he grunts. 'When you killed that bodyguard, *Andeanna* told you he was Axel Nelke?'

'Yes.'

'Then, at the seance, she said through the medium that Nelke was her lover from long ago and she didn't actually know the name of the bodyguard?' When I nod, Gardiner snorts. 'After you butchered the guy in the mansion, did you frisk him for ID, or did you simply leave his cards in his wallet and bury them at sea with him?'

'Of course not. I went through his pockets and took . . .'

I stop, horrified. I'd forgotten about the cards, but I can visualize them now that Gardiner has reminded me. Credit cards, a driver's licence, a membership card for Blockbuster. I only flicked through them, but I got a good look at the name, the same on every card. *Axel Nelke.*

Gardiner chuckles as the penny – one of the pennies – drops. 'The guard you killed *was* Axel Nelke. He was one of my boys.'

'But Andeanna . . . her lover . . . she said . . .'

'She lied.'

'No. There must have been another Axel Nelke, this guy's father or uncle or –'

'Don't insult yourself,' Gardiner snaps. 'She played you. She knew who he was. My guess is she lured him there on purpose.

262

I think he was a guinea pig. She wanted to see if you still had a killer's touch.'

'You're lying. You want to torment me. You're saying this to . . .'

'What?' Gardiner jeers.

'. . . confuse me,' I finish lamely.

'Why should I?' he retorts.

'To throw me off the scent. To stop me . . .' I run out of ideas.

'If I wanted to stop you, I'd have killed you. Even a lovesick lunatic like you must be able to see that. Right now, I'm the one person in the world you can trust, because I in no way stand to benefit from lying to you.'

He's telling the truth. It would be easier if he wasn't, if this was part of some scam to sidetrack me, but it would have been far more straightforward for him to shoot me than set me free and lie to me. The guard was Axel Nelke. Andeanna lied about him.

What else wasn't true?

'Did the Turk kill her?' I croak. Gardiner doesn't answer. He seems focused on the matches. 'Did he!' I shout.

'Do you have an address for Etienne Anders?' he asks.

'Yes,' I reply, befuddled.

'I want it.'

'What does she have to do with –'

'You were set up!' he barks. 'There was no ghost. I doubt if Anders was behind the scam, but she's part of it. If I find her, I might be able to wring the truth out of the bitch.'

'But Anders was only a channeller. Andeanna spoke through her.'

Gardiner slaps me. When I stare at him numbly, he slaps me again, then grabs my neck and pulls my face in close to his. 'Can't you get it straight, you fucking moron? There. Was. No.

263

Ghost. It was a con job. Someone dressed up as Andeanna and tricked you into killing Mikis, then hired a clever psychic to make you believe she was a spirit.'

'No,' I moan, pulling away. The matches drop. He bends to pick them up. I use the few seconds to think of something to prove I'm not a patsy. 'Greygo,' I gasp. 'He saw the ghost too. He'd been to see Anders as well.'

Gardiner's expression softens. 'Poor Greygo. He was so anxious to learn about her, always asking questions, wanting to know. He must have been an easy mark.'

'What do you mean?'

Gardiner plucks loose a match, lights it, watches the flame flicker down, then blows it out. 'Greygo has an active imagination,' he says through the thin stream of smoke. 'Mikis used to say he was away with the fairies. Whoever manipulated you got to Greygo beforehand. I don't know how they did it, but if they fooled someone like you, it can't have been that hard to mesmerize a mixed-up kid.'

'No. You're wrong.'

'Think about it, Brad. Greygo went –'

'*Ed*,' I interrupt. 'My name's Ed.'

'Whatever. Greygo went to lots of mediums. He missed his mother, and nothing we told him about her was enough. He always wanted more. Of all those psychics, only one could put him in touch with his mother? Only one could succeed where the others failed?'

'Logic doesn't work with ghosts. Sometimes shades can only speak through –'

'Can it,' he snaps. 'You were conned. So was Greygo. If you can't see that, you're dumber than I thought, and maybe I *should* finish you off and leave you here with those two.' He jerks an angry thumb at the corpses behind us.

'Why haven't you killed me?' I ask, curious in spite of everything.

'Too complicated. The police won't believe that Langbein and Dash wiped each other out, but they'll accept it because they'll be glad to be rid of the pair. But if I throw in a third body, they won't be able to explain it away, so they'll have to investigate for real.'

I think about that, then shake my head. 'I don't buy it. You could have dumped me in the trunk and killed me elsewhere.'

'*Now* you tell me,' he chuckles, pretending to groan, hoping I'll drop it.

'Why spare me?' I press. 'Why tell me about Nelke? I've admitted to killing the Turk. Why aren't you carving your revenge out of my flesh?'

'Because you weren't to blame. You were a tool in some cunning fucker's hand. When I find him, I'll do plenty of carving, but I don't shoot messenger boys.'

It's a plausible excuse. Another time I might believe him. But Gardiner has been visibly shaken, and I can see through him as clearly as I can see Sebastian Dash's bloody remains through the windows of the car.

'The truth, Bond,' I say softly. 'Let's not bother with lies any more. There's no place for them here. Tell me why you spared me.'

Gardiner stares at the matches, runs a finger over them, speaks without looking up. 'Because I took pity on you.'

I almost laugh. It's his most pathetic lie yet. I open my mouth to berate him, then close it slowly, not having said a word. Because it *isn't* a lie.

'Why, for God's sake?' I mutter.

'Not for God's sake,' he says. 'For Andeanna's.' He lifts his head, and his eyes are hard but soft at the same time. 'You shocked me in the pub when you turned up with talk of

Andeanna having a lover. Since you knew so much, I fed you a half-true story, hoping that would satisfy you. If I'd known who you really were . . .' He steels himself and says, 'Andeanna had a lover, but Mikis never knew.'

My eyes narrow. As bewildered as I am, I understand what Gardiner is saying. 'It was *you*,' I whisper.

He nods with ferocious sharpness. 'That's why you're alive. Because I see the love I felt for her mirrored in your eyes. And although it wasn't the real Andeanna you fell in love with, you thought it was and you were prepared to sacrifice everything for her. I respect that. You killed Mikis and Axel, so I shouldn't, but I can't help myself.'

'Christ,' I groan. 'Mary fucking Mother of God.'

'Don't blaspheme,' he scolds me.

'It was all bullshit,' I mumble. 'The Turk didn't know about her affair.'

'No.'

'He didn't kill her.'

'No.'

'I thought . . . even when I was convinced that she wasn't a ghost, when I assumed I'd been set up . . . I thought only a vengeful lover or relative would go to such twisted lengths to kill a man.'

Gardiner grunts. 'I was closer to Mikis than anyone else on this shitball of a planet. Even if he'd murdered Andeanna, I couldn't have retaliated. I could have hated him, but I couldn't have killed him or allowed someone else to.'

'This is crazy. Why would she lie to me? What does a ghost stand to gain by lying?'

'For fuck's sake!' Gardiner roars. 'When will you get it through your thick fucking skull? She wasn't a ghost. You were conned.'

266

'No,' I disagree. 'You weren't there. You didn't hear the way Anders spoke, the way her face changed shape to become Andeanna's. It wasn't a charade. It was really her.'

'You never met the real Andeanna!' he howls. 'Don't you get it? The woman who seduced you was an impostor. You have no idea how Andeanna talked or how her lips lifted when she was happy or how her nose twitched when she was mad. You know nothing about her.'

'You're wrong,' I defy him. 'It *was* Andeanna. She knew too much not to be. She had access to the mansion. She was there when I killed Nelke and the Turk. She knew about the affair and the story you told me about her husband killing her.'

'Anders could have learnt most of that from Greygo,' he says.

'Did Greygo know about the affair?' I challenge him.

'Well, no, I don't think so, but –'

'*But* nothing. The ghost knew that Andeanna had been unfaithful. She didn't reveal her lover's real name, but that's because she wanted to protect you, like you'd protected her.'

'No,' he growls. 'She wasn't a ghost.'

'She was!' I yell, going face to face with him. He's a head taller and outweighs me by thirty pounds, but I don't care. I could take on the devil himself, the mood I'm in. 'Stop denying it. It doesn't make sense any other way. She was a ghost.'

'An impostor,' he mumbles, taking a step backwards.

'A ghost.'

'Impossible.'

'Why?' I follow him as he retreats. 'Why are you so set against the idea? Because you don't believe in ghosts?'

'It's not that.'

'Then what?' He doesn't answer. '*What?*'

Gardiner stops backpedalling and lets me run into him. 'It can't have been a ghost,' he says flatly, then puts his lips to my ear and hits me with a thunderbolt that sets me adrift once again on the seas of bewildered madness. 'It can't have been a ghost because Andeanna isn't dead.'

TWENTY

St Michael's Psychiatric Hospital lies close to Darlington, in the north-east of the country, not far from Joe's native Newcastle. I toy with the idea of inviting Joe along for the journey – he knows the area and could serve as a guide – but that would mean telling him the truth, and I don't want to do that, not until I've confirmed it.

Gardiner walked me from the glade when he was finished talking. He made a phone call, gave our position, then sat with me on a stone wall to wait. We said little. When the car arrived, the driver gazed curiously at me but didn't ask who I was. Gardiner told him to find a town with a train station, where he left me to make my own way north. 'Remember,' he said in parting, 'you don't tell anyone and you never come back. This is my riddle now. I'll let people think Dash killed Mikis, but I know the truth and I won't forget. If you show your face in London again, you're dead.'

It wasn't an idle threat, but I can't let the matter drop. If my investigation draws me back to the Big Smoke, I'll take my chances where Bond Gardiner's concerned.

I bought a ticket at the station, found a quiet carriage when the train pulled in and settled back to brood. That's where I am now, watching the countryside whip by, trying to make sense of what I was told. Gardiner promised to call ahead to the hospital and clear my visit, but even if he didn't, they won't be able to keep me out. Nothing will bar my way. I have to see. I have to *know*.

Gardiner released me after dropping his bombshell. He stepped aside, a look of shame contorting his features. By that shame, I knew he wasn't lying.

'She *isn't dead*?' I croaked when I was able to make more than a thin gasping cry. 'What the fuck is that supposed to mean?'

He didn't reply straight away. He was disgusted with himself for revealing the truth. He waved me away, and although I wanted to grab him by the throat and choke answers out of him, I said nothing while he took deep breaths and sought control. Finally he calmed down enough to continue, but he couldn't get through the story without mauling his book of matches until it was pulp in his hands.

'There should never have been anything between Andeanna and me,' he began. 'The attraction was there a long time, but we were loyal to Mikis and knew the dangers of betraying him. For years we resisted. We spent a lot of time alone – Mikis trusted me with her – but we never acted on our feelings. Until . . .

'She made the first move. We were watching TV one night. Without warning, she leant over and kissed me. I should have pulled away, but I just sat there, stunned. She took off her blouse and . . .' He blushed. 'We needn't relive *all* the details. We did what we shouldn't have, regretted it the next morning, swore never to do it again.'

'But you did,' I interjected quietly.

His blush deepened. 'Yeah. We planned our encounters carefully, usually when Mikis was out of the country and we had the house to ourselves. A few other times we met when

Andeanna was visiting her parents. We took no chances. I think we could have carried on indefinitely if . . .' He faltered to a stop.

'If the Turk hadn't found out?' I said, to get him going again.

He shook his head. 'Mikis never knew. You think I'd be alive if he'd rumbled us? Our friendship wouldn't have mattered. He'd have killed me.'

'So what happened?' I asked.

'Madness,' he said, and stirred uncomfortably.

I stir uncomfortably on the train as I recall this part of the conversation and think about my destination. I've only been to an institute for the clinically insane once before, researching for *Soul Vultures*. It was a depressing experience. On the back of that visit, I cut out the scenes that were going to be set in an asylum. I wish I could cut out the forthcoming scenes as easily.

'I only realized later that our affair was a by-product of Andeanna's breakdown,' Gardiner told me dully. 'She was strong, not afraid of anything, but Mikis slowly crushed her. He loved her, but he was callous. He was a man of violence, the same as you and me. He let the brutality of his work spill over into his private life. He mellowed in the latter years of their marriage and tried to make amends – that's why she was allowed to visit her parents – but it was too late. Later than any of us imagined.

'You know Mikis cheated on her. Andeanna knew too. She never said anything, but she knew.'

'What does that have to do with –' I began to ask.

'Her name was Christina Whiteoak, wife of Arnold. Know him?' I shook my head, bewildered. 'Arnold Whiteoak was a munitions baron, a total mercenary. He didn't care who he sold to. That's what did for him in the end — he spent so long playing one group off against the other that eventually . . .

'But this isn't about him. It's about his beautiful wife, Christina. She had an affair with Mikis. It was the only time he let his lust get in the way of business. Arnold Whiteoak was a shark, far more powerful than Mikis. If he'd found out, he would have washed the streets with their blood, and Mikis knew it. But he couldn't stop.

'Mikis and Andeanna were due to spend Christmas and New Year in Scotland. They'd been a couple of times before. Mikis loved the kilts, the bagpipes and the rivers of whisky. He used to say he was a Celt at heart. That year he made an excuse to return from the festivities early. Stayed for Christmas dinner, then tore down to London. Told Andeanna he had urgent business to attend to. That shouldn't have surprised her – he often cut holidays short – but this time she was suspicious. She followed him.

'She hit London on the twenty-seventh without telling anybody. Caught a train, then got a cab home from the station. She must have guessed what Mikis was up to, but whether she went in there intending to do what she did, or if it was a spur-of-the-moment reaction, I don't know. I doubt she knew herself.'

It's late when I reach Darlington. Dark, wet, miserable. As I step down from the train, my eight ghosts – a seething Mikis Menderes joined the parade while I was en route – drift out along the platform in a crescent and smile at me smugly, a cool welcoming committee. I'm back to not being sure if they're real or figments of my imagination. I could do without that distraction at the moment – I'm tense enough – but since I can't disperse or claim to understand the shades, I jam my head down and push through, doing my best to ignore them, looking for the taxi rank.

The hospital isn't what I was expecting. A modern building backing on to an industrial estate, no signs out front to reveal its true purpose apart from a small plaque over the door and an ambulance parked in the drive.

'You want me to stick around to take you back?' the driver asks as I step out.

'I'm not sure,' I mumble.

'I'm only saying 'cos it might take a while to get a lad out here this late. It'll cost you a fair bit if I wait, but if I don't, you might be stuck here longer than you'd like.'

I shove a handful of notes into his eager fist. 'Is that enough?'

'Oh, aye,' he says. 'That'll keep me till morning if necessary.'

I walk to the door, stare nervously at the buzzer, then press it. Moments later I'm stepping inside to face the living ghost of an undead past.

'It took her a while to find them.' Gardiner's face was dark as death, defying the glittering beams of the early-morning sun. 'They were in one of the spare bedrooms. Mikis told me, years later, that every door on the landing had been opened. She must have gone from room to room, opening the doors, checking, not closing them, moving on.

'We never found out where she got the knife. Maybe she bought it on the way home, or lugged it down from Scotland. I often imagine her sitting on that train with a bag on her lap, the knife inside, hand in the bag, clutching the handle, focused on what she was going to do. Her right hand was all cut up. She'd been gripping the blade, either on the journey or while she stalked the halls. I don't think she felt the pain. The madness would have numbed her to it.'

He stopped, and his fingers squeezed around the remains of the book of matches. I could guess what was coming and was almost as apprehensive as Gardiner.

'She found them in the end. Mikis felt a draught when the door opened, but he took no notice. He thought he'd forgotten to shut it properly. That was almost ten minutes before she screamed, so she must have been standing there all that time, watching, listening, grasping the knife.'

I wanted him to stop. Despite having forced the issue, risked my life, killed or been instrumental in the murder of four people, I wanted him to leave the story unfinished. I almost asked him to stop but my lips wouldn't form the words.

'Mikis got drunk a couple of years ago and told me that her scream was the most chilling thing he'd ever heard. He said it was like the whistle of a steam engine, only filled with hate. He was crying. Said it was a sound he'd never been able to block out. It echoed in his ears still, often driving him to the verge of suicide. If not for Greygo, he would have topped himself years ago.

'Christina was on top at the time – another detail Mikis only revealed long after the event – and she spun around when she heard the scream. She saw Andeanna framed in the doorway, one hand held to her head, the other hidden by her side. For a moment Christina stared at her, bewildered. Then she laughed.'

Gardiner dropped the destroyed book of matches, fished in his pockets for another, tore it open, lit a match and continued, letting it burn down to his fingers, not flinching when it quenched itself on his hard, callused flesh.

'If she hadn't laughed, it might have stopped with the scream. But this was Andeanna's house. Her home. Her husband. And here was this woman, this slut, fucking Mikis. And she was *laughing*.'

Gardiner lit another match, held it up and nodded at the flame. 'Andeanna flared into life. She moved so fast, Mikis barely saw what happened. She raced across the room. Christina

274

was still laughing. Andeanna sliced through the bitch's breasts with the knife, then whipped it across her throat.

'She didn't stop there,' Gardiner said as the match burnt out. 'She carried on hacking. Mikis lay on the bed, staring at the women, his body and face covered with blood, unable to raise a hand, knowing it wouldn't have mattered if he had. It was over after the second cut. The rest was mere butchery.'

Mere butchery,' I whisper to myself as I wait for Dr Jan Tressman. A young nurse has asked three times if I'd like anything to drink. She looks worried. Maybe it's my appearance. I'm not sure what I look like, but I'm not my normal self. I can't remember the last time I shaved or washed. I spent several hours in the trunk of a car. There are bloodstains on my trousers from Dash's death spray. I've had my world turned upside down, inside out, ripped to pieces and tacked back together with the glue of nightmarish madness. I'm not, I think it's safe to say, at my dapper, dashing best.

'Mikis expected to die,' Gardiner continued. 'Once Andeanna had finished with Christina, he was sure she'd attack him. He lay there anticipating death, doing nothing to avert it. He was hers for the taking. But she spared him.

'She stared at him hungrily, gripping the knife, her chest heaving. Maybe the fact that he made no move to defend himself saved him. Perhaps she was waiting for him to raise a hand or cringe or . . . laugh. But he just lay there, gazing at her desperately, and finally she got off the bed, walked to a corner, sank to her haunches and started to croon.'

'What did she sing?' I asked.

Gardiner looked at me incredulously. 'How the fuck do I know?' he roared. 'Does it matter?'

'Just curious,' I replied, stung by his reaction.

'Why don't we find this mystic of yours and ask if she knows? Perhaps she has a spectral CD player.' He shook his head. 'What a dumb fucking question.

'Anyway, she was *crooning*. Mikis couldn't lie there all night, much as he'd have liked to. He got to his feet, checked to make sure Christina was dead, then edged past Andeanna and rushed for the phone to call the police.'

'I'd have thought they were the last people he'd want to involve.'

'They were. But he was so shaken, he didn't know what he was doing. He was two digits in before he stopped to consider the consequences. Calling the coppers would have been the end of both of them. Andeanna would have been carted away, taken into custody and subjected to the full process of the law. Details would have leaked to the press, Christina's name would have emerged, Arnold Whiteoak would have come gunning for Mikis.

'Going public was out of the question. Mikis put the phone down, sat naked on the floor and thought it through. His survival instincts kicked in and he rang me. He couldn't handle it alone. I was the only person he trusted. He knew I wouldn't milk the fuck-up for all it was worth, or hold it over his head for the rest of his life.

'He didn't tell me what happened over the phone, only said it was an emergency. When I walked in and saw Christina and Andeanna, I knew we were in deep shit. I wanted to rush to Andeanna and comfort her, but I managed to stop myself. Mikis would have known there was something between us if I had. The state he was in, he'd have throttled me with his bare hands there and then.

'Mikis had dressed, but he hadn't washed off the blood. He gave me a rundown of what had happened, explained his basic plan and asked for my input.' Gardiner cracked a half-smile. '*Input*,' he repeated with a snort.

'What was the plan?' I asked.

'Kill two birds with one stone,' Gardiner replied. 'If it had just been Christina, we'd have dumped her body and prayed that Arnold never found out. But . . .'

He stalled, so I said it for him. 'There was Andeanna.'

'Right. As much as he loved her, Mikis couldn't let her walk. We could see that she'd passed way beyond reason. We couldn't help her. There was only one other solution — we had to kill her.'

A middle-aged, grey-haired, chubby doctor steps into the waiting room and casts an eye around. 'Mr Sieveking?' he asks, already stepping forward to shake my hand. 'I'm Jan Tressman.'

'Doctor,' I greet him.

'Please, call me Jan.' He studies my face and clothes. If the nurse didn't spot the bloodstains on my trousers, Tressman does, and his lips tighten. 'Do you need assistance, Mr Sieveking?'

'No. I'm fine. Never better.'

He grunts sceptically. 'So, you're here to visit one of my patients?'

'Yes,' I whisper.

'Our mutual acquaintance —' he's careful not to mention Bond Gardiner's name – 'told me that Miss Emerson does not know you. Is that correct?'

Is it? Beats the hell out of me. But I go along with Gardiner's story. Less complicated that way. 'Yes.'

Tressman chews his lower lip. 'Miss Emerson is unaccustomed to visitors. She is docile most of the time, but reacts nervously to unfamiliar faces. When we have to introduce someone into her environment – a new nurse, for instance – we do so gradually. There is no direct contact to begin with. The nurse remains at a distance until Miss Emerson learns to accept his or her presence, then slowly moves closer and plays a

277

more active role in her life over a period of concurrent days. A stranger walking straight in to see her . . .' He shakes his head.

'Has she never had a visitor?' I ask.

Tressman hesitates, then says, 'Only her son.'

'*Greygo?*' I gape.

'Gregory Menderes, yes. He first came several years ago, before I started here, and has been a regular visitor since.'

I didn't think Greygo knew about his mother. Then again, I didn't ask Gardiner about the Menderes heir. I know that Greygo was desperate to find out more about Andeanna. He must have tracked her down, probably through Mikis, who maybe told him the truth during a drunken bout of self-pity.

'What does Greygo do when he comes?' I ask.

'Sits with her. Talks. Tells her about himself.'

'Does she know who he is?'

Tressman sighs. 'Miss Emerson is beyond the realms of such recognition. Her fragile mental state, combined with her medication . . . You know about that?' I nod stiffly. 'She knows somewhere within the remains of her mind that she has a son – she plays with dolls and often pretends that one of them is her child – but she is incapable of recognizing him in the flesh. Gregory tried jogging her memory when he first visited – he would tell her who he was, bring photos of himself when he was younger, beg her to acknowledge him – but he now knows that can never be. He is satisfied just to come and sit with her.'

I think about that in silence. It's sad, but also troubling. Greygo told me he saw his mother's ghost when he was growing up, that he'd spoken with her. If that had been a cover story, I could accept it, but he sent me to Etienne Anders, who not only backed up his claims but put me in touch with the *ghost*. An elaborate ruse to steer me away from the truth? Or a more calculated ploy? Might Greygo have set me up with the Andeanna lookalike? Could *he* have masterminded the downfall of the father he claimed to love?

All reports contradict that hypothesis – everyone says that Greygo was a model son – but the evidence is beginning to weigh against the Menderes heir. I may have to corner him again and put a few harsh questions his way.

Focusing on the present, I consider the matter in hand. The last thing I want is to disturb *Miss Emerson*. If she's as wrapped up in her own world as Gardiner and Tressman have said, I can gain nothing by questioning her. I ask the doctor if it's possible to view her without revealing myself. 'Of course,' he beams. 'That would be best.' Smiling approvingly, he slips away to set things up, and I'm left alone again, with nothing to do but think back upon the revelations in the glade.

Gardiner couldn't kill her. Even though he agreed that execution was necessary, he'd been Andeanna's secret lover, and when it came to placing a cushion over her face and smothering her, he faltered. He fetched a pillow from the bed, fluffed it up and started forward, but got no closer than a couple of feet. Her blank look, her trembling hands, her crooning, memories of their affair . . . In the end, he could only stand, pillow in hands, and shake his head.

'Mikis howled at me to kill her,' he said. 'In all our years together, that was the only time he turned on me. He struck me, threatened to kill me. I didn't fight back, just stood my ground and told him I couldn't do it.'

Eventually the Turk grabbed the pillow from Gardiner, determined to finish her off himself. He got right up to her, the pillow poised mere inches from her face, before he stalled.

'It was her expression,' Gardiner croaked. 'It never changed. She went on singing softly, no understanding in her eyes. You'd think that would have made it easier to kill her, but it didn't.'

When Mikis tossed the pillow aside, he thought his world had come to an end. He would get rid of the corpse of Christina Whiteoak, confine his wife to home and hire a tight-lipped harridan to nurse her, but he was sure the truth would leak. It was too much to hope that Andeanna would remain comatose. She'd return to consciousness and bring him to ruin. There was nothing he could do to prevent it.

'The idea to swap bodies was mine,' Gardiner said hollowly. 'It hit me when we were discussing ways to dispose of Christina. Mikis wanted to dump her where she'd never be found, but I thought it would be better if we could arrange for her body to be discovered. If she disappeared, her husband wouldn't stop looking for her, but if we made it look like an accident . . .'

'A bit of a problem, given the way she was killed,' I noted.

Gardiner nodded. 'She'd been hacked to pieces. Mikis asked if I meant to throw her down a flight of stairs and claim she'd tripped while carrying a knife. I lost my temper and told him to stop acting like an idiot. It wouldn't be easy, but it could be done. If we started a fire, the flames would destroy the evidence of foul play. Her wounds were flesh deep. Get rid of the flesh, get rid of the wounds.

'Mikis was worried. Too much could go wrong. He didn't see the need to be so elaborate. He'd almost won me over when a new plan struck. And *struck* is exactly the way to describe it. The scheme slammed into my mind in a single sickening second. You could say it was my one real moment of genius.'

It was a dreadfully simple idea — incinerate the corpse but pretend it was Andeanna. They'd have to burn Christina beyond identification to get rid of the stab wounds. Such a body could be anyone's. If they dressed it in Andeanna's clothes, placed it in her car – even at that early stage he saw the need to stage a crash – and said that it was the Turk's wife, who would ever question them?

'Mikis thought I'd lost my mind. The women looked nothing alike. They weren't the same height. They wouldn't have matching dental records. And Arnold Whiteoak — the whole reason we'd considered burning Christina was to throw her husband off the scent. Without a corpse, he'd keep searching for her, and Mikis thought we'd be left with the threat of Andeanna one day blabbing and alerting Whiteoak to the truth. I convinced him that she wouldn't. That she *couldn't.*'

Gardiner talked him through it quickly and convincingly. They could smash the teeth to pieces and the police would believe it was a result of the crash. The ruse wouldn't stand close scrutiny, but if they staged the crash correctly, why should anyone suspect a swap? It would be Andeanna's car, clothes, jewellery. Mikis would say he'd seen her leaving the house. Why would the police believe she was anybody other than who she appeared to be?

'He still couldn't see the point of swapping the bodies,' Gardiner muttered. 'It wasn't until I told him what we could do with Andeanna that he saw the light.'

At that, Gardiner's shame overwhelmed him and he practically shrivelled up.

Tressman sticks his head into the waiting room and whistles for me. I get to my feet and follow him into a long white corridor. He leads the way to a small dark room that looks on to a larger area via a two-way mirror. There's a chair next to the mirror, positioned close to a loudspeaker. The room beyond is vacant.

'She will be here presently,' Tressman says. 'This is one of her recreational zones, so she will feel at ease. You can stay and watch as long as you wish. She cannot see you. A nurse will be waiting outside when you want to leave.'

'You aren't staying?'

'I am busy. I have papers to —'

'I'd prefer if you stayed,' I interrupt. 'I might have questions.'

'What about?'

'Her condition. Her history. Her state of mind.'

He laughs cynically. 'She has no mind. Her previous doctors were most successful in drugging that out of her.'

I stare at him curiously. 'You don't approve of how she's been treated.'

He shrugs sadly. 'I have two children in university and a third with special requirements. My predecessor knew of my need for additional income. He introduced me to Mr Gardiner and I snatched the thirty pieces of silver from his hand. I am all too aware of my faults, but I still know right from wrong, and the way that woman has been treated is as wrong as you can get. I would never have sanctioned what was done to her, at any price.'

'Is there no way you could help her?' I ask softly.

'No. The damage was done long before she passed into my care. God himself could not reverse the effects of what they have pumped into her. Her personality has been erased and it can never be restored.'

The door to the room opens and he stops. We watch silently as a young black nurse leads in a wizened old woman. She shuffles forward with short, trembling steps, clutching a couple of dolls to her chest, lips moving wordlessly in rhythm with the twitching of her neck. With a mix of horror, disgust and pity, I watch.

Gardiner's plan – awful simplicity itself if they could get away with faking the car crash – was to commit Andeanna to a mental asylum and keep her doped up for the rest of her life. They had contacts in the medical profession, doctors who owed them favours or who could be otherwise coerced into following orders.

'He warmed to the idea once I'd explained it,' Gardiner said without pride. 'In a matter of minutes he was on the phone, first to a hospital in Kent, then Darlington, where she ended up. It was expensive, but Mikis didn't care. Anything was better than having to answer to Arnold Whiteoak for the death of his wife.'

'You weren't afraid that he'd find out some other way?' I asked.

'No. Nobody else knew about their affair. Andeanna was the only link.'

They had to act quickly. Early the next day, they bundled Christina's corpse into the trunk of Andeanna's car, having taken a hammer to her mouth and adorned her with Andeanna's clothes and personal items. Gardiner drove to the countryside and Menderes followed. They found a quiet stretch of road and pulled in. Together they prepared the body and the car – it wasn't the first time they'd staged a crash – then Gardiner got in and aimed it down a hill at a group of trees. Once he'd set the corpse on fire, he rode in the flaming car most of the way, taking a dive only when he was within sprinting distance of the trees. Dashing for cover, he hurried through the forest and down to the next stretch of road, where the Turk was waiting. Then it was back to London to collect Andeanna.

'We'd tied her up before we left,' Gardiner said, 'but I spent the entire journey back thinking she'd somehow clawed her way free and would be waiting for us with a knife. The idea didn't frighten me — I was already having regrets. Part of me wanted her to recover, longed to die at her hands.'

But she hadn't escaped. She never would.

Andeanna didn't react when they bundled her into the back of Christina Whiteoak's car and covered her with a blanket. Menderes sobbed and vowed to scrap the plan, keep her with him, nurse her back to sanity and beg forgiveness. If the Turk had made a real attempt to stop Gardiner, he wouldn't have argued, but for all his tears and protests, the grief-stricken husband made no move to detain his partner, who was soon on the road north, leaving his boss to sit by the phone and wait for the police to break the tragic news of his wife's death.

'And that was that,' Gardiner finished gruffly. 'I switched cars along the way, leaving Christina's outside a hotel near Birmingham airport, then made sure Andeanna was safely tucked away. I signed the papers, used her mother's name and paid the first of what would prove to be many instalments. Her doctor – *our* doctor – knew what was expected of him and promised to take good care of her. I didn't ask what that entailed. If I live to be a hundred, I never will. There are some things you're better off not knowing.'

I agreed wholeheartedly with that. There was a lot about Andeanna Menderes, her marriage to the Turk and her life thereafter, that I'd have been happier knowing nothing about. But having come so far and learnt so much, I couldn't stop now. So I pushed for more and asked which hospital she'd been admitted to. Without even pausing, Bond Gardiner reeled off the address, and the rest, as they say, is history.

Until that tired old woman walked into the room, I'd been entertaining hopes that she might be *my* Andeanna. She could have recovered her sanity – perhaps under the guidance of a new doctor – and set out to destroy the man who'd cheated her of so many years. I had visions of her looking through the glass, sensing me on the other side, smiling knowingly. 'Took your time getting here, Ed,' she might chuckle.

Those faint hopes disappear as soon as she enters. This woman is Andeanna Menderes. As broken and haggard as she is, I've studied the photos of her long enough to know the real deal when faced with it. But there isn't a chance in hell that she's the woman who seduced me. Her face is lined with pain and madness, marks that no amount of make-up could disguise. Her hands are thin, twisted spindles at the ends of her bony arms. She walks hunched over. Her hair is grey, poorly cut, the ends jagged and torn. This is the true, present-day Andeanna. My ghost was an illusion, a clever reconstruction of a face from the past. I see that now. More importantly, I accept it. Whoever – whatever – my lover was, she wasn't a rejuvenated, vengeful Mrs Menderes.

Tears stream down my face. So many years of dry ducts, and now here I am, reduced to waterworks for the second time in twenty-four hours. Her beauty sets me off. Because despite her appearance, the empty eyes and the shuffling movements, she *is* beautiful. A woman old before her time, cruelly robbed of her mind and personality, a soul in suffering. But still a beauty to behold.

Something waves at the corner of my vision – Dr Tressman offering a white handkerchief. Smiling sadly, I shake my head. I don't want to wipe away the tears. I enjoy the warmth of them on my cheeks. They're an assurance that in spite of all I've done and been, I'm still partly human.

'How could they do this to her?' I weep. 'Killing her would have been kinder. Leaving her like this . . . destroying her mind . . .'

'I agree,' Tressman sighs. 'Death would have been a blessing.'

'Isn't there something you could do? An injection?'

'Yes,' he murmurs. 'And I have considered it, not only for Miss Emerson, but others like her. But I have sworn an oath to protect life, not take it. Besides, who am I to decide such matters? Miracles *do* happen. I have seen people like Miss Emerson, in some cases worse, emerge from the depths of lost madness and resume their lives where they left off.'

'But you said her brain has been destroyed.'

'It has,' he nods. 'But while we know much about the brain, we know nothing of the soul. I do not expect Miss Emerson to recover. I would class it as an impossibility. But the chance, as slim as it is, exists. Where there is life, there is hope. *That* stays my hand, even in my darkest hours, when I bear witness to pain of the most horrendous degree.'

'Give *me* the choice,' I whisper. 'I'd put her out of her misery.'

'That is why you will never be given such an option,' he says with a wry smile. 'We must trust our weak and damaged to those with the strength to endure their suffering, or else they would be at the mercy of those without.'

'I can show mercy,' I growl, disliking the implication.

'Can you, Mr Sieveking? Can you really?'

I think of the people I've killed. I run my gaze over the ghosts pressed close around me — they seem as fascinated by the woman in the room as I am. I don't answer.

The nurse remains with Andeanna, but retires to a corner to read a creased novel. Andeanna wanders while I watch in hidden silence. She runs her fingers over colourful paintings on the walls (they look like they were painted by children, but are probably the work of the inmates) and smiles a ghostly, stop-start smile. She halts before a picture of a bright blue boy with a huge head and stares at it, her smile spreading, then presses her forehead against the figure's stomach and keens sharply.

'What's happening?' I ask, startled.

'That was drawn by a man who has been here almost as long as Miss Emerson,' Tressman says. 'He is more balanced and experiences spells of clarity. He has a crush on her. When he learnt that she once had a child, he painted that picture for her. She recognizes it sometimes and mourns for what is lost.'

'I thought you said she was beyond recognition.'

286

'She remembers certain things, occasionally, in ways we do not understand.'

'Then she's not entirely brain-dead?'

He shrugs. 'When her real son comes to see her, she does not know who he is. A man paints a surreal picture of a child he has never seen, and it stirs something inside her. Traces of her humanity remain, but they are subtle and impossible to define.' He rests a hand on my shoulder. 'She cannot be rescued, if that is what you are asking.'

Andeanna turns from the painting and shuffles into the middle of the room. Her eyes are wide-open pools of nothingness. She sits on the floor, clears a space and lays down her dolls. She cocks her head and studies them, then picks up the larger doll and plucks at its hair.

'She will play with that until we take her back to her room,' Tressman says. 'She will treat it as her son, feed it imaginary sweets, maybe bare a breast and suckle it.' He coughs discreetly. 'I will have to ask you to leave if that happens.'

As I watch, Andeanna lays the doll in her lap, picks up the other – a girl – and removes its dress, which she slides down over her surrogate son, smiling and gurgling. Next she rocks the doll in her arms and makes choked sounds.

I want to leave but I can't tear myself away. It's not just that I feel sorry for her. Part of me wants to stay. It thinks that I belong here too. I can feel insanity stirring within myself. It would be so easy to surrender, abandon the real world, the quest for truth, the need for knowledge, and just join Andeanna in her aimless, carefree life. Sit in a room, gurgle over childish paintings, dress up dolls, let others do the worrying and planning. In a warped sort of way, it would be heaven.

But this isn't a time for heaven. This is a time for hell. There can be no sanctuary until I've stripped the lie of all its trimmings, revealed the truth of who I fell in love with and lost my soul to. If I gave up now, I'd be haunted for ever. There could be no rest. I wouldn't be sitting with Andeanna, playing with dolls. I'd be locked away where my screams couldn't frighten the rest of the patients.

Andeanna slaps the floor with one hand, clutching the doll to her chest with the other. Her face contorts and she slaps the floor again. The nurse hurries over to a locked cupboard set high on one of the walls, opens it and produces a small bag.

'Drugs?' I ask, preparing to leave, unwilling to be a witness to the deliberate doping of Andeanna Menderes.

'Nothing so monstrous,' Tressman smiles.

The nurse hands Andeanna the bag, the contents of which she shakes out on to the floor. I'm relieved to see nothing more frightening than everyday cosmetics – lipstick, mascara, rouge. Andeanna's fingers scuttle over the tubes and cases, then settle on the lipstick, which she starts to apply with surprising care and precision to the doll's stiff plastic lips.

'Now there will be no shifting her,' Tressman notes. 'When she starts this, she loses herself for hours at a time.' He glances at me. 'If you like, I could take you in. She will not notice anything other than the doll now that she is focused on it.'

I shake my head. 'I've seen enough,' I whisper.

Tressman's lips purse. 'May I ask what your interest in Miss Emerson is? I know I am not meant to, and you do not have to answer, but . . .'

'I was her lover,' I answer softly.

He stares from me to Andeanna and back again. 'Before she was admitted?'

'More recently than that.'

His features crease. 'I do not understand.'

'Me neither,' I reply with a choked, bitter laugh.

One last lingering look at Andeanna and her lifeless baby, then I turn away. 'I'd like to leave now.'

'You are sure?'

'I've seen what I came for. There's nothing more for me here. I don't know if there's anything beyond either, but I can't stay here and hide, can I?' Tressman stares at me, confused. I laugh bitterly. 'It's OK. I don't expect an answer.'

'Do you have somewhere to sleep tonight?' Tressman asks, opening the door.

'I don't know. I might head back to London. Is there a train this late?'

'I doubt it. I can recommend a good hotel instead.'

'Thanks. If you knew the day I've had . . .' I manage a short smile. 'I'm dead on my feet. I think I could sleep through a . . .'

I come to a standstill, not sure why I've stopped. An image of a doll flashed through my mind, but it wasn't the doll Andeanna was holding. It was a doll of the boy in the painting, the one with the enormous blue head. Except the features were different. It was *my* face. And it was laughing at me.

Tressman is closing the door to the viewing room. 'Wait,' I stop him and barge back in, the image seeming to will me on. I can almost hear the laughter. I can't leave without knowing what the doll is snickering at.

'Are you all right?' Tressman asks, following me back inside.

I silence him with a sharp gesture. Thoughts collide like trains deep within my brain. Strands of the puzzle wrap together, unbidden, forming a picture. I can't see the whole of it yet, but I know it has something to do with the woman on the other side of the glass, and more crucially with the doll whose cheeks she is now reddening with rouge. What is it about the bloody doll that so disturbs me?

Then, out of the dark waters of my consciousness, a question surfaces, and I intuitively know that it will lead to answers. I don't know what the question means, or how it acts as the key to the puzzle, but I voice it anyway, giving it the release it demands.

'If she thinks the doll is her son,' I mutter to a bemused Dr Tressman, 'why the hell is she treating it like a *girl?*'

TWENTY-ONE

I spend the night in the hotel recommended by the good doctor, but although it's peaceful and I'm exhausted, I sleep fitfully, tormented by questions and murkily evolving answers.

At first I can't believe what my instincts are telling me. I fear that the madness of the asylum has rubbed off on me, that these are the workings of a deluded mind. I waste hours denying theories I know in my heart to be true. I shy away from the revelations and desperately explore alternate solutions, but I'm damned to return each time to the warped, crazy truth.

I keep fixing on the image of the doll, how Andeanna dressed it in girl's clothes and smeared its face with make-up. If I could escape that image, perhaps I could seek false answers elsewhere. But I can't lie to myself, no matter how hard I try. The truth won't let itself be denied.

By morning, I can fight no longer. I don't know the complete story, but it won't be difficult to fill in the gaps. Dangerous and awful, yes, but not difficult. I know who to turn to, how to find him, how to force a confession from him if he resists. No more screwing around with lies and ghosts. We're done with that shit. Only the hellish pit of the truth remains.

On an express train back to London. Lack of sleep must be getting to me, because I don't remember buying a ticket or boarding. The last thing I recall, I was having an early breakfast at the hotel.

I should be worried about Bond Gardiner's warning, but I'm not. I'm sure I can slip in and out of the city before anyone clocks me. Exhaustion troubles me more than Gardiner's threat. I don't want to spiral out of control. I need to stay focused.

Leaning back in my seat, I close my eyes, tune out the world around me and try to sleep. But I have no more success here than I did in the hotel. The doll haunts me, fills my thoughts, lets nothing distract me. Maybe the mad don't need to sleep. Maybe their insanity is all they require to sustain them.

In a taxi. I've lost track of my movements again — I have no memory of getting off the train. I look out of the window and grunt softly. I'm back in London. I feel a bulge in one of my pockets. Letting my fingers steal in to explore, I trace the outline of a gun. Axel Nelke's. I must have gone to Heathrow, broken into the car and reclaimed it.

Leaning forward, I ask the driver if we'll be much longer. 'Ten minutes, guv,' he answers cheerfully. I don't need to ask for the destination. Sitting back, I smile softly. For the first time since the asylum, I can turn away from the image of the doll and all the questions and answers that go with it. No need to guess any longer. Ten minutes, give or take, and all will be made clear.

I phase out again. Next thing I know, I'm stealing through the grounds of the Menderes mansion. The ghosts trail along beside me, hunched over, expressions intent, as if homing in on a scent. They look like hounds. Hungry, hellish hounds about to be fed.

I sneak around back, quietly break in through a window and glide through the familiar rooms, advancing silently, encountering no one.

I find my target in the pool room, playing solo, a game where losing and winning are the same, where triumph goes hand in hand with despair. I wait for him to pot the black before stepping forward to clap slowly.

Gregory Menderes looks up, startled, raising his cue defensively. When he sees me, the tip of the cue drops, then lifts again, as if he can't make up his mind whether I'm a threat or not. Eventually he lays the cue aside and smiles warily. 'Mr Sanders. May I ask how you got in?'

'The name's Ed Sieveking,' I reply quietly. 'But you already knew that, didn't you?' Greygo's eyes narrow, but he says nothing. 'Who's in the house with us?'

'Nobody,' he says with a smile. I take out the gun and aim. His smile vanishes. 'Nobody,' he repeats, sullenly this time.

'No staff?'

'The cleaners work early. They're finished for the day. So are the gardeners. I cook for myself most nights. There's nobody else.'

'No guards?'

'Not since my father died. I kept some here for a while, to warn off the media, but now that interest in him has diminished, they're not needed.'

That's a bonus. I keep the gun trained on him, readying myself for business. 'I've just come back from Darlington.' The young man's face pales – he no longer has a tan, and I'm sure he never did, that he sprayed it on ahead of our meeting to disguise the natural colour of his flesh – and his jaw drops. It's the reaction I anticipated. Confirmation that I'm not crazy.

'We're going upstairs,' I tell him. 'You're going to take me to wherever you store the outfits. Then you're going to change. If you act like you don't know what I'm talking about, I'll put a bullet through you where it will really hurt.'

'Ed . . .' he begins.

'Walk, Gregory. Don't talk.'

He looks at the gun and my twitching finger, nods glumly and starts for the corridor. I let him pass, seeing so much now, telltale signs I must have subconsciously noted before but paid no heed to. Bile rises up my throat but I force it down as I fall into step behind him, careful not to get too close, taking no risks, not when I'm so close to the truth that I can feel it sliding through the hairs of my nape like a snake.

If Greygo is afraid – and he must be – he masks it well. That doesn't surprise me. He's used to hiding his emotions. His training in RADA, his years on the stage, his preference for character roles. I recall Andrew Moore telling me that his grandson could be a star, that fame was his for the taking. But Gregory Menderes was never interested in fame, only in honing his craft, perfecting the art of getting into the skin of the people he was pretending to be. I wish I'd researched his background more thoroughly, looked into the roles he'd taken over the years. I bet I would have found precursors. Joe and I focused on Andeanna and Mikis. We never dug into their son's past in great depth. Didn't think he was worth the study.

Joe . . . What would he think of this? I can never tell him, whatever the outcome. I can never tell anyone. This is the sort of truth you carry deep in your heart and never reveal. If I walk out of this alive, I'll invent something for Joe. I'm good at that. I carved a living out of stories once upon a time.

Greygo leads me to his mother's bedroom and heads for a built-in wardrobe.

'Hold it,' I snap, edging ahead of him, sliding open the doors. There are four shelves loaded with clothes and boxes. 'Are these the costumes?'

'Yes,' he says. 'But there's also a bag stowed away beneath the lowest shelf. I'll need that to create the full effect.'

I back out of the closet and tap the gun's trigger with my finger. 'Don't come up with anything that looks remotely like a weapon,' I warn him.

Greygo gets down on his knees and reaches into the dark. He emerges with a stuffed plastic bag. I tell him to dump the contents on the floor in the middle of the room. A shower of padding, corsets, bras, tights, knickers. I stare at the under-garments, then clear my throat, forcing back the bile, which is rising again. 'Put them on,' I croak.

He undresses without argument, revealing a smooth, shaven chest, arms and legs. He pauses at his boxer shorts. 'Would you mind looking away?'

'Yes.'

'Ed, please, there's no need to –'

'Just do it.'

Greygo sighs dolefully, then slides down his shorts. His genitals have been waxed bare. His nudity unsettles me. I'm not homophobic, but seeing him like this, thinking of all that has passed between us, I feel nauseous. Though not as much as many men in my position might. I'm surprised by that. I thought I'd be more bothered by the gender side of things. Maybe I will be, later, when I've had time to think and reflect. Right now, everything has the unreal quality of a dream.

'Get dressed,' I snarl, averting my gaze.

It's a complicated process. Each step must be followed in exact order. It looks uncomfortable, especially around the groin, but Greygo seems at ease and takes no notice of the biting straps.

With all the padding in place, in all the right places, he rolls on the tights and fastens the bra over the synthetic but real-looking breasts. Then he returns to the wardrobe. He picks a red dress, steps into it and slides it up over the tights, straps and padding. I expect him to turn and ask me to zip him up at the back, but he manages it himself, then slips into a pair of high-heeled shoes.

Then there's just the wig. He takes it out of a box, fixes it in place, throws his head back and beams at me, turning on his full range of charms.

My breath catches in my throat. I step backwards, shocked, almost dropping the gun. The disguise will need a few more touches before it's perfect. His features are incredibly similar to his mother's, but there's still something masculine about his face minus make-up and lipstick, earrings and eyelashes. And he needs to add coloured contacts. Yet even at this halfway stage, the figure is unmistakable.

'*Andeanna*,' I groan.

Gregory Menderes raises an eyebrow, purses his lips and says in *her* voice, 'The one and only.' He grins sexily. 'A kiss for old times' sake, Ed?'

I can't answer. I can only stare at the face of the man who is the woman I fell in love with and killed for, and wait for the furies of insanity to sweep down from the tormented heavens and take me.

Greygo sits at the dressing table, working on his face. I watch Andeanna swim into being in the mirror, and I'm amazed by the transformation. It isn't just the look. As he progresses, he *becomes* a woman — the way he moves his hands and arches his neck, the frame of his shoulders, the subtle sway of his hips as he leans forwards and backwards on the chair, the way he crosses his legs. Even knowing who it really is, I have to forcibly remind myself that this isn't Andeanna — a he, not a she, a cruel conspirator to be executed, not a restored lover to be adored.

'It was a set-up from the start, wasn't it?' I mutter.

'Of course,' he answers in Andeanna's voice.

'Not like that,' I snap. 'Use your own voice.'

'This *is* my voice, darling,' he answers without changing key.

'Stop it,' I warn him, 'or so help me . . .'

He sighs like Andeanna did when talking about her life with the Turk. 'You don't understand, Ed. When I'm dressed like this, when I have this body and face, I *am* my mother. I can't alter my voice to suit you. If you want me to speak as Greygo, I'll have to shed these clothes. Do you want me to do that?'

'No.' It's difficult facing him in this guise, but if he took it off, I'd spend the rest of the conversation wanting him to put it back on. I don't think I'd be able to believe he's Andeanna – *my* Andeanna – without seeing him as her all the time. 'One question before we start. Did you arrange the murder of your father to get your hands on his money?'

Andeanna shakes her . . . No. I must think of him as he really is. *Greygo* shakes *his* head.

'Nothing that venal,' he says. 'I'm surprised you had to ask.'

'Just wanted to make sure.' Sitting on the bed, I rest the gun in my lap and nod for him to begin.

'I assume you know the full story, how my mother discovered my father in flagrante delicto and lost her head?'

'Yes.'

'Good. That saves us a lot of time. Let's cut to *my* beginning. Love for my mother took precedence over all others. That included love for my father and you.'

'For *me*!' I snort.

He smiles but doesn't press the point. 'My mother always knew that I was . . . shall we say special?'

'Let's say bent as a boomerang,' I correct him.

He shrugs. 'I was never overly bothered about sex, so it's a moot point. I wasn't afraid of what I was, but I was conscious of my father and how the truth would hurt him. It was hard enough telling him I was intent on becoming an actor, but if

I'd told him I was gay . . . I think he could have forced himself to accept me, but it would have stung him to his core. I didn't want to bring more misery into his life, not after what had happened with my mother, so I've been mostly celibate. I even had a few flings with women, to make it look as if I was a hot-blooded hetero. Anyway, my sexual orientation isn't the issue here.'

'Isn't it?'

He shakes his head. 'What my mother saw in me as a child wasn't a craving for cock – pardon me for being so crude – but a desire to be feminine. I loved dressing up, trying on beautiful clothes and undergarments. I wanted to be part of that world of glamour and disguise. Sex had nothing to do with it.

'She knew I used to sneak into her room and raid her wardrobe. In fact, sometimes I'd find clothes that were too small for her, which I'm sure she bought with me in mind. My father, on the other hand, knew nothing about it until he discovered me dressed in one of her outfits when I was nine years old. He thrashed me to within an inch of my life.' Greygo's face softens. 'I never blamed him. It's how people of his generation thought. Hell, it's how many of *our* generation think.'

Greygo smirks at me. 'What about you, Ed? We never discussed it before. Where do you stand on the homosexual issue?'

'Live and let live,' I grunt. 'I've no problem with gays. But I've no interest in them either.'

'That's a shame,' he murmurs, pouting playfully.

I stare at those lips. I think about all the times I've kissed them. The hardcore hetero in me wants me to recoil, to maybe bash them to shreds, to make him pay for what he did. But in truth, I'm not bothered. I should be, but I'm not. I loved Andeanna so much that I don't think I would have cared if she'd turned out to be a tranny, not if everything else had been on the level. I could have lived with that. It was an adjustment I would have been happy to make. For her.

'That was the only time he hit me,' Greygo continues. 'After that, I went underground, with the help of my mother. She took me under her wing and let me dress up when he wasn't around. She taught me how to apply make-up and wear the clothes, but also how to remove all traces of my alter ego when I left her room. Through her, I learnt the importance of separating one's identities.

'She was so brave,' he says softly. 'My father would have beaten her terribly if he'd found out. It was the one time in her life that she betrayed him, and she did it for my sake.'

'Not the only time,' I contradict him. 'There was her affair, too.'

He chuckles. 'With *Axel Nelke*? Surely you know better by now. I don't know where Andrew got the idea that she was having an affair. Bond played along with the lie for reasons of his own. So did I. But you must have come to understand how devoted and loyal she was. She could never have betrayed my father.'

To my surprise, I realize he doesn't know about her fling with Gardiner. A spiteful part of me wants to immediately shatter his illusions, but that would mean a detour, and I don't want to waste time. I came here to learn, not enlighten.

'I was devastated when she died,' he continues, eyes cloudy. 'It wasn't just my mother I'd lost, but my teacher, confidante and friend. She wasn't only a huge part of my regular life, but *all* of my secret life.'

I start to say how hard it must have been, sympathizing with him out of habit, then stop and frown. 'But she isn't dead.'

'I know that now,' he says, 'but I didn't then. At the time I thought, along with the rest of the world, that she'd perished in a car crash. I mourned for many years before I discovered she was still alive.'

'How did you find out?' I ask, then silently warn myself to

be careful — he almost has me feeling sorry for him. I have to remember what he's done. Save the pity for myself.

'I'd known for a long time that something wasn't right with my father, the way he responded when my mother's name was mentioned, the guarded looks he shared with Bond. I began to eavesdrop on conversations and search through his files when he was away, to no avail.

'The breakthrough came when I was arrested.' He laughs. 'I used to visit tranny bars and clubs — for the fashion, not casual sex. I was at a private party when it was raided. Since I was underage, I was taken into custody. I had to phone someone but I didn't dare call my father, so I rang Bond. I knew my mother had relied on him and hoped that I could too. He bailed me out and took me back to his place.

'Bond said nothing about what I'd been up to — he didn't want to know. He mixed a drink for me, let me have a bath, lent me some of his clothes. Then he was summoned away on business. My snooping instincts got the better of me. I found letters from St Michael's Psychiatric Hospital referring to a patient by the name of Deleena Emerson. I got straight on the line to her doctor and demanded to know the truth. I threatened to expose him if he refused to cooperate.

'I was appalled,' Greygo mumbles. 'My father loved her. I couldn't understand how he could have done that to her. I didn't know about Christina Whiteoak at the time, and could think of no reason why he . . .'

Greygo can't bring himself to say 'ruined her life' or 'destroyed her'. It's the first true indication I've seen that Gregory Menderes really did love his father.

'Did you go see her?' I ask.

'Of course. I fled, hailed the first cab I found and offered the driver as much as he wanted to drive me to Darlington. When I got there . . .' He stops, lips thinning.

'It's OK,' I tell him. 'You can skip this bit. I've seen her. I can imagine.'

He nods gratefully. 'Cutting a long story short, I sat down with Bond when I got back and forced the story out of him. I couldn't approach my father. I never did. To the very end he assumed that I thought she was dead.

'I didn't know what to do. I wanted to hate somebody, but who? Not Bond — he was only following orders. Not the staff at St Michael's — they were strangers who had been bullied or bribed. There was only one person I could truly hate, and that was the one person I could never bring myself to despise — my father.'

'Explain how you *couldn't* hate him,' I interject.

Greygo shrugs. 'I loved him.'

'But he stole your mother from you. He wiped her mind and locked her away in a madhouse.'

'I know, but that aside . . . ' He laughs sickly. 'What I mean is, I knew I should hate him, I knew I had to hate him, but I couldn't make myself. I wanted him to pay for what he'd done, but I could no more attack him than I could cut out my own heart then sew it back in again. I couldn't hate or harm him, Ed. But Andcanna Menderes *could.*'

Greygo rises from his chair at the dressing table and turns. He looks so feminine that for a moment I truly forget who he is and almost race across to clutch Andeanna and kiss her and tell her how much I've missed her. I catch myself in time, but only just.

'This isn't a mere disguise,' Greygo says, taking several steps towards me. 'I'm not just pretending to be a woman. When I transform, I transform completely. When I was with you as Andcanna, I didn't know where I ended and my mother began. I wasn't playing. I *was* Andeanna Menderes.'

'Are you pleading innocence?' I sneer. 'Copping some

fucked-up schizophrenic plea? *It wasn't me, it was my mummy.* Is that what you're trying to pull?'

'No,' he sighs. 'I planned the seduction and the assassination. I was behind it all, and self-aware every step of the way. But when I was immersed in the part, it was total immersion. It went beyond role-playing. Look at me. *Listen* to me.' He touches his throat and strokes it sensuously. 'I have to speak like this when I become her. I have no voice of my own right now. If my life depended on it, I couldn't do Greygo's voice or any of the others.'

I stare at him blankly. 'What others?'

He looks surprised. 'I thought you knew.'

I think furiously and it hits me. 'Etienne Anders. *You* were the mystic.'

'Naturally. How else could she have replicated the voice? Etienne was my weakest creation. You would have seen through her if you hadn't been so preoccupied. I never really got under her skin. I threw on a lot of make-up and clothes, but I never felt like a true medium.'

I grin grudgingly as I think back. He's right — I should have seen it. The forced joviality, the heavy make-up, the pitch-perfect voice when she summoned Andeanna, the facial similarities. Last night, when I was putting it all together, I assumed that the mystic was a paid cohort, but of course it was much safer for the master actor to simply assume another disguise and play the part himself.

I frown as I think back to what Greygo said — *others*, plural. 'Who else were you?' I ask, running through all the faces I've encountered recently, searching for any that might have been Greygo in drag.

'Only one more,' he says, his smile slipping.

'Who?'

He hesitates. 'It's not relevant.'

'Tell me,' I growl.

'You won't like it. I had to get close to you, to know what made you tick, to keep tabs on you.'

I don't know what he's getting at. Who could he have been? One of the staff at the Royal Munster? I think of Fred Lloyd and smile at the absurdity. I flash on more faces, as many as I can recall, but none matches. 'I give up,' I mutter.

'You really want to know?' I glare at him archly. 'OK,' he says, removing his wig and lowering his head. He rolls his shoulders and spreads his legs, instantly becoming more masculine, even in the dress and make-up. When he looks up again, he's smiling, and there's something hauntingly familiar in that smile.

In spite of the feeling that I should recognize him, I can't place him until he speaks in a light northern brogue. 'Have a good trip up north, Ed? Should have taken me along. We could have gone to the footie. You haven't seen the beautiful game played properly till you've seen it in the Stadium of Light.'

Regardless of the face, I'd know that voice anywhere. It's the voice of the one true friend I've made since Belinda tricked me all those years ago, the one person apart from Andeanna who I let into my life.

Joe.

In an instant, the rest of the mystery clicks into place. Joe was the one I turned to when I ran into trouble with Andeanna. He was a sympathetic audience, always there for me, except when Andeanna was around. Greygo was both my lover *and* my best friend. What one couldn't find out about me, the other could. As shocked as I am, I have to admire the genius behind it. Gregory Menderes is in a different class. I've known some sly bastards in my time, but Greygo puts them all in the shade. He played me with contemptuous ease. His only mistake was to not finish me off after I'd killed his father. I wonder how

303

he botched such a vital part of the plan. Were there others he wanted me to kill while I was at it?

'I spent months dressing up as her, slipping further into the disguise.'

The words come suddenly out of the silence. Looking up, I see that Greygo is wiping away the make-up. He's still wearing the dress but is speaking as himself now, not as Andeanna or Joe. I must have blanked out for a while, but he hasn't seized the chance to turn on me.

'I'd never tried so hard to become someone else. It had to be perfect if it was going to work. I went on holidays and masqueraded as my mother the whole time, sleeping as her, eating as her, flirting as her. I took men back to my room and made love to them, testing the bounds of my disguise. I made mistakes to begin with, but eventually I learnt to mask every last masculine trace. I discovered how to make a man love me but never know me, how to *be* and not just *be like*. Then I was ready.'

He licks his lips. Small dabs of lipstick cling to them like faded bloodstains. 'You weren't the first,' he says sheepishly. 'There were two others before you, a couple of your fellow assassins. I approached them as I approached you, tried to make them fall in love with me. It didn't work. I could attract them, but I –'

'Wait,' I interrupt. 'I don't get it. Why not just hire someone to kill him?'

'I tried, several times, wheedled names out of Bond and my father, approached a variety of contacts openly and offered them a fortune to accept the hit. They wouldn't bite. In the guise of my mother, I had to be a woman with no history — they all thought that she was dead, so I had to use my Deleena Emerson alias. The trouble was, no assassin would take on a target like the Turk when their would-be employer was a nobody who couldn't offer them protection from the Turk's men when they came gunning for revenge. As Greygo I might have been able to convince one of them, but I couldn't authorize a hit as myself. It had to be as my mother. So I decided to create a scene.'

'A *scene*,' I grunt. 'That's it. You staged a film noir plot. A scheming femme fatale seduces a capable but gullible patsy, spins him a tale of woe involving life with her abusive husband, and . . .' I nod at the cunning of it.

'That's how it was,' Greygo agrees. 'Only it didn't work to begin with. I wasn't able to believe in the scene. I could calmly plot in the safety of my room, but out in the real world I had to become one with the story. I needed to be as convinced by the piece as those I sucked in. I couldn't do that with the first two assassins. I was beginning to think I could never do it with anyone. Then you fell into my life.'

He crosses the room and kneels in front of me. Extends his hands and cups my face. If he dropped his fingers, he could wrench the gun from me and fire before I had a chance to react. But he doesn't.

'If it's any comfort, I really am a fan of your books. I read *Nights of Fear* and *Summer's Shades* before I learnt your true identity.'

I blink. 'Do you really think this is the right time to be praising my work?'

He giggles. 'It's relevant, because that's how it started. I found myself discussing your books with a friend of my father's at a party one night. That friend was Carter Phell.'

'Carter,' I groan. I should have known my old mentor would come back to haunt me. The past is never truly dead and buried.

'To Phell's credit, he changed the subject,' Greygo continues. 'It was only later, after he'd had a few drinks, that he tracked me down and asked if I knew who you used to be. He wanted to share his juicy titbit with the one person he'd met who'd actually read Ed Sieveking's books. He didn't do it to drop you in the shit — he knew I wasn't part of my father's seedier affairs, that I wouldn't try to exploit the information. In his own strange way, he was proud of you and wanted me to know how far you'd come.

'I'd researched the other assassins as best I could, but there's only so much you can unearth about men who operate as hired killers. You can't get close to them. Writers are different. They welcome questions and love to share. It's much easier to get to know a writer, to learn about him, to consume.'

Greygo tells me how he scoured the internet for interviews with me. He attended conventions where I was present, sometimes flying halfway round the world to hear me speak. He tracked down those who knew me, agents and publishers, and carefully pumped them for info about me.

It wasn't enough. He couldn't get inside my head. He didn't want to approach me cold, as Andeanna, so he invented Joe to get close to me. He corresponded with me, taking his time, doing nothing to arouse my suspicions. He had no set plan for luring me to London. But he had a hunch that one day things would fall neatly into place. As they did when I got interested in spontaneous human combustion after he had mentioned it in a few emails.

'From that moment, you played into my hands,' he sighs. 'There was nothing odd about me inviting you to London then — it looked like I was doing it in response to your plans to write a book about a subject I had turned you on to. It was natural that, in my excitement, I'd ask you to come here so that I could share the research with you.

'I made Joe a child of the Troubles, allowing me to cover up — because of his supposed scars, I was able to wear thick clothes and stick padding down the arms and legs to make me

306

seem larger than I am. You accepted the beard because I had a good reason for wearing it. You also didn't look at my face too closely because you didn't want me thinking that you were searching for traces of my scars.'

'You thought of everything, didn't you?' I snort.

'I had to,' he mutters. 'I was nervous the first time we met, but the more time we spent together, the less acting I had to do, until by the end, Joe was every bit as real to me as my mother. You never thought of connecting either of them to Gregory Menderes, because both were real, individual, complete.

'I think you can work out the rest,' Greygo says, rocking back on his heels. 'I juggled the alter egos, careful never to cross my wires. It wasn't easy going from your arms as Andeanna to your side as Joe, remembering what you'd told me as one and trying not to let that knowledge leak through the lips of the other.'

'A virtuoso performance,' I remark bitingly.

He shrugs. 'I don't think you can summarize it that simply. I wasn't acting — like I told you already, I became those people. I created souls, not just faces and bodies, and carried them within me, as separate and whole as my own.'

'Fancy words,' I snort.

'The truth,' he insists.

'What do you know about truth?' I sneer. 'You're one big walking, talking, stalking fucking lie. *Souls?* You have to be human to comprehend the quality of a soul. I'll tell you this, though.' I raise the gun and press the muzzle to his forehead. 'Souls are real. They do move on. And when you die, yours is going all the way to hell, you sick, twisted fuck.'

He doesn't display any fear, just gazes at me with a look that's half pity, half . . . *what?*

'Don't you understand?' I growl. 'I'm going to kill you.'

'Yes,' he says. 'I know.'

'It doesn't bother you?'

He makes a gurgling sound. 'Life hasn't been much to speak of recently. Part of the reason I slipped so easily into character was because I preferred being Joe and Andeanna. They were sweet. They could sleep at night, untouched by nightmares. They didn't look into mirrors and see a monster. I was happier as them. If I could go on being them, maybe I'd fear death. But I'm Greygo now. It's just me. And I hate myself. That's why I'm not afraid. Without my mother, my father, Joe, *you* . . . I'm nothing, just an empty shadow of a man. Death will be a relief.'

Tears trickle down his cheeks. It could be an act – he is, after all, an actor of the highest calibre – but I don't think so. I believe he's truly as miserable and lonely as he claims.

'Why didn't you kill me?' I sob, tears coming again to these once barren eyes. 'Wasn't that the plan, to set me up and have me murdered too?'

He nods. 'Once you'd killed my father, it would have been simple to step into his room and remove the evidence of Sebastian Dash, plant my own in its place. I had articles of yours stored away, to frame you with. And I was ruthless enough. I lured poor Axel to his death to test you, a trial run for the real thing. As Andeanna, I could be as brutal as I needed to be.'

'So why didn't you?' I scream.

'You know why,' he says.

'No. I don't. *Why?*'

He looks down, tears blackening his face. When he looks up again, there's a world of wanting and pain in his eyes. 'I couldn't kill you,' he weeps. 'I turned somersaults to spare you. I knew we were finished as Ed and Andeanna, but I hoped we could continue as Ed and Joe. I wanted you to flee and carry on with your life. I would have followed. We could have been friends. Even though I knew it might backfire on me, I couldn't bring myself to finish you off. I had to . . . let you . . . go.'

He's sobbing deeply. So am I. We're almost beyond words. But I have to know. Before the end, I must have it all explained. 'Tell me the truth. Why didn't you betray me?'

He looks up, locks gazes and says in as close to silence as a whisper can ever be, 'Because I love you.'

I thought I'd fallen as far into the madness as I could.

I was wrong.

'You *love* me?' I splutter, incensed by the disgraceful claim.

'Crazy, isn't it?' he croaks.

'You can't mean that. You can't!'

'But I do. I love you, Ed, and I know you're going to kill me anyway, but you forced me to say it, so I have.'

'You can't love. You're a monster.'

'I wish I was,' he says softly. 'But this was always about love. Love for my mother and father, then love for you. It wouldn't have been so fucked-up if I could have distanced myself emotionally from any one of you. Love's a bitch. You know love brought us here. Deny it all you like, but you *know*. It doesn't make sense any other way.'

I look inside myself for a scathing remark, only to find to my dismay that he's right. About everything. I wish with all my being that he wasn't, that he was an evil, calculating bastard, or a sick fuck who'd put me through hell for kicks, but he isn't. He's a lonely, hurt, resourceful, talented young man whose love for those closest to him has led to the ruin of us all.

'You know the really crazy thing?' I ask quietly. My lips lift in a self-mocking sneer. 'I love you too.' He stares at me wordlessly, not shocked by the revelation, but by my expression of it. 'After all you've done, regardless of your sex, you're still the person I fell in love with, the one I would have given the world for.'

'Ed . . .' he moans.

I look down at the gun, then toss it to the floor. Killing him isn't an option. Manipulator and liar though he is, he's

Andeanna, he's Joe, he's all that has come to mean anything to me. I can hate him, but I can't kill him, just as I couldn't kill Belinda when she betrayed me. Gregory Menderes chose his patsy well.

As if in a dream, I rise and face the door.

'Ed?' Greygo says behind me.

'So long, Andeanna.'

'You're leaving?'

I stop but don't look back. 'You want me to stay?'

'Of course!' He gets to his feet and shuffles towards me.

'No,' I murmur.

He draws to a halt. 'Ed?' he says again, fearful this time.

'You've destroyed me,' I whisper.

'But you said you love me.'

'I do.'

'Then you've got to stay. We can make this work. We can save each other. It won't be easy, but if nothing good comes of this, we're finished, the two of us.'

'We're finished already,' I sigh.

'No!' he protests. 'Is it because I'm a man? I can change that. Everything's possible. If you're patient, I can alter my sex, become Andeanna for real.'

'No.' I smile bitterly. 'Like I said, that isn't a problem for me. I thought it would be, but it's not. Guess I'm more metrosexual than I assumed. Don't become someone else again. Be yourself. It's time.'

'But if you leave . . .'

'Goodbye, Greygo.'

'Ed!' he howls.

'You've destroyed me,' I whisper again, only this time to myself, and I make for the door.

'Ed! No! We can . . .' he starts, but he's too late. It's over. I'm gone.

EPILOGUE

London is a cold, cruel city in the winter. Dark streets. Dark people. Dark ghosts.

The ghosts are everywhere. I see not just my own gaggle now – who mock me jubilantly at every turn, rejoicing in my downfall – but just about everyone who died here and remained bound to the buildings and streets. Old, young, innocent, guilty, from the distant past and the recent present. They reveal themselves wherever I go. Their resigned eyes follow me sadly, patiently, knowingly, as I stumble by, unwashed, unshaved, clothes torn and filthy, sobbing, moaning, gibbering.

Are they real or am I imagining them? I don't know. That doesn't seem to matter any more. Answers are for wise men, not fools like me.

I have no idea how long it's been since my showdown with Greygo. A week? A month? I've been sleeping rough, in old warehouses or under bridges. Not that I've been catching much sleep. The ghosts I have to face during my waking hours are a thousand times preferable to those that drift through my dreams — Andeanna, Joe, Greygo and Etienne. The fourth not as frequently as the first three, but the mystic has her moments, when her features dissolve in bubbling pools of flesh and blood to reveal a jeering skeleton, which in turn crumbles away to display the sad, haunted face of Gregory Menderes.

I think of Belinda sometimes too, and wonder if she misses Dash or ever thinks about me. I no longer hate her. There are worse than Belinda Darnier in the world.

I could go back. Track down Greygo and stop the suffering, kill or forgive him, crush or embrace him. But I won't. I've been consumed by madness. I no longer have the strength to take control of my life. All along I've been a figure in a tragic play. Now I must accept my fated end with dignity and resignation. There can be no other way.

The one comfort in this cold city of callous spectres is that my death is certain. My days and nights are numbered. Bond Gardiner will find me and keep his promise. He's a man of his word. Even if he doesn't want to kill me, he will. He's bound to his destiny as surely as I am to mine. It's only a matter of time.

So through this city of ghosts I crawl, broken and alone, trying in vain to hide from thoughts of Andeanna. Cut loose from God and man, I seek refuge and comfort among the shades of the dead, and wait for them to claim me.

THE END

written between 5th april 1999 and 29th may 2012